HIS HONOR

DALE F. SHAFFER

First published by Dog Ear Publishing
4010 W. 86th Street, Ste H
Indianapolis, IN 46268
www.dogearpublishing.net

ISBN: 978-1-4575-1219-3

This book is printed on acid-free paper.

Printed in the United States of America

To law enforcement officers and their families,
who serve and sacrifice to keep us safe.

ACKNOWLEDGMENTS

The individuals who provided valuable advice in a classroom setting were Dennis Hensley and Gayle Roper. The editors who made it a better read were Joan Alexander and Anne Grant.

1

CHICAGO ALDERMAN STEVEN Bryan exited City Council chambers, claimed his silver Chevy Blazer, and headed north. Snow had been falling for over an hour but that wasn't unusual for mid-December in the Windy City. No more boating or Cubs' games until spring. Anyway, City Council's heavy workload would keep him occupied through the cold winter.

Some in the Council resented his recent change of position on the upcoming vote concerning the development in his neighborhood. He knew he had taken a risk, but he had decided to represent his community this time and not be pressured by special interests. Council would just have to live with it. He was eager to get home to his beautiful wife and two great sons.

Traffic was light as the alderman moved north on Halsted through Chicago's north side. He slowed and entered the left lane as he approached the light at Wellington on the south side of the Masonic Medical Center, preparing to make his left at Clark. He stopped as the light changed at Wellington. Just as he reached to increase the wiper speed his SUV was rammed hard in the rear. The impact threw his head back violently against the headrest, stunning him. He glanced in the mirror, placed the Blazer in park, and reached for his door handle.

Hector Ruiz was watching his first ever snowfall in Chicago and catching a smoke on the roof of the medical center when he heard a crash. He hurried to the edge of the roof and looked down at the well-lighted intersection four stories below. He watched a large man wearing a dark jacket jump out of a black Cadillac that had rear-ended a Blazer. The big man ran to the driver's door just as the Blazer driver was getting it opened.

Ruiz stared in disbelief as the big man grabbed the driver's head with both hands and twisted sharply. He saw the smaller Blazer driver go limp. He watched the big man push the driver's upper body over onto the passenger seat, lower the driver's headrest, and run back to the Caddie. Then he watched the Caddie pull out around the Blazer, and drive north, its punctured radiator leaking reddish antifreeze on the snow-covered street.

Ruiz had thought Chicago would be safer for his family than Ciudad Juarez, Mexico, but now he wondered. He had just witnessed a murder.

THE FOLLOWING APRIL the case concerning the death of Alderman Steven Bryan went to trial. Opening statements had been made and witnesses had testified, but now the courtroom was silent except for Assistant State's Attorney Stambaugh raising his voice to the judge.

Judge W. C. Hayes pointed at Stambaugh and raised *his* voice, then motioned the two attorneys away from his bench. ASA Stambaugh clenched his teeth and shook his head as he strode back to his seat. Defense attorney Toney Marcello smiled as he nodded toward his client.

The judge leaned forward slightly and pulled himself up to his full height. "After hearing the opening statements and the testimony of all witnesses, I find that the State has failed to establish probable cause for a charge of homicide in the death of Alderman Steven Bryan. Therefore, I will not waste the jury's time on the closing arguments or deliberation, but give a directed verdict of not guilty." He rapped his gavel once. The bailiff's face appeared to register surprise at the announcement.

Judge Hayes stood then and announced, "Court is adjourned."

Defendant Frankie Carbonaro smiled broadly as he turned toward Marcello and shook his hand. ASA Stambaugh glared at

3

Judge Hayes as he watched the short man in his black robe with its purple trim leave the bench.

Detective Schneider turned to Stambaugh and raised his voice. "That's bullshit. We had his ass nailed."

Stambaugh's jaw was set tight and his face flushed as he turned. Facing Schneider and his partner, Dolsi, he spoke slowly and distinctly. "That, detectives, was the worst miscarriage of justice I have ever experienced!"

"Even if the witness was weak, we still had the Medical Examiner, the accident reconstruction report, the Council's meeting minutes on the pending vote, and our investigation," Schneider said.

Dolsi said, "The jury would have convicted his ass!"

"We did our best, detectives."

"Let's appeal," Schneider said.

"Let me cool off and we'll discuss it." Stambaugh reached for his briefcase beside his chair and jammed his paperwork into it. He rose and had taken just a few steps to the rear when an intent woman stepped into his path.

"What does that mean, 'a directed verdict'?"

Stambaugh stopped and locked eyes with the beautiful young woman for several seconds without speaking. "It means, Mrs. Bryan, that the judge did not believe we presented enough evidence to show your husband's death was a homicide."

At first Candice Bryan didn't respond. Then, "Do you mean that no one will be punished for Steven's murder?"

"Judge Hayes felt we didn't have enough."

Candice Bryan struggled to speak. "So ... in Chicago ... you can kill an alderman ...for saying he would vote the way his community wanted him to vote ... and get away with it?"

"I'm sorry, Mrs. Bryan. We did our best." Stambaugh stepped around her.

Candice Bryan caught up with him. In a shrill voice broken with sobs she screamed, "How can you let this happen? How do I raise two kids alone?"

Stambaugh kept walking.

ED SLATE ARRIVED early at Area 3's Robbery/Homicide Unit on Chicago's north side on the morning of April 19. Shift change was approaching and many of the two shifts of his fifty-four detectives were at their desks or milling about talking or copying reports. Holding a paper bag in his left hand and some reports he'd picked up under his left arm, he unlocked the door to his office at the right rear corner of the large detective squad room.

He set the bag and reports on his desk and hung his blue blazer on the hanger at the bookcase on the rear wall. He grabbed his cross draw holster on his left front and his belt on his right and pulled his gray trousers up a little before sitting.

The Starbucks coffee was still hot as he popped the lid off and tossed it into the basket beside his desk. The Danish smelled good. He ate and drank as he began shuffling through some of the robbery and homicide investigation reports. With six hundred homicides annually and countless robberies in the city of three million, the paper flow never stopped.

After reviewing and signing off on several reports he sat back, loosened his tie, and grabbed his coffee again. In seven months as Robbery/Homicide's new lieutenant he'd become a paper pusher. He wondered if he had done the right thing by leaving his detective sergeant role. Home life was better and Rebecca seemed happier with his day shift and the weekends off. But he missed working a good case. And now he was seeing city and department politics in a new light that showed more clearly the justice system that many times rendered no justice to the average Joe. Especially in one particular felony court.

He didn't remember a judge being charged with bribery in Chicago, but he remembered the Florida case of a judge who appeared to be tough on criminals, imposing large fines and long sentences. The PD believed justice was being served. Then they learned this judge was later contacting certain defense attorneys and—for a fee—ruling that time was served and releasing the criminal.

Even when dealing with just the cases he and his former partner, Joe Barona, handled Slate knew there were problems in one felony court. Seeing hundreds of robberies, homicides, and the human misery moving through this maze was depressing.

He had enjoyed most of his career, but the culture and city had changed in those two decades. Chicago had always been too political. Plus the Outfit had a long history of corrupting construction unions, truckers, waste haulers, casinos, and even some cops. But the Mob hadn't gotten inside the court system. This morning he was beginning to wonder.

It seemed like he was always the one catching the tough cases. He knew Rebecca considered his pursuit of justice a compulsion, but he figured he was just a better cop than most. His clearance rate proved that. Yeah, doing things his way had caused some pain, but that went with bucking the system. He could live with it.

Slate sipped his coffee and turned to study the photo on the wall to his right, the one featuring the platoon of Marines he'd led in Vietnam. It was on display with other photos of Marines, police officers, detectives, and a Distinguished Police Service Award.

After a difficult home life Ed Slate had proven himself in the Marine Corps, and that training focused him on the mission regardless of the risks. He was four years short of that magic age for retirement. Rebecca would welcome that change. But what would he do at age fifty? He'd never worked as a civilian.

———

Detective Schneider knocked before he entered Lieutenant Slate's office at Robbery/Homicide. Slate looked up from a pile of investigations. He was impressed with Schneider, also a Vietnam vet. Still fit, Schneider stood about six-two, a couple inches taller than Slate, but he was balding. Even with the gray showing on his temples Slate was relieved that he still had his full head of hair. "What's on your mind, Schneider?"

"Dolsi and I lost the Carbonaro homicide case yesterday, Lieutenant. With a directed verdict."

Slate frowned and sat back in his chair. "The alderman's homicide? Whose court?"

"Hayes. He said we failed to establish probable cause for a homicide. We'd like to discuss the case."

Slate jumped up and threw his pen on the desk. It slid off the front to the floor. "Damn! Who is that guy working for? Cook County, or the Outfit? The city is overrun with crime, and this jerk lets another one walk!"

"We had him. The jury would have convicted him," Schneider said as he bent down and retrieved the pen and placed it back on Slate's desk.

"Who was the ASA?"

"Stambaugh prosecuted it. He did a good job."

"What'd he say?"

"He was pissed and left right away. Mrs. Bryan was crying and yelled at him."

Slate studied Schneider. "Did you talk to Sergeant Waddell? He's running your day shift."

"He said you would have more information since he just moved back to the Unit."

Slate nodded and sat back down. "Okay. I need to move some paper. How about 10:00 a.m.?"

After Schneider left, Slate picked up his Starbucks and the last piece of his Danish. He leaned back and reviewed the events of the past eight months. Unlike the previous lieutenant, he had decided to operate with an open door policy. But he moved the two chairs from in front of his desk to the side table to ensure short, to-the-point meetings. Morale and clearance rates had improved since he took over.

But Robbery/Homicide was losing too many cases in Judge Hayes's courtroom. All were strong cases, each carefully investigated and screened by the department and the State's Attorney's office. How did two experienced detectives lose another homicide case that an experienced ASA had accepted and prosecuted? The system was screwed up.

CHAPTER

4

JUST BEFORE 10:00 A.M., Detective Schneider returned to Slate's office with his partner, Dolsi.

"Let's use the table." Slate shut the door and motioned to his right. He looked the men over as he moved toward the table to join them. Dolsi was short, stocky, about ten years younger than Schneider. A very good detective. Schneider and Dolsi grabbed two of the padded swivel chairs at the front of the table. Slate placed his white tablet on the table and took the rear chair so he could face both detectives.

"So," Slate said, frowning, "Hayes threw out your homicide charge for lack of PC?"

"I couldn't believe it!" Schneider said. "We had plenty of probable cause to arrest his ass, and the jury should have decided the case."

Dolsi moved forward in his chair. "The witness was just one piece of the evidence, but Hayes didn't let the jury consider all the rest. Carbonaro was guilty as hell!"

"This was the Alderman Bryan case involving a vote and you guys thought he got whacked?"

Schneider nodded.

Dolsi and Schneider were both seasoned detectives and Slate knew that if they said a death was homicide, it was homicide. "Okay, it's been awhile since I read the case last winter. Give me an overview."

Schneider led off. "City Council was debating the construction of a condominium unit versus a casino on Sheridan Road between Addison and Belmont. I guess the group that wanted a casino thought it would attract business from the Chicago Yacht Club and Wrigley Field and increase the city's revenue. The other group of aldermen said that was no place for a gambling joint and wanted a condo development built there."

"Was this where an entire block was razed of old three-flats?"

"Yeah. They needed a two-thirds majority. Bryan was with the casino group originally. Then according to his wife, after the *Tribune* ran the story he began getting a lot of calls complaining about a casino in the neighborhood. So Bryan changed his mind and the casino backers lacked a vote to make it two-thirds. Then Bryan is killed and a new alderman will decide the issue." Schneider looked at Dolsi. "Nick has more on the accident."

"Bryan was on his way home about 6:20 p.m.," Dolsi said. "He lived south of Wrigley Field on Newport. It was mid-December and the roads were bad but traffic was very light, as most commuters were already home. His Chevy Blazer was rear-ended when he was stopped for a red light on Halsted beside the Masonic Medical Center."

Slate nodded and continued making notes.

"The second driver fled the scene, but Traffic had a squad nearby and tracked the other driver from the antifreeze trail in the snow. The crash punctured the radiator. Alderman Bryan ends up with a broken neck and his headrest is completely down, so his head supposedly went back over the top of it. Traffic handles it as an accident and charges the second driver, Frankie Carbonaro, with vehicular manslaughter and leaving the scene."

"How big a guy was this Bryan?" Slate asked.

"Maybe five-nine, kinda small," Dolsi said.

Slate nodded and kept writing. In his ten years in Robbery/Homicide he hadn't heard of Carbonaro working for the Outfit. He wondered if he was their hitter or just a punk.

Dolsi continued. "A few days later we hear from the Masonic Medical super that one of his Mexican cleaning crew may have seen something. So we talk to this Hector Ruiz at his job. He says he was on the roof taking a smoke when he heard the crash and saw the guy killed. We bring him in for a written statement."

Dolsi looked at Schneider. "His English is limited," Schneider said, "but he tells us that after the crash the second driver runs up to Bryan's SUV. Bryan starts to get out. Carbonaro grabs Bryan by the head and twists, then pushes him over on the passenger seat and lowers the headrest."

"How many stories is the hospital?" Slate asked.

"Just four, so he's not too far away."

"But it's dark?"

"Yeah, well, but it's pretty well lighted in front of the medical center."

"Any forensics?"

"Nothing. They checked the headrest for prints," Schneider said.

"How big is Carbonaro?" Slate asked.

"Big, maybe six-three and about two seventy-five. He did some professional wrestling in his younger life, I guess."

Slate nodded. A pretty sloppy hit if the driver was working for the Outfit, he thought. Maybe it was a hit from someone working for a casino, or someone on City Council ordered it to change the vote.

Schneider continued. "So we get a translator and get Ruiz's statement, then file a homicide charge."

"What about the manslaughter?"

"We amended the affidavit."

"Is your janitor witness legal?"

"He had the papers, but we're not sure they're real and we didn't ask. He lived in a dump in Rogers Parks with his wife and two kids."

"Lived?"

"Yeah. We looked for him after court yesterday but they've moved."

"What was your other evidence?" Slate asked.

"We had the accident reconstruction guys investigate and we had the Medical Examiner," Dolsi answered.

"Did the accident guys and ME testify?"

"Yeah. Traffic said it was a simple rear-ender and would not have been fatal. The ME testified that the break was not consistent with the head snapping back, but sideways. And we subpoenaed the Council secretary with the voting discussion record. He testified that the casino vote was one short after Bryan changed his mind. And we testified concerning our investigation. The reconstruction crew doubted that the damage would have broken his neck even if the headrest was down, and his wife said he never drove with it down."

"Anything else? Exactly what did your witness, Ruiz, say?"

Schneider responded. "Under oath he wasn't as clear about what he saw, and he was scared."

"What he said under oath was different than his written statement?"

"Everything was the same, except he hedged on seeing Carbonaro snap Bryan's neck. Marcello got him to say he was four stories up, it was dark, and he might have been mistaken. Carbonaro testified he was holding Bryan's head because he knew he was hurt, and he lowered the headrest to allow him to lay back until paramedics arrived."

"But Carbonaro fled the scene, huh?"

Schneider nodded. "Said he got scared when he saw the guy was dead."

"Assistant State's Attorney Stambaugh thought the case was strong?"

"He said it was a miscarriage of justice."

"Bryan's wife was crying and she stopped Stambaugh on his way out," Dolsi added.

"So this witness, Ruiz, accident reconstruction, the ME, the city council secretary, and you two testified. Is that it?"

Schneider nodded. "Yeah. And this little jerk, Hayes, still wouldn't let the jury have it."

Slate studied both Schneider and Dolsi. "What do you think?"

"I think somebody got to Ruiz," Dolsi said. "Not only because of the way he testified but the way he disappeared right away after the trial."

"And maybe someone got to Hayes," Schneider added shaking his head. "We've lost other strong cases in his court."

"So an alderman is dead. And we'll have a casino with a new alderman's vote rather than a condo?"

Schneider and Dolsi both nodded.

"I read where Bryan had a wife and two kids," Slate said.

"A beautiful wife," Schneider said. "She was really hurting when we talked to her, and she was crying after Hayes threw out the case."

Slate nodded. "I can imagine. Her husband is killed so somebody can get a casino built and Hayes lets the killer walk."

"Must not have been married long, the kids are small," Dolsi said. "She's young, a real knockout."

"Had problems with Hayes before?"

"No more than anyone else," Schneider paused. "I'd like to get his little ass alone in an alley some night."

Slate studied Schneider and Dolsi, trying to decide how much he wanted to share. If his concerns got out, the department would shut him down. Still, he had to know if Hayes was Mob-connected. "I raised the issue with Commander Arnold last fall. He said he keeps getting elected."

Schneider nodded, "Yeah. A damn pity."

"Going to appeal or re-file on the manslaughter charge?"

"We'll talk to Stambaugh," Schneider said.

"Let me give it some thought. It sounds like the jury had plenty to consider, especially with the ME's testimony." Slate looked at his notes. "Your homicide clearance rate is okay at seventy-seven percent but you're not clearing many of your cold homicides."

"Most are gangbangers," Schneider defended. "We're trying to beat your record, Lieutenant. Was it eighty-five percent?"

Slate nodded slowly.

"And the Unit was under seventy before you took over?"

"We were at sixty-seven and now we're at seventy-four, but that's sad considering we cleared about eighty-five percent of homicides when I started twenty years ago."

"Back then, most homicides were domestics or between people who knew each other," Schneider said.

Dolsi said. "Gangbangers has hurt us, and a court decision like this don't help."

"See what you can learn about this Frankie Carbonaro."

"He's a trucker now."

"See if he's Outfit-connected. They've been pretty low key in recent years."

Schneider said, "They're still around, just a little more careful. They're still into casinos, street tax for those wanting to stay in business, trucking, construction jobs, strip clubs, and contract hits on those who get out of line. And now, after the new vote, they'll own a piece of a new casino, or skim their take."

"And some of the politicians will get their piece," Dolsi said.

Slate nodded. "If this was a hit, it was pretty sloppy."

"Maybe their regular hitter was out of town," Schneider said.

"Anything else?"

Both men shook their heads. Then Schneider offered, "Lieutenant, it's not related but have you how you noticed how Detective Angelino dresses? He looks like hell to be representing Robbery/Homicide."

Slate nodded, "Yeah, but he clears his cases. I'll say something to Waddell."

"Can't believe he's really Italian," Dolsi said. "They'd run his ass out of my neighborhood with clothes like that."

Slate thought about his own gray trousers and blue blazer. Unlike his former partner, Barona, he wasn't going to ruin his best suit chasing robbers and killers through alleys and over fences. He nodded to Dolsi. "Maybe he was adopted."

Dolsi raised his eyebrows. "I hope so."

Slate stood and the detectives followed. Slate looked at his notes. "Let me know what you dig up on Carbonaro."

Slate moved to his desk and dove back into the stack of paperwork, but his mind kept returning to Judge Hayes. Why would Hayes let a guy charged with the homicide of a city alderman walk instead of allowing the jury to decide? There was clearly probable cause for the charge.

Commander Arnold, his boss over Robbery/Homicide, Sex Crimes, and Juveniles/Gangs for Area 3, would not approve taking on a duly elected felony court judge, nor would the brass downtown. The State's Attorney's office would no doubt discourage such a move unless the evidence was overwhelming. The ASAs already screened out some good cases, trying to build a reputation for convictions that would get them into some high-paying law firm.

And there would be risks to his career, to himself, and maybe even his family if the Outfit had bought Hayes. The Chicago police department had come a long way during his twenty-plus years. More officers were degreed and training had improved, but Slate had grown up on the northwest side like many police and firefighters. Rebecca was a Wisconsin farm girl and the stress of his career choice, along with the four shootings he had survived, had affected their marriage, sometimes severely. When they visited her folks, he always found the area scenic and peaceful. He knew Rebecca would welcome a return to that quieter life. The lower cost of living would help if he left early, but Sarah was in college, and Tim was still in high school.

He thought of his tour in the jungles of Vietnam. There were very strict rules, but when he found a better way, he did it. The Corps would have to catch up! So damn the risks! If Hayes was dirty, he'd make the case. Just before noon Slate placed a call to make an appointment for the next day with Assistant State's Attorney Paula Lyon, the lead attorney assigned to handle Area 3 cases.

———

Slate left the Area 3 building for lunch and walked west on Belmont Avenue toward Smokey's, a small Greek restaurant about two-thirds of a block west of his office. It was a basic eatery and the clientele were mostly police. The paneled walls were a light wood tone and the floor was dark blue tile. Several pieces of police memorabilia from retirees and active officers hung on the walls. There was a small counter area at the front, with tables lining both side walls. Rick Waddell, who had replaced Slate as the day shift sergeant, waved from a table toward the back. Waddell had been in Sex Crimes before moving back to Robbery/Homicide.

"You alone, Rick?"

"I am." Rick gestured to the other chair. "So, how do you like the lieutenant spot by now, Ed?"

Ed hesitated before answering. "Well, the hours and the income are better, but the paperwork is a pain."

"That goes with all the money and fame."

"Right. What are you having?"

"The gyro and soup, and coffee."

The server arrived with Rick's order. "I'll have the same, but just water."

"How's things with you and Bennett, Rick?"

"We're doing okay. He's getting better at sorting things out."

"What do you know about the homicide case Schneider and Dolsi lost?"

"Very little other than what I've read. I told them to see you."

"They were in this morning. Any indication their investigation was sloppy?"

"Not from what I read. I can tell the morale is much better than when I left, Ed."

Ed nodded. "And clearance is improving. But we shouldn't be losing cases like this Alderman Bryan homicide."

"Some of the guys figured you might come back to working cases."

"Really?" Ed paused and smiled. "I do miss being out there digging."

"So why did Hayes let this Carbonaro walk?"

Slate shook his head. "Don't know, Rick."

IT WAS AFTER 5:00 p.m. as Ed Slate headed for the northwest side and home. The houses were smaller conservative brick ranches or older two story wood-sided homes, dating to the 1950s and 1960s. Housing was affordable for the many police and fire personnel who lived in the area and the streets were fairly safe, even with the higher crime rates on the west side and south end.

Rebecca was at the sink as he entered the kitchen.

"Good. You're on time."

"Having trouble getting used to that, Babe?" He walked up, put his arms around her waist, and gently placed his lips on the left side her neck. He had always liked the natural smell and the taste of her body.

"Stop. You know what that does to me."

"I do. We could eat later?"

"Maybe you should go back to the street, then you won't be so frisky."

"You don't like my . . . energy?"

"I plead the fifth," she said, turning to kiss him.

Ed still remembered when he first saw this five-seven blue-eyed blond at a Fellowship for Christian Athletes event in Milwaukee when they were both in college. She made a serious effort to stay fit and could probably pass for thirty-five, ten years younger than he knew his wife to be.

He stepped back. "So, what are we having?"

"Salad, a rib-eye, baked potato, and some fruit."

"Sounds good. That steak will give me more strength."

Rebecca turned and smiled. "You don't need it, lover boy."

"Do I have time to change?"

"It won't be long. The steaks are ready to turn."

"Tim home?"

"He's going to Brandon's after we eat. A school project."

"Any word from Sarah?"

"No."

At dinner Ed asked Tim, "You're going to Brandon's?"

"Yeah, I need help with my algebra."

"Maybe we can shoot some hoop tomorrow night."

After dinner, Rebecca got her sweater while Ed grabbed a sweatshirt and they took their coffee to the glider on the porch.

"How's things going with being Christian Ed director?"

"Pretty good. It's quite different from teaching school, but I've completely reorganized the place. We're still revising curriculum."

"That sounds like a job."

"It is, but it was overdue. The old lesson plans don't address the issues kids are facing today. I'm really enjoying the work. It makes me feel useful again."

She turned sideways to face Ed. "And that's been good for both of us. How's Lieutenant Slate doing?"

Ed paused, thinking if he wanted to get into it again. They didn't see it exactly the same. "Enjoying the regular hours and weekends, but still a little frustrated."

She smiled. "So, are we ready for Captain and a Commander assignment?"

"Not this soon, but the money would be better now and at retirement, if I last that long."

"Same problem?"

"Yeah."

"Ed, you don't have to prove anything to anyone. Certainly not to me."

They had been over this before and things never changed. He tried to keep the worst from Rebecca, but the corruption and politics drove him crazy and he couldn't talk to the troops about it.

"I know. You think it relates to my stepfather and trying to prove myself. The Marine Corps and Vietnam were places I could prove something. Then the politicians ran the war and screwed that up. And look at how the vets were treated, and the suicide rate. Now, the PD politics, the courts don't really protect the little guy without a high-powered attorney, and there's the assistant State's attorneys who are just getting experience to get into a big law firm. You bust your ass out there, survive some shootouts, work the shifts, weekends, and holidays on a case, and you still get a bunch of crap from the department and the system. We're damn sure not getting rich, Becky." He paused. "And . . . well, now we may have a judge on the Outfit's payroll."

"Really? And you can't let it go, right?"

Ed hesitated wondering how much more he should say. Their marriage had already been through some rough spots. He turned on the glider to face her. "The department won't approve taking on a judge. The State's attorney won't act unless it's a slam dunk. And there could be some risk . . . If he's dirty, the Outfit will protect him."

"That retirement is looking better all the time, Ed. What if you leave early and we both start second careers in Wisconsin?"

Ed shook his head. "I don't know. The mission and policing is in my blood. It's all I know."

"Ed, as a Marine you were awarded a silver star. And you are a very skilled detective. The men have always looked up to you. Now you're heading Robbery/Homicide."

"I guess, but it could be so much better if people were more dedicated! The city was fairly safe when I was growing up here."

"I'm afraid that most don't take their work that seriously."

Ed studied her for several seconds. "Is it me, or the damn system?"

"Probably both. Your standards or expectations are higher than most . . . you're focused on justice for all, Ed. We all have our hang-ups, but you expect too much, hon."

Ed reached over and laid his hand on her thigh. "That's just me, Becky. When I see something wrong, I have to fix it. And I'm too old to change. Ready to walk?"

She stood and put on her sweater. Ed grabbed his sweatshirt and pulled it on as they left the porch.

After thirty minutes of walking in the neighborhood they were back at their porch. Ed moved in front of Rebecca, turned around to tip her face up so he could look deeply into her eyes. "I appreciate your support, and I want a better life for both of us, but I feel policing is my calling." He paused.

"With Tim gone we could go to bed now . . . and you can be as noisy as you like."

Rebecca slapped him lightly on the shoulder then placed her arms around his waist, pulling her body tightly to him. He placed his arm around her shoulder, leading her to the bedroom and whispered in a husky voice, "I love you, Rebecca Slate."

SLATE ARRIVED AT ASA Lyon's office about 1:15 p.m. She waved him in.

"Have a seat, Ed."

"Thanks for working me in, Paula." Slate had first met this attractive, long-legged blonde several years earlier when she was interested in leaving the medical malpractice business for a State's attorney spot. Her interest was in homicide and some of the ASAs had suggested she talk to him. Ed knew she was a military brat, which he figured accounted for her toughness. But he could never figure why, at thirty-five, she hadn't married. She was tough, but polished. Maybe she was too tough for most men to handle, but she was the kind of woman he would have checked out if he were single.

"What does the new lieutenant need today?" She paused. "But you've been a lieutenant before."

Ed smiled. "Yeah, but it didn't take as long to make lieutenant in the Marine Corps. Paula, how well do you know Judge W. C. Hayes?" He noticed a quick flicker across her face at the judge's name. She didn't speak for a long moment.

"I see you lost a homicide case," she finally said.

"We did. And from what the two detectives told me, the jury should have had the case."

19

"I heard a little from Stambaugh. I've never seen him that upset. What do you think?"

"Now that I see all the dispositions Paula, we're losing too many cases in Hayes's court. What do you know about him?"

Ed watched Paula hesitate, as if weighing her answer. He figured her to be clean, but he wondered what she knew to act like that. "The first case I tried in his court, we won the case. He asked me to see him when court was adjourned. I thought he might chew me out for coming on too strong with the defendant. Instead, he gets me into his office and comes on to me."

"Really. Is he married?"

"Several times. Do you remember a homicide in Lake Point Towers a few years ago?"

"I don't think so."

"Hayes's second wife was stabbed and killed by a burglar."

"Remember her name?"

"No."

"Was it cleared?"

Lyon shook her head no.

"Any more trouble from him after he came on to you?"

"No. I thought I might lose some cases after that, but he seemed okay with the rejection. Fortunately, I haven't drawn his court very often."

Slate smiled. "Maybe he hasn't given up on you."

Paula shook her head. "He's not my type. What was your case? "

"This casino versus condo vote in City Council. It looks like a hit on the alderman who had the swing vote. Appears to be a staged auto accident where the alderman's neck was broken. A witness saw the second driver snap the alderman's neck. Then someone must have gotten to our Mexican witness, who may have been illegal. Judge Hayes gives a directed verdict rather than letting the jury have it. We also had the ME's report, accident reconstruction, the Council's secretary to testify about the vote count, and my two detectives." Ed paused before adding, "So I'm wondering if he's also on the Outfit's payroll. I want to check him out."

"You're on dangerous ground, Ed. Nobody wants to take on a judge, including this office."

"I know. Not even my department. But I need to know what we're dealing with when a clear case of homicide is tossed. The damn system is screwed up enough without a corrupt judge! We both know the Outfit has its fingers in a lot of places in the city. We can't

have them in our court system. What does the W.C. stand for, any-
how?"

"Wilbur Clarence. And you may be just the guy who could pull it
off, Ed."

"I guess I'd use W.C. too with a handle like that."

"This conversation is just between you and me. Nothing in your
case report," Lyon emphasized.

Ed raised his hands. "You have my word, Paula."

"After he came on with me, I did some checking. Hayes is from a
working class family on the north side, Irving Park. They had a combination grocery and liquor store and I guess some of his family still
runs it. His grandfather put him through college. Then he worked in
the liquor store and went to John Marshall Law School at night for
several years. In his early thirties he finished law school, became a
public defender for a few years, continued working at his family's
store part-time. Then he was an assistant State's attorney, starting in
traffic. From there he filled in some in the criminal division. After
several years he was appointed to fill a vacancy in Circuit Court, then
ran for the office and won. So he's had his Circuit Court job for
maybe ten or twelve years."

Paula paused. "He's on his third marriage."

"You did check him out." Slate considered asking if she had ever
been interested in being a judge's wife, but thought better of it.

Paula read him. She sat back on her chair. "I just wondered what
kind of guy this was on the bench in a Circuit Court, hearing felony
cases and coming on to an ASA."

"And I want to know why we're losing cases in his court." Ed
stood. "Thanks, Paula. Let me know if you come up with anything
more."

"Sure, but nothing on the record . . . It could be risky, Ed."

Slate nodded.

———

Slate weighed his options as he made his way back north. He'd
known Sergeant Hal Lewis in Intelligence since their academy days but
had never worked with him. The Intelligence Section was under the
Organized Crime Division and operated from the headquarters building on South Michigan Avenue. He parked at the side of a loading zone
in the rear then placed his blue light on the dash of his Ford.

The Intelligence Section was on the fifth floor. He went in the rear door with another detective after displaying his ID. He took the elevator to five, and as he got off he saw Lewis in the hall talking to another person. Slate stopped a few feet away and waved. Lewis finished talking and moved toward Slate.

"Hey, Lieutenant, congratulations on the promotion. You always were a go-getter. You lost, or looking for work?"

"Hal. How's the Intell business?"

Hal looked carefully up and down the hall. "I can't discuss it, Ed."

Slate grinned and nodded. "Okay. I have one question, off the record."

"Oh, those are the most dangerous kind."

"What you know about Judge W. C. Hayes in Circuit Court?"

"What's the problem?"

"Just lost a homicide case on a directed verdict."

"He's raised a few red flags, I hear, but nothing solid. I haven't been personally involved as a sergeant. It's just what I've heard."

"Suppose the Crime Commission would be any help?"

"Can't say, but you don't want it getting back to Hayes." Hal paused. "And I doubt the department wants to take on a sitting judge, Ed."

"I know, but I've got to know. I'll appreciate a call if you hear anything more. And stop when you're in Area 3."

"You buying?"

"Sure."

Back at Area 3, Commander Arnold followed Slate into his office. "How's it going, Lieutenant?"

Slate turned and met Arnold eye to eye, as they both stood six feet. "We're doing some good, Commander." Slate knew Arnold had about twenty-five years on the job, had served with the Airborne in Vietnam.

Slate moved a chair from the table over to the end of his desk and motioned for Arnold to sit. Slate sat down at his desk and waited for Arnold to initiate the conversation.

"Looks like you're doing a lot of good. Morale is up in the last, what—eight or nine months. And you're at seventy-four percent now for homicides cleared. Your career high was what, eighty?"

"I was running eighty-five percent when Bricker was here."

"I hated to see Bricker retire," Arnold said. "What was his secret?"

"He was a cop's cop and he knew how to pair up detectives. He was low key, but you better know what you're talking about when you discussed a case with Bricker or he'd make you look stupid."

"How's he doing? Have you talked to him?"

"Not since last year. He got the pacemaker when he retired and was pretty down when I saw him."

"That's rough after a good police career." He paused. "Let's hope we're in better health than Bricker when we hang it up."

Slate thought about Hayes, but he knew Arnold wouldn't endorse an investigation. He didn't know Arnold well enough yet to be sure where he stood. With over thirteen thousand coppers, there were always some dirty ones. But who? If the Outfit had penetrated the court system, they could also be in the PD, and it would likely be the brass.

After Arnold left, Slate grabbed his mug and went to the squad room for a coffee. On his way back he paused at the window facing east toward Lake Michigan and stood looking out over the EL track and the city. After twenty years of dealing with crime his police blood told him that W. C. Hayes was dirty. But he needed more than police savvy to make a case.

He moved back to his office to unlock and open the doors covering his whiteboard on the side wall near his desk. He adjusted the window blinds to the squad room, then shut his office door. This way there would be no investigation report he was holding back in violation of CPD rules.

He sat on the end of his desk, viewing his board and thinking about building his case. Four years from minimum retirement. Sarah in college. Tim in high school. And Rebecca not making big money as Christian Education Coordinator at their church. Where did Commander Arnold stand? And how about Arnold's boss, Urbanski, Deputy Chief of Detectives? Sure, he had a good record with the PD, but city and department politics were ruthless and Slate had seen them ruin some very dedicated public servants.

Was it worth the risks? He finished his coffee and set the mug on the desk. No, it wasn't worth the risk. Most would let it ride. But he'd never been a conformist and that had caused some trouble with supervisors through the years.

He thought of his firefighter dad, killed when Ed was eight. His mother had married his step-dad, Douglas Norton, two years later. A

CPA didn't think like a firefighter or a cop. It was obvious that Douglas could not relate to a kid like Eddie Slate and so he chose not to adopt him. Feeling the coolness and rejection, Ed always felt the need to prove himself. In the university the Marine Corps ROTC provided an opportunity, then the police department working the street, and the last ten years as a detective arresting killers and robbers.

He knew Rebecca didn't share his passion for justice and thought he expected too much from himself and his peers. But a good challenge and the risk fed his very soul. The Corps, then the PD fulfilled his need. He couldn't tolerate more rejection. And he knew how John Q public felt rejected at times, especially when an innocent man didn't have somebody to stand up for him and his case.

Slate always worked better when he made notes and studied them. He stood and moved to the whiteboard and recorded the information on the Bryan homicide, the latest case to be lost in the court of W.C. Hayes. Then he added information provided by ASA Lyon. If CPD got word, he could be transferred or demoted. If he got demoted, he would leave early. But then what? He stepped back and studied his notes, made some adjustments, then closed and locked the doors.

———————

Slate decided to visit Mrs. Bryan, the alderman's wife, on his way home. He found the address on Newport just west of Halsted, and south of Wrigley Field. Steven Bryan's obituary had mentioned he was a big Cubs fan. The neighborhood was made up of well kept older homes.

Slate rang the bell and waited. He knew Candice Bryan had a couple small kids, but the house was quiet. After Slate's second ring, he could see a woman wearing a purple knit long-sleeve sweater and bone colored slacks brush her long dark hair to the side as she approached the door. Tall, slim, long legs. And she was a beauty, the kind of woman who didn't need makeup to look good.

"Lieutenant Slate, Robbery/Homicide," Slate said, displaying his star and ID when Candice Bryan opened her entrance door to speak through the storm door. "Did I wake you?"

"Yes, but I needed to get up."

"I need a few minutes of your time."

She unlocked the storm and stepped back. "Is there something new?"

"Not exactly, but I have a few questions."

She gestured to her right. "Is the dining room table okay?"

"Sure." Slate took the closest chair and Mrs. Bryan sat facing him.

"Kids asleep?"

"No, my mother has them."

"I see you're in purple and white. A Northwestern grad?"

She nodded. "Yes. Are you?"

"No. University of Illinois at Circle. NU didn't fit my budget."

"Were you at the trial?"

No. I'm in charge of Robbery/Homicide, but Detectives Schneider and Dolsi briefed me."

"I could not believe what I was hearing. I thought sure that Carbonaro would be found guilty. That would have given us some closure."

Slate pulled his notebook out and laid it on the table. "Give me some background on your husband and this voting issue. Did your husband receive any threats during the council discussion on the condo versus casino issue?"

She was silent for several seconds. "Steven and I were married five years. We have—or I have sons, two and four years old. Steven married the first time right after serving six years as an Air Force officer. His wife was from Winnetka and a very well-off family, but she didn't like sports, didn't want children, and wanted nothing to do with Chicago politics. The marriage only lasted a year.

"Steven was single for eight years until we met. He was thirty-seven and I was twenty-six. Being from this neighborhood, I like the city and the lake. We attended some NU games. Steven liked the Bears too. We followed the Cubs, and had a boat at Benton Harbor. And, we had our two sons . . ."

She looked down at the table and paused. "Steven did confide in me some, but not on the everyday things about how City Council works."

Slate asked, "He was threatened, then?"

"He received many calls from the Ward saying they didn't want a casino in the area. That's when he changed his mind about the upcoming vote. Originally, he thought the city needed the casino revenue. His change made them one vote short of the two-thirds needed. Originally he had been told by a ranking alderman, and later by the Committeeman, that the casino people would reward him for his vote. We weren't sure whether that meant money or some future favor. He also had a couple phone calls he wouldn't talk about. I think they were threats. He did seem worried, but he kept it to himself."

"Anything recorded that you know about?"

"No. Your detectives checked here and at his office. What do you think happened?"

"At the trial?"

She nodded.

"Not sure. But I'm checking some things. So please do not mention to anyone that I have been here. If it gets out, the department will order me off the case since we have no evidence to go to court again with our homicide case tossed."

She nodded and studied Slate. "Do you think the trial was rigged? Did the Committeeman get to the judge?"

"Hard to say at this point. Anything else you can think of?"

Mrs. Bryan stared into the distance for a moment again and Slate knew she was somewhere else, probably thinking about her future alone.

"No, I guess not." She shook her head slowly. "I thought the Committeeman and other aldermen might not support him for re-election and might endorse another candidate, but I never imagined they would murder him over a vote. It still doesn't seem possible that at thirty-one I'm suddenly alone with two little boys."

THE NEXT DAY Slate decided to visit Judge Hayes's courtroom at the Cook County Courthouse, on California Avenue, southwest of Area 3. He arrived just before 1:00 p.m. and took a seat in the back behind several other people. The ASA, detectives, defendant, and defense attorney were seated at their tables, ready to proceed.

At 1:30 p.m. Judge Hayes entered the court and took his seat at the bench. Slate was surprised at how small the man appeared as he stepped up to the platform behind his desk. The bailiff called the court to order.

Hayes looked at the assistant State's attorney. "Are we finally ready to proceed, Mr. Morgan, or are you still going to waste the court's time?"

"All witnesses are now present, your honor."

"And is the defense ready?"

"We're ready, your honor."

The case was an armed robbery at an ATM station. The defendant had been identified from the video. Hayes was loud and demanding with both attorneys. Slate thought back to his time on the street. It was seldom the big guy that gave him trouble. He had come to believe that little men were much like little dogs. They tried to compensate for their insecurity by being loud and acting tough.

He watched for about ten minutes, then decided to visit the court's personnel office.

As he approached the young woman behind the counter, Slate decided not to identify his position in CPD as he displayed his ID. "Lieutenant Slate, Internal Affairs. I need to see some records to locate a witness who worked in Circuit Court, for Judge Hayes, during the last three years. I've lost the name, so I need to see all of the former employees during that period."

"I'll have to ask the supervisor."

Slate waited, then a middle-aged man approached.

"Glen Connors, Lieutenant. What is it you need?"

Slate repeated his request.

"You have ID?" Slate displayed his star and ID card again, using the Internal Affairs title.

"This will take a while. You can wait in that interview room over there if you want." Connors motioned.

Ms. Hare brought three personnel folders to the interview room. "These are the former employees in that office for the last three years. Just three people."

"Okay, I'll see if I can find the right one."

The folder on top was for Harriett Stevenson, who lived at 3612 Central Park, about twelve blocks west of the Courthouse. The second, Sammy Vincent, lived at 4805 Cermak Road in Cicero. The other former employee, Bernice Delaney, was at 6031 Taylor in Oak Park. Slate recorded the information and returned the files to Ms. Hare.

Harriett Stevenson lived close so he decided to check her out before returning to Area 3. Slate made his way west on Twenty-ninth Street then south on Central Park. Checking the address, he found that the Stevensons had moved to St. Louis.

Since he hadn't made contact with Stevenson and Cicero was in the area, he decided to check on Sammy Vincent. At a check at his home he learned that Mr. Vincent was now working at the Galione Insurance Agency on Austin Boulevard, a few blocks west.

Slate parked in the alley beside the agency and placed his blue light on the dash. He approached the first desk and displayed his ID to a young woman. "Looking for Mr. Vincent."

She called a number and relayed the message. Coming from the rear area, Slate saw a short, heavyset man walking to the front. He was in his fifties with thick gray-black hair.

"Mr. Vincent? Lieutenant Slate, Internal Affairs, Chicago PD. I need a few minutes of your time."

Vincent studied the ID suspiciously, then said, "Come on back."

As they entered the small office to the rear where there were two desks, Vincent motioned to a chair. "Have a seat." He rounded the desk and sat down. "What's on your mind, Lieutenant?"

"You worked at the Cook County Courthouse a while back?"

"Yeah. For Judge Hayes."

"Did you supervise the office?"

"No. That was Mario DeMeo."

"You reported to him?"

"Yeah. What's this about?" Slate had already determined that Sammy was not likely going to be a good source. He obviously didn't like police. Slate wondered about his record. "I'm checking for someone I can trust to check out a detective and his possible relationship with a woman in that office."

Vincent gave a phony smile. "DeMeo would be the one. He runs the place and he's been with Hayes for years."

"Are you aware of a relationship between a detective and a woman in that office?"

"No. I've been gone over a year."

"Are you still on friendly terms with DeMeo?"

"Not really. Haven't seen him since I left."

"Think he would work with me on my investigation?"

"I don't see why you're talking to me."

"Trying to learn about the woman and who I can trust there. This detective may be involved in more than just a relationship."

Vincent stood. "Afraid I can't help you, Lieutenant."

––––––––

Back at Area 3, Slate had just sat down at his desk when his former partner, Detective Joe Barona, knocked and entered. Slate looked him over, thinking of the tailored clothes Barona liked and his telling Slate where to find the best suits.

"How's it going, Lieutenant?"

"Pretty good, Joe. How about you and Ingram?"

"We're doing okay. You're not missing being out there digging?"

"Yeah. Some."

"I was hoping to get partnered with Sergeant Waddell like I was with you, so if you decide to come back, I'd like to be your partner again."

"How about the Sergeant's exam?"

"I got most of the questions, but I don't expect anything soon."

"How about you and Maria?"

Barona shook his head. "Not good. She's still working on her MBA and neglecting me."

Slate hesitated. He knew the marriage was already shaky when he and Barona worked together. "Maybe things will improve after she graduates."

"Or she'll take her MBA and be a career gal and I'll be another police divorce statistic." Barona moved closer to the desk and raised both arms. "It pisses me, Ed. We talked about a couple kids before we married, then she decides she doesn't want kids and a family life. I come from a big family. We had Sunday dinners with twelve, fifteen people every week and Ma cooking lasagna, chicken parmigiana, or calzone. She always had Italian bread and a great dessert. Now I come home to nothing or a note that says a microwave dinner is in the fridge."

"The MBA study has to be tough. Have you asked her how things are going for her?"

"She's either at school or at the library, or when she's home I'm on a case. It's no way to live, Ed, alone and not gettin laid." He turned and walked toward the door then stopped and turned back toward Slate. "I tell you, Ed, some of our tomboy detectives are looking better every day."

"Don't get yourself in trouble, Joe. Talk with Maria."

The next morning Slate moved the paper, but Hayes was still on his mind. He shut his door and called Bernice Delaney in Oak Park, the other former court employee. She agreed to meet with him.

SLATE MADE HIS way south on Western Avenue then west on North Avenue toward Oak Park. Morning commuter traffic was gone. The day was bright and sunny but still cold. He wondered if it would be another year without a spring, like many he had experienced in Chicago.

As he drove he thought about how to investigate Judge Hayes without tipping him off or alerting the CPD. If he could develop a strong enough case, the State's attorney would have to prosecute and the department would have to go along with that. He made a left on Taylor and quickly found 6031, a modest home in a middle-class neighborhood.

As Slate approached the door he still hadn't decided how to handle the interview. He rang and an older woman came to the door. Slate displayed his star and ID.

"Lieutenant Slate. I called." He noted that Mrs. Delaney was tall, trim, in her late fifties to early sixties, and wore her snow white hair short.

"Yes, come in, Lieutenant. Have a seat." She motioned to a chair at the end of the couch while she sat on the couch and pulled her sweater close together in front. Slate removed his trench coat, laid it on the back of the chair, sat down, then pulled his notebook from his inside sport coat pocket. Pictures of a teenage boy and girl hung on the wall, apparently high school graduation photos.

"How did I get involved with your investigation, Lieutenant?"

"Well it doesn't really involve you, Mrs. Delaney, but you worked in Circuit Court, in Judge Hayes's office?"

"Yes, but I retired at the end of 1991, four years ago, when my husband retired.

"How long were you there?"

"About four years. I retired from teaching at fifty-two. Then I worked in the Circuit Court office until my husband retired. We did some traveling the first year after retirement, then Howard passed away. Traveling alone hasn't been much fun, so I'm thinking of looking for something to help fill my time."

"My wife taught, and now heads Christian education at our church."

"That should be a good fit."

"Mrs. Delaney, my investigation involves the Circuit Court office. What can you tell me about the operation there? Anything ever bother you during your time there?"

She took a long look at Slate and frowned slightly. "Like what?"

"Did you ever feel like anything was wrong?"

"Is there something going on there?"

"Not sure. But I need to know a little more how the system works and I thought a former employee like you could help."

Delaney seemed to consider Slate's question and his explanation very carefully before she started to reply. "There was one thing I wondered about. Normally, when an attorney called for a continuance of a case, one of us handled it and gave Mr. DeMeo a note. Mario DeMeo, the administrator.

"But when certain attorneys called, they would only talk to Mr. DeMeo and it was a longer conversation. Normally an attorney wanted to change a scheduled trial for a few days later or wanted a time change due to a conflict. However, the ones who would talk only to DeMeo would ask for the date being moved up several days, and they seemed to be arguing about how many days to move it." She paused. "But DeMeo never told us to change the date."

"And DeMeo had the final say on all docket changes?"

"I don't know. He met with Judges Hayes at the end of each day."

"What do you think of DeMeo?"

"Well, he knows the court system, but he wasn't the type of man I enjoyed being around."

"Why is that?"

"I can't put my finger on it exactly, but I never felt he was sincere. I may be wrong; it was just how he struck me."

"How about Judge Hayes? Did you have much contact with him?"

"Very little. Mr. DeMeo was the administrator. The judge normally talked only to him." She paused. "The word was that Hayes was a chaser. Three marriages. You probably know about his wife being killed?"

"That was when their home was burglarized?"

She nodded. "And I heard his first wife just left him."

"Has he remarried?"

Mrs. Delaney nodded. "He remarried. She came in sometimes. She looks more like his daughter."

"Pretty young?"

"Can't be over her mid or late twenties, and he's past fifty."

"Mrs. Delaney, if sometime later I ask you to talk to a State's attorney or a judge about what you have told me, would you do that?"

"What would you want me to talk about?"

"Just what you told me."

"I guess so. What's the problem?"

"It may be nothing, but I need to check it out."

"Corruption?"

"I don't know yet, so please don't mention our conversation to anyone because it could impede my investigation, and that would be a crime."

Mrs. Delaney studied Slate before she nodded slowly.

Slate stood and put on his coat and moved toward the door. "Thanks for your time."

Delaney followed him to the door. "I know Chicago has its share of corruption, and I expect Oak Park has some too."

"I'm afraid that's true. Again, thanks for your time. I may want to talk to you again."

As Slate left Oak Park and headed back east, he mentally reviewed his investigation and decided to visit the Recorder of Deeds Office at the Cook County Courthouse. Ms. Shay there had been very cooperative while he worked a serial killer case the previous year.

Slate parked in a police stop on California in front of the building. At the Recorder's office he displayed his ID and asked for Ms. Shay. The clerk made a call then directed Slate to an office to the rear. He knocked and entered.

"'Lieutenant Slate' now, huh?"

"Since last fall." He remembered Ms. Shay well, a middle-aged black woman with a quick smile and mind.

"You're not after another serial killer, are you?"

"No. I need your help again, Ms. Shay, but on the QT without a warrant this time."

Shay leaned back and raised her eyebrows. "It better be legal, Lieutenant."

Slate smiled and raised both hands. "Nothing but legal. It's a public record but it may take some digging. I want to know all the properties Wilbur Clarence or W.C. Hayes owns or has owned in the last fifteen years."

Shay made notes as Slate talked.

"A Hayes owns a grocery and liquor store on the north side on Irving Park and I also need that information."

"Can I just look at the north side?"

"I think that's the place to start. I wonder how many Hayes there are on the north side."

Shay looked up at Slate. "Too many, I expect, but the Wilbur Clarence or W .C. should narrow it down."

"Do you have any contacts in the Recorder's office in Michigan?"

"You thinking about a summer home?"

Slate nodded.

"Let's see what we find here first. Who is this Hayes, one of your suspects?"

"It's a very confidential investigation. I can't say until I learn a little more. So let's keep this name just between the two of us."

"That means I have to do the digging."

"I'll pop for a nice lunch if that helps."

"No, that's okay. That serial killer case you had last year was a doozy!"

Slate nodded. "Call before you fax copies of the deeds so no one on my end sees them but me."

"Sounds like you're into another big one."

"Maybe. And thanks."

————

Slate picked up a sandwich and fries at Wendy's, then dug into the paper in his IN box, pausing occasionally to consider his questions about Judge Hayes and the risks in going after the answers. Being the Unit lieutenant over twenty-seven pairs of detectives, each pair working several cases, didn't allow him much time to dig for the answer to the question of whether they were appearing before a dirty judge. Still, the case dispositions and his gut told him that justice wasn't being served in one Chicago felony courtroom.

Detective Schneider knocked and walked in. "I did a little more checking on Frankie Carbonaro, Lieutenant."

Slate waited.

"He does drive truck like we said yesterday. He's also a bouncer at the Peacock on Rush Street, a strip joint where a lot of hoods hang out." Schneider paused and stepped closer to Slate's desk. "And the word is that he does some work for the Outfit, mostly with union truckers."

Slate nodded. "Interesting. That makes your case on Alderman Bryan's death even stronger." As time permits, see if you can connect him to any particular 'made guy' in the Outfit."

"Okay, Lieutenant."

The next morning Slate called Chuck Rizzo at the police garage and requested the use of a confiscated car from the Narcotics pool. He had used the cars before when conducting surveillance.

———

About 10 a.m. he headed for the police garage on Lincoln, but first double-parked at May's Bakery for some glazed whole wheat donuts.

At the garage he sounded his horn. Rizzo's partner, Skip Claywood, peeked out of the small window in the door. The door went up. Slate pulled in and proceeded to a stall at the far end.

As he walked back toward the office at the left front, Rizzo came out from between two cars. "Mornin, Ed. Or should I say Lieutenant Ed?"

"Chuck."

Rizzo glanced at the bag Ed was carrying. "Whole wheat glazed?"

"If I brought anything else you wouldn't take care of me."

Chuck grinned. "I'll make a fresh pot."

They entered the small office. Rizzo dumped the stale coffee and started a new pot. Slate sat at the table and placed two donuts on two pieces of paper towel. While the coffee was brewing, Rizzo sat across from him.

"So, did you find me a good set of wheels?"

"Don't I always take care of you?' Rizzo studied Slate and grinned. "You wanna bet on the Cubs' next game?"

Ed shook his head. "You're a stronger fan, Chuck."

"Yeah, but a detective is suppose to be able to detect!"

Ed nodded and took a bite from a donut. "But now I'm in management."

"Yeah, and more money to bet with. Did ya hear 'em take Milwaukee"?

"No. What was the score?"

"Three to one. A great game."

Rizzo got up and poured two cups. "I still got that black Dodge you used last year on the serial killer case."

"A 1994, wasn't it?"

"Yeah. And in good shape."

"That's good."

After coffee, Slate moved his gear from his Ford to the Dodge.

Back at Area 3, Slate took a call from Ms. Shay in the Cook County Recorder of Deeds office. "You have something on Hayes?"

"Yes, several properties, in fact. At 3214 Irving Park, near Pulaski a grocery/liquor store was owned by Wilbur Hayes, then transferred to Dewayne and Clarence Hayes, then to Dewayne Hayes."

"Okay, that's apparently where W. C. Hayes got his first two names."

"Then, Wilbur Clarence Hayes owned a place at 437 Racine near Wrigley Field."

"Okay, got it."

"He also owned a condo in Lake Point Towers, off Lakeshore Drive, near the Loop. And he now owns a townhouse on Fullerton, near Halsted."

"Anything else?"

"That's all we have on file. Am I going to be reading about another serial killer you shot?"

"You can never tell. Fax all of that and I'll grab it now. Thanks for the quick response."

Slate processed the necessary case reports, kicking back two investigations for more details. Most cops didn't like a lot of paperwork, but they had to make the adjustment when they became detectives and entered the Robbery/Homicide Unit. Some were excellent investigators but not great writers and this drove the ASAs crazy when vital information, which the detective no doubt had in his notes or his head, was not included in the investigation report.

———

He couldn't get Hayes off his mind and decided to check out a former neighbor of the judge. Near the Loop he pulled off at Lake Point Towers. Using the phone at the front door he rang four condos on the sixth floor before a lady answered. "Lieutenant Slate, Chicago Police, ma'am. I need to get in. Can you see my identification?"

"What do you want?"

"I need to talk to you about a crime in this building."

"I'll release the entry door, but I'll have to come down and let you in the hall." A few seconds later the entry door lock snapped open.

Slate waited in the lobby. In a couple moments a small older woman opened the hall door.

Slate displayed his ID. "Thanks. I need to talk to you." They stepped inside the elevator.

"You are?"

"Vera. Phillips. What crime problem?"

"Did you know the Mrs. Hayes who was killed on your floor?"

"Yes, a little. We had coffee a few times. Have you found her killer?"

"No, it's still an open case. I head Robbery/Homicide."

They arrived on the sixth floor and she keyed into 603. As they stood inside the door, Slate asked, "What can you tell me about the Hayes couple?"

"He's a judge."

"Yes. What was her background?"

"She worked in a law office before they married."

"What was her name, and where was she from?"

"You must have that in your report."

"I thought you might come up with some new information."

"Her name was Juanita." Mrs. Phillips shook her head. "She wasn't a very happy person, then she gets killed."

"Do you know where she was from?"

"Somewhere on the northwest side I think."

"Marriage trouble?"

"She wasn't happy. He was cold and very demanding. She said that he wanted a pre-nuptial agreement when they married but she wouldn't go for it."

"Have you talked with any neighbors about her death?"

"Some, at that time. A guy was seen in the lobby and hall on the night she was killed, but that's all I heard. They thought she surprised a burglar."

"Did Mr. Hayes stay here long after his wife was killed?"

"No. I understand he remarried pretty soon after that. It's easier for men than women to start over."

"Okay. I appreciate your time Mrs. Phillips. Here's my card in case you learn of anything new."

"I hope you get her killer. Juanita was a nice person."

———

Back at Area 3 he found a note from detectives Barona and Ingram requesting a meeting the next morning to discuss a case. Slate cleaned out most of the paper in his IN box. The day shift had left after 4 p.m. and most of the second shift had hit the street.

SLATE WAS IN early the next morning with a fresh Danish and a large Starbucks. As he ate and drank, he pulled his notebook out. Starting at the front he reviewed the many bullet statements he had recorded.

- Solid cases lost in the courtroom of W. C. Hayes
- Alderman Bryan's homicide
- Lyon's court experience with Hayes
- Delaney calls to DeMeo ref days continued
- Hayes, Juanita, wife #2 killed by burglar? (homicide?) Wife #1?
- Grocery/liquor store on Broadway
- Property in city

He had nearly finished when Barona and Ingram arrived.

"Morning, Lieutenant," Barona said. "You ready for us?"

"Sure. Have a seat." Slate motioned toward the table, then closed his office door. He grabbed his tablet from his desk and moved to the table. "Pam, Joe, what's on your minds?"

"We lost a case a few days ago we wanted you to know about. Sergeant Waddell said to see you," Barona said.

"Whose court?"

"Judge Hayes's," Ingram said.

Slate didn't react. "What case?"

Barona responded. "A robbery and vehicle theft."

Slate nodded. More notes for his whiteboard.

"Last year we had an armed robbery in the office of a refuse hauler, G & G Waste Management. They were counting the monthly income, much of it in cash, when they were hit."

"Where's G & G located?"

"On North Avenue, but far west. They had just bid on a city contract and had received some threatening calls. The loss of a month's income almost put them out of business. During the robbery, two of their five trucks were stolen." Barona looked at Ingram.

"Two guys did the robbery while two others drove the two trucks out of the lot. Those were later found in Lake Michigan off the North Avenue beach. They winched them out but the motors were ruined. The oil had been drained in the lot, then driven to the lake."

"Part of the bidding war?"

"Looks that way. We found one of G & G's drivers who had pulled into the lot during the robbery and thefts. He saw one guy standing on the running board of a truck parked in the lot but didn't think anything about it at the time. While he was parking, the two stolen trucks pulled out. Forensics lifted good prints from the door of the truck the one guy had apparently been checking out."

"The keys were left in the trucks?" Slate asked.

"The ones being used that day."

Barona jumped in. "So we filed truck theft on this Frank Ruggiero, whose prints were on the truck still in the lot. He works for Central Waste Management. It's owned by a couple guys who apparently have Outfit connections. They were bidding on the city contract against G & G."

"And if Central Waste didn't get the contract, the Outfit wouldn't get its cut," Slate said.

Barona nodded.

"The case just went to court?"

"Right. Pam and I tried to move this Ruggiero while he was waiting trial, but he wouldn't give us anything. He didn't ask for a jury trial, which we found unusual. The witness and driver for G & G identified this Ruggiero in court as the man standing on the running board. And his print was on the truck door. Ruggiero takes the stand and says he did touch the truck, but it was early in the week out on their route when he jumped on the running board to ask the driver what G & G paid, as he thought he might switch jobs. The G & G driver verified that he had asked what they made. Ruggiero denied being in the lot when the robbery and theft went down."

"And he was found not guilty by Hayes?"

Barona and Ingram both nodded. Slate finished his notes.

Ingram continued. "We approached this Ruggiero the next day at Central Waste Management and tried to get him to talk. We threatened to put out the word that he was cooperating. He laughed and said we had the wrong guy."

"Is that it?"

"One more thing," Ingram said, "apparently someone saw us talking to Ruggiero and a day later he's found in an alley off of North Avenue, near work, with a bullet hole behind his ear. Later, Central Waste Management got the city bid. We heard Ruggiero was talking about working for the Outfit. So we don't know if it was that or our contact that got him killed."

"What did Judge Hayes say when giving the verdict?"

"That we had failed to prove it was Ruggiero the driver saw on the day of the theft."

"But the witness IDed him from a mug spread, or a lineup, and in court?" Slated asked.

"Six mug shots," Ingram said, "and in court, and the prints matched."

"So, no more leads?"

"None," Barona said.

"And the robbery is also still open?"

They both nodded.

Barona continued. "We know the Chicago Outfit is into waste management, Lieutenant. We figure it was an Outfit job, but how do we prove it?"

Slate looked at his notes, thinking about his own concerns.

"I've had little experience with the Outfit, Lieutenant," Ingram said. "How are they organized?"

Slate knew Ingram was a new detective and that it takes awhile to adjust from working in uniform to a detective position. "They have been more low key in recent years, but to start with, you must be Italian. The gangster is like a street cop. A racketeer is like middle management, and a family head is an administrator. This Ruggiero is probably more of a wannabe who was used by some gangster type. The family head has to authorize a hit on a 'made man,' a person recognized as a part of the family. It's unlikely Ruggiero would have been hit that soon after you talked to him if he were a made guy. So the Outfit used Ruggiero to get rid of the competition and their company got the contract, and at a higher rate, no doubt. And they had to hit Ruggiero because he was shooting off his mouth playing the role."

Slate leaned back. "In a city of three million with fifty wards, three thousand voting precincts, with committeemen and council aldermen, you have many opportunities for corruption."

Barona looked at Ingram. "The aldermen vote, but the committeemen have the clout."

Slate continued. "The committeemen are unpaid but they get paid by handing out jobs for political support. So the Chicago Outfit is a whole different world, and difficult to penetrate, Pam."

Slate paused. He dare not share his concern about corrupt judges, at least not yet. He knew Barona was okay, but he didn't know Ingram that well. "Okay, I'll give this some thought. You can keep working it as a cold case for now."

Slate tried to finish the paperwork in his IN box but he couldn't stay focused. He got up and shut his office door then leaned back in his chair and placed his feet on the corner of his desk. Two good cases lost since he headed Robbery/Homicide, plus the others that were lost before his promotion. And all in Hayes court.

Alderman Bryan's death, and this waste hauler case were a good starting point but could he proceed without alerting the judge or the department? He could give what he had to the Chicago Crime Commission, or to the FBI for a Racketeer Influence and Corruption case, a RICO. But he didn't know enough about the Commission to trust its members. The Bureau was more cooperative than they had been earlier in his career but he still could not be sure they would be totally open with him, probably fearing a leak within CPD. And where did his own boss, Commander Arnold, and the other brass stand?

The phone rang.

"Slate."

"Lieutenant Slate?"

"Yes."

"Bernice Delaney. I just had a call from Mr. DeMeo from Circuit Court, asking if I would be interested in working twenty hours a week."

"Interesting. What did you tell him?"

"That I would let him know in a couple days. I've been thinking about some part-time work since my husband died."

"If you decide to work, I want to meet with you again. This could be very helpful to my investigation."

"I think I'll try it. I already know the job, so it will be easier than starting over someplace new. And if they're doing something crooked, maybe I can help."

"That would be great, Mrs. Delaney. And call me when you get settled in." Slate sat back and breathed out a sigh. This could be the break he needed.

————

He grabbed a sandwich at McDonalds and decided to visit an old acquaintance up on Broadway. Just south of Addison he parked in an alley beside Mike's Sporting Goods. Slate had known Michael Vansant since their high school days. Mike had started working in the family's business back then and took it over after earning a business degree from Loyola University.

Slate entered the store and found Mike talking to a customer looking at a slalom ski. Mike waved and Slate looked around until Mike was free.

"Ed, it's been a while. Where have you been?"

"Trying to keep the city safe, Mike." They shook hands.

"I heard you made lieutenant."

"Heading Robbery/Homicide."

"A social visit? Or do we have trouble?"

"No trouble. Just some information. How's the family?"

"Okay, but we have two in college, so the money is tight. How about you?"

"One in college and one in high school."

"So the good-looking Wisconsin girl is still putting up with you?"

"Rebecca's doing fine. She's the education director at our church."

"She taught, didn't she?"

"Yeah, until we started our family."

"You near retirement?"

"Could go in four, but I may be good for thirty."

"What's on your mind today?"

"How well do you know the C & D Grocery and Liquor people down the street?"

"The Hayes family? One's a judge."

"Right. What's the family makeup?"

Mike paused and gave Slate a thoughtful look, probably trying to figure out where this was going. "It's been in the family a long time. Dewayne owns it now."

"Dewayne is the judge's brother?"

"Yeah. W. C. and his first wife worked in the store but Dewayne bought out his share. I guess W. C. didn't want anything to do with the store, and he never was close to the family according to Dewayne. W. C. worked there a long time during college and law school. He went to night school for many years to get his law degree. They in trouble?"

"It's a long story, Mike. It may be nothing, so please keep it confidential. What's their reputation?"

"They are part of the merchants association and seem to be okay. I guess W. C. is difficult."

"How so?"

"Dewayne and I talk sometimes. W. C. resented being poor, not able to go to a better school, and going to night school for many years. Like I said, he was never close to the family. I guess he's pretty well off now. Dewayne said he has a place in Benton Harbor, Michigan, that he uses on the weekends. And a place in Naples, Florida."

"Do the judge and Dewayne socialize?"

"No, but they talk once in a while, according to Dewayne."

"I hear W. C. has been married several times."

"Yeah. That bothers Dewayne too. The first one, who worked in the store, left him and went back to Wisconsin, I guess. He helped run the liquor store and she helped run the grocery. You may have handled the homicide of W. C's second wife."

"No. I didn't catch that one."

"Dewayne's a family man but W. C. isn't. And all of his wives have been a lot younger."

Ed nodded. "I appreciate your help, Mike. But nothing to Dewayne, okay?"

"Sure. Let me know if I can help further. I know you must be on something."

"Maybe. But just a little research for now. Say hello to Ginny."

As Slate drove back toward Area 3 he thought of the Hayes family. It sounded like W. C. Hayes had done well, given his background. Slate wondered how much snooping he could do without raising a red flag. What would be his best approach? He wished he still had Barona with him to do legwork. That wouldn't raise the attention that Slate's inquiries would.

At Area 3 he moved more paper from his IN box and recorded the information on the first wife, and the Benton Harbor and Florida homes on his whiteboard. He had just finished and shut the doors over his whiteboard when Commander Arnold walked in.

"How's it going, Lieutenant?" Arnold slid a chair from the table over to the end of Slate's desk. "I heard your people just lost another case."

Slate thought about confiding in Arnold, but decided against it. "Yeah, a waste hauler's war I guess."

Arnold studied Slate. "Ever wished you had stayed in the Corps and retired?"

"No, but maybe I should have stayed in the reserves for more rank and another retirement check."

"Yeah, I didn't either. But if we had we might be in the Middle East now. I still think about my 'Nam time. How about you?"

"Not much. I have a bad dream now and then and some of the firefights are still with me, especially after Roger Daniels and I get together and reminisce."

"He's the insurance PI that was wounded?"

Slate nodded. "My radioman. Sniper got a piece of his skull and left him disabled on his left side. He was in the hospital at Great Lakes Navel for nine months. He can walk but his left leg and arm are weak, kind of like a guy who's had a stroke."

"The military time was good for us. We learned discipline and a dedication to the mission. I wish our younger officers here had more of that."

"Yeah, but it was a stinking war, fifty-nine thousand killed, and there's been many suicides since it ended."

"A lot of disrespect when we came home and some couldn't handle that, I guess." Arnold paused. "You've been out of the office a lot. Are you keeping on top of things?"

"I have over ten years in the Unit, Commander. Investigations are moving and the paperwork is current."

Arnold stood up and slid the chair back to the table. "I got your report on Kaminski and Mercer but haven't read it. They're not making it, huh?"

"No. And my talk didn't help."

When Arnold was gone Slate stretched back in his chair and thought more about his boss. Arnold seemed to be more curious lately. Why had he really stopped by? Had something about his contacts gotten back to him? He didn't want to jeopardize Arnold's position by investigating a sitting Circuit Court judge if, in fact, Arnold was clean. He would keep the investigation to himself for now.

Slate shut the door to his office then partially closed the window blinds to the squad room. He unlocked the doors on the whiteboard on the wall to the left of his desk, then stood there thinking. He figured that no one but Arnold would have a key to his whiteboard door, but just to be safe he would not title the notes on the board or refer to Hayes by name.

He pulled his notebook from the inside pocket of his sport coat. Looking through his bulleted statements, he listed the possible investigation points in more detail on the board, then made a few adjustments. He liked to record the details but it wasn't a hang-up, or even being a perfectionist, like Rebecca had said. He was just being a careful investigator.

Rebecca was right about one thing, he had nothing to prove at this point in life, but still, he had to know if the justice system he was part of was corrupt, even with the risks to himself and maybe his family. He closed and locked the doors over the board, then reopened his door to the squad room.

Slate was at his desk getting ready to end his day when Detective Brandi La Rue knocked and entered. "How's Lieutenant Slate doing?" Brandi stepped close to the front of the desk.

"Hello, Brandi." Slate had always been impressed by this brunette's natural beauty, a beauty that Brandi didn't seem to be aware of, or at least didn't try to exploit. Maybe that was because she came from a large police family and she had natural police instincts. His mind flashed back to their work on the serial killer case last year. "How's business in Sex Crimes?"

"Lusty!"

Slate chuckled. "I'm sure. So what's on your mind?"

"Just wanted to say hello, and tell you to keep me in mind for Robbery/Homicide."

Slate's mind immediately went to his problems with Kaminski and Mercer. He had just written them up for a move back to Traffic due to their lack of productivity and their low clearance rate. Commander Arnold hadn't yet approved their demotion back to uniform but he had mentioned Slate's report and Ed felt sure they would be moved.

"Your timing may be good. Make a request to Commander Arnold. Tell him you've worked with me and I encouraged you to apply."

"You have an opening?"

Slate smiled. "Maybe."

"Okay. He'll have my request tomorrow." La Rue stepped forward and shook his hand. "Thanks."

CHAPTER 10

AFTER SHUFFLING THE necessary paper the next morning Slate ran driver's license checks on Wilbur C. Hayes and Mario DeMeo. Hayes came back with a DOB of 4/3/1945, so he was fifty. DeMeo was born 2/11/1950, forty-five years of age. He then ran a check with the state Law Enforcement Automated Data System and the National Crime Information Center on DeMeo. He was clean with both LEADS and NCIC. He was afraid to run Hayes, as it might raise a red flag. But he figured he was probably clean.

He shut his door and placed a call to Lieutenant Phelps, Kalamazoo, Michigan, PD.

"Lieutenant Ed Slate, Chicago PD."

"Ed, you made lieutenant!"

"I did. Heading Robbery/Homicide for Area 3."

"That's where you worked before? No transfer. Is that normal?"

"No. I was surprised too."

"Congratulations. What's on your mind?"

"I have one going now that I need your help with."

"Sure."

"Do you have a contact at Benton Harbor PD?"

"Yeah. Pete Morrison, a detective sergeant."

"Good. I need to know if a Wilbur Clarence Hayes, or W. C. Hayes, owns a place there, where it is, date of purchase, its value, and if there's a mortgage. Also, if Morrison has any info on activity there."

"A drug case?"

"No. I'm not sure what I have yet, maybe nothing."

"Okay. It may take a while to get Pete on it."

"No problem."

"One of us will be in touch, Ed."

Slate placed a call to ASA Paula Lyon.

"What's on your mind today, Lieutenant?"

"Need some help. Your line's not recorded, is it?"

"Not that I know of."

"I need a favor, Paula."

"Those are always dangerous."

"Could you check on the guy we discussed the other day to learn his salary and where his political donations came from for the last election? It's police work I know, but you'll raise fewer red flags than I will."

Paula was silent.

"You still there?"

"Let me check. I will if I can do it through someone else and not use my name. Or by making a wider inquiry of several individuals. It could impact my position otherwise."

"I understand."

"I'll let you know."

He had just leaned back in his chair to consider how Lyon could approach his inquiry when the phone rang.

"Slate."

"Bernice Delaney, Lieutenant. I start at the court next week and I thought you should know."

"Good. I appreciate the call. We won't meet until you get settled in there. What I would like you to do is listen to any calls that only DeMeo takes and make some notes without being noticed. Note whose court case it involves and when it's being heard, if the court date changes, and any contacts DeMeo has with Hayes following those calls."

"Okay, I'll try. But I can't guarantee anything."

"When you've worked a while and have heard such a call, let me know and I'll meet with you, perhaps for dinner on your way home."

"Can you tell me anything more?"

"Not really. I'm just suspicious at this time."

"I'll call when I know more."

"Thanks again, Mrs. Delaney."

A few days later Commander Arnold stopped by Slate's office again. "Morning, Lieutenant."

"Commander."

Arnold shut the door and stood in front of the desk. "I approved your recommendation on the transfer of Kaminski and Mercer."

"Good. It was obvious that my talk had absolutely no effect."

Arnold nodded. "Kaminski got hot and talked about his union, but their clearance rate tells the story."

"Good."

"Now, how well do you know Brandi La Rue?"

"I've known Brandi and Ted for years. She worked with me last year on the serial killer case. She's a dedicated investigator who can handle the details and I think she can make it in Robbery/Homicide."

"She's attractive. That hasn't influenced you, has it?"

Slate smiled. "I never even noticed, Commander."

"Sure. Okay, let's give her a shot."

"Moving Kaminski and Mercer will help our clearance rate."

"If I go with La Rue, we need one more detective," Arnold said.

"You must have several requests, but Waddell might have someone in mind."

"I have a list, but tell Waddell to tell me about anyone he recommends that's coming from Sex Crimes. I'll move La Rue ASAP. Think about how you want her and the other new detective assigned. Then I've got to find one to replace La Rue in Sex Crimes."

Slate nodded.

He left a message for Sergeant Waddell that Kaminski and Mercer were moved and to decide which senior detectives La Rue and a second new detective would work with. And to tell Arnold of anyone in Sex Crimes that would be good in Robbery/Homicide to fill the other spot.

Slate then called the Intelligence Unit to talk to an old academy friend, Sergeant Hal Lewis.

"Which of my secrets are you interested in today, Lieutenant?"

"Just one, Hal. Do you have anything on a Mario DeMeo, DOB 2/11/1950. He's Judge Hayes's administrator, so let's keep this just between us."

"Okay, Ed. I'll be in touch."

Slate then headed down to records and pulled the homicide case on Hayes's second wife, Juanita Hayes, killed by a burglar in Lake Point Towers.

Back at his office, Slate shut his door then unlocked his white-board. He sat on the end of his desk and opened the case folder. It was a homicide in February 1992, Lake Point Towers, condo unit 611, which occurred sometime between 10:00 p.m. on February second and 2:00 a.m. on the third.

Judge Hayes had been at a conference in Miami and had talked to his wife on the second but could not reach her on the third so he called the police to check the condo. She was found lying in the living room near the bedroom door with one stab wound to the heart. The photos showed her wearing pink pajamas. There were no other wounds, and no sexual assault. Forensics determined there was no forced entry. So the door was unlocked, a key was used, or the lock picked.

Jewelry had been taken and the drawers and closets searched. Closed circuit cameras in the lobby and hall showed one small white male with a short beard and wearing a hooded coat. He was not identified.

Hayes had insisted that police check several people he had sentenced in the past couple years, but nothing developed. Detectives Testaverde and Ryan had worked the case. Juanita Hayes was thirty, dark haired, and attractive even in her final pose. Judge Hayes had said he would notify her parents, a Mr. and Mrs. Leslie Jameson, on Linder on the northwest side. Slate added several notes to his board.

He stepped into the squad area and left a note on Testaverde's desk asking to see him regarding the cold homicide case of Juanita Hayes in 1992.

The next day Lieutenant Phelps at Kalamazoo PD called.

"Hey, Lieutenant. That was quick."

"Pete Morrison, at Benton Harbor was able to get right on it but he's in a trial now, so I told him I'd call."

"What'd he find?"

"Hayes does own a place. Actually a very nice home on the shore of Lake Michigan. Purchased in 1989 for three hundred and forty thousand. Not a big place, but it's on the shoreline with a good beach. No mortgage recorded. That's all Morrison has now, but he'll see what he can learn about how the place is used."

Slate had just hung up when Testaverde and Ryan knocked and came through the doorway. "You wanted to see us, Lieutenant?"

"Yeah." Slate motioned to the table, then got up and shut the door. He took the seat facing the detectives and laid the Juanita Hayes homicide case and his tablet on the table. He glanced at both detectives. "Our homicide clearance rate has improved and you two are in the average, but we need to do more. I'm looking at cold cases. How much follow-up did you do on the 1992 homicide of a Ms. Juanita Hayes in Lake Point Towers?"

"The judge's wife?" Testaverde asked.

"Right." Slate slid the folder in front of them. "How about an ID on the guy recorded by the camera?"

"We determined he wasn't a resident," Ryan said. "And we checked with all Unit detectives, posted it for all roll calls, at Narcotics, and talked to the Intelligence people. No one could ID him."

Testaverde said, "And neither the FBI nor DEA could make him."

Slate nodded.

"How about your CIs?"

"We tried our informants too," Ryan said. "We figured he wasn't local."

"You think he's just a burglar?"

"We wondered about that. There are easier places to hit than a sixth floor condo at night. We thought it might be a revenge hit from someone sentenced in Hayes's court," Testaverde said.

"And Hayes was afraid of that," Ryan added.

"That didn't work?"

"We couldn't make a tie-in."

"How about the jewelry?"

Ryan said, "We checked with pawn shops and with some cons but came up cold."

"How about Gary or Milwaukee?"

"Didn't check that far," Testaverde said.

"Do that. It's too old for the jewelry, but someone may recognize this guy. Also, check St. Louis and Kansas City. Somebody has to know him."

"We hear Kaminski and Mercer are going back to uniform," Ryan said.

Slate nodded.

"Who's replacing them?"

"Commander Arnold will announce that."

Slate stood. "Let's get this guy IDed. It was a judge's wife."

"We're on it," Testaverde said.

Slate shut the door then placed a call to the Naples, Florida, PD.

"Violent Crimes, Detective Reese."

"Lieutenant Slate, Robbery/Homicide Chicago. I need to talk to your OIC."

"That would be Commander Russell. Hold on."

"Commander Russell, Lieutenant. How's business in the big city?"

"Need a little help, Commander. Could you have someone check with your county Recorder of Deeds and tell me if a Wilbur Clarence Hayes, or W. C. Hayes owns property there?"

"What kind of case?"

"Not sure. Just checking some concerns."

"Okay, what's your number?'

Slate gave his number. "Give it only to me or my machine. What's your homicide clearance rate down there?"

"We run nearly ninety percent."

"Whoa! No gang activity, I guess."

"Not really. What's Chicago run?"

"We're at seventy-four percent."

"I'll take our crime rate and our weather, Slate."

"Our retirees tend to agree with you. You local?"

"No, Pennsylvania. But I like warm weather. Someone will get back to you."

Slate took a call from Hal Lewis in Intelligence. They had nothing on Mario DeMeo.

Slate made notes in his notebook, then unlocked his whiteboard. He added the property in Michigan and the Florida check.

When he returned to Area 3 from lunch at Smokey's he had a message from ASA Lyon to call. Slate shut his door and returned the call.

"Ed Slate, Paula."

"I have some information."

"Go ahead."

"He's making around a hundred and sixty-five thousand. In regard to political donations, there are many, but the majors ones are Central Waste Management, the law firm of Profacci and Bellino, a local Teamsters Union, and the Lucky Star casino on the west side."

"Good. That's the law firm that Frankie Carbonaro used on his arrest for the death of Alderman Bryan, and a guy named Frank Ruggiero used them on the Central Waste case where Ruggiero beat a truck theft charge during a robbery—and then turned up in an alley with a bullet behind his ear."

"Really? Are you finding anything solid?"

"He also owns property in Michigan and maybe Florida."

"On a hundred sixty-five K, huh? In our weekly meeting Stambaugh was still pissed about losing the Carbonaro case."

"I appreciate your help, Paula."

"You did it on your own, Lieutenant."

"I understand. You're not in my investigation."

"Have you thought of people who work in that office, Ed?"

"I'm working on that. Let me know if you think of anything else."

"Will do."

Slate had Forensics blow up the photo of the suspect in the Juanita Hayes homicide. He sent it to Sergeant Hal Lewis in Intelligence, suggesting a check with the State Police and another check with the FBI.

11

THE NEXT MORNING Slate was reviewing the investigations for homicides and robberies, and the required monthly supplemental reports for all cold cases when Detective Brandi La Rue knocked and walked in. She stepped close to Slate's desk and extended her hand. "Thanks for the recommendation, Lieutenant, I'm now in Robbery/Homicide."

Slate stood and shook her hand. "Congratulations, Brandi. Shut the door and have a seat." Slate moved to the table and La Rue joined him. "Sergeant Waddell is still working on getting you partnered up but until then, I have some work." La Rue pulled her notebook from her shoulder bag.

"Need a marriage license check on Wilbur Clarence Hayes, or W. C. Hayes. Should have a record of three marriages."

"The judge?"

"That's the one. But that's between you and me. Use your Sex Crimes ID to keep the focus away from me and Robbery/Homicide."

La Rue nodded.

"You're the only one in the Unit that knows about this."

"I understand."

Slate stood.

"Should I ask Sergeant Waddell about my partner?"

"After this assignment."

La Rue had just left when he took a call from a Detective Honeycutt. "Lieutenant Slate."

"Returning your call to Commander Russell, Naples PD."

"Right. What do you have?"

"W. C. Hayes owns a condo in the northwest corner of Naples. It's called Gulf View. He has unit 317. Bought it in 1987. No mortgage. We have nothing on him in our file."

"Good. Thanks for your help, Honeycutt. And call if you need something up here."

Slate opened his whiteboard and added the confirmation on the Florida property.

The next day Detective La Rue came by. "I have the marriage information, Lieutenant. You ready, or I should stop back?"

"Now's fine. Shut the door." They both moved to the table.

Slate laid his tablet on the table.

"Okay, here's the list." She slid it over to Slate and read from her copy. "His first wife was Karen Olson, Stevens Point, Wisconsin. She listed herself as a paralegal. Married in 1978. She was twenty-four, Hayes was thirty-three. Hayes obtained a divorce in 1986 based upon abandonment. Wife number two was Juanita Jameson, twenty-five, from the northwest side on Linder. They married in 1987. Hayes was forty-two. No occupation listed. She's the one killed in 1992. And wife number three is Carmel Destazio, Benton Harbor, Michigan, paralegal. They married in 1993, when she was twenty-eight and he was forty-eight."

Slate studied the notes.

La Rue asked, "Anything more you can tell me so I know what to look for as I work here?"

"Not now, Brandi. And this is just between us. Rick Waddell isn't involved. Nor is the Commander. It's a very sensitive case, but I knew I could trust you."

"Okay. Where to now?"

"I haven't heard from Rick yet, so see him about your partner." Slate stood. La Rue followed and moved toward the door, then paused. "Let me know if you need anymore work on the judge."

Slate sat at the table considering what Brandi La Rue had just reported when the phone rang. He moved back to his desk. "Slate."

"Ed, Hal Lewis."

"What do you have, Hal?"

"We still had nothing on your photo, so I ran it by the State Police and Bureau as you asked. The Bureau can't be sure but it may be the Professor, a hit man from Miami. With the hood it's not a sure ID, but his side profile matches some other cases."

"I haven't heard of this one. Why 'the Professor'?"

"They said he looks more like a prof than a hit man. But he's never been IDed. And he always uses a knife. He hit one recently in Boston in broad daylight while the guy was walking a crowded street. Just what is my old academy buddy working on?"

"Can't say just yet, Hal."

"Now you're sounding like me. Maybe you should be in Intell."

"I'll leave that to you deep thinkers."

"You wouldn't BS me would you, Ed?"

"Never. Thanks, Hal."

Slate sat back in his chair and considered the facts he had gathered so far. He got up to shut his door and move the widow blinds to block a view from the squad room into his office. He then unlocked the doors on his whiteboard. He added Hayes's marriages and the possible ID to the video photo from the homicide of Hayes's second wife. He then sat on the end of his desk, studying all the notes. When someone knocked, he shut the doors on the board and opened his office door.

"Hey, Rick, what's up?"

"Here's a few more case reports. And I've assigned La Rue with Max Yeager."

"Sounds like a fit."

Waddell looked at Slate for several seconds like he was waiting for something, then waved and left. Slate figured that Waddell recognized he was on to something but had decided not to ask.

He went back to the board, opened the doors and studied his notes. After all the research, what did he really have? Losing solid cases in one felony court, a judge on his third marriage and owning three properties with one salary. One wife left, one was killed while the judge was in Florida. Why would a burglar be working a sixth floor condo, and during the night, when people are most likely to be home? Was she really killed by a burglar or by a hit man IDed as the Professor? And Hayes's election support was from some questionable sources, including the law firm involved with defense in two trials recently lost in his court.

He shut and locked the doors over the board and went to Records to confirm that the law firm of Profacci and Bellino had defended Frankie Carbonaro on the death of the Alderman Bryan over the casino vote and if they had also defended Frank Ruggiero on the theft of the waste hauler trucks. When he returned to his office he kept the office door closed so he could add Profacci and Bellino to his board as handling both trials.

Slate sat on the end of his desk and studied the information. What a challenge, a dirty felony court judge and a law firm! He found himself remembering the rush he felt in Vietnam when the birds became quiet, the monkeys stopped moving, and he knew the enemy was close.

From his conversation with Mike Vansant Slate knew that W. C. Hayes was not close to his family and apparently resented his background and his struggle to make something of himself. The risks in pursuing an investigation of someone like that were not to be taken lightly.

About a week later Bernice Delaney called.

"How's the new job, Mrs. Delaney?"

"I've been able to settle in pretty quickly. I had a call yesterday that may be of interest."

"Good. Can we meet on your way home?"

"I suppose so. Where?"

"You name it."

"How about the China Buffet on Washington at Kedzie? It's on my way home and that's as close as I get to the north end. Do you like Chinese?"

"Sure. What time?"

"About 5:15 p.m."

"Good. I'll try to be on time."

Slate was thinking about what Delaney might have when the phone rang.

"Slate."

"Sergeant Pete Morrison, Benton Harbor PD, Lieutenant."

"Good. How's business on your side of the lake?"

"Not bad. Had a chance last weekend to check on the Hayes property. Three cars there. You ready to take them down?"

"Go ahead."

"A 1995 Mercedes, Illinois WCH, comes back to W.C. Hayes, 4592 North Avenue, unit 349, Chicago. The second vehicle was a 1994 Lincoln EKS 1853. Comes back to a Mario DeMeo of 714 Clinton, River Forest, Illinois. And the third vehicle was a 1995 BMW, LAW APJB, to Profacci and Bellino at 5112 Roosevelt Road, Cicero, Illinois."

"Very good, Pete. Can you spot check it occasionally?"

"Sure. What am I looking for?"

"Right now, just info like this. Not sure what I have yet."

"Okay. Talk to you later."

Slate knew the BMW must belong to Anthony Profacci and Joseph Bellino. So Hayes, DeMeo, and the lawyers were social friends.

Slate called and left a message for Rebecca that he wouldn't be home for dinner.

SLATE FOUND BERNICE Delaney waiting in the lobby of the Chinese Buffet.

"So, Chinese is okay."

"Sure. It'll be a nice break." After they were seated Slate said, "Brief me on the call. We can discuss it while we eat."

"The caller asked for Mr. DeMeo. I asked who was calling. He said Profacci and Bellino Law Firm. DeMeo took the call so I moved over to the copier to listen where I wouldn't be noticed while I was doing something."

Slate thought he might have a teacher-detective here. "The caller mentioned a case and apparently wanted it moved ahead ten days. DeMeo asked what kind of case it was, then said, it would probably be forty or fifty days. It seemed like the caller didn't like that, and DeMeo said he would let him know."

"Any contact with Hayes after the call?"

"They meet after the judge comes off the bench."

"Are you still in the office then?"

"Yes, but they meet in the judge's chambers."

"It would be great if you could hear the meeting." Slate thought about a bug, but he didn't have enough yet for ASA Lyon to be able to get that.

"What did DeMeo do with the information he took?"

"Put the note in his shirt pocket."

"Any idea of which case they were referring to?"

"No. DeMeo wrote it down but I was too far away to read it."

"Anything else?"

"That's all. Does it mean anything to you?"

"Not sure. Let's get our meal and I'll think about it."

As they were seated again Slate said, "Find out which case is moved ahead forty or fifty days if you can. Then call me with the defendant's name and the court date. I'll sit in on the trial if I can. The question is, is this call about moving a court date, or is it the Outfit's code talk?"

Bernice Delaney's eyebrows went up as she took a deep breath. She stared at Slate. "The Mafia?"

"Could be."

She sat back and stared out the window for a minute. When she made eye contact with Slate she said, "This is what you expected all along, isn't it?"

Slate nodded.

"Am I going to get detective pay, Lieutenant? This could be dangerous."

"It could be dangerous, but I need to know if we have criminal activity. Don't take any risks. And yes, I can pay for information."

Obviously concerned for her safety, Mrs. Delaney poked at her meal without speaking for several minutes. Finally she said, "I'm not sure I should get into this, Lieutenant. Who knows what could happen? I could be killed!"

"It's up to you, of course, but without an inside person how will we know if we have a corrupt Circuit Court in our city?" Slate went back for seconds to allow her time to think.

When he returned to the table, he asked, "Mrs. Delaney, does DeMeo drive to work, or take public transportation?"

"He used to drive, when I worked there before, but I'm not sure now." She moved forward and whispered, "You think they may be fixing cases?"

"We're losing important cases, including homicides. I'm not sure what's going on."

Mrs. Delaney shook her head. "I wish Howard were alive. I could talk it over with him."

"If you could continue to watch, listen, and make notes, I'll appreciate it. But don't do anything obvious. And don't call me from an office phone. Your cell, or a public phone will be better."

"You think they're monitoring the calls?"

"Can't be sure. So another phone is safer."

"Oh, my. What have I gotten myself into?"

He didn't tell her how much more he might ask of her or how risky it could become.

———————

The next morning Slate reviewed new case investigations and kicked back a few of them for more detail. He was checking the homicides more closely than the robberies since a cold robbery was more difficult to clear. He wanted to tap DeMeo's phone but he needed more.

After lunch he checked out a Tele-Track monitor system to monitor vehicles from Technical Services. A Tele-Track device worked off strategically located towers within the city to a range of about a twenty-five mile radius. He asked Ernie Shimp not to show it issued to him.

Toward the end of the day Slate proceeded southwest to the Cook County Courthouse on California and Twenty-Ninth Street. He circled the parking lot in his Dodge, looking for DeMeo's 1994 Lincoln, with plate EKS 1853.

On the first round he found it parked in the row closest to the courthouse. He circled again, debating whether the monitor could be attached without being seen. A court order was not required if the vehicle was in a public place and there was no intrusion to the vehicle or its wiring.

He tried to remember what offices were on the south end of the building and who might see him from there. On the second circle he stopped in the lane behind the Lincoln and pulled his hood latch. He got between his Dodge and the rear of the Lincoln, quickly got down on one knee, placed the four by six inch box with four magnets on the bottom of the Lincoln's trunk. The magnets grabbed the metal even through the undercoat and snapped into place.

Slate stood up and moved to the front of the Dodge then lifted the hood. He shifted to the side, as if checking his motor, his back to the building. He then closed the hood and pulled out of the lot. As he headed north on California he checked his monitor. The signal was strong.

From there he drove up to North Avenue, made a U-turn, and pulled to the curb to wait while watching his monitor. About 5:55 p.m. the monitor showed the Lincoln moving north toward him on

Harlem. As the Lincoln got closer it turned west on Chicago Avenue. Slate pulled out and proceeded south, then west on Chicago Avenue. Finally the signal stopped and Slate wondered if DeMeo was at his home on Clinton in River Forest.

He kept moving in that direction and the signal led him to 330 Locust, one block west of the Clinton place. The Lincoln was parked in the driveway. Slate passed the home, made a U-turn at the next intersection, and pulled to the curb. He noted the address in his notebook, then called Communications by his cell, not wanting to be monitored using the radio. The listed owner of 330 Locust was a Carmine Vaccaro.

The next morning Slate called Sergeant Hal Lewis in Intelligence. Carmine Vaccaro was a made guy in the Outfit, an administrator type who could to give orders, including murder. He added the information to the whiteboard then got started on the paperwork generated by the twenty-seven pairs of detectives. More cases were being cleared and moral was getting better, but he had become a paper pusher. The morning moved along with phone interruptions, and an occasional question from a detective.

He had just leaned back to evaluate something he was reading when Commander Arnold came in, looking tense. He slammed the door, moved to the side of Slate's chair, and stood close, facing him.

"What's going on with you and Judge Hayes, Slate? I know we're losing some trials, but like I said, he keeps getting elected."

Slate stood up to meet Arnold's piercing gaze. Was his boss clean? That was no guarantee in a department of over thirteen thousand coppers.

"What's bothering you, Commander?"

"I just talked to Testaverdee at the coffee pot and asked how it was going. He said he's checking on the homicide of Judge Hayes's second wife."

"It's a cold case."

Arnold leaned closer. "Don't bullshit me, Slate. We're from the same school. The Airborne isn't that much different from the Marine Corps and I've been a cop longer than you have. What the hell are you up to?"

Slate lifted both hands, palms forward. "Cool it, Commander. I didn't want to get you in trouble, but I think this guy may be dirty. So I've done a little checking."

Arnold didn't speak for several seconds. "And you were going after a judge on your own?"

Slate didn't respond.

"Do you realize what Deputy Chief of Detectives Urbanski would think of that? Not to mention the brass on Michigan Avenue. I don't want you on an elected judge!" Arnold moved closer and pointed. "You work for me and if the shit hits the fan, we'll both get axed or be back in uniform!" Arnold then stepped back.

"I didn't want anyone else involved because of this very reaction. Are you ordering me to violate my oath of office and ignore a felony?"

Arnold moved close again and shook a finger in Slate's face. "I'm telling you to lay off this judge before we both regret it."

Slate's face flushed but he managed to rein in his anger and decided to try an explanation. "Cool it, Commander. I'll explain.

"I know that we'd lost cases in Hayes's court before I took over here. Now I see all court dispositions and it's much worse than I thought. Just recently we lost the Carbonaro homicide on Alderman Bryan. His wife is a widow with two boys to raise alone because someone didn't like the way Bryan was going to vote. Then the robbery and truck theft in a waste haulers bidding war. The guy who stole a truck in that case talks about being an Outfit guy and gets himself whacked after we talked to him.

"Hayes is on his third wife, and the death of the second one— which Testaverde is looking at—doesn't stack up with a burglar working a sixth floor condo during the night when people are home." Slate decided not to reveal his other information on DeMeo, the law firm, Mrs. Delaney, or the properties Hayes owned since he could not be sure if Arnold was on the take.

Arnold relaxed a bit. "I don't want you investigating a sitting judge unless you have a solid felony case. Understand?"

Slate knew Arnold was thinking about his captain rank with his Commander assignment and being very close to retirement. "If you're telling me to violate my oath of office, Commander, put it in writing!"

Arnold moved toward Slate.

Slate waited.

"I was told you were obsessed with your 'justice for all' thing, but not this department, nor the city, nor the courts, are perfect. You're going to get in some deep shit if you keep it up!" Arnold paused. "I knew you were a hard-ass, but I figured you could straighten out Robbery/Homicide so I got you promoted."

"And I appreciate that. But I'm not going to let a felon walk—judge or cop! If he's dirty, his ass is mine! You do what you have to do and I'll do the same. Maybe you can put me back on the street. I've been there before. But don't think for second that I won't take you or anyone else in this department with me that tries to obstruct justice! I'll tell a grand jury everything I know about this crap . . . that you want to protect!"

Arnold shook his head. He turned and started toward the door then stopped and turned back to Slate. "Any of our brass involved?"

"Not that I know of."

"You think Hayes's second wife was a hit?"

"It doesn't look right."

As Arnold left, Slate thought of Testaverdee and wondered if he was dirty, or was he was trying to impress the Commander. He wondered what Arnold would do. Maybe Rebecca would get her place in Wisconsin sooner than she had thought.

———————

Slate went to the squad room to get a coffee and tried to relax.

Through the afternoon he moved his paper, but before leaving for the day he shut his door, unlocked his whiteboard, and reviewed his notes. Should he add something about the confrontation with Arnold? He wanted a phone tap, but Paula Lyon would need more before her boss, the State's attorney for Cook County, would pursue going after a judge. He was still studying his board when the phone rang.

"Slate."

"Bernice Delaney. I may have something of interest."

"Where are you calling from?"

"I'm at home."

"Good. Tell me about it."

"I answered a call from the Profacci and Bellino law firm again. They asked for Mr. DeMeo. DeMeo took the call, and I took a project and moved to the copier and listened. They wanted to move a case up twenty-five days. DeMeo asked what kind of case, then said it maybe could be moved a hundred days.

"The lawyer must have been upset. DeMeo said he would get back with him. I left as usual at 5:00 p.m. then came back and listened near the partially open door to Judge Hayes's office. I heard the judge say 'twenty-five for an arson and homicide.' Then they both laughed. I left before anyone saw me."

"Good work. What were you going to do if someone saw you?"

"Tell them I forgot something in my desk."

"This is good information. Do you know what case it was?"

"No. I think I could get it though."

"Keep your ears open but don't take big risks."

"Okay. What do you think this means?"

"I'm not sure, but I want to check on a couple things."

The next morning Slate got an appointment with ASA Lyon for 1 p.m. He reviewed investigation reports all morning, but his mind was on his own case.

During his lunch at Smokey's he thought about Hayes and Arnold and wondered who in the department might be involved. Even an assistant State's attorney could be involved by refusing to prosecute, presenting a defective case, or not objecting or appealing a dismissal. But Schneider said Stambaugh presented a solid case and Lyon said he was still pissed about losing it.

He also worried about Bernice Delaney. She was a retired teacher and a widow, but she would be expendable if they thought she put them at risk.

———

Slate was in the lobby when Lyon returned from lunch. Lyon extended her hand. "Lieutenant Slate. How's it going? "

Slate gave a once over to her short blond hair and the fitted green suit that complimented her figure.

"Need a little help, Paula."

"Come in." She motioned him to a chair. Slate closed the door and took a seat.

Lyon removed her suit coat and placed it on a hanger at the end of her bookcase behind her desk, then sat down and slid a yellow pad in front of her. "I thought lieutenants were stuck in the office, but you keep finding work, Ed."

Ed nodded. "I never have been much of a conformist, Paula."

"Maybe that's why you've had some outstanding cases. What's on your mind?"

Slate briefed her on the two cases lost, then on DeMeo and his visit to Carmine Vaccaro. Finally, his informant's report of calls going to DeMeo for moving a case up so many days.

After Paula finished writing, she studied Ed. "Let's make sure I got this right. You lost a case involving the death of Alderman Bryan, who had the swing vote on a casino or a condo development?"

"Right. A faked accident and broken neck. But the only witness was likely an illegal and was probably threatened. So he changed his testimony and moved immediately after the trial."

"And Hayes gives a directed verdict?"

"Right. But your guys had accident reconstruction testify, the ME, and the two detectives testify. Oh, and the Council secretary regarding the upcoming vote."

"I'll talk to Stambaugh if I need to. Then you have a refuse bidding war with an armed robbery and two trucks stolen and run into the lake. And one truck thief's prints are on one truck they didn't take and he is found not guilty, but turns up dead later?"

"We had his print, and an employee saw him standing on the running board the day of the crime. But another G & G driver testified that the suspect did ask him a few days before what their drivers made. Not sure who drove the second truck or pulled the robbery. Then G & G lost the bid to a company with Outfit connections."

Lyon continued. "Then DeMeo, Hayes's officer manager, visits the made guy, Carmine Vaccaro, in River Forest." Lyon checked her notes. "And DeMeo takes calls from Profacci and Bellino about moving a case up by twenty-five or one hundred days?"

"Right. Delaney has heard this same firm calling DeMeo before but she wasn't close enough to hear anything. This time though, she comes back to the office while DeMeo is in with the judge and hears Hayes say to DeMeo 'twenty-five for an arson and homicide,' and they laugh."

Lyon shook her head. "River Forest is full of hoods."

"And Melrose Park and Oak Brook," Slate added.

Paula studied her notes. "Any evidence of a cop involved?"

"Not at this point."

"Who else knows about this?"

"Commander Arnold got on it from a detective I talked to about the death of Hayes's second wife. I said I was checking cold cases, but Arnold didn't buy it. He told me to back off and we had words. I didn't tell him much but he told me to get off Hayes, so I may be back on the street. But I'll still work the case."

"Would he really move you?"

Slate nodded. "He may if he's dirty or too worried about offending someone over him. Detective La Rue did some work on marriage records for me, but he doesn't know about that."

"What about wife number two?"

"A guy on the video in the condo may be 'the Professor,' a hit man out of Miami. He uses a knife."

"'The Professor'?"

"The Bureau says he looks more like a professor than a hit man."

"Hayes had an alibi?"

"He was at a conference in Florida. I need to tap DeMeo's phone, Paula."

She stared into Slate for several seconds then studied her notes. "This is a very sensitive and dangerous one, Ed. A Circuit Court judge and his employee."

"And if we have people involved, I may need to leave before I get my last four years in."

"We both know that some of your people are dirty." Paula paused. "And at this level it would be the brass."

"What about an ASA?" Ed asked.

"It's happened, but rarely. Stambaugh was really pissed over losing the case on Alderman Bryan, and still is."

"Apparently DeMeo is the contact."

"You think the number of days is code for what?"

"Thousands of dollars for the judge's verdict, because the case is never moved up."

"So twenty-five K offered and DeMeo counters with one hundred K?"

Slate nodded.

"We need to know what case this refers to, Ed. Can you learn that?"

"I'll try, but I don't want to get my witness killed."

"I know, but we need more if we want a judge to order a tap in another judge's office."

"And we need a judge we can trust to keep it quiet, not to mention that judge's staff."

"We're into some dangerous stuff here, Ed."

He nodded. "But, if he's dirty, he pollutes the whole justice system, and I want him. I'll see if my witness can ID the case."

Ed stood.

"I'll do the application when you get more info, but the judge will want to hear from both you and your witness on one this sensitive. In the meantime I'll work on the question of which judge to use."

Lyon stood and extended her hand. "We may both have to retire early, Ed."

As Slate returned to Area 3 he wondered if Delaney would be able to determine what case the law firm and DeMeo were discussing without getting herself killed. And if she would stay in the battle long enough to make the case.

THAT EVENING ED and Rebecca took their coffee to the porch.

"What's on your mind, hon?" Rebecca asked.

"Is it that obvious?"

"You're too quiet."

Ed turned in the glider to face her. "Arnold and I had a round today. We were both pissed. He wants me to back off my judge investigation. So we may be in Wisconsin sooner than you expected."

Rebecca studied her husband's face for a long moment. "Why is he concerned?"

"His job, I guess. I don't think he's dirty, but he's close to hanging it up and doesn't want to get in trouble with headquarters. If he's demoted, it cuts his retirement."

"And you're not going to let it go?"

Ed looked deeply into Rebecca's eyes. "Do you want me to?"

"Would it matter?"

Ed jumped up and stood facing his wife. "I'm going to arrest and convict his ass, even if I get forced out early," he declared quietly and firmly.

Rebecca put her face into her hands and sighed but said nothing.

After their walk, they tried to watch television but they both had other things on their minds. Ed's mind was on his investigation and his confrontation with Arnold.

He normally was asleep within a few minutes after hitting the bed but this night was different.

Around two in the morning he awoke to Rebecca yelling and shaking him. "What's wrong?"

"You were having a nightmare and yelling."

Ed used the sheet to wipe perspiration from his face.

"Vietnam?"

"What did I say?"

"Hold it, hold it . . . Fire!"

Ed took a deep breath and wiped his eyes.

"You've done that before. What's it about?"

He hadn't shared much of his one year in the jungle, but he did have dreams at times, mostly after talking to his former radioman, Roger Daniels, or when he had a lot of stress.

"We ambushed a bunch of VC and killed them. We'd lost a six-man scouting patrol the day before. So I took this patrol out. We were deep in the jungle when I spotted a tunnel opening just off the trail, one they forgot to cover. I moved the patrol ahead about a hundred yards and set up on one side of the trail, and waited. It wasn't long before VC came looking for us. We got all nine of them." Ed swallowed, and exhaled loudly.

"Then when we moved ahead, we found our guys. They were stripped of everything but their shorts . . ." His voice broke. "The bodies were mutilated. We carried them back and when we reached the VC we had just killed . . . my guys took their machetes and beheaded all of them and tossed their heads into the tunnel. I didn't stop them . . . and I didn't report it."

Rebecca was silent for several seconds, then rolled over against her husband and laid her head on his chest. "My brave Marine. No wonder you have nightmares."

CHAPTER 14

SLATE SHUT HIS door, checked his IN box, then unlocked his whiteboard beside his desk. Judge Hayes's first wife was from Stevens Point, Wisconsin. Her name was Karen Olson. He called information and then began calling Olsons in that city, asking those for relatives with other names too. After the third call he found Karen's sister, Sherri Herman.

"Mrs. Herman. This is Lieutenant Slate at the Chicago Police Department. I understand that you are the sister of Karen Olson Hayes?"

"Yes. But I haven't been in touch with her for years. Has something happened to her?

"No. I'm in charge of Robbery/Homicide on the north side and looking at some cold cases and I have some questions. I've been told that your sister, Karen, left her husband, W. C. Hayes."

"I guess she did. Karen and I were never close. She was a surprise baby when Mom was forty-six and I was in college. Mom is the one she kept in contact with."

"Is your mother living?"

"Yes, but she has dementia."

"She's not able to talk about Karen?"

"No. She doesn't even know who I am sometimes. She hasn't mentioned Karen in a long time."

"Do you know if Karen has had contact with your mother since she left W. C.?"

"No, I really don't know."

"Okay. If you learn anything at all about Karen, please call me."

Slate finished the day in the office, but he was tired. He hadn't rested well the night before.

———

That night he called Bernice Delaney at her home.

"Lieutenant Slate, Mrs. Delaney. Can you talk a bit?"

"Yes."

"Did you learn what case DeMeo was talking about regarding moving it twenty-five or a hundred days?"

"No."

"See what you can learn from the other staff. If the Profacci and Bellino office calls back, ask them what case they are referring to before you transfer the call to DeMeo."

"I'll try. But I can't promise anything."

"I appreciate your help, and I'll see you're rewarded with some payment."

"It's not that. I just don't want to get myself murdered!"

"I understand."

The next day Bernice Delaney called on her lunch hour. She told Slate she had asked if the docket had to be changed for the case Profacci and Bellino had called about. She was told the defendant was Danny Fischetti and the date didn't have to be changed unless Mr. DeMeo told her to change it. The trial was to be in a couple weeks. She also reported that the charges were arson, homicide, and manslaughter.

Slate called ASA Lyon and relayed the message. Paula told him she had picked Judge Burnett for the phone tap since he had just been elected last year, that he was in his early forties, likely not a close colleague to Hayes. When the appointment with Judge Burnett was set, she would call.

Through the day Slate moved the paperwork but stopped twice to open the doors over his whiteboard and study and change some notes. He wondered where pressure from the CPD brass would come from if Arnold reported his investigation up the ladder.

Late in the afternoon Lyon called to tell Slate they had a meeting with Judge Burnett for 11:00 a.m. the next day.

―――――

At 11:00 a.m. the next morning Lyon and Slate met Judge Burnett in his chambers. Lyon made introductions. "Lieutenant Slate heads Robbery/Homicide in Area 3 on the north side. He'll give you the facts."

"What we need, your honor, is an order to tap a telephone in the office of a Circuit Court Judge and his office administrator."

Burnett raised his eyebrows and shifted in his chair. "Really. And what's the PC?" Slate pulled his notebook from his jacket pocket and laid out the two cases lost, the telephone calls to DeMeo, DeMeo meeting with Vacarro, the three marriages, and the properties owned debt free by Judge W. C. Hayes.

"The detectives came to you complaining about the dispositions on the two trials lost?"

"Yes, sir."

"And how did you learn about the calls from the law firm to this DeMeo?"

"From an employee of his."

"This employee came to you?"

"No, I went looking for former employees and found this one. Then by chance, she was asked to come back to work a twenty-hour week."

"And you think this talk regarding days of continuance is code talk for money to fix the case. Do you know what trial the call refers to?"

"Yes, sir. I did more research since talking to ASA Lyon. It's an arson case where a person died in the fire. The charges are arson, homicide, and manslaughter."

"And who's prosecuting this case, Lieutenant?"

Before Slate could answer, Lyon said, "That would be me, your honor."

Slate looked at Lyon.

"Lieutenant Slate didn't know that until now."

Judge Burnett looked at Lyon, then Slate. "And why is that?"

"He just learned what case it involved. We haven't talked since he received that information except to make this appointment," Lyon said.

73

"Do you know Judge Hayes?"

"Only slightly," Lyon said. "I've tried a few cases before him."

"Lieutenant?"

"I may have been in his court years ago, but I'm not sure. I didn't remember him when I sat in on a trial recently."

"The death of an alderman involved a condo-versus-casino vote? And a robbery and truck theft that was likely a bidding war?" the judge asked.

"Right," Lyon said.

"Do you have any officers involved, Lieutenant?"

"Not that I know of. I'm keeping it to myself as best I can. Commander Arnold, my boss, became aware after I talked to a detective about a cold case involving the homicide of Hayes's second wife. The Commander doesn't want me to pursue the case. We had a heated discussion but I told him I was working the case." Slate paused. "He may get me moved out of Robbery/Homicide, especially if he's dirty or his boss orders it."

"So Hayes's second wife was murdered?"

Slate nodded.

"Was Hayes a suspect in her murder?"

"No, he was in Florida. But it might have been done by a hit man rather than a burglar."

"It sounds like the jury should have heard the case on the alderman's death. On the truck case, the witness identified the man at the truck and the print matched that man?"

"Yes, but the suspect denied being there and said the print was from talking to the driver of the truck earlier in the week when he was inquiring about switching jobs. A driver confirmed that they had talked."

"That one sounds less solid, but you had a witness for the day of the crime." Judge Burnett checked his notes. "You have this DeMeo and Hayes talking and laughing about twenty-five versus one hundred for an arson/homicide after a phone call from the Profacci and Bellino law firm?"

Lyon nodded.

"You need to take a deposition from the lieutenant's witness, Ms. Lyon. And if that's solid, you have your tap."

"Thank you, sir."

Slate nodded.

As Lyon and Slate stood, Burnett said, "If you're wrong, Lieutenant, we will all suffer. But if you're right, you'll have rendered a great service to the city and to our justice system."

In the hall, Lyon got more information on Delaney from Slate and asked him to have her call Lyon for an appointment.

Slate thought about the possible consequences of a case against a Circuit Court judge as he drove back to Area 3. Even if Arnold was clean, CPD brass above Arnold would not like it. And what were the risks from the Outfit? To himself? To his family? Bringing a case like this into the public eye clearly wouldn't help his marriage. Rebecca had been close to leaving him before.

He contacted Bernice Delaney that evening and persuaded her to give a deposition to ASA Lyon and to allow Slate to copy her office key. He mentioned casually that if any legal action was taken against DeMeo, she would have to quit her job. He didn't mention appearing in court if charges were brought against W. C. Hayes.

A few days after the deposition of Bernice Delaney, ASA Lyon called to say the telephone tap was a go. Slate called Ernie Shimp in Technical Services and asked him for a lunch meeting at Smokey's.

———

Shimp was at the entrance when Slate arrived and extended his hand.

"Lieutenant. Is the Tele-Track working okay?"

"Yeah, but now I have another one for you." After they were seated and ordered, Slate briefed Shimp.

"What time do you want to do this?"

"The office closes at 5:00 p.m. but the cleaning people are in later. I'll meet you in the parking lot at 10:00 p.m. How long will it take?"

"How many phones?"

"I don't know, so bring enough for several."

"Maybe I can pick them all up at a terminal box."

———

At 10:00 p.m. that night Slate met Shimp at the Cook County Court House on California.

"Got everything you need, Ernie?"

Ernie grabbed the bag from the seat beside him. "This should do it."

"I'll get us past the security people on the door for a telephone repair. I'm not sure how many cameras we have, so pull your cap down and look down as we go through the building."

Slate's ID got them past the security officer at the door, and the copy of Delaney's key opened the office suite. Shimp worked quickly while Slate monitored the exit doors. Within a few minutes Judge Hayes's, De Meo's, and the three other office phones were bugged.

"Do you still want the recorder here, rather than your office?" Shimp asked.

"Yes. And keep this installation off your records for now. It's a highly confidential investigation. Equipment at my office would raise questions."

They moved to a maintenance room where the telephone terminal boxes were located. The room was locked. Slate went back to the security officer and asked to borrow his key for the room, assuring him he would bring it right back. The officer hesitated, then gave him the keys and went back to reading his newspaper. Slate unlocked the door to the terminal room and then made a clay impression.

While Shimp worked in the terminal room, Slate went to an unmanned side door of the building and found the key that fit on the officer's key ring. He made an impression of it then returned the key ring to the security officer.

Shimp made the connections to a recorder that he hid on the floor behind some boxes.

⸻

The next few days were tense. Each night Slate entered the courthouse through the side door, went to the terminal room, switched tapes, then listened to the previous day's calls. Six days later he heard DeMeo and Anthony Profacci talking.

"Mario, Anthony Profacci."

"What can I do for you, Anthony?"

"On the Danny Fischetti case, remember how we wanted to move it up twenty-five days?"

Mario laughed. "Yeah, that's not gonna happen."

"Well, how many?"

"We can move it seventy-five days if you want. The court docket is set."

"Damn, Mario, this isn't the only move we've moved or will move."

"Arson and homicide are tough to move. I did what I could."

"Maybe I should go with a jury."

"It's your call."

There was a long pause on the tape. "Okay. Seventy-five it is."

Slate smiled to himself. Profacci was hired to protect one of the Outfit's street tax collectors, and they wanted their guy found not guilty.

———

The next morning, he took the tape to ASA Lyon.

"It looks like you have something, Ed. You going to the trial?"

"Sure. I want to watch this Profacci and see how Hayes decides your arsonist and murderer is not guilty. And I haven't seen you in action for a while."

"This will be tough, knowing the fix is in."

"Yeah, but it is a building block, Paula."

Lyon nodded. "I interviewed and subpoenaed Detective Leary from your Unit. His partner, Manacowski, passed away. How will Leary do on the stand?"

"Leary has some experience. He should be okay."

———

Slate continued to manage his load at Area 3 Robbery/Homicide but he recognized he was less focused. He was surprised he hadn't heard from Arnold. Maybe the Commander had decided to play dumb when the thing broke.

A few days later, Bernice Delaney called Slate and asked to meet him again for dinner.

"Do you have some new information?"

"No. I just walk to discuss a few things."

"Okay. Chinese Buffet today?"

"Are you up to Chinese again?"

"Sure. About 5:30 p.m.?"

"Good. See you then."

He called home and left a message for Rebecca.

———

When he stepped into the restaurant Bernice Delaney was waiting just inside the door. She acted tense and Slate knew she had reason to be. When they were seated, Slate said, "Shall we get our food, then talk?"

Slate felt anxiety coming out of her eyes as she studied his face. "I've thought more about this position you've put me in and I don't like it. Judge Burnett told me about the risks."

Slate waited.

"When you came to me looking for help, I had no idea that this could get me murdered. You know better than I do how brutal the Outfit can be, and still you got me involved. Why did you play on my sympathies and involve an innocent ordinary citizen like me?"

Slate weighed his answer. He spoke quietly as he leaned forward. "I think we have a corrupt office administrator, a corrupt judge, and a corrupt law firm, all responsible for allowing murderers to go free. A society can't survive with that kind of greed and injustice, Mrs. Delaney. In just a few months we've had an alderman murdered so the Outfit would have a casino or get their take. We've lost an armed robbery and truck theft case over a waste haulers bidding war with Outfit connections. And that just scratches the surface.

"Do you want Chicago's children and grandchildren to live in that type of society? This is a war, Mrs. Delaney, not World War II or Korea or Vietnam, but a war of good and evil. Chicago has over six hundred homicides every year and over thirty percent of those victims' families never see justice. We also have assaults, rapes, robberies, burglaries, thefts, and many other kinds of criminal activity. We don't have a future if we have corrupt judges."

Bernice Delaney seemed taken aback by his response. Her eyes fastened on his face as he continued making his case for her help.

"I went looking for former employees of that man's office because I needed someone honest on the inside. One employee had left the state, the second was not cooperative and I didn't think he could be trusted. Then I talked to you, Mrs. Delaney, and I recognized someone who cares about what's not right in our city. I need your help to fight this war. One cop for every three hundred citizens, spread over an area thirty-five miles long and fifteen to twenty miles wide can't protect and serve three million citizens without support from the people." Slate waited for her to think a little.

"The police are your representatives. We have officers killed every year. I've been in four shootouts myself, and wounded once. What happens to one of us affects every police family for the rest of their lives. Justice can't be someone else's problem. Citizens have to get involved." Slate paused.

"If you want to skip the meal, that's perfectly alright. I understand why you're concerned."

When Bernice Delaney broke her stare at Slate, Slate thought he saw a new kind of awareness in her eyes. "No. Let's eat."

They got up and moved around the buffet in silence. Slate wondered if he still had an informant. They returned to their seats and were eating for several minutes before Mrs. Delaney spoke.

"I see you point, Lieutenant Slate, but I hope you also see mine. What happens if you're right?"

Slate bent closer and spoke softly. "The deposition you gave for the phone tap has already paid off. A recording pretty well proves what I thought."

"Really? They're fixing cases?"

Slate nodded.

"Now what?"

"Just continue as you have been. But don't do anything out of the ordinary. We don't want you to risk drawing any attention to yourself. If things get hot, we'll get you out of there. And I'll pay for the information when we're done. It won't make you rich, but it will show our appreciation."

The next day Slate was moving investigation reports and supplements when Commander Arnold entered Slate's office and stood in front of his desk. "How's it going, Lieutenant?"

"Moving the paper, sir."

"How's your case moving?"

Slate looked up to meet Arnold's eyes. How much should he reveal? He could not be sure at this point where his boss stood. He decided not to mention the tape. "I still think that we have a dirty judge, but proving it may be tough."

Arnold didn't appear satisfied but didn't push it.

In the afternoon Sergeant Pete Morrison called from Benton Harbor, Michigan PD.

"What's new, Sarge?"

"Checked on your house last weekend, Lieutenant. Same cars were there early Sunday afternoon. The Mercedes, WCH, the Lincoln, EKS 1853, and the BMW, LAW APJB."

Slate made notes. "Okay, Pete. My case is moving, so I'll appreciate your continued reports."

"Anything you can tell me?"

"Maybe corrupt public officials."

Morrison laughed. "Not in Chicago."

"Maybe a couple."

He leaned back. Were they there to plan for the preliminary hearing in Hayes's courtroom? But they were in another state and another department's jurisdiction. He was still trying to figure his next move when the phone rang again.

"Slate"

"Paula Lyon, Ed. The arson/homicide preliminary hearing is set for next Monday, 9:00 a.m."

"That soon?"

"It is quick. Maybe there's some pressure from the outside to clear the arsonist. Are you still sitting in?"

"I'll be there. How long after the preliminary before the regular trial?"

"Hard to say. He still hasn't filed for a jury trial."

"And if he doesn't, that makes my case for payoffs stronger."

"Anything more on the tapes?"

"No. I'm checking every night."

"How about the security officers getting wise?"

"I copied the key to the unmanned side door."

"See you in court."

THE FOLLOWING MONDAY Slate came in early and moved the paper so he could get to W. C. Hayes's Circuit Court before 9:00 a.m. He took a seat near the rear of the courtroom, hoping he wouldn't be recognized. ASA Paula Lyon was at the table on the right side in front of the seating area. A man in his fifties sat beside her. Slate figured he must be Mr. Yost, owner of Yost Furrier. Two men sat at the table on the left. He assumed the one on the right was either Profacci or Bellino. The other man was the defendant, Danny Fischetti.

At 9:05 a.m. Judge Hayes entered, wearing his black robe with the purple trim. The bailiff called the court to order.

At the preliminary hearing ASA Lyon presented just enough brief facts to show there was probable cause for an arrest and trial. She explained Danny Fischetti's attempt to collect street tax, or protection money, but Yost had refused to pay. The furrier's building was torched and the video showed the defendant and only the defendant in the alley to the rear of the building just before the fire was recorded on the video.

Anthony Profacci claimed that his client was patrolling the area and just happened to be in the vicinity of the camera when the fire started. The hearing was brief and Hayes found that there was, in fact, sufficient evidence of the crimes being committed to go to trial. Slate knew Hayes would accept the charges. How else could he collect for a not-guilty finding? Lyon nodded slightly in Slate's direction once, but they did not acknowledge one another.

———

After the hearing Slate checked his IN box and found a note to call a Lieutenant Detwiller in the Deputy Chief of Detectives Office. He considered what the call would be about. Deputy Chief Urbanski was Commander Arnold's boss. It had to be the Hayes investigation. Slate returned the call.

"Deputy Chief Urbanski's office."

"Lieutenant Slate, returning Lieutenant Detwiller's call."

"Slate?"

"Yes."

"The Deputy Chief wants to see you at 8:00 a.m. tomorrow."

"What's the subject?"

"He'll tell you."

"What's the room?"

"It's 208, near the reception area."

"Okay."

Slate didn't know Detwiller, but he didn't like his attitude. Power went to some officers' heads, he knew. He suspected Detwiller was one of those, with all the power in the Deputy Chief of Detectives Office. Urbanski would only know about his questions concerning Hayes from one of two sources, Arnold or the Outfit.

Could DeMeo and Hayes know? He didn't see how, unless the telephone tap had been discovered. Had someone . . . maybe the security officer or a janitor in the courthouse . . .discovered the phone tap recorder?

Was Arnold dirty, or just covering his own ass? How much should he tell Urbanski? And was Urbanski clean? What he needed was someone higher up, to tell him about Urbanski.

He called Sergeant Hal Lewis in Intelligence.

"What's on you mind today, Ed?"

"A quick one, Hal. Do you guys have anything on Paul Urbanski, Deputy Chief of Detectives?"

"Whoa! That's dangerous ground, Ed. What is my old academy buddy up to now?"

"Just a little snooping."

"Right. I know you too well, Ed. Seriously, I know nothing about Urbanski, but they may not tell me at my level if they did have something."

"Thanks, Hal."

Slate called ASA Lyon with the same question. She had nothing. He also briefed her concerning his dinner meeting with Mrs. Delaney.

"So is she still with us?"

"For now. I think I struck a nerve with my comments. But we've got to keep her safe."

"I'll have to rely on you to do that, Ed."

"If we get in much deeper, I'll see what I can do."

"On Urbanski, what do you make of that?" Lyon asked.

"Either Arnold told him, or someone in the Outfit, or Hayes's office is wise."

"Could that be?"

"I doubt it."

"So is Arnold warning his boss of a possible problem, or protecting the Outfit?"

Slate paused. "Arnold could be just covering his own ass, or you could be right, he's dirty and he thinks Urbanski will shut me down. Or Urbanski is dirty and after Arnold's heads-up, he wants to know what I've got. Either way, it puts me in a tough spot, Paula."

"Does Arnold know about the tap or the taped exchange?"

"No."

"Good. Are you going to talk to him before meeting with Urbanski?"

"I thought about that. Normally I would, but then I'd have to get into more detail."

"You'll have to make that call, Ed."

chapter 16

AT 7:50 A.M. THE following morning Slate was waiting in the reception area of room 208 on State Street. At 8:10 a.m., a lieutenant came out of the Deputy Chief's office. He was a slim-built man, maybe forty years old. A paper pusher rather than a street cop, Slate thought as he stood. "Lieutenant Slate."

"Lieutenant Detwiller," he said, extending his hand without smiling. "This way."

Slate had seen the Deputy Chief of Detectives at the annual awards meetings but not recently. Chief Urbanski seemed heavier than when he had last seen him, and wearing a gray suit with a blue tie. Slate wondered if the thick gray hair was actually his. Urbanski stood and shook hands.

"I don't think we've met, Lieutenant, but I remember seeing you in the paper and at the award banquets. You've had a colorful career." He motioned to the chair.

"How many shootings have you been in?"

"Four, Chief."

Slate could tell Detwiller's eyes had opened a slit wider when he heard that answer.

"Commander Arnold tells me you served in Vietnam."

Slate nodded. "Marine Corps Lieutenant."

"I did too, but on a carrier as a naval reserve officer. I was recalled for that war."

"It was a tough war but we could have won it if the politicians in Washington hadn't tried to micromanage."

Urbanski didn't miss the point. "You don't like politicians, Lieutenant?"

"Only if they know their limits and respect the responsibilities of their subordinates."

Urbanski paused and leaned back in his leather chair. "I called you in to discuss your investigation of a Circuit Court operation."

Slate waited.

"Commander Arnold wanted me to be advised of possible repercussions."

Slate nodded. "I just raised a question, Chief."

"What makes you think something is amiss?"

Here it was. Ever since the phone call from Urbanski's lieutenant, Slate had been trying to decide how far he had to go to stay out of trouble in his answer and still make his case. How much had Arnold revealed?

"Since I took over Robbery/Homicide, we've lost two solid cases we should have won. One was the death of Alderman Bryan."

"But that was ruled an accident."

Slate nodded.

Urbanski studied Slate, then glanced at Detwiller, then back to Slate. "So where are you at this point with the investigation?"

Slate had thought about what he'd have to say to answer that. Shimp, in Technical Services hadn't recorded the Tele-Track on DeMeo's car or the phone tap, but Communications would have logged his cell call on Carmine Vaccaro, the made guy DeMeo contacted in River Forest.

But that log entry would get lost in the daily volume of radio and telephone traffic. If it went completely wrong, there was the FBI and a RICO trial. But he was four years from the minimum retirement age. And if Arnold was in fact clean, he would have covered his tail with the notice to his boss but left the details to Slate.

"Lieutenant."

"My detectives have been complaining about losing some good cases. You don't want to hear the details."

Urbanski leaned forward and placed both hands on the desk. His voice rose as he responded. "This is my area of responsibility. I want to hear some details, and I want of copy of your investigation, Slate!"

Slate locked eyes with Urbanski. Who could be trusted? Urbanski was the boss, but Slate knew that one leak could blow his investigation.

"At this point it's more a gut reaction. I was wondering why we lost two good cases and shared that concern with Commander Arnold. I don't have an investigation report."

Urbanski nodded and sat back. "Commander Arnold seemed to think you had more. You need to understand, Lieutenant, that you are responsible for not only Robbery/Homicide performance, but also the morale of the detectives. Don't allow your concern over a couple court cases to affect the detectives' morale and their work."

"Homicide clearance is up since I took over, Chief. I cleared eighty-five percent as a detective sergeant, so I understand our mission."

"Have you talked to Intelligence?"

"No." Slate didn't consider Hal Lewis an official contact and he decided not to mention the arson/homicide trial, just in case he wasn't among fellow cops. "I haven't discussed much with the Commander. The ASA who prosecuted the case involving the death of the alderman was also upset, and I passed that on to the Commander."

"You realize the department could be damaged by a false accusation or charge. That could have severe repercussions for promotions, pay raises, and the entire department. Our budget could suffer if our aldermen thought we were on some kind of crusade."

"I've been on the job twenty-plus years, Chief. I understand."

"Anything else?"

"No. I'm surprised that Commander Arnold raised the issue."

"He didn't want me to get surprised." Slate felt the penetrating look Urbanski was giving him. "You must keep Commander Arnold appraised of your every move, Lieutenant. Heading Robbery/Homicide is much more sensitive than being just a detective sergeant."

Slate slowly nodded but had no intention of following Urbanski's directive.

Slate wondered what his future held as headed north to Area 3 after the grilling from Urbanski. Most officers in his position would have leveled with the Deputy Chief. He knew that. But he had seen too much.

At his desk, he moved the necessary paperwork, then got up and shut his door. He unlocked the doors to his whiteboard beside his desk then added the meeting with Urbanski and added Detwiller with a question mark. He studied the notes, then added Testaverde's name and a question mark. The events of the next few weeks would determine if they had a corrupt judge, and if that corruption included members of the Chicago Police Department.

When a knock sounded at the door, he quickly shut the doors over the board, then opened the office door.

Commander Arnold walked in. "Thought you might be in a meeting."

"No, just trying to get caught up." They stood in front of the desk.

Arnold studied Slate for several seconds without speaking. "How'd the meeting with the Deputy Chief go?"

Slate watched Arnold for reactions as he answered. He figured Arnold was concerned about his own position and didn't want to go back to a captain's spot, but if there was something more, he wanted to be sure his eyes were watching for any trace of personal involvement. "Okay. But I wish you had warned me."

"You're not sure who you can trust, right?"

Slate didn't answer.

"I had to give my boss a heads-up, Ed."

Slate nodded. "I still should have been warned."

"You didn't want to talk to me. Remember?"

Slate didn't respond.

"So what did you tell him?"

"That I was concerned about the cases we had lost and had complained to you. Apparently you didn't tell him much. And I appreciate that, Commander."

Arnold nodded. "Okay. My boss has been warned. Now keep me posted if anything develops."

Slate didn't respond.

When Arnold exited, Slate locked the doors on his board, then sat back and placed his feet on the corner of his desk. He was trying to figure his next move when the phone rang.

"Slate."

"Paula Lyon, Ed. The arson/homicide hearing is set for next Monday, 9:00 a.m.

"I'll be there." Slate was surprised how soon the trial had been set following the preliminary hearing. "They may be getting the case heard early so their collector can get back to work, Paula."

"It is sooner than I expected. Oh, how about your meeting with the deputy chief?"

"He's concerned, but I hedged on everything. I'd rather retire early than let a dirty judge walk. Then the Commander was just in to see me about it. Fortunately he didn't tell the Chief much."

"You may be on something big, Ed. Watch your back—and your witness and your family. There's a lot of risk in what you've taken on."

"I know, Paula. I know."

The remainder of the week was uneventful as Slate moved the paper and weighed different scenarios that could arise from going after a Circuit Court judge with Outfit connections. And who in CPD might also be on the Outfit's payroll? Maybe some of his fifty-four detectives? They would be an excellent information source.

Then there was Bernice Delaney to protect. The Mexican witness to the Alderman Bryan homicide had skipped town after the trial. The testimony of Delaney was vital to his future case, if they could prove this arson/homicide trial was fixed. Delaney was worried, even without knowing all the facts. When they filed on Hayes, Profacci, and DeMeo, Bernice Delaney would be expendable.

BEFORE 9:00 A.M. on Monday Slate was seated in the back and to the left in Judge W. C. Hayes's Circuit Court. The courtroom was nearly full. Slate figured many in attendance were concerned area merchants. Anthony Profacci and his client, Danny Fischetti, were seated up front at the table on the left. Slate could see ASA Paula Lyon at the table on the right.

He thought about Alderman Bryan's trial and the fact that Carbonaro had requested a jury. Apparently the fix wasn't in at that time, but most people in Fischetti's position today would have certainly requested a jury trial. He pictured what it might be like to testify against Hayes when the judge was charged for taking bribes. That would be a great day. He felt for ASA Lyon, knowing she was going to lose this one.

At 9:05 a.m. the judge entered the courtroom and the bailiff called the court to order. The judge asked if the State's attorney and the defense were ready to proceed.

Lyon stood and approached the bench with her tablet. Slate noted her black suit and white blouse. Maybe black was appropriate for this trial. "Your honor, the State will present a case of arson, which resulted in a death. We will show that the defendant tried to extract a monthly street tax from Yost Furrier for alleged protection during the hours when the retail store was closed. The furrier owner, Mr. Carl Yost, refused. His son was sleeping in the rear of the store when a fire was set. That fire killed Mr. Yost's son and caused extensive damage to the building and merchandise.

"We will show that the defendant," Lyon stopped and pointed at Mr. Fischetti, "was the person demanding street tax and was photographed by the camera at the rear of the store at the time the fire was set."

Lyon returned to her seat.

"Mr. Profacci," Judge Hayes summoned the defense attorney.

Profacci stood and approached the bench. Slate didn't know Profacci, but as he approached the bench Slate figured him at about fifty. He was wearing a navy blue suit with a wine floral tie. He had dark, rather long hair. Slate thought about Barona's suits and Dolsi's comment about Angelino's poor clothes. Italians liked their clothes.

"Your honor, the defense will show that Mr. Fischetti offered a service to Mr. Yost for his store and that he declined the service. Then a fire occurred and my client was blamed, based upon this earlier conversation and a video of a man in the alley that they claim shows my client before a fire is recorded. The State has no direct evidence of a crime being committed by Mr. Fischetti, a local businessman who offers security services for retail stores where the traffic is very light after business hours and over the weekend." Profacci sat down.

"Ms. Lyon, do you still have five witnesses?"

"Yes, your honor."

"Call your first witness."

"I call Mr. Carl Yost."

Slate noted that Mr. Yost was a tall man, maybe mid fifties. He walked to the witness chair, took the oath, and sat down. Lyon approached. "Please state your name and business."

"Carl Yost. I own Yost Furrier on Huron Avenue."

"Is that a new business?"

"Yes. We opened last fall."

"And what did you do before opening this business?"

"A career in the U.S. Navy."

"How long was your career?"

Profacci stood and objected to the relevance.

"I'm simple trying to establish the witness's competence, your honor."

"Overruled. Proceed."

"How long was your tour and what was your rank?"

"Twenty-seven years. I retired as a captain."

"And a naval captain is equal to a full colonel in the Army, Marine Corps, or Air Force, is it not?"

"That's correct."

"So you commanded others?"

"Many. I was the executive officer on a carrier of nearly six thousand sailors and Marines. The exec is second in charge."

"Now tell the court how you met the defendant, Mr. Fischetti, and when."

Yost leaned forward in his seat. "Last winter he came in and wanted to provide security protection during the hours we were closed. I said I wasn't interested. He explained the dangers when the Loop area is lightly populated. I still declined.

"Then this spring he was back with the same pitch. Only this time, he talked about vandalism and fires, and what that would do to our furs. I declined again, then talked to my son, Keith."

"And did the defendant, Mr. Fischetti, offer to provide you with a written contract stating what services he provides for this fee?"

Yost looked at Fischetti. "He did not."

"And your son, Keith, was how old?"

Yost took a deep breath. "He would have been twenty-eight in July."

"And what was his career?"

"He served as a Naval officer and a Seal for a six-year tour. Then he became a stock broker."

"And what did the two of you decide about this street tax offer."

"Objection," said Profacci "This payment was for security services."

"Rephrase your question."

"What did you do when you declined this extra protection?"

"We had three wide-angle video cameras installed viewing the front, the inside, and rear of the store. The rear one was placed outside to view the loading dock area."

"What did these cameras look like?"

"Like a spotlight. They were a combination light with a motion detector and a camera."

"So you were offered this alleged protection twice by the defendant and you refused, then installed the three cameras after discussing your concerns with your son?"

"Yes. Then after the second protection offer, Keith began sleeping at the store periodically. He was single and commuted by car to Deerfield. So when he worked late, he stayed there."

"How did you learn of your son's death?"

Yost glanced at Fischetti, then to Lyon. "A fire department captain called me at home. Then the detectives talked to me."

"What happened then?"

"The detectives had their forensics people take a gas can found in the area and all three videos from the cameras."

"What was the extent of your losses?"

Yost hesitated, then spoke with difficulty. "The fire killed our son . . . our only child, and caused half a million dollars worth of damage to our store and the furs."

"Did your wife also work at the store?"

"Yes."

"And how did you feel when this happened?"

"My wife and I spent twenty-seven years of our lives to make sure our country and our way of life was secure. Then we come back home and find that no one is protecting us or our business!"

Lyon returned to her seat.

"Mr. Profacci."

Profacci approached Yost. "Mr. Yost, did my client threaten you or you son in any way?"

"In his own way he did."

"Did he brandish a weapon or tell you what he would do if you didn't want security protection?"

"No. But I knew what he was implying."

"Did you see my client other than at the two contacts several months apart?"

"No."

"Did you have any problems at the store until the fire?"

"No."

"Did you see him set the fire?"

"No, but the camera did."

"I move that latter answer be struck."

"That will be covered in other testimony, Mr. Yost," Judge Hayes said.

"So you're upset about a fire that, regrettably, killed your son and you're blaming my client."

Yost moved forward in his seat and pointed at Profacci. "And you're defending a murderer!"

"I move to strike that."

"So ordered."

Profacci returned to his seat.

"Anything more, Ms. Lyon?"

Lyon approached Yost. "Since the offer for this extra protection, have you talked to other merchants in your area?"

"Yes, and several pay the costs. There're afraid not to."

"Objection. The witness doesn't know what they think."

"Restrict you testimony to what you know, Mr. Yost," Judge Hayes said.

"The defendant collects this protection money from some store owners on Huron Street?" Lyon asked.

"Yes. It's street tax for the Mafia!"

Profacci jumped to his feet. "Objection!"

"Strike that statement."

Lyon entered the cost of the fire into evidence as exhibit #1. She turned toward her seat, then turned back to Yost. "In Chicago, Mr. Yost, it's not known as the Mafia, but the Outfit." She then took her seat.

"You're excused."

"Call your next witness."

"I call Chicago Fire Department Captain O'Rourke." O'Rourke was in uniform. He was sworn and took the stand. Slate remembered seeing O'Rourke years ago when he was working the street but didn't know him.

"Please state your name and occupation."

"Captain Michael O'Rourke, Chicago Fire Department."

"And how long employed?"

"Eighteen years."

"What is your education and training, Captain?"

"Associate degree in Fire Science, graduate of the Chicago Fire Fighter Academy, and Arson Specialist training."

"How many hours of arson training did that involve?"

"Eighty hours at the Illinois Institute of Technology."

"Have you testified as an expert witness and Arson Specialist in other criminal trials?"

"Yes, many times."

"In what jurisdictions?"

"Mostly in Chicago and the suburbs."

"Now, did you respond with your crew to the fire at Yost Furrier?"

"Yes. After I viewed the scene and talked to Mr. Yost, I suspected arson."

"And what did you investigation reveal, Captain O'Rourke, regarding the early morning fire at Yost Furrier?"

"It was immediately suspicious due to the location and materials in the area."

"Please explain."

"There were no flammable materials like papers or cardboard boxes outside the rear of the building. It's an old building with paneling over old wood shingles. One piece of paneling showed a fresh crack where it had been pulled out from the building. The fire started there, in the old dry wood shingles and burned into the building.

"There was no insulation, so once it burned through the shingles and wood sheeting it quickly came in contact with cleaning fluid stored along the rear wall. There was evidence of a major explosion. Mr. Yost's cot was on the other side of that room, and he . . ." O'Rourke glanced at Mr. Yost, "he was basically cremated by the explosion and intense fire from the highly flammable cleaning fluid."

Slate noticed Yost staring down at the floor with his head in his hands.

"How do you believe the fire was started?"

"With rags soaked in a flammable liquid, then placed between the paneling that had been pulled out to expose the dry shingles."

"How did you conclude that?"

"Part of the rag burned off and fell to the ground. That piece was recovered and tested for an inflammable liquid."

Lyon walked back to her table and picked up an evidence bag. "Is this the piece of rag, Captain O'Rourke?"

The Captain examined the bag. "Yes."

"What was the inflammable liquid?"

"Gasoline."

"And was any type of gasoline container found in the vicinity of the fire?"

"After I determined it was an arson, and Mr. Yost's son had been killed, I radioed for detectives. Detectives Leary and Manachowski showed me a gas can they found in a dumpster just across the street in the next block. It was laying on top of other trash, so it likely hadn't been there long. It still had some gasoline in it."

"Objection. There is no evidence that the can was connected to the fire."

"The can was in close proximity to the fire, your honor, and the fire was started with gasoline." Lyon said.

"Overruled."

Lyon entered the fire investigation report and the partially burned rag as exhibit #2.

"So, it is your position that this was a set fire?"

"Yes."

"Have you seen other cases where a merchant refused to pay for this security protection and a fire occurred?"

"Two others. Those were small and caused little damage."

"Do you know what those store owners did after the fire?"

"No, I don't."

"So there were no papers, boxes or flammable material at the rear of the Yost store, or weather conditions that would have accidentally started this fire?"

"No."

Lyon returned to her seat.

"Mr. Profacci."

Profacci approached. "Can you prove that this fire was intentionally set?"

"Yes, by what I testified to."

"And can you prove who set the fire?"

"I have viewed the video of the defendant, the only person on the video."

"But does that video show my client setting the fire?"

"No, but—"

"You've answered the question."

Profacci took his seat.

They broke for lunch from 11:40 a.m. to 1:15 p.m.

After lunch, Judge Hayes said, "Call your next witness, Ms. Lyon."

Lyon called Detective Leary. Slate watched Leary walk to the stand. He was about Slate's size, six feet, and trim. He had been in Robbery/Homicide for five years and had a reputation as a capable detective. Leary was sworn and took the stand. Lyon walked him through his education and training.

"Did you work the fire death of Keith Yost?"

"Yes, along with Detective Manacowski. We were called by the Fire Department."

"And Detective Manacowski is since deceased?"

"Yes."

"Did you call Forensic Services?"

"Yes."

"And why was that?"

"Because Captain O'Rourke, Manachowski, and I all saw it as an arson."

"And did Forensic Services supply you enlarged photos from the video camera?"

"Yes."

Lyon retrieved an evidence bag from her table and handed it to Leary "Detective Leary, is this the photo?"

"Yes."

"And were you able to identify who the person was recorded by the surveillance video?"

"Yes." Leary pointed to Fischetti. "The defendant, Danny Fischetti."

"And, did the videos record any other persons in the alley that night?"

"No. Only the defendant was recorded."

Slate knew that Lyon couldn't get Fischetti's record in, even though that was the way he was identified from the video.

"While searching the area after the fire, did you find any evidence?" Lyon returned to her table and picked up a gas can.

"Yes. In the alley just across the street in the next block I found a two-gallon gasoline can in a dumpster."

"And is this the can?"

Leary checked the tag. "Yes, it is."

"Any fingerprints on the can?"

"No prints were found."

"Was there any gasoline remaining in the can?"

"Yes. A little."

"Your investigation then concluded what, Detective Leary?"

"That the fire was an arson and was set by the defendant, Danny Fischetti, based upon his attempt to collect a fee for protection, the video of Fischetti in the alley just before the fire was recorded, Captain O'Rourke's investigation as to how the fire started, and our own investigation."

"And did that the fire cause the death of Keith Yost?"

"Yes. He never had a chance once the cleaning fluid exploded."

Lyon entered the investigation report and gas can as exhibit #3, then returned to her seat.

"Mr. Profacci."

Profacci approached Leary.

"Does the video show my client setting the fire?"

"No, but—"

"Just answer the question, detective. Does just seeing Mr. Fischetti patrolling the alley for his customers, make him guilty of a crime?"

"No."

"Do you know if this gas can was in any way related to the fire at Yost Furrier?"

"No, but it was on top and still had gasoline in it."

"So it could have been placed there by anyone?"

"Yes."

"In other words, detective, you have no direct evidence that Mr. Fischetti set the fire?"

"We have the video that places him, and no one else, in the area at the time."

Profacci returned to his seat.

"You may step down. It's now 4:20 p.m. We will resume tomorrow at 9:00 a.m." Hayes struck his gavel once.

Lyon spoke briefly with Mr. Yost and Captain O'Rourke. After Hayes had left the courtroom, she walked back and sat down next to Slate. He thought the ASA looked tired. Knowing she was going to lose this case due to the fix with Hayes's office certainly didn't help.

"What do you think, Ed?"

"Looks good."

"But I'll still lose."

"But it's a building block in our bigger case."

Lyon gave Slate a sober look and nodded as she stood and left the courtroom.

———

The next morning everyone was in place by 9:00 a.m. "Call your next witness, Ms. Lyon," Judge Hayes said.

"I call Forensic Technician Howard Bauer." Bauer took the oath and was seated.

Lyon walked him through his education, training, and experience. He testified that the video in the camera in the rear of the building recorded a man in the alley walking toward the loading dock, but on the other side of Keith Yost's car at 3:40 a.m. At 3:44 a.m. the man walked back into the alley, carrying something in his right hand.

Lyon asked if the object could have been a gas can. Bauer said it could have been. It was a square object, but visible for only a fraction of a second before he moved out of view. At 3:53 a.m. or nine minutes later, the camera picked up a glow from a fire coming from the rear of the building and on the other side of the car. He also testified that the video images were blown up and given to Detectives Leary and Manachowski.

Lyon entered the forensic report and video as exhibit #4.

Profacci approached Bauer. "Did the film show my client setting the fire?" the defense counsel asked the witness.

"No."

"And did you identify Mr. Fischetti from the film?"

"No."

"So you have a film that shows a man in the alley. Later a fire starts at the loading dock where boxes, paper and other flammable material may been thrown."

"Objection," Lyon said. "The fact there was no trash stored behind the building has already been covered."

"Sustained."

"But the video does not show my client setting the fire, does it?"

"No, but the fire was visible within nine minutes after the defendant was recorded in the area."

"But it doesn't show him setting the fire does it?"

"No"

Profacci took his seat.

Slate wondered how Hayes could toss this case due to its strength, Lyon's presentation, and with the death of Keith Yost. It was clear that Fischetti was the arsonist, even if the death was unintentional.

"Call you final witness, Ms. Lyon," Judge W.C. Hayes said.

"I call James Kim." Slate had not met Mr. Kim and wondered how Lyon was going to use this witness. The small Asian man approached the witness chair with some hesitation. He was sworn and took the stand.

"Please state your name and occupation." Lyon said.

"James Kim, owner of Loop Cleaning, 112 Huron Street."

"How long at that location, Mr. Kim?"

"Six years."

"Do you know the defendant, Mr. Fischetti?"

Kim nodded his head.

"Please answer for the record, sir."

"Yes."

"How do you know him?"

"I pay for security for my business."

Slate could see Kim becoming more confident.

"How much, and when?"

"Every month. A hundred dollars."

"Did you receive a contract from the defendant for this service?"

"No, but I asked for one."

"What is the hundred dollars to cover?"

"He said he keeps my business safe at night and on weekends."

"Why do you feel you need to pay this fee?"

Kim paused. He avoided looking at Fischetti as he answered. "I thought my place might be damaged or burned down if I didn't."

Profacci jumped up. "Objection. No basis for that has been established."

'The witness responded to his concerns, your honor."

"Overruled."

"Do you know that others pay for this protection?"

"Yes."

"Mr. Kim, during your six years of paying for this security protection to Mr. Fischetti, have you received written reports from him?"

"No."

"Photographs of a risk at your store?"

"No."

"Any contacts by the defendant to discuss security concerns?"

"I never talked to him after his first stop, but I saw him a few times around my store in the daytime."

"In six years of payments of one hundred dollars per month, you receive nothing from him?"

"Objection. My client patrolled the area when Mr. Kim was closed."

"If I may, your honor."

"Proceed."

"Mr. Kim. Did you ever stop at your store after hours and on weekends?"

"Many times."

"Did you ever see Mr. Fischetti there?"

"No."

Lyon took her seat.

"Mr. Profacci."

"Nothing, your honor."

"You have just one witness?" asked the judge.

"Yes, your honor."

"Call your witness."

"I call Danny Fischetti."

Slate watched the defendant walk to the witness chair. Fischetti was short and heavy. The only hair on his head was at the sides and rear, and worn long. Slate watched Fischetti swagger as he walked to the front. The defendant took his seat in the witness chair and was sworn.

Profacci approached the witness.

"State your name and occupation."

"Danny Fischetti, Security Services."

"Explain the services you provide."

"I check on businesses at night, over the weekends, and holidays. I check to see if doors are locked, and that flammable materials are not stored near the building. I take photos of any risks and report them to the owner."

Profacci continued. "On the night in question, were you patrolling in the area of Huron Street?"

"Yes, I was."

"And do you carry equipment with you when you are on patrol?"

"Yes. A small bag with my list of customers, a flashlight, my camera, and maybe a sandwich and bottled water."

"So if you were seen in the area, it was while you were patrolling to protect your customers?"

Fischetti nodded. "Yeah. Checking around each property."

"So you could be photographed by any camera used in many different parts of the city?"

"I guess so. I walk around many buildings and down many alleys during the night and on weekends."

"And during your patrols do you ever encounter street people or vagrants walking or sleeping in the allies or along buildings?"

"Yeah, all the time in good weather, and even in bad weather if they can find an exhaust vent to lay on or near."

"And did you find any of them starting a fire to stay warm?"

"Yeah, in bad weather, they'll have a fire in a barrel or a metal bucket."

"So, it's common at night to find all kinds of people roaming, sleeping, or warming themselves in these alleys."

"Yeah, all the time."

Slate knew this was true and could give Hayes an out.

Profacci sat down.

Paula Lyon approached Fischetti. "Did you, on two occasions, contact Mr. Yost to offer this security protection?"

"I may have. I contact many businesses with my security services."

"And do you point out the risk of a fire or theft if they don't pay for your services?"

"I explain the risk at night and on the weekends when the area is lightly traveled."

"Why did you walk to the rear of Yost Furrier on the night of the fire and not just stay in the alley?"

"Checking on security problems and the rear door."

"But Mr. Yost had not paid for your services."

Fischetti hesitated, then grinned. "I still check on potential clients. Then if I find a problem, they may change their mind."

"And if you encounter so many of these vagrants in the alleys, why are none of them recorded in the alley behind Yost Furrier on the night of the fire?"

"I don't know."

"Do you have any other employment or income other than this security service, Mr. Fischetti?"

"No. I stay pretty busy with it."

"I'll bet you do."

"Objection."

"Sustained."

"How do you explain the fact that a security camera shows you walking to the rear of the store, then within nine minutes a fire is recorded?"

Fischetti shrugged. "I have no idea."

"Do you carry a gas can as a part of your equipment?"

"Objection."

"Strike that."

Lyon sat down.

"You're excused. Let's take a short recess before final arguments."

In the hall Slate thought about Lyon's closing argument as he waited for the recess to end. She had grounds for a strong one. He gave her credit for presenting a solid case even though they both believed the trial was fixed. He wondered how the payments were made. Likely from an Outfit guy to DeMeo, then to Hayes. All in cash, of course. He would see Lyon after the verdict, but he didn't expect it today. It would look more legitimate to take the case under consideration, then rule later.

The bailiff called the court to order.

Lyon approached the bench with her notes to summarize the case. "Your honor, the street tax, or security fee, was solicited. Mr. Yost declined to pay and he was approached a second time. His store was burned. Although the arsonist may not have been aware that Keith Yost would die, he is at least guilty of arson and manslaughter."

Lyon turned and grabbed another paper from her desk. "The defendant was identified at the rear of Yost Furrier and nine minutes later the fire is recorded. And he is recorded on video carrying an object that appears to be a gas can. Danny Fischetti is the only person recorded that night in the alley behind Yost Furrier. A gas can is found in a dumpster near the scene of the fire. The defendant does not provide a genuine security service evidenced by the lack of a contract, reports, or photographs over a six-year period, as testified to by Mr. Kim."

Lyon moved to another position and pointed at Fischetti. "His guilt in the arson fire at Yost Furrier and the death of Keith Yost, and the damage of five-hundred thousand dollars, has been proven beyond a reasonable doubt. Therefore, your honor, the only disposition the court can render is guilty."

As Slate had predicted, Profacci countered that his client was a businessman providing security services to merchants and just happened to be in the area protecting his customers at the time of the fire. He could understand Mr. Yost's grief over his son, but Mr. Fischetti was not responsible. Perhaps a fire used by street people to warm their food or themselves had accidentally led to the explosion and the death of Keith Yost.

"I will consider all the facts and render a verdict within a few days," Judge Hayes announced. He rapped the gavel once.

"Court is adjourned," the bailiff announced.

Slate waited in the hall for Lyon. "Good work, Paula. You covered all the bases."

"But I lost."

"What's our next move after the not-guilty?"

"I think we should talk to my new boss, Mark Erwin."

"What happened to Chet Crawford?"

"He decided to return to private practice. His public service salary wasn't paying the bills."

"Will Erwin take on the Outfit?"

Paula exhaled a weary breath before she answered. "We'll know very soon, Ed."

"I'll call if we get anything on the tape."

ON WEDNESDAY SLATE had two days of paperwork to push through the system but his thoughts kept replaying the two-day trial that was surely fixed. Who was involved besides Hayes, DeMeo, and Profacci? How many in CPD?

At 5:20 p.m. he was sitting along North Avenue at Pulaski, watching his monitor. At about 6:00 p.m. the signal showed DeMeo's Lincoln moving north, maybe on Kedzie. The signal then went west. Slate moved south, then west on Chicago Avenue. The signal stopped in River Forest. Slate found the Lincoln in the driveway of Carmine Vaccaro, the same made guy DeMeo had contacted before. Apparently Vaccaro was the Outfit's contact for Hayes, but Profacci and Bellino were the law firm doing the trial work.

From River Forest Slate drove back east and then south to the courthouse to change the tape. He pulled into the lot at the side of the building to avoid the security staff posted at the doors on the north and south ends, keyed into the side door, into the telephone terminal room and quickly changed the recorder tape.

As he drove toward the northwest side and home he wondered about the safety of his family when it became clear who had initiated the investigation of Hayes. The Outfit would do what ever was necessary to protect their family. It was time to discuss the risks with Rebecca.

———

After dinner they stayed at the kitchen bar since it was later than usual and the evening was exceptionally cool for late spring. Ed turned left to make full eye contact with his wife. "I'm still on my judge investigation, Becky, so we need to be a little more cautious."

He summed up the major points of his investigation. "This one is big—a judge, his office guy, a law firm, and the Chicago Outfit—so there are some risks. I want you to be alert to any unfamiliar cars or strangers in the neighborhood or to being followed when you're out. I'll warn Tim, and Sarah at Northern Illinois."

Ed watched his wife's shoulders sag as the weight of his words sank in. Worry lines creased her face. "Of all the men I had to choose from, I married a Chicago cop."

Ed tried to lighten up her mood. "Wisconsin was never this way, huh? We'll be fine."

"Now what?"

"I'll move the weapon in our bedroom to the kitchen, and get you back on the firing range if you want. Keep the doors locked and be alert. I'll also warn District 16 and ask their tactical officers to spot check our house. If this goes to the grand jury, we'll take other precautions. People in our department may be involved."

"In your old cases that were big, you expected me to live in fear for you. This time you're telling me that your wife and children at risk too, wherever we are. This is no way to live, Ed."

"I know Rebecca, but let's hang tough and see this through. As I told my witness, it's a war between good and evil." Rebecca didn't make eye contact with Ed and didn't respond to his words.

———

The next morning Slate called District 16 to request checks of his home. After he processed the pile of paperwork he shut his door and listened to the tape from Wednesday, the day after the trial. DeMeo had called Anthony Profacci that morning.

"Anthony, we have a problem. The Fischetti case needs a fifty-day extension; the docket is very tight, given the new information."

"We already agreed on seventy-five days."

"I didn't know then how tough the schedule was. Things have gotten tighter this week."

"Is this from the man who sets the schedule or you, Mario?"

"He told me to reset the schedule after the past two days."

"This is bullshit. The schedule was set."

"Things have gotten worse. And we have a guy watching the docket, Anthony."

"Maybe I'll go with jury trials in the future."

"You could do that—talk to Carmine—he understands our docket—the problem if Danny can't work."

Slate stopped the recorder. As he suspected, Danny Fischetti was collecting street tax for the Outfit. The fee had been raised because the case Lyon presented was stronger than what Hayes had anticipated. And Slate was probably the guy they were referring to as watching the docket. He called ASA Lyon and let her hear the tape.

"That's great stuff, Ed, if we can convince them the days are code talk for money. We'll need more to do that."

"Like some financial records?"

"Right. There will be risks, Ed."

"I've warned my wife and the kids. A question, Paula. Do I remove the recorder now, or after a grand jury indictment? Also, I have a bug on DeMeo's car."

"The indictment will make them check everything," Lyon said.

"I think it's time to give Delaney some money for her help and have her resign."

"You could get Delaney out now, but leave the tap and the bug on the car until I see how long it will be before the grand jury is set. Erwin may require the financial records to match the telephone calls. We have an informant fund and I can get five hundred dollars for Delaney."

"Okay. I'll pick it up soon and warn her."

How far would corrupt people go to stop him and his witnesses? Given the threat of prison, he knew that no one was safe.

Delaney didn't work in the judge's office on Mondays so Ed called and asked to meet at her home, then stopped at the ASA's office for the cash.

———

He pulled up to Bernice Delaney's house before 5:00 p.m. She quickly answered the door and stepped back for Slate to enter. He could see that she was tense.

"I wanted to stop on the way home and give you this for your help, Bernice." He handed her an envelope. "The five hundred dollars is from Assistant State's Attorney Paula Lyon. Her fund is larger than mine. It's for your help with information about the judge's activities and for giving your deposition. This case will likely go to a grand jury. To be safe you need to resign now. If the jury indicts DeMeo and Hayes, you should not be working there. We'll keep you safe."

"I'm afraid your money isn't enough to take care of the problems that are ahead for me, Lieutenant. They already know where I live. I wish I had known what I was getting into before I agreed to meet you and then to help you."

"I understand. There are risks for my family too. I briefed my wife last night."

"Maybe I should move to Denver near my son, or Phoenix near my daughter."

"You'll be needed here for the trial. After that, you'll be free to relocate wherever you want to be."

Mrs. Delaney lowered her head into both her hands then lifted it to look Slate in the eye. "Why didn't you tell me things would go that far, Lieutenant?"

That was one question Slate didn't want to answer. He wondered himself how he could have handled his investigation differently without involving an innocent citizen so directly. He didn't want to give her the entire picture of the risks that were building but decided to give her one more caution. "Don't answer the door unless you know who it is. And call 9-1-1 if you think you're in any danger. We'll keep you safe."

The next afternoon Slate was shuffling departmental paperwork when ASA Paula Lyon called.

"What do have, Paula?"

"Hayes found Fischetti not guilty."

"Your case was strong."

"He ruled that a video showing him in the alley didn't prove he set the fire, and there were no fingerprints or other direct evidence to Fischetti."

"A jury would have convicted him with his two attempts at the street tax, then him going up to the building, then the fire nine minutes later."

"Sure. That's why they didn't request a jury. They knew they could buy Hayes."

"Right, and after DeMeo's call to Profacci and likely his call to Vaccaro, the fifty thousand was added so Fischetti could get back to work for the Outfit."

"I'll talk to Erwin. I think you and I can handle the grand jury request, along with Delaney's deposition. Is she okay?"

"I gave her the informant's fee last night and let her know it's time to resign. She's nervous. She talked about moving near one of her kids, but I said she was needed for court."

"Can you keep her safe? The tap might get tossed without her. That's our probable cause."

"I'll cover her before the indictment is published. You'll call when we're ready to meet with Erwin?"

"Right."

Slate got up and shut his door, then unlocked his whiteboard and added the call between DeMeo and Profacci, and the arson/homicide trial being lost. He also noted delivering the cash and his warning to Delaney to resign. He then stood back and tried to decide on what steps had to be taken to get DeMeo and Hayes convicted while still keeping Mrs. Delaney and his own family safe.

The next day Lyon called to say they had a meeting with State's Attorney Mark Erwin at 9:30 a.m. the following morning. Slate already had a full day of paperwork to catch up on. It was good to have his notebook current on the corruption investigation. Somehow he would carve out the time he needed to study the way he had the details arranged on his whiteboard to prepare for that meeting.

CHAPTER

19

SLATE ARRIVED AT the Cook County Courthouse on California about 9:25 a.m. Lyon made introductions in Erwin's office. With the State's attorney's dark hair just starting to gray, Slate figured Mark Erwin in his mid forties, about his own age. He wondered about Erwin's background. Most SAs were just average prosecutors, and some were clearly in the wrong business. That's when the police and the public suffered. He sometimes wished he had gone to law school himself after his Marine Corp tour rather than marrying right away and going with the PD.

They moved to the conference room adjacent to Erwin's office. Erwin shut the door and took the seat at the end of the table. Slate moved to the right side and Lyon to Erwin's left. "Paula tells me we have a problem with a Circuit Court judge, Lieutenant."

Slate nodded.

"She gave me some of your background. Twenty years with CPD, ten as a detective, and now heading Robbery/Homicide. And one hell of an investigator. I'm sure you'd like to know where I'm coming from."

"That's always helpful."

"I graduated from Norte Dame and the University of Chicago. Practiced criminal law four years with Gilbert and Mitchell, then fifteen with Louis, Morgan, and Van Winkle.

Slate nodded. The guy knew criminal law and criminals.

"So, give me an overview of what makes Judge W. C. Hayes corrupt."

Slate looked at Lyon. "Shall I lead off?"

"Sure. I'll cover any gaps."

Slate briefed Erwin on the death of the alderman who had the swing vote, the robbery and truck theft in the waste haulers bidding war, and the arson death at furrier who refused to pay the street tax. Then the phone tap with Mrs. Delaney's help, and the code talk with the Profacci and Bellino law firm, the trial lost and the follow-up call from DeMeo for more money before a verdict was announced. Erwin nodded and kept writing. Slate also explained Judge Hayes' several wives and the properties he owned in three states.

Lyon jumped in. "And Profacci and Bellino, and a casino, have been Hayes's largest campaign contributors."

Slate then mentioned DeMeo's contacts with Carmine Vaccaro.

Erwin nodded. "Vaccaro, huh? River Forest, Melrose Park, and Oakbrook have some Outfit guys. Can we show any money changing hands?"

"Not at this point," Lyon responded. "Maybe if we subpoena some bank records."

"And Hayes's, Profacci's, and the administrator DeMeo's cars have all been seen at the Michigan place," Slate added.

"You saw them?"

"No. A detective from Benton Harbor."

"What's Hayes make?"

"About a hundred and sixty-five K," Lyon said.

Erwin looked at his notes for several seconds. "I could get this through a grand jury." He paused. "But with a sitting judge, we're on dangerous ground politically if we lose. And if you're correct, our lives are in danger."

Slate nodded. "That's the risk of war, sir."

Erwin studied Slate, but didn't speak.

"I say put him away," Lyon said. "We'll deal with the side issues as they arise. I'd love to put him in with the kind of guys he's letting walk."

"You're ready to prosecute this one, Paula?"

"I am. Ed and I have worked on other tough cases." She glanced at Ed. "And we'll make this one."

"That's right. I don't think this one can be ignored."

"You have the PC, no question about that, but can we convict them? I wish we had proof of the money move."

"We'll get the bank and telephone records after we get a secret indictment," Lyon said.

"That may or may not yield something," Erwin said. "We have your witness in the office and her deposition, of course. You need to keep her safe, Lieutenant."

Slate nodded.

"What judge did you use for the tap, Paula?"

"Burnett. He's fairly new and I don't think he knows Hayes."

"See him and get subpoenas for the bank records now for Hayes, his administrator . . . what's his name, again?"

"DeMeo," Lyon said.

"Right. And Profacci and Bellino. See what the bank records show at the time those three cases were lost."

Slate also wanted a PEN register to see Arnold's and Urbanski's calls, but without some proof, he knew Erwin won't go for it.

"You want to see the bank records before we try for an indictment, then?" Lyon asked.

"With a sitting Circuit Court judge, I think we have to see what we find."

"How, about a PEN register on Carmine Vaccaro and DeMeo?" Slate asked. "See who they're talking to, and if anyone in CPD is involved."

"Old Vaccaro, he's been around a long time, but no rap sheet last time I checked."

Slate nodded.

Erwin looked at his notes. "DeMeo is the administrator for W. C. Hayes?"

"I tailed him to Vaccaro's place twice."

"You think DeMeo may be the messenger, and if it's cash, is picking it up and delivering to the judge?"

"Right. And that would prove the connection with the Outfit. Vaccaro is on our list of made guys."

"Okay, get those two also, Paula. Your tap will cover the calls DeMeo makes from his office."

Slate nodded.

"Then, we'll see where we go from there." Erwin paused. "You realize that if this goes wrong, my political career will be very short."

"I'm four years short of my retirement age," Slate said, "and my Commander and Deputy Chief are asking questions that make me wonder if either of them is involved."

"We're on a slippery slope folks, so let's get it right."

———————

Slate arrived the next morning with his Starbucks and a Danish. He hadn't slept well, but no nightmares. However, this case posed all kinds of risks. Not only to himself and his career, but also to Rebecca and Tim. He thought Sarah was safe out at Northern Illinois University at DeKalb. Even with the risk, he couldn't walk away from a corruption case involving a judge and the Outfit. He actually enjoyed the challenge.

Slate wondered what Lyon would find in the bank and phone records. Considering the political risks, would Erwin actually take the case to the grand jury? Would Delaney hang in there? And could he keep her safe? Who might be on the Outfit's payroll in Area 3? He thought about the heated discussion with Commander Arnold and his meeting with Deputy Chief of Detectives Urbanski.

He reviewed several homicide and robbery investigations and kicked back a few for more detail, but his mind kept circling back to his own case. It could be his biggest case, or a major disaster. On his way home he monitored DeMeo, but the judge's administrator went directly to his home in River Forest. Slate then turned back east to the Cook County Courthouse and slipped in to change the tape in the recorder.

———————

The following afternoon ASA Lyon called.

"Good news, Paula?"

"Right. Have the orders from Judge Burnett for the bank checks on Hayes, DeMeo, and the Profacci and Bellino law firm, and the phone checks on Vaccaro and DeMeo."

"Great. Nothing of interest on the tape I picked up last night, and DeMeo went straight home."

"I'll be in touch when we get the records. You're taking care of Delaney, right?"

"I told her to resign, and I'll put people on her before an indictment is published. One more thing, Paula, would you prepare an introductory letter for me to present to the State's attorney in Benton Harbor, Michigan? Give them a brief summary of our investigation without giving anything away, but with Hayes's involvement. I'll see if I can get my detective friend over there to go with me to meet the SA and get some bugs in Hayes's summer home. I think that's where the planning occurs, and maybe the payoffs."

"We may have to use the FBI and RICO on that, Ed."

"I know it could end up with a racketeering charge, but the information from there could help our case first, even if I can't use it in court, and I don't want to hand the Bureau all my work."

"Okay, Ed. I'll write the letter. When you going?"

"A soon as I can get a meeting set for over there."

"I'll call."

Slate moved the paperwork, but his focus was still on his own investigation. He was thinking about Hayes when the phone rang.

"Slate."

"Lieutenant Slate, this is Scott Delaney in Denver. My mother, Bernice Delaney, tells me she has been helping you on an investigation."

"That's true, Scott. What can I do for you?"

"She's really worried, and wishes she had stayed out of it. Can you get along without her? She doesn't need this stress and risk after all her years of public service as a dedicated teacher, Lieutenant."

"I understand, Scott. I explained to your mother about a citizen's duty, and the risks to all of us."

"Yeah, she told me. And she feels some obligation, but she is afraid."

"I promise to protect her. I've told her to quit the part-time job, and I'll put detectives at her home before anything goes public."

There was a long pause. "So you can't keep her out of it?"

"I can't, Scott. This is a critical investigation and it's too late to turn back. She's a critical part of it. We will keep her safe."

"Okay, Lieutenant. I'll try to reason with her."

Two days later Lyon called to say her letter for the State's attorney with jurisdiction in Benton Harbor was ready. Slate scheduled an appointment to pick it up. Then he called Sergeant Morrison in Benton Harbor and explained his plan for bugging Hayes's house. Morrison agreed to arrange a meeting with his State's attorney. Morrison called back when he had set the meeting for 1:00 p.m. the next day.

SLATE WAS IN the office until 10:00 the next morning then headed for Michigan to meet Sergeant Morrison for lunch before their meeting with the State's attorney. It was a warm, sunny day and it felt good to get out of the office. He took the Skyway through Gary, then back onto I-94 in Michigan and into Benton Harbor. He arrived at the Red Lobster Restaurant just before noon. Morrison was waiting in his car and got out with Slate.

"Lieutenant Slate?"

Slate extended his hand. "Ed Slate."

"Pete Morrison."

Slate was always curious as to whether his impression of a person on a phone matched the real person. Sergeant Morrison was a shorter man than he had expected, maybe five-nine, and in his late thirties.

"You like seafood?"

"Sure. How's business in Benton Harbor?"

"Well, it's not like Chicago, I'm sure, but we have our problems even in a city of twelve thousand." They were seated at a rear corner table that provided some privacy and allowed them to see who entered.

"We're set with your SA for 1:00 p.m.?"

Pete nodded. "Todd Orr, late forties. Been in office only three years."

"Any background in criminal law?"

"Some, but he moves slowly and carefully. He wants to be reelected."

"What did he do before?"

"Career Army guy, then in a local practice that handled some criminal work."

The server took their orders.

"You head Robbery/Homicide?"

Slate nodded.

"How many detectives?"

"Fifty-four."

"That's more than our entire department."

"With twelve thousand you must have about thirty officers?"

"Thirty-four, but we use about fifteen more auxiliaries in the summer when many of your folks show up. Sounds like an interesting case you're on, Ed. A bad judge?"

"It is. How long you been on, Pete?"

"Started in 1980, so fifteen years. Eight as a detective."

"And you report to who?"

"Lieutenant Ferrell."

"Is he okay?"

"You mean can he be trusted?"

"Yeah. Just to be safe, let's keep the details between the two of us. We're hoping to get enough to go with the grand jury and I'd like to strengthen our case with intelligence from here. I don't want the FBI involved, at least at this point. I appreciate your help with spot checking the home." Slate pulled a note from his pocket. "Here's one to add to your list. He's a made guy in the Outfit. Carmine A. Vaccaro. Driving a 1995 Mercedes, Illinois plates, CAV." He handed the note to Morrison.

The server brought their orders. They ate for several minutes without comment.

"How much experience has your department had with bugging a place?" Slate asked.

"We handle it unless it's a tough one. Then we use the State Police."

"So, either way you can do it?"

"We'll likely use the State Police on this one due to the sensitivity of the case, and they have better equipment that's tougher to detect."

"Good. Once an indictment is out, these guys will get someone to do a sweep of their offices and homes. We're checking bank and phones now. If that's good, I may have other names for you."

"You figure they're doing their planning here?"

"And maybe some payoffs. A good bug could provide a wealth of information."

"You don't want to do a RICO, with the two states involved?"

"I don't want the FBI in on this unless I have to. They always take over, and I've done too much work to give them the case."

"How did you get on to this judge?"

"I knew we had lost some good cases in this one felony court, but when I took over the Unit about nine months ago, I saw all the dispositions. So I began my own investigation, knowing my department would not approve taking on a sitting judge. But if he's dirty, his ass is mine!"

Morrison nodded and grinned.

———

Slate followed Morrison to State's Attorney Orr's office. The sergeant made introductions and they moved to a small conference room down the hall. It appeared to be a general meeting room.

The SA still wore his hair in a military cut that did nothing to mute his piercing eyes. Slate liked a guy who could look him in the eyes while talking. He figured he was getting the truth then. He wondered how sharp Orr was, given his limited criminal experience. "Here's a letter of introduction from Assistant State's Attorney Paula Lyon. We've worked together on several cases over the years. And she's working this particular case."

Orr read the letter. "You head the Robbery/Homicide Unit and have a corrupt judge?"

Slate nodded.

After Slate thanked Sergeant Morrison for his help, he briefed Orr and gave his deposition. On the basis of Slate's statement the SA thought a judge would approve the bugs for Hayes's summer home. He would have Morrison contact Slate when it was ready. The monitor would be at the Benton Harbor police department.

Slate thanked Orr for his help and headed back to Chicago. As he drove through Benton Harbor he thought about how different it would be to work here. Compared with Chicago's three million, small towns were a different world. He knew that some large city officers thought they were the "real police," but there were about seven hundred thousand law enforcement officers in the U.S., and during his twenty years Ed Slate had worked with many good cops.

The inept politicians were a problem in many places, both in the villages and the big cities. He had always thought that a metro police concept, absorbing many of Chicago's hundred and sixty-plus suburbs, would provide better policing and greatly improve communications in the Chicago area. But the local politicians would resist that.

21

SLATE CONTINUED TO review the homicide and robbery investigations from Area 3 Robbery/Homicide detectives, but his mind was on his own investigation and the risks involved. He changed the tape on the phone tap to Hayes's office again after several days but there was nothing significant. He wondered whether Mrs. Delaney's resignation from the part-time job had aroused any suspicion in the office.

A few days later Sergeant Morrison called to say the bugs were in place and tested in the Hayes house in Benton Harbor. He would keep Slate informed.

He had hung up the phone and was wondering about ASA Lyon when the phone rang again. It was Lyon.

"I have some information, Ed. When can you meet?"

"You name it."

"How about in the morning, maybe at 10:00 a.m., so we can both move some things first."

"See you at 10, Paula."

Slate wondered if the bank and telephone information was good. He then thought about his own phone. Could it be tapped? It certainly could be if a superior ordered it. Probably being too paranoid, but he unscrewed the handset and checked. It looked okay at that point, but the tap could be anywhere in the building's wiring or at the Illinois Bell switch building.

———

After dinner that evening Ed was still thinking about what Lyon might have when Rebecca came to the family room. Ed looked up as she sat on the arm of the sofa, facing him in his recliner.

"What would you think if I took a leave of absence and Tim and I went to my folks' place for a while?"

Ed studied her. "You that worried? This Hayes case could go on for months. The church won't go for a long leave of absence."

"And we have to live in fear here all that time?"

"I notified District 16 to watch our house. When the indictment is published you can ride with someone from church, and we'll pay them. Or you call a different cab each day."

"Each day?"

"So they aren't able to pinpoint the cab company you're using."

Rebecca raised her voice. "Edward, no one should have to live this way!"

Ed placed his hand on her knee. "I'm sorry, Becky. A judge is letting murderers walk for a fee. The city can't survive with that kind of justice. Mr. Delaney, my witness's son, called me the other day. He's worried too, but I need her testimony."

"How do you get into these kinds of cases, Ed? Robbers, murderers, serial killers. Now a corrupt judge."

Ed looked over at Rebecca. "What do you think?"

Rebecca looked at him with teary blue eyes for a long time before speaking. "Because you're very good at what you do I guess. But it's so hard on the rest of us Ed!"

He nodded. "I know, Becky."

———

Slate was in ASA Lyon's waiting room by 9:55 a.m. At 10:05 a.m. a woman left the office and Lyon waved him in. Erwin was in her office.

The SA stood and shook hands, "Lieutenant Slate."

"Mr. Erwin."

Slate shut the door and took a seat in front of Lyon's desk beside Erwin.

"How's it going?" Erwin asked.

"The bugs in Benton Harbor are in place."

"Good. Nothing so far?"

"They'll call."

"They were able to handle it?"

"They do some, but the Michigan State Police did this one. I had to give a deposition."

"I would have required that."

Lyon looked at the reports in front of her. "The bank checks were good with Hayes and DeMeo. Couldn't tell anything with Profacci and Bellino. Just too much money moving there." Lyon handed a copy of the records to Erwin and Slate. "They settled on seventy-five days before the Yost arson trial, then DeMeo demanded another fifty before Hayes gave the verdict."

Slate studied the records. Hayes had deposited $56,250, and DeMeo $18,750, before the trial. So, the split was 75% and 25% and they both deposited all of it.

"Now, check the record after the trial and before the verdict," Lyon said.

Slate flipped the pages. After the renegotiation Hayes deposited another $37,500, and DeMeo deposited $7,000. So, Hayes deposited all of his again, but DeMeo kept back $5,500 of his twenty-five percent.

Erwin turned toward Slate. "Looks like your code-talk theory was on target."

Lyon continued. "On the pen register for Carmine Vaccaro, he called DeMeo's home several times in the last three months. And he called a CPD member at his home." Lyon paused and looked at Slate.

Slate studied her face, thinking about the options. Commander Arnold. Deputy Chief of Detectives Urbanski. Or Lieutenant Detwiller, Urbanski's staff officer.

Lyon continued, "Urbanski."

Slate shook his head and looked at Erwin. "Paul Urbanski, our Deputy Chief of Detectives. I thought about him, but I also wondered about Arnold, or Dewiller, Urbanski's staff lieutenant. I thought he might be profiting from all he hears in that office. Urbanski has nearly thirty years in. I didn't think he would risk it." They all sat without speaking for several seconds, trying to figure how to handle the information.

"You report to who?" Erwin asked.

"Commander Arnold, and he reports to Urbanski. We need a check on Urbanski's calls from home."

"I agree," Lyon said. "Urbanski could claim that many people call him. He can't control that."

"How many calls from Vaccaro to Urbanski's home?" Slate asked.

"Four over the last three months."

"Urbanski called me in after Arnold found out I was looking at the homicide of Hayes's second wife. Detective Testaverde told Arnold."

"How did he know?" Lyon asked.

"I had Testaverde in to discuss the homicide of Mrs. Hayes, the second wife, letting him think it was just an open cold case. This puts me in a tougher position, Paula."

She nodded. "But it's better Urbanski than Arnold."

"Urbanski is downtown?" Erwin asked.

"Right. I have to live with Arnold up at Area 3. I feel better about him, but we didn't check his phone."

Erwin asked, "You think he was just giving his boss a heads up on the possibility of a judge being investigated?"

"Yeah. I didn't tell him very much, but he told Urbanski even less than I shared with him. Maybe Commander Arnold is wiser than I thought." Slate paused. "I have a bunch of names and facts on my locked whiteboard in my office...should anything happen to me."

Lyon and Erwin looked at him.

"Also, my wife is worried and wants to take our son and go to her folks' place in Wisconsin until this is settled."

"Ed has been in several shootouts." Lyon said.

Erwin studied Slate and nodded.

Over the next week things were quiet, but when time permitted, Slate was using his whiteboard to analyze the options. He noted what it would take to get Hayes, DeMeo, the attorney Profacci, the made guy Vaccaro, and Urbanski. Vaccaro would be hard to make without a paper trail or phone tap. Then there was Fischetti, who torched the furrier and killed Yost's son and was found not guilty. How could he get Fischetti? Arnold probably would not help to get his own boss, Urbanski, unless it was a rock solid case.

He stepped back and sat on the end of his desk, studying his notes. Then there was Rebecca's frame of mind. They had faced many stressful issues in his years with CPD, but she had never before suggested leaving him and going to Wisconsin with their children. He could give all of it to the FBI, but damn, it was his case!

––––––––

He was just finishing his lunch and reading the *Chicago Tribune* in Smokey's near the rear when someone stepped up close. He looked up to see the former Deputy Chief of Detectives, Larry Seryak who had retired several years earlier.

"I noticed you back here alone, Slate. Mind if I join you?" Slate nodded to the other chair and laid the paper down.

"I hear you're now heading Robbery/Homicide."

The server arrived and Seryak ordered coffee.

"I've had the Unit for several months. How long have you been retired?"

"Five years. Paul Urbanski has my old spot. So how's business?"

"Homicides are down a little since you retired, but we're still overloaded."

"You've increased the clearance rate considerably, I hear."

"I paired up detectives that could work together. What about you? Working, or fully retired?"

"I'm with Vaughn Security. We cover a number of places in the city."

"Was Vaughn one of ours?"

"Herb worked in several places, but he was a Commander in Area 4 on the west side when he retired." Slate remembered hearing that Vaughn's retirement may have been encouraged but kept quiet.

"You can't be too far from that magic age yourself, Ed."

"Four years."

"Then what?"

"I may be good for thirty."

"I could put you in a good spot with us."

Slate evaluated the comment. Was Seryak making him an offer?

"Either then, or now, if you want to get out early. We have some interesting cases."

"Who's your major clients?"

"Oh, banks, retail stores, warehouses, casinos, trucking companies."

"Sounds a little tame after working homicides."

Seryak got serious, leaned closer. "We have to slow up sometime, Slate, and working security after twenty years with CPD is much safer than some of the things you can get into out there."

Slate studied Seryak's face. Was he speaking for the Outfit, for Urbanski, or was it a legitimate offer? He felt his insides tighten. The thought of knocking Seryak's ass off his chair crossed his mind. But that would be taking the bait.

Slate stood. "I'll keep that in mind, Seryak." He leaned over and got closer to Seryak. "But in my twenty years, four guys have tried me and they're all dead."

Seryak picked up his coffee without responding.

As Slate walked back to Area 3, he could feel the tension in his body. Decking Seryak would have been a pleasure, but he would have been suspended and charged. Why Seryak's offer? Had Urbanski made a call? He wasn't worried as much about his safety as he was for Rebecca, Tim, and Sarah. Silently he prayed for their safety and his own.

Back at his office he shut his door, unlocked the doors over his whiteboard, and noted Seryak's threat. He thought about his Dodge Charger in the lot and Rebecca's car at church. In spite of his comment to Seryak, he knew there were many ways to get a person. One call from a guy like Vaccaro, and a hit man would be looking for the target. He was relieved that Arnold still appeared clean.

———

On Monday, Sergeant Morrison called to report that Hayes and his wife had been in Benton Harbor, but the bugs picked up nothing other than a noisy romp in the bed. Slate commented that things could get very interesting once an indictment was published.

It had been about ten days since he talked to ASA Lyon regarding more phone records. Nothing more had been found on the recorder in the courthouse. He had monitored DeMeo's travels several times, but there were no more contacts with Vaccaro. He expected more on the tap once an indictment was issued and published. If they were smart, though, they would cool it and have their cars and homes swept for devices.

He wondered again about pulling the recorder in the courthouse and the Tele-Track from DeMeo's car before an indictment was published.

Tuesday morning ASA Lyon called to report she had the additional phone records, and that a meeting with her boss, State's Attorney Erwin was set for 1:00 p.m.

Slate moved the paper, then shut the door and opened his white-board. He added the information about Hayes and his wife at Benton Harbor but skipped the bedroom scene.

To prepare for the meeting with Erwin and Lyon he took out his notebook and recorded one name below another on the left side of the page: Hayes, DeMeo, Profacci, Vaccaro, Urbanski, Fischetti, Ruggerio, and Seryak. Then to the right of each name he noted their status and any crime he believed he could prove, including bribery, conspiracy, extortion, robbery, arson, truck theft, manslaughter, and maybe tax evasions if the feds got involved. He decided to add Arnold, but left the space blank beside that name.

CHAPTER

22

AT 1:00 P.M. Slate entered the State's attorney's conference room. Erwin and Lyon, already in a discussion, nodded to greet him. Slate sat down across from Lyon, opened up his notebook, and waited.

"We've been discussing DeMeo's and Urbanski's calls from home," Lyon said.

"Anything good?"

"DeMeo called Vaccaro twice in the last two weeks."

"Erwin checked his notes. Your Deputy Chief of Detectives, Urbanski, recently called Vaccaro from home."

"Are we ready for the grand jury?" Slate asked.

"I think so," Erwin said, "but let's decide how we approach this. We have Hayes and DeMeo fixing trials for Profacci even if we can't identify Profacci's cash moves. Your tap showing the payoffs changing while the arson case verdict was pending will get Profacci even without a bank record. If we nail Hayes, DeMeo, and Profacci, one of them may give up Vaccaro. He's likely paying, but we couldn't find any bank trail."

"You checked his too?" Slate asked.

"We figured we needed that," Erwin said, "but he's too smart to leave a trail, at least locally."

"Maybe give him to the Bureau on a RICO after we're done, if we pick up something in Benton Harbor," Slate said.

"That may work," Lyon agreed.

"On Urbanski," Erwin continued, "I think we let him wait also. Get Hayes, DeMeo, and Profacci indicted, then see if any of them will give us Vaccaro or Urbanski. If not, we go after them separately and build what we can in the meantime. Or do like the Lieutenant says and try for a RICO. Even if we can't make Urbanski, we can get him retired, I'm sure."

Slate nodded.

"By the way," Slate said, "I was approached at lunch recently by a retired cop. Larry Seryak. Urbanski replaced him. He works for Vaughn Security. Vaughn was Commander in Area 4. Anyway, Seryak offered me a job...either now, or when I retire. He said it would be 'safer.'"

Erwin and Lyon looked at Slate. "And?' Lyon asked.

"I wasn't sure if it was a warning or an offer, but I think it was a warning. So I told him there had been four others who tried me and they were all dead. I figure Urbanski talked to Seryak."

"I'll check the record for Seryak's number," Lyon said.

"This is a can of worms, Lieutenant," Erwin said.

"Yeah, with over thirteen thousand cops you always have some misfits, but when it's the Deputy Chief of Detectives, that's another matter."

"Urbanski reports to whom?" Erwin asked.

"The Chief of Detectives, who reports to a deputy superintendent."

"So, he sees everything from Area 3?"

Slate nodded.

"Then are we agreed on our approach?" Erwin asked.

"We go after W. C. Hayes, Mario DeMeo, and Anthony Profacci now," Lyon said. "Then see what we get from those cases or can develop on Vaccaro and Urbanski."

"And, maybe Seryak, if we can develop more," Slate said.

"Right." Erwin checked his notes and looked at Slate.

"Fine with me, Paula," Slate agreed, "but let's get Urbanski out of there as soon as we can. He can monitor all of my official actions."

"Okay," Erwin said. "We'll get our grand jury together and let you know, Lieutenant." Erwin rose and shook Slate's hand.

Slate pocketed his notebook. "How soon will it be?"

Erwin looked at Lyon. "A couple weeks, I guess."

"I'm going to put people on Delaney before the indictment is published. Her son called me. What should I do about the phone tap, and my bug on DeMeo's car?"

"What do you think, Paula?" Erwin asked.

"I would leave the phone recorder. The worst thing that could happen is they find it and Ed loses some equipment. But we may still get something good."

"Okay. Leave the tape."

Slate waved and left.

───────

At Area 3 he checked his IN box and reviewed investigation reports. That afternoon he was in position to monitor DeMeo but the suspect went directly to his River Forest home. Slate changed the tape at the Courthouse before heading to the northwest side and home.

───────

When he tried the rear door of his house it was locked, as he had coached his family. He knocked and Rebecca checked to see who it was before unlocking it. In her right hand was the pistol from the bedroom. She laid it on the counter beside the refrigerator, then turned and gave her husband a quick kiss.

"How's my main squeeze?"

"Dangerous."

"Good. You remember how to use it?"

"Just point and pull the trigger."

"Right. It's double action only. Hold it with both hands. Remember how it recoils. Any problems?"

"No. When will it be in the paper?"

"A couple weeks, they say." He decided not to mention Seryak's threat.

Ed removed his gun belt and hung it on the knob to the basement door, then sat at the breakfast bar. Rebecca worked at the counter and range, preparing dinner.

She turned toward Ed. "You know the scripture about turning the other cheek?"

He nodded.

"What do you think about that?"

He thought of the many firefights in the jungles of Vietnam, and his first kill. He had hardened himself to the life-or-death risks after that but he did his best to block the memories out. Like Roger Daniels his radioman had said, a movie could remind him and cause a restless night. He also thought of the shootings he had been in. "I guess it makes sense with the family, friends, and neighbors. But, if we applied that to soldiers and law enforcement, we would be speaking Japanese, German, or Russian. And the Outfit would be running Chicago, probably the whole country."

"I don't like the idea of killing someone."

"When it's us or them, what choice do we have?"

"I know you have nightmares, Ed, and I don't want to have to live with a conscience like that." She paused. "So, even as a Christian, you can pretty much forget about shooting a man?"

"Yeah, when it's me or him."

A look of resolve began to form on Rebecca's face as she said, "If someone comes after me, or Tim, I'll use it."

"Good. Take care of business Becky, and let God sort them out."

———————

The next week was tense, but finally ASA Lyon called with the grand jury date. They would meet in one week, at 9:00 a.m. the next Monday. She had subpoenaed Bernice Delaney, Detective Schneider on the death of Alderman Bryan, Detective Barona on the waste hauler robbery and truck case, Detective Leary on the Yost arson and death, and Slate for the overview. They couldn't file on the first two trials lost, but citing those cases would provide some background as to how the phone tap came about. Lyon would oversee the presentation and present the case to the grand jury.

Slate decided it would be best to cover Delaney early just in case there was a leak from the grand jury. He called Sergeant Waddell and asked him to come to his office for a meeting. He was still moving paper when Waddell arrived.

"Shut the door, Rick." They moved to the table. "I have an assignment for some of your people, to start next Monday night. I want you to use Leary and La Rue, and Barona and Ingram." Rick took notes.

"They are to give 24/7 protection to a Mrs. Bernice Delaney, at 6031 Taylor in Oak Park. Here's the info." He slid the name and address across the table.

"She's a witness in a major case and I told her, and her son who called me, that we would protect her. Her life may be in danger. We were going to wait until the indictment is published, but I'm afraid of a leak. This is between the two of us for now. You need to tell Oak Park PD that you have a detail there.

"Schneider, Barona, Leary, and myself will be subpoenaed to the grand jury for next Monday. Nothing to the detectives until they get their subpoenas. By Tuesday or Wednesday it will hit the papers and all will know what's happening. I know taking this many people off their assignments will impact our clearance, but it must be done. You can figure out how you're going to handle the extra eight hours of overtime for four detectives to cover the entire week."

"I knew you were on something big. How long does this run?"

"Probably weeks."

"Ed, this kills us."

"I know, but we don't have a choice. Oak Park is not going to cover our witness. Have the others pick up the pending cases that the four I've assigned to Delaney are working."

Rick looked at his boss. "You'll fill me in when the jury finishes and it goes public?"

"There's still some loose ends."

AT 8:45 A.M. ON Monday Slate was at the Cook County Courthouse in the lobby near a conference room being used by the grand jury. Bernice Delaney sat tensely next to him. Barona came in and took a seat on the other side of Slate. The other witnesses arrived within about ten minutes. Slate talked quietly with Mrs. Delaney about the 24/7 coverage on her home beginning that evening. She didn't respond.

At 9:10 a.m., after ASA Paula Lyon had given the opening statement to the jury, she came to the doorway and called Detective Schneider. He would cover the investigation of the death of Alderman Bryan in the phony auto accident. About twenty minutes later Detective Barona was called to cover the robbery and truck theft in the waste haulers bidding war. Then Detective Leary went in to cover the arson and death at Yost Furrier and Fischetti's not-guilty finding by Hayes. Bernice Delaney was next.

About 11: 50 a.m. Lyon came out into the lobby.

"We're breaking for lunch until 1:30 p.m., Ed. Then you're on, then I'll wrap it up."

"Okay, Paula. What do you think?"

"It went well. Mrs. Delaney was tense but remained in control of herself. Her testimony went just like her deposition earlier in your investigation."

"I told her we would cover her home beginning tonight, Paula. I'm afraid of a leak."

"Good."

"You're still okay with me pulling the bug from DeMeo's car? Once this hits the media, they'll have their cars, homes, and offices checked and I'll lose an expensive piece of equipment."

"You're leaving the phone tap?"

"Right. How do we handle arresting and booking them if we get a true bill on all three?"

"Whoever represents them will surrender them for booking."

A little grin played at the edges of Slate's face. "That takes all the fun out of arresting, cuffing, and searching a corrupt judge, Paula."

"You can have your fun in court. I expect both Hayes and DeMeo will be put on leave with pay until they're tried."

————

After the indictments Attorney Nicolas DeCenzo brought Hayes, DeMeo, and Profacci in for booking. Slate instructed Sergeant Waddell to have them processed. Later, when Slate went to the squad room for coffee, he saw them waiting to be fingerprinted. Hayes spoke to Profacci, who looked toward Slate and nodded.

Hayes strode over and stopped very close, facing Slate. "When I'm found not guilty, Slate, I'm going to sue your ass for everything you have or ever will have. Then I'll sue your department and you'll be done!"

Slate was surprised that Hayes had the guts to confront him and hesitated while looking down at the man standing too close. His first thought was to deck him right there.

He leaned closer to Hayes's face and raised his voice for all to hear. "I'm not your biggest problem, Hayes. Your biggest problem is staying alive long enough to stand trial. If you survive that long, then it will be trying to stay alive in the pen. The Outfit knows your whoring days are over!" Hayes recoiled a step and some detectives in the squad room clapped.

"I'll take everything you own!" Hayes turned and moved back to the line.

Slate glanced at Profacci and DeMeo as he moved toward the coffee pot. DeMeo appeared worried and intimidated.

After prints and mug shots were taken and bonds posted, all three men were released. Since the department had not been called by any reporters, Slate figured the media either had not yet seen the grand jury action, or were still evaluating it.

However, on Tuesday, the *Chicago Tribune* and the *Sun Times* covered the story. CIRCUIT COURT JUDGE AND ADMINSITRATOR INDICTED the *Tribune* announced on page one. The *Sun Times* read, JUDGE W. C. HAYES INDICTED. Slate read the *Tribune* story at home, then the *Sun Times* at the office with his Danish and Starbucks. Profacci's coverage appeared later in the articles. The squad room was noisy with the night shift staying over to talk and the day shift not leaving on investigations.

He was reading about Hayes and DeMeo's being put on paid leave pending the trial when Commander Arnold walked in, shut the door, and pulled a chair from the side table to the end of Slate's desk. Slate waited, not sure what to expect.

"I should chew your ass, Ed, but I admire your guts." He shook his head. "Taking on a Circuit Court judge! You should have been more open with me. But you didn't know if I was dirty too, right?"

Slate weighed his words before he spoke. "I figured it was my neck, and you couldn't get blamed if you didn't know."

"But do you have the goods to convict them?"

"I think so, and the State's attorney, and the grand jury agree."

"This could get hairy. I expect we'll hear from Urbanski. Hayes will fight this to the end, and you're at risk, Ed. And maybe your family. The Outfit may try to hit you and your witnesses."

"I know. Hayes threatened me yesterday. I have my witnesses covered, but my wife is worried."

Arnold nodded. "I don't blame her."

"Do you know Seryak?" Slate asked.

"He had Urbanski's spot before retirement. He and Vaughn, from Area 4, have a security business."

"I think he delivered a threat to me the other day in Smokey's."

Arnold sat back. "That so?"

"It was a job offer, but it was a threat. And that was before the grand jury."

Slate could tell Arnold was gauging what he heard before he spoke. "He has an inside source."

Slate nodded.

"Damn, Ed! This is bad. You still carry your backup piece on your ankle?"

Ed nodded again.

"Maybe I better carry mine."

"If you or I get called in to see Urbanski, let's keep our comments to what's in the paper," Slate said.

Arnold got up, slid the chair back to the table. "Okay. Watch your back."

Slate moved the paperwork that had built up during his grand jury appearance. Waddell came in for a more detailed briefing and reported the detectives assigned to Mrs. Delaney's home were in place starting last night.

Slate called Sergeant Morrison in Benton Harbor and gave him a heads up on the indictments. He pointed out that now was a critical time for a meeting there by the suspects and reminded Morrison to watch for Vaccaro's Mercedes too.

Just before lunch, Arnold called.

"Yes, sir?"

"We have a meeting with Deputy Chief Urbanski for 1:00 p.m. He's really pissed."

Slate considered telling Arnold about Urbanski's calls but decided to wait until he was sure about Arnold. "You want to go with me?" Slate asked.

"Right. Let's leave by 12:15 p.m."

"I'll be at the back door."

CHAPTER 24

A LITTLE AFTER 1:00 p.m. Urbanski opened his door and called them in. Slate noted that Lieutenant Detwiller wasn't present. Clearly this was going to be tough. He hoped Arnold would hang in.

The two men took seats in front of the desk. Two newspapers were folded on the side of the desk.

Urbanski leaned forward and fixed a glare on Slate. "I asked you the other day to brief me on this investigation, Lieutenant, and instead, I got a bunch of bullshit!"

He looked at Commander Arnold. "You're the Area Commander, Arnold. I expected you to keep me informed."

"He didn't have anything to pass along, sir," Slate said.

"You kept it from both of us?"

"It came together quicker than anticipated, and I never reveal anymore than necessary during an investigation, Chief."

"Well you better start when you're dealing with me! I'm the Deputy Chief of Detectives. If you can't follow orders, you'll be back in uniform directing traffic on Michigan Avenue or working in the south end where you'll have some real crime!"

Urbanski glanced back and forth from one to the other. Wondering how much trouble he was in, Slate thought.

"This is a very serious charge, Lieutenant, and it's on you. We all know a grand jury is led by the State's attorney and the detectives. And like they say, a grand jury will indict a ham sandwich if the State's attorney asks it to. If you're wrong, think of the damage to our department image and our relations with judges. No one will trust us. Then, if you're right . . . and we had a corrupt judge, things could get dangerous for you and your witnesses."

Slate didn't respond.

"Wait outside until I finish with the Commander."

Slate stepped outside the Deputy Chief's office to wait in the small lobby. About five minutes later, Arnold came out.

As they rode back to Area 3, neither spoke for several minutes. Then Arnold said, "He's dirty, right?"

"Time will tell, Commander."

Slate dropped Commander Arnold at the back door, then parked his Dodge near the doorway, figuring there would be more foot traffic there than in the lot, making it more difficult to place a bomb. He wondered about an explosives detector. Technicians used gas monitor probes when searching for a buried body, and dogs could detect explosives, but he wasn't aware of a portable explosives detector. That would be worth checking with Technical Services.

As he climbed the steps to Robbery/Homicide on the second floor he was feeling a rush. What a challenge! A dirty judge, his administrator, a defense lawyer, and maybe their Deputy Chief of Detectives.

He called Technical Services and learned that if such portable explosives detectors were available, CPD didn't have them. Slate asked them to check and get one for him if possible.

He found two notes. One from Barona, and the other from ASA Lyon. He returned Barona's call. "What do you have, Joe?"

"I wish I had been with you on this grand jury case, Lieutenant."

"I do too."

"Late this morning I spotted the same car passing Delaney's home three times."

"What time?"

"Between 3:00 a.m. and 4:00 a.m."

"Get a plate?"

"No. The light over the plate was out. Think I should get a Narc car from Rizzo?"

"Sure, but run it by Sergeant Waddell first, and this information on the suspicious car."

"Okay. It's a boring detail."

"I know, but we have to keep her safe, Joe."

"How's things with you after the media blitz on the grand jury?"

"Tense. Very tense. Keep my witness safe."

"We'll do our best."

He also had notes from several media people regarding Hayes. He gave Arnold a call, then returned the media calls, referring them to Deputy Chief of Detectives Urbanski or Media Relations. As soon as he'd handled those details he called ASA Lyon.

"You as popular over there as I am, Paula?"

"Afraid so. Who's after you?"

"The Commander and I were called to Urbanski's office. He chewed me."

"I had a phone call yesterday, Ed. The male caller said, 'Are you going to let Slate get you killed?'"

"Whoa! Could you trace it?"

"No. The other thing that's developed is that the law firm of DeCenzo, Hennesy, and Dobrowski are representing all the defendants."

"Do you know the firm?"

"Not yet, but I'll be checking them out. Also, Ed, I'm going to move for a change of venue to Lake County."

"Good move if you can get it done."

"They'll fight it. It will be easier for them to get to the jurors in Cook County."

Slate thought about the threat called to Lyon. "You're still carrying your piece, aren't you, Paula?"

"Yes. Like the one in your Columbo coat."

"Good." He had recommended a 2-inch snub-nosed Smith/Wesson with a hammer shroud like the one he carried in a pocket holster in his trench coat.

"You had any more threats, Ed?"

"Hayes threatened to sue me while he was being booked."

"Really?"

"I told him his big worry wasn't me, but him staying alive."

It seemed that everyone was still evaluating the charges and their respective risks. Slate moved the routine paperwork but continued to plan. He opened his whiteboard and recorded the Hayes threat, the meeting with Urbanski, and Arnold's comments. He moved back and sat on the end of his desk. Urbanski could move him out of Robbery/Homicide, but the charge was set. It would go to court, and he would testify.

After the media coverage wore off things settled down a little for the remainder of the week, but Slate knew he might be transferred at any time. The weekend proved no relief due to the risk to both him and his family.

HE WAS STILL moving the pile in his IN box on Monday morning when Sergeant Morrison, from Benton Harbor, Michigan, PD called.

"Morning, Pete. What do you have?"

"Your grand jury indictment hit our paper too. What a case!"

"It's causing waves here."

"Do you have time for me to give you an overview by phone?"

"Sure. Let me shut my door." He shut and locked the office door. "Okay."

"They were busy over the weekend. I'll brief you, then send the tape. Hayes, DeMeo, Profacci, and the new guy...Carmine something...were all there Saturday afternoon until Sunday afternoon. They had their homes and cars checked for electronic equipment and also found the phone tap at the courthouse. They talked about bugs over here. This Carmine and DeMeo looked around the place but didn't find anything."

"Where are they?"

"In the electrical outlets. The bottom receptacle is a mike. They want a Delaney hit, and Carmine was to call someone in Florida. He mentioned that you were warned by Ser– something."

"Seryak, a retired cop."

"If it goes to trial, they want it in Chicago. And somebody in your department is getting nervous. I couldn't make out the name."

"Maybe I can have the tape enhanced."

"This DeMeo is scared," Morrison continued. "The Carmine guy didn't say much. He did talk about an offshore bank account. They figure if Delaney is gone, the basis for the phone tap is gone and the case will be dismissed. That's it, Lieutenant."

"Thanks, Pete. Send the tape express and a chain of evidence form and stay in touch."

"Will do."

Slate shifted in his chair. How did they finger Delaney? Her resignation? A grand jury leak? Or had someone seen him meet with her?

Slate called Sergeant Waddell and asked him to meet regarding the Delaney assignment. Waddell came through the door a few minutes later.

"Shut the door, Rick. This won't take long." He stood as Rick stepped to the front of the desk.

"Delaney is marked for a hit. Move her to a motel in Lake County today ASAP."

"Whoa! This is getting heavy."

"Yeah."

"You think the trial will be held in Lake County?"

"That's Lyon's plan, and I agree. They'll fight it though."

"Where's the court there?"

"Waukegan."

"A motel near there?"

"Right. She'll resist, but tell her that her life is in danger. I've already heard from her son, so I expect he'll call again. And Rick, only you, me, and the four detectives are to know where she is. Don't put it in your report. Just say 'moved to another location.' You've talked to Oak Park PD, I guess."

Rick nodded.

"Better tell them she's moved. Maybe to Colorado to be near relatives, in case the Outfit has a source in the Oak Park PD."

"You know, I can't remember a case against a Circuit Court judge, Ed."

"I don't either. Hayes probably isn't the first one to bend the law, especially for political reasons. But he's into fixing homicides, likely more than one."

"Does this involve any of our own?"

Slate hesitated. "To be safe, just assume for now that it does."

"Okay. Watch your back, Ed."

Later, Sergeant Waddell called and said Bernice Delaney was refusing to leave her home.

————

Traffic was heavy as Slate moved west toward Oak Park. He called his wife to check on her day and tell her not to wait dinner.

Barona was in an older Lincoln in front of Mrs. Delaney's house. He got out as Slate pulled into Delaney's driveway.

"Lieutenant."

"Anything more on that car casing the place, Joe?"

"No, but it's early. We have a motel in Lake County, but now she says she not going."

Slate stepped onto the porch and Detective Ingram let him in.

"Pam. Where is she?"

"In the kitchen." Slate walked into the kitchen and found Bernice Delaney searching through papers in her home office area to the side. She turned toward Slate. "I'm not leaving my home!"

Slate turned a chair toward her and sat down on it. "I understand how you feel, but I told you at our dinner meeting awhile back what we're up against. Crime control is the responsibility of every citizen, not just the police."

"I should have stayed out of it."

"Mrs. Delaney, I won't kid you. We're all at risk. When you take on a judge, and the Outfit, everyone is a risk. They risk facing a death sentence or spending their lives in prison, and we risk being killed in order for them to avoid that. I told you about my wife."

"Yes. But you're a police officer."

"My wife isn't."

Delaney gave up on the papers and sat down to face Slate.

"I'm going to be straight with you, Mrs. Delaney. We have no choice but to move you. You are marked for a hit and we spotted a car casing your place."

Mrs. Delaney stared at Slate in disbelief. "You're just trying to scare me."

Slate raised his right hand. "I swear this is the truth. I wish we could avoid the move, but we cannot. So pack enough for a while. We'll get you to a laundry at your new location if necessary. It will be a while before the trial is held. My detectives will keep you safe, and Oak Park PD is aware of the threat.

"If you don't pack, I'll have Detective Ingram pack for you, and order the detectives to take you forcibly. You are the major witness in a felony case. Your deposition to the State's attorney, and then your testimony before the grand jury is the probable cause that allowed us to file the charges. Without you we've wasted our time, and because of that your life is in danger. . . . So, we're too far along to be changing anything now."

"My son warned me. He didn't want me to be involved."

"You did the right thing, and there is no turning back now."

"You tricked me. You knew what I was getting myself into!"

Slate didn't respond. He got up and went into the living room and spoke loud enough so Delaney would hear. "Detective Ingram, see that she is out of this house by dark, even if you have to pack for her." He paused. "And handcuff her if you have to, but I want her out of here!"

"Yes, sir."

Out front, he directed Barona to ask Oak Park PD to spot check the empty home.

———

On Tuesday ASA Lyon called.

"How's it going, Paula?"

"Two items Ed. I think we're okay on Lake County, but we'll know for sure tomorrow. Secondly, guess who wants to talk to me?"

"DeMeo."

"How did you know?"

"They had a meeting in Michigan over the weekend and he was scared."

"I see. He wants to meet tomorrow but not here. I want you with me."

"Fine. He won't want to meet here either."

"I suggested the Medical Examiner's office and told him to grab a cab from some place away from his home."

"Good. I'll meet you there."

"Right. Can you clear it with Dr. Griffin?"

"Okay. What time?"

"I told DeMeo 1:30 p.m."

"One more thing, Paula. Delaney is marked for a hit. So we've moved her moved to Lake County."

"The Michigan bugs?"

"Yeah. Vaccaro was to call someone in Florida. Probably the Professor."

"This may get ugly. Any more from your brass?"

"No. I figure everyone is focused on protecting their own tails."

"See you tomorrow, Ed."

Slate called ME Griffin regarding the Wednesday meeting with Lyon, then moved more paper, but his mind would not stay focused. He hoped he wasn't missing too much as he processed the paperwork on various investigations.

He leaned back to think about his own investigation, then shut the door and added to his whiteboard the threat on Delaney, her move, and the trial moved to Lake County. Sitting on the end of his desk he studied all the notes for several minutes, rising to remove something or to add a detail. The phone rang and he shut the doors over the board.

It was Sergeant Hal Lewis, Slate's buddy in the Intelligence Unit.

"How's Mr. Intell?"

"I should be asking that. You're into some heavy doo-doo, Ed."

"You think so?"

"Seriously, this is a good case. They're talking here about it making us look bad."

"Hadn't thought of that, Hal."

"A Circuit Court judge, huh?"

"And a few others."

"We just had a call from the Bureau. They have an agent at O'Hare reviewing video tapes every day, and he says it looks like the Professor, the Miami hit man with a knife, may be in town."

"Interesting."

"Do you think he's after you or one of your witnesses?"

Slate decided not to share the threat on Delaney or the car Barona spotted.. "They didn't say if he might be connected to one of their investigations?"

"The FBI doesn't share much, Ed."

"I know, but they're better than they used to be. We don't have a mug shot or photo, other than that one I gave you?"

"That's it."

"Okay, I'll get that one to my guys. Thanks, Hal."

Slate dug into his file for the photo of the Professor taken by the camera in the lobby of the condo building where Hayes's second wife had been killed. He walked it down to Waddell, briefed him on the Bureau's call, and instructed him to copy the photo for the four detectives on Delaney. It didn't show much detail about the man's build or other features but it would have to do.

Just before he was ready to leave for the day the tape from Sergeant Morrison's bugs in Hayes place in Benton Harbor Michigan arrived. Slate had intended to have Technical Services enhance the portion of the recording about someone in CPD, but then decided it was too hot an issue internally. He would have to farm it out to a local company, or give it to the Bureau. It would be easier for the FBI to prosecute Urbanski if it was the deputy chief on the tape, rather than trying to fight the city politics. He would see what Arnold thought of the idea.

He shut his door and listened to the tape.

SLATE MET ASA Lyon Wednesday at the morgue on Harrison Street south of the Loop, near the Dan Ryan and Eisenhower expressways. Slate keyed in the rear door off the alley and he and Lyon walked the hall to the front, where Doctor Griffin worked.

"That smell!" Lyon said.

Slate turned, trying to avoid breathing in the direction where the odor was strongest. "You really know how to pick the spots, Paula."

"I guess. Is it always this bad?"

"Pretty bad, at least in the hallways."

They came to the last room on the right. Dr. Harry Griffin was standing over a young black male on the table.

"Hello, Doc," Slate greeted. "You know Assistant State's Attorney Paula Lyon, I guess."

Doc Griffin looked up at Paula and nodded.

"Gang-banger?" Slate asked.

"Another senseless death."

"What room can we use?"

"My conference room. Across the hall."

"We have one more coming." Slate looked at Lyon. "If you want to get ready, I'll meet our guy at the front."

Slate waited just inside the front door, where he could see the street. About 1:25 p.m. a Yellow Cab pulled up and DeMeo got out. He peered around, then strode toward the door. Slate remembered that DeMeo was forty-five, but he looked older given his weight and he was only about five-eight. His thin dark hair was combed straight back.

DeMeo startled when Slate opened the door.

"Lieutenant Slate. Come in." DeMeo stepped into the hall.

"Turn around," Slate said.

DeMeo paused.

"You packing?"

DeMeo then turned his back to Slate. "I have a permit."

Slate removed a 380 caliber pistol from DeMeo's right pocket of his sport coat. "I'll keep it until you leave." He then completed his pat down.

"Let's see your carry permit."

DeMeo pulled his wallet and displayed the permit.

"Okay, we're right down here." Slate led DeMeo to the conference room and introduced ASA Lyon seated at the end of the small table.

DeMeo took a chair to her right, and Slate to the left. The odor was less noticeable here, but the smell of death was still present.

"I'll be recording this, Mr. DeMeo," Lyon started. "To start, I'll need some ID, a couple in fact." DeMeo showed his driver's license and the carry permit.

"I have the pistol," Slate said.

"You said on the phone that you could help us for the right deal."

DeMeo glanced to Lyon, then Slate. He leaned forward in his chair and placed both arms on the table, like a used car salesman about to offer a deal Slate thought.

"I can give you several people, but I want to walk. And get into a witness protection program, including my wife, and daughter. My son's raised. You have to understand what risks I'm taking. And you'll have trouble with your case without me."

Lyon said, "I think our case is solid, so enlighten me. Just why do I need you?"

"Your witnesses aren't safe. Jurors can be bought." He looked at Slate. "And there are other ways."

"We need to hear specifics before any deal."

"But where am I then if you don't agree? I'm dead!"

"You're looking for a deal, DeMeo. It's your move. We will not give you up, but we can't make promises until we know you have something we need. Right now, the police department, the State's attorney's office, and the grand jury think we have a solid case."

DeMeo glanced around nervously, Slate observed, before he made his pitch. "Okay. I will testify that Hayes and I have taken money in exchange for a not-guilty finding. I can tell you who our contacts are in the Outfit." Slate figured he was holding the PD information as a backup.

"How many trials could you testify about?" Lyon asked.

"More than the one you know about."

"How much money have you accepted?"

"I'm not sure, but hundreds of thousands."

"For how many years?"

"Maybe five or six years. Hayes refused at first." Slate added that detail to his own notes. Maybe the judge's marriage troubles had created the need for cash.

"How does the system work?" Lyon asked.

"I get a call, then I talk to Hayes and we negotiate the fee."

"How is the fee referred to?"

"As days to move a trial ahead."

"So a day represents what?"

"A grand."

"How is payment made?"

"Cash, or to an off shore account."

Lyon looked at Slate. He asked, "Who has paid you and Hayes?"

"It depends."

"The Profaci and Bellino law firm?"

"Yes."

"Who in the Outfit pays you?"

"Carmine Vaccaro, most times."

"You're the one who always gets the payment?"

"Yes. Hayes would never go to them."

"And who in my department is involved with the Outfit?" Slate asked.

DeMeo shifted in his seat as he looked at Lyon, then Slate. "I'm going to hold that for now."

"How can you prove the payments from Vaccaro?"

"Only my word."

"From Profacci?"

"Just my testimony, and the way the case came out. And some of my deposits, I guess."

"Your cut?"

"One fourth."

"What do you know about Hayes's various marriages?"

"He likes them younger, and he's been married three times. That's about all I know."

"Did you know his first or second wife?"

"I knew Juanita, his second wife."

"What do you know about her death? That could maybe get you a walk."

"I don't know anything about that."

Slate glanced at Lyon. Lyon continued, "Okay, Mr. DeMeo. I'll have to talk to my boss, but I'll at least recommend a reduced sentence based upon your testimony, and that you are placed in witness protection."

"I want to walk if I give your Hayes, Profacci, and Vaccaro. Otherwise I'll be killed in the pen."

"You have no evidence on Vaccaro, so it's your credibility versus his, and we already have you, Hayes, and Profacci. In the meantime, think about what records you could provide and if you're willing to wear a wire with Vaccaro and Hayes."

"And who you can make in CPD," Slate added.

DeMeo didn't respond, but Slate thought he had more. He was obviously anxious and disappointed.

Lyon was still at the table in the conference room when Slate returned from escorting DeMeo to the door and returning his gun. "What do you think, Paula?"

"He's afraid. But not much solid evidence. You're sure Delaney's covered?"

"Right. 24/7 in Lake County."

"This guy isn't dependable at this point. We need her, or we're in trouble."

"Maybe he'll come up with some records, and some of my superiors' names."

They stepped into the examining room to thank Doctor Griffin then went to their cars. "The trial in Lake County should help us with the jury," Paula said.

"Anyplace is better than Cook County."

The next morning Slate worked with pending details. Technical Services could find no portable explosives detector. He unlocked his whiteboard and updated it with the DeMeo meeting.

Sitting on the edge of his desk, he reviewed all the notes. This trial could be very good for the city of Chicago. It would not only put away a dirty judge, his crooked administrator, and a corrupt lawyer, but maybe allow him to get a made Outfit guy and even some corruption in CPD.

On Thursday morning Slate went directly to the police garage to switch his black 1994 Dodge for a silver 1995 BMW 525. He figured that the Dodge was becoming known at Area 3 and at his home. Since he couldn't get an explosives detector, the BMW would keep a hit man from readily identifying his vehicle. He would have to switch cars every few weeks.

At Area 3, he parked near the rear entrance. As he was on his way to his office Sergeant Waddell stopped him to report that Bernice Delaney was still upset and complaining. Slate thought of the risks not only to Delaney but also to Rebecca and Tim. It would be easier to hit his witness or his family rather than him. He hoped the trial in Lake County would be set soon.

Sergeant Morrison in Benton Harbor, Michigan, called.

"What do you have, Sarge?"

"Bad news, I'm afraid. The bugs went dead."

"Really. What do you think? Could it be an equipment defect?"

"No. State police say that they work independently and are all dead now. They say the place was swept clean. They want to know who's going to pay for the lost equipment."

"How much?"

"Several thousand, I guess."

"Have them send the bill to me. I'll give to the State's attorney."

"I'll continue to log the vehicles there, but I'm sure that will slow down too."

"You're right. More information could have really been valuable, but we got our witness protected. Thanks for the help, Morrison."

The next morning Slate stopped for coffee and a Danish near Area 3. He had just keyed in to his office when Sergeant Waddell arrived.

"Morning, Lieutenant." He handed Slate a report.

Slate placed his bag and cup on the desk and paged through the report River Forest PD had faxed to Waddell because they knew of DeMeo's arrest. "DeMeo was killed last night?"

Waddell nodded. "His wife said she heard the garage door open but she didn't hear it close and he didn't come into the house. She went to the garage and found him lying beside the car in a pool of blood. River Forest says his throat was cut. His pistol was still in his jacket pocket. The guy must have got him just as he stepped out of his car."

Slate glanced through the report again, then at Rick. "DeMeo talked to Lyon and me about a plea bargain and witness protection."

"Really."

"And he took a cab and we met at the morgue."

"So he was tailed."

Slate studied the report as he spoke. "Or the cabby knew who he was and sold the information. Or maybe his place or his phone was bugged by his own people."

"The guy from Miami?"

"My guess is that the hit on Delaney was paid for when it was ordered. But with us there he couldn't get to her. Then they learned about this problem with DeMeo and changed the target."

"Good thing you got Mrs. Delaney moved when you did."

Ed nodded, still evaluating the problem. "Okay, Rick. Warn your crew on Delaney about DeMeo and the Professor. They got the photo, right?"

"They have it. Has the trial date been set?"

"No."

ASA Paula Lyon called to advise Slate the preliminary hearing was set for Monday morning in Waukegan. He briefed her on the DeMeo hit.

"How did they find out he talked to us?" she asked.

"Maybe his phone was bugged, or the cabby recognized him and sold the info. Or maybe they have had a tail on him."

"There's always a risk when you agree to be a State's witness, but I'm surprised they got him so soon."

"I figure it was the Professor, with a knife used. From intelligence from Michigan we knew they had planned to hit Delaney, but we had her covered. Then they somehow learned about DeMeo, and their man was already in town."

"You're probably right, Ed."

"They know we have a solid case Paula, so they want to stop it before we go to trial."

"I'm glad you had the bugs in Michigan, or Delaney would be dead."

"My guy in Michigan called yesterday to report that all the bugs went dead."

"What do you make of that?"

"The State Police are sure the place was swept. Each transmitter was self-contained, so they found all of them. And the recorder for Hayes's office is gone. I removed the monitor from DeMeo's car before the grand jury indictment was published."

"Maybe when you put people on Delaney, they figured out the Michigan place was bugged."

"Michigan State Police will send me a bill for the lost bugs, which I'll pass on to you."

"How much?"

"Several thousand, I guess. But your office has a better budget than mine. Right?"

Slate noticed that Paula didn't respond to that comment but changed the subject.

"This case is even bigger than we anticipated, Ed. Have you had any more contacts?"

"No, but I just switched to another Narc car. And I'm concerned about my wife and son. Why don't you do another pen register, Paula, to see if you can find Vaccaro's call to the Professor in Miami. Oh, did you find any calls from Urbanski to Seryak?"

"No. I checked the list after we met with Erwin. I'll tell you, Ed, I have so many cases going, it's hard to keep track."

"We may have to get our Internal Affairs guys and the Bureau involved, Paula."

"Maybe. Eventually."

———

As Slate drove to the northwest side and home he thought more about his safety and his family. He stopped at Ace Hardware and purchased three bags of lime.

Just as he reached the rear door of his house, Rebecca unlocked it. When she stepped back, Ed immediately recognized the expression on her face.

"What's wrong?"

"Got a call just after I got home."

Ed waited.

"A man said, 'Are you prepared to be a widow?'"

"That's it?"

Rebecca nodded.

"So much for unlisted numbers. Could you trace it?"

Rebecca shook her head.

"We're about ready for trial," Ed offered.

"What about this DeMeo? The paper says his killing is tied to the grand jury indictment."

"He was an inside man, Hayes's administrator. He met with Lyon and me, looking for a deal to be a State's witness and get into witness protection. Someone found out. The Outfit may have his place bugged."

Seeing his wife's face when she heard that, Ed wrapped his arms tightly around her. "We're okay, Rebecca," he assured her.

She turned back to the bills she had been sorting and changed the subject. "I see you switched cars."

Ed nodded, then suggested, "Why don't you pay someone at church to give you a ride to work?"

"I may still go up to the folks and take Tim with me."

Ed studied Rebecca, thinking she might be right. "They might give you a leave for the summer. Things are slower at church then. But I'll hate to see you go."

"No one should have to live this way Ed, not in America!"

"Why don't you ride with someone for now?"

They tried to watch a movie after dinner, but neither one of them could get into it. After dark Ed went to his car and moved two bags of lime to the garage. He would use them on the yard. He opened the third bag and used a shovel to spread a thin layer of lime on the blacktop driveway around the BMW. He left the rear light off and told Rebecca why.

Ed checked around the BMW over the weekend but found no footprints.

———

On Monday morning he called his daughter, Sarah, at Northern Illinois, then called the University PD with an update. He had just started his coffee and Danish when the phone rang.

"Slate."

"Lieutenant Kachovec, Oak Park PD."

"What's the problem, Lieutenant?"

"The Delaney house was torched early this morning."

"Torched?"

"Yeah. The fire captain said a fire started in the rear and the front at the same time. It's a total loss. You had a witness there but she was moved, right?"

"She was moved. Do you know about the DeMeo hit in River Forest?"

"Was that connected?"

"He was looking for a plea bargain. So let me know if you learn anything more on this arson, or from River Forest on the DeMeo hit."

"Sounds like you better watch your own ass, Slate."

Slate informed Waddell of the arson and instructed him not to let anyone tell Delaney unless she saw something in a paper or on the news. He felt pretty sure that the media would not connect the Oak Park arson with his pending trial involving a judge in the city. He also called ASA Paula Lyon with the information.

Slate had just finished moving the pile of paper when Commander Arnold called. "The FBI just called and wants to meet with us at 1:00 p.m."

"About the Hayes case?"

"Right. They mentioned the Florida connection."

"I don't want them involved in my case, Commander."

"Let's talk to them and see what they've got."

"I'll be surprised if they reveal anything. In your office?"

"Right."

Slate sat back to collect his thoughts before the meeting. The Bureau never was keen on sharing information, although things had improved in recent years. And they liked to get into a local case they could run with and look good. Most city detectives hated this since the Bureau always took the credit.

CHAPTER

27

AT 12:50 P.M. he was at Commander Arnold's office.

"You're early."

Slate shut the door, then leaned on the back of a chair in front of Arnold's desk while he laid out his concerns about the meeting with the FBI. "I have a few questions. I have a tape from a bug in Hayes's place in Benton Harbor, Michigan. They mention someone in our department but it's not clear enough to tell who they're referring to. I don't want Tech Services to enhance it because of possible leaks." Slate watched for any reaction from Arnold.

"Whoa. That would be serious."

"And I don't want the feds in my case now. Eventually we can give them some of it, especially with the Illinois, Michigan, and Florida connections."

"RICO?"

"Right. The conspiracy to hit Delaney was planned in the Michigan meeting with Vaccaro, Hayes, and DeMeo. Apparently this 'Professor' hit man in Florida was contracted. Then when they couldn't get to Delaney, they hit their new problem, DeMeo. Then we have the Delaney arson. But I don't hear that mentioned on the tape."

Arnold drummed his fingers on his desk. "You're in some heavy shit, Lieutenant."

Slate continued. "I recommend we listen to what the feds have to say and not give anything away."

Slate felt Arnold sizing him up as he weighed the recommendation. "Okay. It's your case. But let's give them the possibility of help on a RICO case to keep them happy. And they can handle anyone dirty within our department better than we can."

Slate nodded.

At 1:00 p.m. two agents entered Arnold's office.

Arnold stepped around his desk and extended his hand as he made introductions. "Commander Arnold, and Lieutenant Slate."

"Special Agent Jerry Milburn, representing Assistant Director in Charge, Dennis Wisner." Milburn turned to the other man. "Special Agent Bill Dodd."

"Let's use the table." Arnold gestured and took his seat at the far side of the table. Slate shut the door then sat to Arnold's right. Milburn sat on the end facing Arnold, and Dodd across from Slate. Milburn placed his notebook on the table, checked his notes, and glanced at Arnold. Clearly the feds had come with a plan to get involved, Slate concluded.

Arnold addressed Milburn. "You said the Bureau is interested in Lieutenant Slate's corruption investigation."

"Yes. You have your local judge, but we have the Professor coming in from Florida, DeMeo being hit, and maybe an Outfit connection here in Illinois. With two states involved, it sounds like a RICO case. We could pick it up for you and work it nationally."

Arnold looked at Slate.

"Why would we want to do that to prosecute a local judge?" Slate asked.

"Who hit DeMeo?" Millburn asked.

"Someone that didn't want him to talk. But can you prove your hit man did it?"

"He was in town, and a knife was used."

Slate nodded. They didn't know about Vaccaro, or they weren't going to reveal it. And they didn't know about his Michigan investigation. He wondered how close the Bureau was to the State's attorney in Benton Harbor. Due to the city's size he doubted they had a source there.

"Do you feel your department can handle this two-state investigation?" Dodd asked.

Slate responded. "We can handle the Hayes and Profacci prosecutions, and maybe clear DeMeo's homicide. It's still early. And I don't see how you have a basis for a RICO without our corruption prosecution. Unless you can prove the Professor hit DeMeo, you don't have another state involved, and thus no RICO. When we finish our case, there may be a RICO case we can help you with. But not now."

Milburn focused on Slate. "By charging them, someone looking for a deal may admit to hiring the Professor. Then we could get several of them on a RICO, then you could finish with your local prosecution. Being an FBI National Academy grad, Lieutenant, you know how the Bureau operates."

Slate nodded.

"I think Lieutenant Slate is right, gentlemen," Arnold said. "It's our case. We'll finish our work, then if there's still loose ends, we'll give you what fits RICO."

"We could have gone to the State's attorney or your superintendent," Milburn said.

Arnold fixed a stare on Milburn as he answered. "You could, if you thought that wise."

Milburn got the message and stood. Dodd followed. "Okay, gentlemen. Let's hope we can both do some good."

Arnold and Slate nodded and stood to shake hands.

When they left, Slate shook his head. "They're still desperate to look good, rather than creating their own case."

"They didn't mention Vaccaro or Urbanski," Arnold said.

"Or Seryak and Vaughn."

"I wonder if either of them ever worked the street," Arnold mused.

"They recruit some from local departments, but most are recent college grads."

"What did you think of your FBI National Academy experience?"

Slate hesitated. "Good forensics and labor relations courses but not enough on management and budget. And too much on firearms for officers at the lieutenant rank and above."

Arnold nodded. "I figure part of the reason the FBINA was created was to improve communications with local departments after many years of poor relations."

Slate went to Technical Services and found a vacant room in where he could listen again to the tape from Hayes' Michigan property. He could not make out the name of the cop they were referring to but he noted the spot where it occurred.

The next day Slate found a local electronics store on Western Avenue, and had them amplify just that portion of the tape. The name they were referring to was Urbanski, Arnold's boss, the Deputy Chief of Detectives. For the present, he decided to use it only to keep Urbanski from interfering in the Hayes trial.

ON MONDAY SLATE went directly to Circuit Court in Waukegan for the preliminary hearing. Judge Secrest was on the bench. With a full head of dark brown hair, Slate gauged him in his late forties. He wore rimless glasses that were difficult to see looking straight at him.

Slate appreciated the concise way Lyon covered the three trials lost in Hayes's courtroom, the code talk of days representing thousands of dollars, DeMeo's admission of a payoff and offer to be a State's witness before he was killed. She presented only enough to demonstrate there was probable cause to believe a felony had been committed in the third trial, where Mr. Yost's son had been killed in the arson fire.

Sidney DeCenzo of DeCenzo, Hennesy, and Dobrowski denied any code talk or payoffs and insisted the case was a result of an overzealous police lieutenant and a gullible State's attorney's office. He pointed out that money was never mentioned on the recordings from Hayes's office nor was any money seen. Judge Secrest ruled there was sufficient PC and announced the trial date would be set soon.

After the brief hearing Lyon approached Slate. "What do you think?"

"Sounded good, Paula. And Secrest seems sharp enough. The defense had nothing."

————

By late afternoon day was still crisp and clear as Slate made his way to the northwest side and home. He watched for a tail but saw nothing suspicious. It was good that Delaney was safe in Lake County, but after Seryak's threat and the call to Rebecca, he knew the Outfit would do anything necessary to avoid a conviction. The Mario DeMeo homicide proved that. After dark that evening he spread fresh lime around the BMW parked in front of his garage.

Wednesday morning he went out to retrieve the *Chicago Tribune* from his driveway and to check for tracks around his car. There were footprints coming from the street to the car, then a smeared area below the driver's door, and footprints going out toward the street. He checked the street for cars nearby but saw none. In the garage he grabbed his tarp and placed it on the driveway along the driver's door, then laid down to view the underside of the BMW. A small package of dynamite had been placed against the floorboard.

Using the house phone he called Area 3 and requested the bomb squad.

"Stay in the house and get out of the kitchen and keep Tim inside until it's removed," he directed Rebecca.

"What if the house is blown up?"

"It might damage the kitchen, but we'll be okay in the den."

"This is insane, Ed!" Rebecca skrieked. "Let's leave for Wisconsin now while we're still alive!"

"We'll talk about it tonight."

The bomb squad van soon arrived and parked at the edge of the street. Two officers approached the house. Slate went out to meet them.

"Lieutenant Hanson and Sergeant Weber."

"Lieutenant Slate, Robbery/Homicide." They shook hands.

"You're sure it's dynamite?"

"I'm sure. There's several sticks up against the floorboard."

"See any strange cars parked nearby?"

"No. I thought about a remote detonation."

"Okay. We'll get our gear on and take a look. You're the one that charged the judge?"

Slate nodded.

"Why don't you wait in the house. With some switches, a strong wind might set it off."

Hanson and Weber returned wearing their protective suits. Slate knew the suits would not save them if the explosives went off. He went into the den and watched through the archway to the kitchen and through the kitchen door window. Rebecca and Tim had gone to the bedroom at the far end of the house.

Hanson laid on the tarp and used his flashlight to examine the device. Weber handed him a tool, then Hanson worked at the device and then handed something to Weber. Then he appeared to be prying the device from the underside of the floorboard. Hanson got up and handed the dynamite to Weber then retrieved something from Weber. Hanson waved to Slate.

As Slate approached, Hanson said, "Good thing you're a careful man Slate. I assume the lime is yours."

"It's mine."

"Four sticks of dynamite taped to a large magnet and a tilt switch. I removed the detonation device." He held it up in his gloved hand for Slate to see.

"Looks like a carpenter's level."

"That's the principle. If you'd opened the door and put your weight on the seat, the mercury would have floated to one end, and that would have been it."

"You'll check it for prints?"

"Sure, but they don't leave any on jobs like this. Looks like you got somebody pissed, Lieutenant."

"Any way to trace the purchase of the stuff?"

"Doubt it. Common dynamite, but it's rare to see switches like this. He's no amateur. Normally, hitting the gas pedal or brake is what detonates it."

———

On his way to the office Slate stopped at the garage and switched his BMW for the black Dodge he had previously used. At Area 3 he briefed Sergeant Waddell and Commander Arnold, then called ASA Lyon with a warning to check her car and to be alert. Lyon informed him of a meeting she had scheduled for Friday morning in preparation for the jury trial in Lake County.

He moved paperwork the rest of the day, but his mind was on the risks to himself and his family. Maybe the time had come to move the family to Wisconsin and then leave CPD after the trial was over.

———

After dinner that night as Ed and Rebecca sat on the porch with their coffee, Ed faced the decisions he needed to make for his family. He turned to make close eye contact with Rebecca. "I guess maybe it's time you tell the pastor about the risks and you and Tim go up to your folks until things settle down."

Rebecca looked deeply into her husband's eyes. Ed felt time standing still and felt her reading his soul. "I know I've talked about that. But marriage is for better or for worse. Still, I never expected 'worse' to include a car bomb. I'm going to take Tim to my parents and come right back. You shouldn't be alone with all this pressure you're going through."

Ed's eyes watered up as he studied his wife. Silently he leaned into her and held her tightly.

———

ASA Lyon had called for all witnesses to meet on Friday morning at her office. Slate waited in the lobby.

"I may not testify," Bernice Delaney announced.

ASA Lyon looked at her in surprise. "You have reason to be upset Mrs. Delaney, but we need your help to put away a corrupt judge, an attorney, and others."

"Lieutenant Slate got me into something I would not have gotten into if he had been honest with me."

Slate turned toward Delaney. "I'm sorry you feel that way. I didn't lie to you, but it's true that I didn't tell you everything that might happen. I wasn't sure what we had, and I needed your help." Slate paused and looked at Lyon. She waited.

Slate continued. "You were upset when we made you move to Lake County, but you see the risk. The hit man was originally hired to kill you."

Delaney shook her head. "I should not have gotten involved."

Lyon briefed all the witnesses as to how she would call them and what they would testify to.

———

Back at Area 3, Slate went to Commander Arnold's office. The door was open so he knocked and entered. Arnold looked up from his paperwork.

"Lieutenant. What's on your mind?" Slate shut the door and stepped up close to the desk. "Something you should know, Commander. On the tape from Michigan, the name we couldn't make out about an information source until I had it enhanced is Urbanski."

Arnold laid down his pen. "Really? Where was the meeting?"

"Benton Harbor, Michigan."

"Hayes's place?"

Slate nodded.

"And a Pen register shows calls between Urbanski and Carmine Vaccaro, a made guy." Arnold didn't change the expression on his face, Slate noted.

"I'm off to home, unless you have something."

Arnold appeared in heavy thought. "Watch your ass, Ed."

———

Rebecca unlocked the rear door when she saw him drive in. Ed noted that the pistol was on the counter near the door, but she greeted him with the words, "You switched cars."

"Yeah. How's my main squeeze? Any more problems?"

She kissed him lightly and returned to the project she had laid out on the table.

"No."

"What's for dinner?"

"Leftovers from the roast."

"Good."

Ed hung his gun belt on the basement doorknob and sat down.

"What's the word on Tim? Is he okay with the move?"

"Seems to be. He's reconnected with some of the boys he played with in the neighborhood during the summers when he stayed with Mom and Dad for several weeks at a time. "

After dinner, they took their coffee to the porch and sat on the glider.

"Do you feel okay riding with Nancy to work?"

"I guess. I still watch for someone following us. When will your trial begin?"

"Soon. We had our pre-trial briefing today."

"I feel for Mrs. Delaney. She must be going crazy."

"She said she might not testify. Lyon and I talked to her. I guess she's thinking about moving to Phoenix near her daughter. Has a son in Denver."

"Do you still have the District checking our home?"

"Yes, spot checks by a tactical officer."

"A guy in plain clothes."

"Right, but driving a Ford, so he stands out."

They took their cups into the kitchen and Ed put his gun belt back on. After a thirty minute walk they neared the house. "Are you still marking the driveway around your car?"

"Yeah, but they won't try the same thing again."

"What about after the trial?"

"What do you mean?"

"Are we safe then?"

"Sure." But Ed wondered about that too, knowing the Outfit liked to settle scores and that he was on their list.

CHAPTER 29

ON MONDAY MORNING Slate headed north to arrive at the Circuit Court in Waukegan before 9:00 a.m. Lake County was the first county north of Cook County, and home to many professionals who worked in the Chicago area. He knew police departments in Lake County were well paid and equipped and crime rates were low. He also knew that ASA Paula Lyon had reasoned that since the Outfit had little influence in Lake County, and a trial was much less likely to be fixed.

As he headed for a seat on the right side and to the rear of ASA Lyon's table, he passed Candice Bryan, the alderman's widow, sitting about a quarter of the way back on the same side of the courtroom. They made eye contact and Slate gave a short nod of recognition. As Slate took his seat he thought of Hayes letting Carbonaro, her husband's killer walk.

At exactly 9:00 a.m. a man in a black robe with blue trim entered the courtroom. "The honorable Jason Secrest presiding," the bailiff announced. Even though Lyon had talked to local ASAs, Slate did his own checking with detectives in Waukegan and the Lake County sheriff's office after he learned Secrest would be hearing the case. Both departments were satisfied with the judge.

Secrest had grown up in Wilmette, the second suburb north of Chicago, and got his education at Norte Dame and then the University of Chicago law school. He had been an assistant State's attorney for five years, and a judge for six or seven. All of his professional experience had been in the suburbs, but Slate figured he would have been exposed to the rougher side of life while at the University of Chicago in Hyde Park, due to the high crime area on Chicago's south side.

Slate was feeling better now after all the work, the risks, and the department politics. W. C. Hayes was going to pay for his crimes, and the people of Chicago would be better served by his successor.

Assistant State's Attorney Paula Lyon was joined at the table in front of Slate by Detective Schneider and Sergeant Utley. In the first row behind them sat Dr. Kimball, the Assistant Medical Examiner, and a man Slate thought was Neil Metcalf, City Council secretary. Those witnesses would cover the trial involving Alderman Bryan's death that had been lost in Hayes's courtroom. The witnesses for the other two cases that had been lost were sitting in the section in front of Slate. Lyon had been able to use the first two cases for background even though new charges had not been filed.

At the table on the left sat Nicholas DeCenzo, of the law firm of DeCenzo, Hennesy, and Dobrowski, Anthony Profacci, and W. C. Hayes. Slate reflected on Hayes's personality when he had watched him during the trials, and Hayes confronting him while being booked. The judge had in fact survived to stand trial, but his life in prison would be short unless he was separated from the main population, which would be a lonely existence.

Judge Secrest asked if the State and the Defense were ready to proceed. Both attorneys responded in the affirmative. Lyon was instructed to proceed.

Carrying a notebook, Assistant State's Attorney Paula Lyon stood and stepped to her right to face the twelve potential jurors seated in the jury box. Slate knew she had accumulated a considerable amount of data on each juror from the prospective juror list. He admired, again, the professionalism in her look and manner.

She questioned each juror by number as to line of work, experiences with the legal system and the police, and the desire and ability to serve. She excused one male attorney who had been a public defender in Chicago before beginning his practice in the real estate field. And a man who had worked at a casino was excused.

Mr. DeCenzo approached the jury. Slate figured him at about sixty. He was no taller than Lyon and heavyset. He wore a black suit, white shirt, a wine tie, and large gold cuff links. The law firm of DeCenzo, Hennesy, and Dobrowski had carefully covered the majority of the white ethnicities of Chicago with an Italian, an Irishman, and a Pole, Slate noted. DeCenzo questioned jurors and challenged several. Slate wondered if the juror pool would be large enough to handle all the challenges.

Then Lyon excused some for cause. She used her peremptory challenges to remove several others without revealing the reason. At 11:40 a.m. the court broke for lunch.

Slate drove to a restaurant near the courthouse and reviewed some of his Area 3 paperwork while he ate.

At 1:15 p.m. DeCenzo continued his screening of potential jurors. He removed several for cause, but seemed to be saving his peremptory challenges for his final screening as he and Lyon went back and forth whittling away at the long list.

The juror selection process continued until midafternoon on Tuesday. Slate was a little surprised that it was over that quickly, as he had seen some very long screening sessions in the city. He figured the large number of professionals in the north suburbs accounted for that.

The final jury makeup was seven men and five women. Two men were retired, he noted, four were professionals of various fields in the Chicago area, and one was a businessman in Chicago. Of the five women, one was retired, one was a homemaker, and three were professionals in the city or suburbs.

It was 4:20 p.m. by the time the jury was impaneled. Slate was confident that this jury would not appreciate the performances of Judge W. C. Hayes or Attorney Anthony Profacci in a Cook County Circuit court. The case would have been stronger with DeMeo's testimony and the conspiracy in Michigan, he knew, but better DeMeo getting whacked than Bernice Delaney.

"Court will resume at 9:00 a.m. Wednesday with my instructions to the jury, then the State's opening statement," Judge Secrest announced to conclude the day.

CHAPTER

30

ON WEDNESDAY MORNING the Waukegan Circuit Court-room was called to order. Judge Secrest gave the jury some instructions and explained that their charge would not be given until all testimony was heard. ASA Lyon was told to proceed.

Paula Lyon stepped to face the jury box for her opening remarks. Slate noted her black suit, gray blouse, and dark shoes. She appeared confident and ready.

"Ladies and gentlemen, what you're going to hear in this trial is a travesty of justice that, fortunately, is still rare in America. The charges against the defendants are: Official Misconduct; Bribery; and Failure to Report a Bribe. Judge Secrest will explain these statutes when he gives you your charge before you leave to deliberate. Under Federal law it would be a Racketeering charge, commonly referred to as a RICO case.

"You are going to hear about three felony cases that were carefully investigated by the Chicago Police Department's Robbery/Homicide Unit, cases that were professionally prosecuted by the Cook County State's Attorney's office. But all three trials ended with the defendants walking out of court free to continue their life of crime. The first two trials caused the Chicago Police Department to begin their investigation, but we have only filed charges on the third trial that was lost. Still, you need to know how the investigation developed, so you will also hear testimony about the first two trials lost, but evidence will only be submitted for the third crime that has resulted in charges being filed."

Lyon flipped to the next page of her notes and moved to another spot in front of the jury. "The first trial involves the homicide of a city alderman in Chicago who held the swing vote on a condominium development versus a casino operation. The second trial is an armed robbery/truck theft case during a waste haulers bidding war where one of the bidders had 'Outfit' connections, as the Mob is known in Chicago.

"The third trial is an arson that killed a merchant's son while he slept in the building to help protect his father's business. His father, a retired Navy captain, had refused to pay street tax, or a monthly charge to the Outfit, supposedly for security protection. But no contract is used and no credible protection is provided.

"No one was convicted for any of these crimes in Judge W. C. Hayes's courtroom. And that, ladies and gentlemen, was because this judge accepted bribes rather than fulfilling his oath of office. Thereby he engaged in a criminal conspiracy, or Official Misconduct, and Bribery."

Lyon moved to another position in front of the jury. "You'll hear from the detectives who investigated each crime, a Fire Department arson specialist, forensic experts, the lieutenant in charge of the Robbery/Homicide Unit in Area 3 on the north side, who initiated this investigation, a former employee of the Circuit Court who had the civic duty to report the corruption she saw, an assistant medical examiner, and an expert witness.

"I will present the evidence in several pieces but in the chronological sequence of events so that you can see clearly how the investigation began and developed. Due to the complexity of this trial, I suggest that you take good notes. Then you will decide if this is the way you want America's criminal court system to function, where money and special interests rule, rather than justice."

Lyon stepped back and took a position at the front and center of the jury box. "If this is not the way you want our courts to function, you will find both defendants guilty as charged. And by your guilty verdict you will send a clear message to other judges and attorneys that if they violate the public trust and condone murder, robbery, and arson, they will pay the full penalty of the law just as any ordinary citizen must pay." Lyon sat down.

Slate tried to predict where the defense would start as he watched DeCenzo grab his pad, pull his trousers up over his belly, and approach the jury. "Ladies and gentlemen, what the State will present regarding the nature of crimes will not be in question, nor will the integrity of the detectives be an issue. They carried out their sworn duty to investigate these events.

"However, what we will show is that the facts in all three of these cases did not establish probable cause that a crime had been committed, or guilt beyond a reasonable doubt. The detectives' supervisor and the assistant State's attorney should not have allowed these cases to go to trial until they had the evidence to win the cases. A just and correct verdict was rendered in each case. The State will allege that there was something dishonest about these decisions."

DeCenzo moved to another position in front of the jury. "We will show how a boy from a poor working-class family on the north side of Chicago went to night school for many years to educate himself, then chose public service rather than a more lucrative position in one of Chicago's law firms. He did that to serve his community."

DeCenzo checked his notes while moving to a new position in front of the jury. "Therefore, as you hear the testimony, please do not allow your loyalty and respect for your own police and State's attorney to cause you to fail to see the errors made by some in the Chicago Police Department and the Cook County State's Attorney's office.

"A trial judge educated and experienced in the law must follow that law. That law requires probable cause that a crime was committed, and probable cause will be defined by the court before you retire to deliberate. Every defendant is innocent until proven guilty beyond a reasonable doubt, and reasonable doubt will also be defined. These cases cited did not meet these legal requirements."

DeCenzo hiked his trousers up again and moved to a new spot in front of the jury. "Also, you may hear a recording of some of the defendants joking on the phone. Before you judge them for some of this talk, remember your own comments, sometimes made in jest. Would you want your telephone tapped and recorded, then have to answer for those innocent comments in court? I think not." DeCenzo sat down.

Judge Secrest said, "Call your first witness, Ms. Lyon."

"I call Detective Schneider." The detective took the stand and was sworn in.

"Please state your name, occupation, and assignment."

"Detective William Schneider, Chicago Police Department, Area 3, Robbery/Homicide Unit."

"And how long employed?"

"Eighteen years."

"And how long a detective?"

"Seven years."

"And were you the lead detective on the investigation of Alderman Steven Bryan's death?"

"Yes."

"Please explain to the court and jury the investigation."

"It was originally handled as an auto accident, but due to the suspicious nature of the death, Detective Dolsi and I were assigned to investigate.

"The alderman was driving home when his vehicle was struck in the rear by another vehicle. There was minor damage to both vehicles, but the alderman had a broken neck, and his headrest was in the lowest position. We found a witness who saw the driver of the second vehicle get out and approach the alderman. The alderman tried to get out of his vehicle but the second driver grabbed his head and snapped his neck by twisting it. He then lowered the headrest."

"Tell the court about the size of each man, Detective."

"Mr. Bryan was small, maybe five-nine. Carbonaro, the man in the second vehicle, was about six-three and weighed two seventy-five. He had done some professional wrestling."

"What action did you take then?"

"We learned that Alderman Bryan had the swing vote regarding whether a condominium development or a casino operation would go up on some vacant lots on Sheridan Road."

"And did the Medical Examiner rule on Alderman Bryan's death?"

"Yes."

"What other investigation was conducted?"

"Our Traffic Unit had already asked for an accident reconstruction team to investigate."

"Any other witnesses used?"

"Yes. The secretary of City Council testified about the upcoming vote concerning condo versus casino."

"Was this case heard by a jury, or by Judge W. C. Hayes?"

"It was a jury trial, but the judge did not let the jury consider the evidence and gave a directed verdict instead."

"What was the judge's directed verdict?"

Schneider glanced at Hayes at the table beside Profacci. "Judge Hayes ruled that we had failed to show probable cause for the charge. He dismissed the case."

"How did you feel when that occurred?"

"That a killer had been set free."

"Objection," DeCenzo said.

"That's his opinion," Lyon said.

"Sustained."

"What did you do then?"

"Talked to Assistant State's Attorney Stambaugh, who prosecuted the case, asking him to appeal, then met with Lieutenant Slate."

DeCenzo stood and approached Detective Schneider. "Detective, isn't it true that the witness you claimed to have seen the neck twist changed his story when he appeared in court?"

"He wasn't as confident, but he told the same story."

"Didn't he finally agree that from four stories up on the roof, where he had been smoking, he could have been wrong."

"He was a Mexican guy with little English and—"

"Just answer the question, Detective."

"He was scared. I think somebody got to him. He disappeared after the trial."

"Objection to the last statement."

"Strike that," Judge Secrest said.

"He changed his story, didn't he?"

"Some."

"So, the only witness that a crime had been committed was from a person on a roof four stories up?"

"Is that a question?"

"Yes."

"Yes, as far as witnesses, but—"

"You've answered the question, Detective."

DeCenzo took his seat.

Judge Secrest announced, "We'll resume at 1:30 p.m. with the State's second witness."

———

Slate kept to himself with his paperwork as he ate lunch. But he paused occasionally as thoughts of the repercussions from CPD when Hayes was convicted kept coming to mind. How far did the internal corruption go? What would he do in Wisconsin after twenty years on the PD?

———

After lunch Judge Secrest directed, "Call your next witness, Ms. Lyon."

Lyon called Sergeant Utley. He was sworn and took the stand.

"Please state your name and position, Sergeant."

"Sergeant Herbert Utley, Chicago Police Department, Traffic Unit, Accident Reconstruction Team Supervisor."

"How is your team trained in accident reconstruction?"

"It's an eighty-hour course at Northwestern University's Department of Public Safety."

"Is that both classroom and field training?"

"Yes."

"Please explain your training."

"In the class we covered the formula for the co-efficiency of friction as it relates to different types of tire tread and pavement surfaces. Then in the field, we run tests in all kinds of conditions, wet and dry pavement, on various types of pavement surfaces, and with various tire treads. We evaluate the damage to each vehicle and determine their speed at the time of impact."

"And did your team evaluate the collision involving Alderman Bryan?"

"Yes."

"And what was the conclusion?"

"We determined that due to the minor damage to the vehicle that struck Alderman Bryan's vehicle and the small damage to the rear of Bryan's vehicle, it was unlikely that the collision would have resulted in serious injury."

"Objection. He's not a medical expert."

"I'm asking for his professional opinion from the accident damage, your honor," Lyon said.

"He may give his opinion based upon his training," the judge said.

DeCenzo stood at his table. "Sergeant, if the driver's headrest was down low enough not to provide support for the driver's head, could not that result in an injury even with the impact of this accident?"

"The headrest was up, according to the witness."

"The witness changed his mind, Sergeant. Could not an injury occur even at this slower speed with the headrest down?"

"Some injury might be possible, but I don't think it would have resulted in a broken neck."

"Do you have any nursing or medical education or experience, Sergeant?"

"No, sir."

DeCenzo sat down.

"Call your next witness, Ms. Lyon."

"I call Doctor Gary Kimball."

Slate had known Kimball for several years. Doctor Kimball worked with Doctor Harry Griffin, the Cook County Medical Examiner. Slate watched the medium-build bald-headed man in his fifties walk to the witness stand.

Lyon approached the box after the witness was sworn.

"Please state your name, profession, and training in your field."

"Doctor Gary Kimball, Assistant Medical Examiner for Cook County. Graduate of the University of Illinois at Champaign, and the University of Michigan Medical School."

"And how long have you served as a medical examiner?"

"Six years in Ann Arbor, Michigan, and twenty years for Cook County."

"Did you examine the body of Mr. Bryan?"

"Yes, I did."

"How many autopsies do you personally conduct in a year, doctor?"

"Hundreds. I counted them when I first came to Chicago, but soon stopped counting."

"So you work with some of the six hundred homicides per year, plus natural deaths?"

"Yes."

"And what were your findings on Alderman's Bryan's death, Doctor Kimball?"

"He died from a fractured neck. The fracture was not consistent with an impact from the rear, but more from a side impact or twisting action."

Slate wondered about Candice Bryan sitting behind him.

"Could this auto accident have caused this fracture?"

"It is my opinion that the impact from this collision was not sufficient to fracture his neck."

"So, is it your expert medical opinion that Mr. Bryan was not killed by this vehicle accident?"

"Yes, it is."

DeCenzo approached. "Doctor Kimball, if the victim's head was turned sideways at the time of the impact, could that have resulted in this type of fracture?"

"No. There was more damage to the neck vertebrae than a simple snap could cause."

"Doctor, you do not really know how the head might have twisted in this accident, do you?"

"My testimony is that the fracture appeared to be from a twisting action rather from an impact from the rear."

"Doctor, has a medical option ever been wrong?"

"Yes."

"Isn't it a fact that over one hundred thousand people die each year in our country due to medical errors?"

"Object. Not relevant," Lyon said.

"Strike that," Judge Secrest said.

DeCenzo took his seat.

Judge Secrest said. "Can we hear one more witness without running late, Ms. Lyon?"

"Yes, your honor. I call Neil Metcalf."

Metcalf was sworn and took the stand.

Lyon approached. "Please state your name and position."

"Neil Metcalf, Secretary for the Chicago City Council."

"Did you record the Council deliberations regarding a vote for the construction of a condominium or a casino on Sheridan Road last year?"

"Yes, I did."

"And what was the outcome of the discussions?"

"Originally, there appeared to be enough votes for a casino. Then it seemed that Alderman Bryan was getting pressure from his neighborhood against a casino and it sounded like the motion would lack one vote for a necessary two-thirds majority."

"What happened after Alderman Bryan's death?"

"The vote was put on hold until a new alderman could be elected."

"So Alderman Bryan's vote was the difference with a condominium development or a casino operation on Sheridan Road near the Chicago Yacht Club and Wrigley Field?"

"Yes."

"No questions," DeCenzo responded.

Judge Secrest checked his watch. "We'll adjourn until 9:00 a.m. Thursday." He struck his gavel once.

As the court cleared out Slate approached Lyon at the table. "What do you think, Paula?"

"Maybe I should have kept Kimball on there longer. How'd it all sound to you?"

"I thought it went well. And your opening to the jury yesterday was solid."

"They seem to be alert."

AT EXACTLY 9:00 a.m. Thursday the courtroom of Judge Secrest was called to order.

"Call your next witness, Ms. Lyon," the judge directed.

Lyon called Detective Joseph Barona. Slate watched Barona stride to the stand in his sharp black suit, white shirt, red floral tie, and black shiny shoes. The money Barona spent on clothes still amazed Slate.

Lyon walked Detective Barona through the armed robbery and the theft of two trucks at G & G Waste Management. Barona testified that G & G was in a bidding war with Central Waste Management and that Central Waste Management had ended up with the city contract. Barona said that he and his partner Detective Ingram had contacted the defendant Frank Ruggerio after he was found not guilty by Judge Hayes. Ruggiero had been bragging about being connected to the Outfit, and he was later found shot to death.

DeCenzo confronted Barona about the fact that no one saw the trucks driven from the lot, and that the fingerprint on the door could have occurred, as Ruggiero had testified to, earlier in the week while visiting with the driver. Barona admitted that could have happened, but Ruggerio was also seen there the day of the crimes.

DeCenzo then asked if there was any real proof that the armed robbery and truck theft were related or that Ruggiero was involved in them. Barona answered that the bidding war, the armed robbery, truck thefts, and the print on the truck established probable cause to charge Ruggiero.

"At least in your mind," DeCenzo said.

The G & G employee Harry Vess testified to seeing Frank Ruggerio standing on the running board of a truck next to where the two trucks were stolen then driven into Lake Michigan. The oil had been drained from the motors before they were driven off the lot so even though the stolen trucks were recovered, the motors were ruined.

DeCenzo offered no cross-examination.

Fingerprint Technician Sharon Jackson testified that Ruggerio's print was found on the truck adjacent to where the two trucks were stolen.

Again DeCenzo offered no cross-examination.

"Call your next witness, Ms. Lyon."

The ASA called Slate to the stand. He was sworn and took his seat. He noted that as Lyon approached the witness box she glanced to the jury to see that all were alert.

"Please state your name and position."

"Lieutenant Edward Slate, Chicago Police Department. I head Robbery/Homicide in Area 3, on the north side."

"How many detectives in the Unit?"

"Fifty-four."

"And there are how many Areas in the city?"

"Five."

"And an Area is responsible for how many Police Districts?"

"Five."

"So there are twenty-five Districts?"

"That's right."

"How long have you been with the department?"

"Over twenty years."

"And as a detective?"

"Ten-plus years."

"Please tell the court your education and training."

"Bachelors in police administration, U. S. Marine Corps Officer Candidate Training, Chicago Police Academy graduate, graduate of the FBI National Academy, and many shorter training programs relative to investigations and forensic science."

"How many homicides are recorded each year in the city of Chicago, Lieutenant Slate?"

"About six hundred."

"And in Area 3?"

"About a hundred fifty."

"During your career of over twenty years, and more than ten years as a detective, how many investigations have you conducted?"

"Hundreds."

"And how many investigations will fifty-four detectives conduct in a year?"

"Each pair will carry four to six active cases, plus many cold cases. So, several hundred cases are investigated each year."

"By cold cases you mean an older investigation that is not yet solved but is followed up on each month?"

"Yes."

"Lieutenant Slate, were you the officer in charge when the two cases that were just testified to were prosecuted?"

"Yes."

"And how did you become involved in this investigation of Judge W. C. Hayes?"

"I knew our detectives had lost some solid cases in his court, but when I was promoted to head the Unit, I saw all the trial dispositions and saw that many more cases being lost in that particular court."

"How were the final dispositions of the first two trials we covered here brought to your attention?"

"By the detectives who had investigated and filed the charges."

"Did you have any input on these charges being filed?"

"No. They were filed before I was promoted."

"What did you do when the detectives complained to you about the trials being lost?"

"I began an investigation."

"And where and to whom did that investigation take you?"

"To several places and persons. Mrs. Bernice Delaney, a former court employee, was able to provide some vital information."

"So you went to her, versus her calling you?"

"Yes. She didn't intend to be involved at all."

"And did what you learned from her make you more suspicious?"

"Yes. It sounded like the conversations with a particular attorney about extending a trial by a certain number of days in the court of Judge Hayes was actually code talk."

DeCenzo jumped to his feet. "Objection. No foundation about codes has been established."

"There will be, if I may finish."

"Overruled."

"Do you, from your twenty years of experience, Lieutenant Slate, have knowledge that the Mafia—or Outfit, as it's known in Chicago— sometimes talk in a code known only by members of the crime family?"

"Yes. That has been established in several federal and state prosecutions."

"So we have case law, criminal case decisions, to establish that the Outfit does use code talk?"

"Yes."

What happened then, Lieutenant Slate?"

"My contact with Mrs. Delaney revealed that after she had retired as an educator, she worked full time in Judge Hayes's office for about five years, then retired from that position. Shortly after I met with her, she was asked to return to work in that judge's office on a part-time basis."

Lyon turned to Judge Secrest. "Your honor, I will recall this witness following more testimony by other witnesses."

"Mr. DeCenzo, your witness."

"Nothing at this time, your honor."

"We will adjourn until 1:30 p.m." Judge Secrest struck his gavel.

Slate left the stand and joined ASA Lyon at her table. "Satisfied so far?"

"Yeah. It's a little awkward with all these pieces, and bringing you in and out, but the jury will see the pattern more clearly this way."

At 1:30 p.m. the court was called to order and Judge Secrest instructed, "Call your next witness, Ms. Lyon."

"I call Bernice Delaney."

Mrs. Delaney arose and stepped forward to the stand. Slate noted her light brown suit with a dark blouse. Her short hair looked good with the suit, but she looked very uncomfortable. He noticed her fleeting glance in the direction of W. C. Hayes while being sworn in.

Lyon said, "Please state your name."

"Bernice Delaney."

"Please tell the court of your education and experience."

"Bachelors and masters of education. I taught high school English in the Chicago public school system for thirty years."

"And how do you come to be employed in the Cook County Circuit Court?"

"After I retired from teaching I worked full time in the court office until my husband retired, then I retired again and we traveled. Then after Howard passed away, I didn't work at all until I was asked to return to the judge's office and work part-time."

"So you worked full-time, how long in the court?"

"Nearly five years."

"So you clearly understand the court system and the scheduling of trials?"

"Oh yes."

"Then you worked part time how long?"

"Less than two months."

"Please tell the court what you heard in Judges Hayes's court office while working under Mario DeMeo, the office administrator."

Delaney shifted in her seat. "Law firms call frequently with requests to move a court time or date due to a schedule conflict or some emergency, and any of us in the office would handle that. However, when the law firm of Profacci and Bellino called," she paused and looked at Profacci at the table beside Hayes, "they would always ask specifically for Mr. DeMeo. They would ask about moving a trial up so many days and then seemed to argue about how many days."

"What did you conclude from this?"

"I wondered why Mr. DeMeo always handled the calls from this law firm about moving a trial up by so many days, and then the trial dates were never changed."

"Were you contacted by Lieutenant Slate regarding the possibility of some illegal activity in the court?"

"Yes."

"And after you meet with Lieutenant Slate, what did you learn and what did you hear Mr. DeMeo and Judge Hayes say?"

"Soon after my meeting with Lieutenant Slate Mr. Profacci called and talked to Mr. DeMeo about moving a case twenty-five days. Mr. DeMeo asked what kind of case, then said maybe one hundred days."

"Where were you when this conversation occurred?"

Delaney glanced at Hayes. "At the copier near Mr. DeMeo's desk."

"What did you do then?"

"I left the office at closing time as usual, then came back and stood at Judge Hayes's partially open door."

"And what did you hear?"

Delaney glanced at Hayes again. "Judge Hayes and Mr. DeMeo were talking in the judge's office as they did at the end of each day. Judge Hayes said, 'twenty-five for an arson/homicide?' and laughed."

"What did you do then?"

"I told Lieutenant Slate what I had heard."

"Then what happened?"

"He told me to find out what case the conversation was about."

"And did you?"

"Yes. It was the arson case that killed a man."

"Your honor, I will recall this witness later."

DeCenzo waived his right to cross examine until the recall.

"I now recall Lieutenant Slate."

Slate took the stand again and the judge reminded him he was still under oath.

"Lieutenant Slate, what was the outcome of your contact with Mrs. Delaney?"

"I learned enough with her deposition to obtain a court order to tap and record the office phone calls of Judge Hayes, of Mr. DeMeo, the office administrator, and his staff's phones."

"Your honor, I will recall this witness one more time."

DeCenzo again said he would cross examine Slate later.

"Your next witness, Ms. Lyon."

"I call Mr. Carl Yost."

Lyon walked Mr. Yost through being approached by Danny Fischetti for a monthly street tax payment to protect Yost Furrier, and his refusal to pay, their installation of security cameras, his son's death, and the loss of his merchandise from the fire.

DeCenzo asked if Mr. Fischetti had threatened him in any way. Yost replied that he mentioned the possibility of burglaries or fires when the business was closed. DeCenzo countered that these were valid concerns. Yost agreed that they might be.

Captain O'Rourke of the Chicago Fire Department testified that the fire was definitely an arson. DeCenzo countered that there was no direct evidence that the defendant set the fire and O'Rourke acknowledged that to be so. Lyon submitted the fire report as Exhibit #1.

Detective Leary testified to his investigation, to identifying the defendant Danny Fischetti on the video, and the subsequent charges of arson, homicide, and manslaughter.

Lyon submitted the police investigation as Exhibit #2.

DeCenzo asked Detective Leary if, since the camera did not show the fire being set, could it not be that Mr. Fischetti was simply patrolling the business places he was paid to protect in that neighborhood during the night time when they were closed? Leary admitted he could be, but the evidence said otherwise. DeCenzo moved to strike the latter part of the response.

Forensic Technician Bauer covered what the film in the security camera revealed, and the gas can found in a nearby dumpster. DeCenzo pointed out that the video did not show Mr. Fischetti setting a fire but patrolling in the area. Bauer agreed, then tried to point out the time sequence but DeCenzo cut him off.

Lyon submitted the forensic investigation as Exhibit #3.

She then called Mr. James Kim, owner of the Loop Cleaners. She led the businessman through an explanation of how he was paying street tax to keep his place safe, that he had received no contract for this service and had never seen Fischetti at his place in the evenings or on weekends when the place was to be checked. He also testified that he never received a receipt for payments, or any written or verbal notices or photos concerning conditions around his dry cleaning business.

In his cross-examination DeCenzo asked Mr. Kim if any threats had been made to him. Kim said not directly.

Court was adjourned until Friday morning.

Slate checked around and under his Dodge before heading west to I-94, then south to the city. He wanted to go directly home, but he needed to check his IN box at Area 3. He called Rebecca and gave her a quick update.

At Area 3 Sergeant Waddell followed him into his office "How's the trial going, Ed?"

"Good so far, Rick."

"Any trouble getting the jury together?"

"No. That went well and they look good. Little Hayes is sitting there looking innocent. What's happening here? Anything more on DeMeo?"

"Haven't heard a thing. Was the Bureau in to see you?"

"Yeah. They wanted to take over the case."

"Make it a RICO?"

Slate nodded. "But they wouldn't tell me how much they knew, so I didn't tell them what I had. I told them I would give them everything after we finish this trial, but they still wouldn't help. I wish we had DeMeo to use in Lake County, but we should be okay."

Rick studied Ed. "See you switched cars again. You're checking for bombs, I guess?"

Slate nodded.

"Any more threats?"

"Not recently. My wife is still worrying. A male caller asked if she was ready to be a widow."

"Whoa, that had to shake her."

"It did."

Rick checked the hall, then came back toward Slate. "Is Arnold clean?"

Slate nodded. "I think the Commander's okay. Well, it doesn't look like I have to move this stack of paper tonight. I'm out of here."

———

As he drove to the northwest side he reviewed the day's testimony of all witnesses. The case was solid. Hayes and Profacci would be convicted.

Rebecca let him in. "I would have waited to eat if I had known you were coming home this soon."

"I thought my IN box might take longer, but the things in it can wait."

He kissed her. "How's things here? Any more calls?"

"No, thankfully. You're checking your car, aren't you?

"Yeah."

"How's court?"

"Looks good, but I wish we had DeMeo to testify. How's Sarah and summer school? Any problems?"

"We talked Sunday night. She's okay."

After Ed ate, they walked for thirty minutes, but his mind was on the trial. After dark he spread fresh lime around the Dodge and they went to bed early. But details of the case and the evidence kept rolling through his mind.

Sleep evaded him for the first hour. He wondered again if they had missed anything. He knew that sometimes the stress brought on the Vietnam nightmares.

ON FRIDAY MORNING at home Slate checked for footprints around his car, then headed north.

Court resumed at 9:00 a.m. and Lyon recalled Slate to the stand.

"Lieutenant Slate, you have already testified that after the second trial, involving the waste haulers, was lost you used Mrs. Delaney's deposition of what she had heard about moving a trial by so many days to obtain a court order to tap and record the court office phones of W.C. Hayes. What did you learn from the recordings?"

"The first tape recorded Mr. Profacci calling again about moving the trial twenty-five days and DeMeo said that wasn't going to happen. Then they agreed on seventy-five days. After the trial, the tape recorded DeMeo calling Mr. Profacci, insisting on an additional fifty days."

"How do you know this was code talk for a payoff, Lieutenant Slate?"

"Because before the trial the discussion was about twenty-five or one hundred days, but it was settled at seventy-five days or seventy-five thousand dollars, and the court date never changed. I attended the trial. And a later subpoena of bank records showed major cash deposits made to Hayes's and DeMeo's accounts."

"And what were those amounts?"

"Before the trial, Hayes deposited fifty-six thousand and two hundred fifty dollars and DeMeo, eighteen thousand seven hundred fifty dollars."

"And what did you conclude from those deposits?"

"It confirmed that seventy-five days meant seventy-five thousand dollars, and DeMeo's share was twenty-five percent."

"What did the bank records show after the trial was held and before a verdict was given by Judge Hayes?"

"After the trial DeMeo called Profacci, asking for another fifty days, or fifty-thousand dollars. Soon after that Hayes deposited thirty-seven thousand five hundred dollars and DeMeo seven thousand dollars."

"And what conclusion did you draw from those deposits, Lieutenant?"

"That Hayes deposited his full seventy-five percent but DeMeo kept fifty-five hundred back out of his twenty-five percent."

"And how, beside the bank records, do you know that the days stated equaled a payment?"

"When DeMeo met with you and me looking for a deal, agreeing to be a State's witness, he admitted that one 'day' equaled one thousand dollars."

"And how do you know that DeMeo's share was twenty-five percent?"

"He also admitted that when we met."

"And did DeMeo say how long this had been going on and how much money was involved?"

"He said payoffs had been made for five or six years and involved hundreds of thousands of dollars."

"And, do you know the source of these payoffs?"

"I placed a Tele-Track device on DeMeo's car and tracked him to the home of Carmine Vaccaro in River Forest on two occasions during this same time frame."

"And what do you know about this Carmine Vaccaro?"

"He's a made guy in the Outfit, the Chicago Mafia."

"Objection," DeCenzo said. "This is pure fabrication."

"If you will hear us out, your honor."

"Continue."

"What do you know about this Mr. Carmine Vaccaro, Lieutenant?"

"DeMeo admitted that Vaccaro had made some payments to him and Hayes. We checked phone records and found that he and

DeMeo had called each other. And he's listed by our department as one of the Outfit's made men.

"Objection. Nothing about 'made men' has been established."

"Your honor, that term and its meaning have been well established in both state and federal trials."

"Overruled."

"What do you mean by being a 'made man'?"

"He has authority to act as a member of the Outfit. He's an administrator or boss with authority, and he can order a hit."

"And by 'hit,' you refer to a person being killed?"

"Yes."

"So, Judge Hayes's administrator, Mario DeMeo, had contacts in person and by telephone with a Chicago Outfit member who is a made man, and DeMeo said that Vaccaro made payments to Hayes and to himself?"

"Yes hundreds of thousands of dollars over a period of five or six years."

"What did you conclude from all of this, Lieutenant?"

"That the fix was in for seventy-five thousand dollars. Then when Hayes saw how strong the arson and death case was, he had DeMeo demand another fifty thousand, for a total of one hundred twenty-five thousand dollars to get a not-guilty finding."

"Did the defendant, Danny Fischetti, ask for a jury trial in the arson trial?"

"No. He did not."

"Did you find that unusual?"

DeCenzo jumped to his feet. "Objection. Pure speculation."

"Overruled," Judge Secrest said.

"Yes, I found that unusual due to the gravity of the case, and the possible sentence that Fischetti faced for the arson and the death of Mr. Yost's son."

"Why was a not-guilty finding important to the Outfit?"

"To protect their street tax collector, Danny Fischetti, and the Outfit's monthly income."

"Did you find any other relevant evidence of a payoff and a conspiracy when meeting with Mr. DeMeo?"

"Mario DeMeo offered to give us Hayes, Profacci, and the made guy, Carmine Vaccaro."

"At this time I introduce Exhibit #4, the court order for the phone tap; Exhibit #5, the bank records; and Exhibit #6, the recording of the meeting Lieutenant Slate and I had with DeMeo, which I will now play for the jury."

DeCenzo jumped to his feet. "Request a sidebar, your honor."

The judge motioned DeCenzo and Lyon to his bench.

Slate knew that DeMeo's confession on the tape of Hayes and himself accepting hundreds of thousands of dollars to fix cases over a five- or six-year period and admitting that a day equaled one thousand dollars would seal Hayes's and Profacci's fate with the jury. He was certain DeCenzo was arguing that since DeMeo was now dead, the tape could not be admitted as evidence.

After a short discussion both attorneys moved from the bench.

Judge Secrest said, "Overruled. Proceed Ms. Lyon."

Lyon played the tape for nearly twenty minutes. The jury listened with great interest, Slate observed, and many took notes the whole time. When the tape ended, ASA Lyon approached Slate.

"Now, after that meeting with us, what happened to Mario DeMeo?"

"He was killed."

"Where and how?"

"In his garage at home. His throat was cut."

"From your investigation, Lieutenant Slate, what have you concluded?"

"That the Chicago police department has been losing cases in one Circuit Court because of a corrupt judge and his office administrator who were taking bribes. As a result, Alderman Bryan's killer went free on a directed verdict by Hayes. And Hayes gave not-guilty findings in the robbery and truck theft, and also in the arson death of Mr. Yost's son. And those payoffs, or at least some of them, came from the Outfit's made man, Carmine Vaccaro."

"Why would the Outfit be interested in each of these cases, Lieutenant Slate?"

"Alderman Bryan's death will likely allow a casino to be built, and that casino could be owned or partly owned by the Outfit, or they would receive kickbacks from the owners. And the same with the waste hauler contract. The Outfit would get a kickback if their man got the contract. The arson case also was income-related. Mr. Yost would not pay the monthly fee, or street tax, like many other business owners paid just to be left alone by the Outfit. When a merchant refuses to pay, the Outfit loses the income that Fischetti otherwise collects monthly."

"Objection. All speculation."

"Overruled."

Lyon submitted Slate's investigation report as Exhibit #7, and the River Forest Police report on DeMeo's death as #8.

DeCenzo approached Slate.

"Lieutenant Slate, did you hear any mention of money on the phone tap?"

"Only by the code talk."

"Just answer my question. Did anyone ever say anything about dollars?"

"No."

"Did you ever witness any money being exchanged?"

"No."

"Could it not be that Mario DeMeo and Mr. Vaccaro are just friends who happen to both live in River Forest?"

"I'm sure they were close friends."

DeCenzo glared at Slate. "You have no idea why they met, do you?"

"Yes I do, and I testified to that belief."

DeCenzo raised his voice. "You saw no money exchanged, did you?"

"No, but I heard the conversations before and after the trial, and saw the trial lost. I saw the bank records and telephone call records, and DeMeo admitted that in their code talk 'day' equaled a thousand dollars."

"Your honor, please tell the witness to restrict his answers to the question."

"I think he has, counselor. Maybe you could be more specific."

DeCenzo's face reddened as he walked back to the table. He picked up his pad, then returned to Slate. "Do you know who killed Mr. DeMeo, or why?"

"I have a good idea."

"Did you ever hear Judge Hayes on the phone tap?"

"No."

"So what you have is speculation that an attorney's call to move a trial date was, in your mind, some reference to a payoff."

"Is that a question?"

"Yes."

"Yes, because the date of the trial was never changed, bank deposits for substantial amounts of money were made, and the case was lost, and DeMeo admitted a day equaled one thousand dollars, and that payoffs had been made for years, with seventy-five percent to Hayes, and twenty-five percent to himself."

DeCenzo shook his head. "We need real evidence in court, Lieutenant, not your zealous crusade to ruin a judge's career because you don't agree with the trial dispositions. I think you're just trying to establish a reputation in your new position with your detectives. In other words, your new job has gone to your head!"

Lyon jumped up. "Objection. He's harassing the witness, your honor."

"Strike that."

DeCenzo returned to his seat.

Slate left the witness stand.

ASA Paula Lyon called her next witness and stated he would serve as an Expert Witness. Slate watched the older man walk to the stand, take the oath, and sit down. Lyon approached him. "Please state your name and former position."

"Stanley Jeffers, retired Circuit Court Judge in Lake County, Illinois."

"Please tell the court your education and experience."

"Bachelor's degree from the University of Illinois, Chicago. Doctor of Jurisprudence from Northwestern University. Practiced law for twenty-two years, five as a criminal lawyer, and served as a Circuit Court Judge for seventeen years."

"You are now retired?"

"Yes, just two years."

"Have you reviewed the three investigation reports the detectives have just testified to, as well as the court transcripts?"

"I have."

"Let's take them one at a time. On the trial involving the death of Alderman Bryan. How would you have ruled on that trial?"

"There was sufficient evidence to establish probable cause. And since the witness on the roof top was only one piece of the evidence, I would have given the case to the jury to decide."

"So, the witness, medical examiner's report, the accident reconstruction report, and the pending City Council vote would have been enough?"

"I would have liked to hear the witness on the roof, but I would have allowed the jury to decide the case."

"Now, on the armed robbery and truck theft case, what is your expert opinion of that trial?"

"That trial is not as clear, given the driver's testimony that the suspect had talked to him earlier in the week. However, another driver testified to seeing the defendant in the lot and on the running board of a truck at the time the two trucks were stolen. So I can't say how I would have ruled there without seeing and hearing all the witnesses."

"Okay. On the arson and the death of Mr. Yost's son, how would you have ruled on that trial that was heard by Judge Hayes without a jury?"

Judge Jeffers shifted in his chair and leaned forward, looking at the jury. "I would have liked to hear all the testimony and evaluated all the witnesses. If I had been satisfied with the testimony, I would have rendered a verdict of guilty. Some is circumstantial evidence, as regarding the street tax issue. But the testimony, along with the video of the defendant at that exact spot just nine minutes before the fire, and carrying the object from the scene, would have resulted in a finding of guilty. And that's without considering the emotional aspect that the fire resulted in a death, which was probably unintentional."

"So, based upon your education, and experience as a lawyer and judge for a period of nearly forty years, is it your expert opinion that the two cases should have definitely resulted in a finding of guilty?"

"Yes. Justice was not served."

"And on the case involving a robbery and two stolen trucks, you are unable to reach a definite opinion without having heard all the witnesses?"

"That is correct."

Lyon returned to her seat.

DeCenzo approached Judge Jeffers. "Mr. Jeffers, isn't it a fact that it's difficult to stay current on the law unless you are practicing every day and staying up with the various court opinions?"

"There is nothing in any of these trials that was highly controversial. Also, even if there were, I've only been retired two years, and I still read the law and trial transcripts almost daily."

"But reading a transcript is not the same as being in court and hearing and observing a witness, is it?"

"That's true, but that doesn't alter the facts as they are recorded." Jeffers pointed to the court recorder.

"You will be paid for this professional opinion, will you not?"

"Yes. That's a common practice."

DeCenzo sat down.

Lyon re-approached Jeffers. "Judge Jeffers, is there anything regarding the evidence used in these three cases that could be successfully appealed?"

"You could try, but I seriously doubt that an Appeals Court would accept a review of any of them. They were pretty straightforward."

"So the defense is blowing smoke by implying these are difficult cases and you are out of touch in just two years after practicing law for nearly forty years?"

"One could conclude that." Jeffers was excused.

They broke for lunch.

As the courtroom filled after lunch on Friday afternoon, Slate studied Lyon. He knew she would have normally closed with her expert witness but probably figured that Mrs. Delaney's testimony would have a better emotional effect on the jury.

"Call your next witness, Ms. Lyon," Judge Secrest ordered.

"I recall Mrs. Bernice Delaney." Slate watched Mrs. Delaney take her place in the witness chair. She was wearing a medium blue suit and a white blouse and walked with a little more confidence. She reminded him some of his teachers and the memories caused him to wish he had put more into his studies.

"Mr. DeCenzo is claiming there were no Mob connections in these three trials, Mrs. Delaney. Tell the court what has happened to you regarding your safety and your home after the grand jury indictment against Judge Hayes and Attorney Profacci."

"I was told by Lieutenant Slate that a hit man had been hired to kill me, so I was moved from my home in Oak Park by the Chicago police."

Lyon paused, apparently deciding how to form the next question. "And after Mr. DeMeo's throat was cut in his garage at home, what did you learn about that contracted hit?"

Delaney glared at Hayes. "That the man who killed Mr. DeMeo was the one hired to kill me!"

"And while you were living in a motel awaiting this trial, what happened?"

"My home was burned down."

She glared at Hayes and her faced flushed. "Everything is gone! Everything from my marriage and family—every memento I had saved over forty years." She stood and pointed at Hayes. "And that little jerk who calls himself a judge is responsible!"

"Please be seated Mrs. Delaney," Judge Secrest instructed.

Lyon waited and glanced at the jury. Delaney then sat back down. "You lost everything in the fire?"

"Everything. My wedding pictures, my children's photo albums, and the photos of my thirty years of teaching. Everything but the clothes and personal records I had taken with me."

"Did you want to be involved in this investigation, Mrs. Delaney?"

She sat up straighter in the chair. "Heavens no. I really didn't realize what I was getting into when I agreed to help. I tried my best to get out of it." She looked at Slate. "The Lieutenant convinced me I had a civic duty . . . and I guess I do. But I had no idea of the risk."

DeCenzo approached. "Mrs. Delaney, in all the five years you worked in the office prior to what you just testified to, did you ever see or hear anything that was dishonest?"

"I wondered why the Profacci and Bellino law firm always had to talk to Mr. DeMeo about changing trial dates without the dates ever actually being changed."

"He was the office administrator, wasn't he?"

"Yes."

"So it was only after Lieutenant Slate talked to you that you decided this sort of phone call was dishonest?"

"I already explained that trial days were never changed," Bernice Delaney answered.

DeCenzo looked at the jury as he asked, "Do you watch police shows on television, Mrs. Delaney?"

The witness seemed to take her time to answer. "Sometimes, but I didn't imagine this."

"But it was Lieutenant Slate who decided that an innocent call to change a trial date . . . something that's done many times . . . was actually something dishonest. Did you every see any money change hands?"

"No."

DeCenzo returned to his seat.

Judge Secrest riffled through the papers in front of him, then looked at DeCenzo. "Do you still have just two witnesses, Mr. DeCenzo?"

"Yes, your honor."

"It's a little early, but we'll close for the day, then hear your witnesses Monday."

———

Slate called Sergeant Waddell from the car and confirmed that all was quiet in the department. As he drove to the northwest side, he reviewed his testimony and the trial in general. He thought of the list on his whiteboard as he drove. What about his Deputy Chief of Detectives, Urbanski, the Outfit's guy, Vaccaro, and the CPD retiree Seryak, who gave him the warning at Smokey's restaurant? Did Seryak call Rebecca? And who ordered the car bomb? He figured that was Vaccaro.

Could he make the others on a State charge? Or would he have to rely on the FBI and a RICO case? Then there was Carbonaro, who killed Alderman Bryan. He was still out there.

As he neared home he thought of the risks to Rebecca. The shootouts were one thing, but a car bomb at home was different. Maybe he should hang it up when Hayes and Profacci were convicted and get out of the corrupt city. Let some other detective get the rest of the Outfit and the corrupt cops.

CHAPTER 33

SLATE ARRIVED AT the Waukegan courtroom early on Monday morning and took a seat with Lyon at the right front table. The court was called to order at 9:03 a.m.

Judge Secrest said, "Call your first witness, Mr. DeCenzo."

DeCenzo stood. "I call Anthony Profacci."

Profacci took the oath and sat down in the witness chair. Slate noticed he had worn a different suit each day. Today was no exception. As Slate studied the defendant, he knew the oath to tell the truth, the whole truth, and nothing but the truth meant nothing to the man who had just taken it.

DeCenzo stepped in front of Profacci. "Please state your name and profession."

The defendant acknowledged his attorney with a smile then stated, "Anthony Profacci. Attorney at Law."

"Please tell the court about your education and years of experience."

"Graduated from the University of Iowa, then John Marshall Law School. I've practiced law for twenty-six years in the city of Chicago."

"And how long have you been associated with Mr. Bellino?"

"Louie and I have been together for seventeen years."

"And what type of law do you specialize in?"

"Strictly criminal law."

"During your twenty-six years, Mr. Profacci, have you ever been charged with a crime or sanctioned by the Illinois or American Bar Associations?"

"Never," he answered as he met Slate's eyes.

"Now to the case in point. How often is it necessary to change a court appearance date?"

"It's almost a daily event. We represent many clients and appear in several different courts each week or month. There may delays due to a client's schedule, sickness, or the schedule of a witness, or a trial date in another court that is close to an upcoming trial, and the first trial takes longer than expected."

"So, calls for trial date changes are a regular and frequent necessity in your trial work?"

"Absolutely."

"Now, in the case of the trial involving the Yost Furrier fire, you called for a change in the trial date then went to trial on the originally scheduled date."

"Yes. The conflict that caused me to request a later trial date was resolved."

"So you went ahead as originally scheduled?"

"Yes."

"At any time have you ever paid for a date change or discussed such a payment?"

"Absolutely not."

"So you never tried to change a trial by calling and paying the late Mr. DeMeo?"

Profacci looked toward the jury and answered confidently. "No. We joked on the phone with each other, and that may have been misconstrued. I wish Mario could be here to confirm what I'm saying."

"By Mario you refer to Mario DeMeo, the office administrator to W. C. Hayes, Mario DeMeo who was killed by a robber?"

Lyon stood. "Objection, Mr. DeMeo was not robbed. His throat was cut in his own garage after he met with Lieutenant Slate and me, offering to be a State's witness."

"Strike the reference to his death by a robber," Judge Secrest directed.

"So the tape played for the jury by Ms. Lyon was simply you and Mario DeMeo joking about the trial dates?"

Profacci nodded. "Yes. We did that and we bet on our golfing scores and even some Cubs games, but it was always as friends. It had nothing to do with the court or a trial."

"Then how did you win the trial of arson against Danny Fischetti?"

"Mr. Fischetti was not seen setting a fire, but was doing his job of patrolling the stores in that area on Huron Street. He was protecting them while the businesses were closed. He just happened to be caught on a camera in the area that night."

DeCenzo turned and sat down.

Lyon stood and approached Profacci.

"I'm sure the jury finds your explanation of the taped conversation of code talk to fix the arson trial very ingenious Mr. Profacci, but it won't fly. On that tape you argue about giving twenty-five thousand dollars and DeMeo wants seventy-five thousand to fix the trial. Isn't that right? Remember, you are under oath, Mr. Profacci."

"No, it's not right. We were joking and we were not talking about money."

"And the later call, when DeMeo said he had talked to Judge Hayes and the case was a strong one, that someone was watching the trial, and he needed another fifty thousand was also a joke?"

"Objection. Judge Hayes's name is not on that tape," DeCenzo said.

"The reference to 'the schedule setter' is clear with the call, and the bank deposits show money deposited to Judge Hayes's account, your honor."

"Overruled."

"Mario and I joked all the time."

"And the bank deposits by DeMeo and Hayes just after that call were also a coincidence?"

"I know nothing about other people's bank records."

Lyon checked her notes. "How much did you contribute to W. C. Hayes's reelection campaign last time, Mr. Profacci?"

"I don't remember."

"How about two hundred and thirty thousand dollars. Does that sound about right?"

"Our firm supports a number of candidates. It's the American way." Profacci's confident tone with the jury began to grate on Slate.

"But isn't it true that Hayes is the only judge you supported?"

"I don't know."

Lyon returned to her table and took her seat beside Slate. "I wish we had DeMeo's testimony and your Michigan tape, Ed," she whispered.

"I'll let the Bureau have that when we're done. Too bad we had to warn Vaccaro," Slate whispered back. "How did you know Profacci only supported Hayes?"

"I didn't."

"Call your next witness, Mr. DeCenzo."

"I call Judge W. C. Hayes."

Lyon rose where she was seated. "I object to the 'judge' title, your honor. Mr. Hayes is appearing as a criminal charged with Official Misconduct and Failure to Report a Bribe."

"Sustained."

Hayes stood and walked to the witness stand. He was sworn and took his seat.

Hayes appeared nervous when he glanced at the jury, Slate thought. That little lack of confidence made him smile to himself. Seeing Wilbur Clarence Hayes as a defendant seemed worth the risks.

DeCenzo approached the defendant. "Please state your name and profession."

Hayes shifted in his seat, to sit taller Slate guessed. "W. C. Hayes, Circuit Court Judge, Cook County."

"Tell the court about your qualifications and the positions you have held."

"I graduated DePaul University then attended John Marshall Law School at night for about seven years. After I received my Doctorate of Jurisprudence I worked part time as a public defender, and then in traffic court. I was appointed to serve the remainder of a judge's term upon his death. Then I was elected to that position."

The other judge's death. Slate wondered if that was that something he should note on his whiteboard board.

"How long have you served as a judge?"

"Fifteen years."

"And during that fifteen years, have you ever been charged with a crime or sanctioned by the State or National Bar Associations?"

"No. Never."

"Now, to this charge filed by a newly promoted police lieutenant."

Lyon jumped to her feet. "Objection. The charge was filed by the Cook County State's Attorney's office after a careful review of all evidence."

"Strike that," Judge Secrest said.

DeCenzo glanced at Lyon, then back to Hayes. "On the first case involving Alderman Bryan, why was that case not given to the jury?"

"The State's main witness changed his mind under cross examination and he was the only witness. Therefore, there was not enough evidence to show a homicide had been committed."

"Does the court transcript clearly show his testimony?"

"Yes."

"I now play that cross examination for the jury to hear."

The tape was played, showing Hector Ruiz being examined and it was damaging to the case.

"Now, Judge Hayes, on the trial involving the waste hauler truck theft . . . "

"Objection," Lyon said jumping up. "That was an armed robbery and a truck theft."

"So state." Judge Secrest pointed to the recorder.

"On this trial, with the robbery, truck theft, why did you find the defendant, Frank Ruggiero not guilty?"

"A driver testified that Mr. Ruggiero had stood on his running board to talk to him earlier in the week, so the case lacked solid evidence as to when the fingerprint was placed on the door."

"And, on the trial of the fire death . . ."

"Objection. The fire was an arson that killed Keith Yost."

"So note," Judge Secrest ordered. "Mr. DeCenzo, let's deal with the facts."

"In the trial of the arson and death at Yost Furrier, why was the defendant Danny Fischetti found not guilty?"

Hayes sat up a little taller. "The defendant was not observed by the video camera starting the fire but only walking in the area before the fire was recorded."

"So, again, another case that did not have sufficient evidence to prove the charge?"

"That is correct."

DeCenzo returned to his table for a second pad. "Have you, in your position as a Circuit Court judge, ever discussed court date changes with Mr. Profacci?"

Hayes moved in his seat, glanced at the jury, then said, "No. My office administrator, Mario DeMeo handled all of that."

"Would you have any way of knowing if Mr. DeMeo were requiring money for doing favors for attorneys wanting to move a court day?"

"No. I only heard about the new trial date."

"How do you account for the bank deposits referred to by the State?"

Hayes shifted slightly again. "I don't always deposit extra money until it builds up."

"And what is the source of that extra money?"

"I still work as an attorney occasionally in other jurisdictions in the state."

"And that would be to avoid a conflict of interest by not working in the jurisdiction of your court?"

"Yes."

Slate could see the portrait of his defendant that DeCenzo was building. It contrasted sharply with the facts.

"So, you have no knowledge of any payments to Mr. DeMeo for any favored treatment of any kind?"

"No. I do not."

"But if Mr. DeMeo had collected some money for doing an attorney a favor, you would not have known about that?"

"No. But I trusted Mario and I seriously doubt he would have done that."

DeCenzo glanced at his notes one more time, then sat down.

ASA Lyon approached Hayes.

"If you are honest, and DeMeo was honest, how do you account for the conversation overheard by Mrs. Delaney between you and Mr. DeMeo where you two were laughing about Profacci wanting to pay twenty-five thousand for an arson death case that was worth a hundred thousand dollars?"

"Objection. The talk about changing a court day did not represent paying anything," DeCenzo said.

"Sustained."

Lyon paused and looked at Judge Secrest. "Mr. Hayes, why were you and DeMeo laughing about moving a trial date twenty-five days for an arson death?"

Hayes moved in his seat. "I don't remember any such talk. Your witness must not have heard the entire conversation."

"Are you aware that Mrs. Delaney's home was torched after she testified before the grand jury?"

"I know nothing about that."

"Do you know a Carmine Vaccaro, a made guy in the Chicago Outfit?"

Hayes hesitated. "I know Mr. Vaccaro from golfing at the same club."

Lyon nodded knowingly. "I see. Just a golf buddy who happens to be a made man."

Lyon stepped over toward the jury then looked back at Hayes. "So, this jury of Lake County citizens is to believe that the code talk was really about moving trial dates and not about thousands of dollars to toss a case or buy a not-guilty finding, even though Mario DeMeo admitted on the tape I played earlier that the word 'days' equaled a payoff, one day equaled one grand, that you two had been doing this for five or six years, and this procedure involved hundreds of thousands of dollars.

"Even though, in the Yosts' case, the trial date was never moved. And the deposits made by you and DeMeo just after that call were not bribe monies. And the call from DeMeo to Profacci before you rendered a verdict in the arson death case was not to swindle another fifty thousand dollars from Profacci and the Outfit, on top of the seventy-five thousand you and DeMeo had already received. And after three marriages and child support payments, buying three homes that are debt free, you weren't in need of extra money?"

"Objection," Dezeno said. "That was a speech, not a question, and these issues are not a factor here."

"It goes to motive, your honor."

"Overruled."

"Well?" Lyon asked.

Hayes again sat up taller and raised his chin. "This was about moving trial dates. And I have been a good money manager all of my life, due in part to my humble upbringing."

"But you resented that humble upbringing and decided that you would live the good life even if it required selling your judgeship and consorting with the Mob, didn't you?"

"Objection."

"To what?" Judge Secrest asked.

"She's badgering the witness."

"Overruled. Answer the question."

"I have overcome my upbringing through education and sound management."

Slate caught himself shaking his head.

Lyon moved to another position in front of the jury. "Sure you have," she acknowledged. "Now, Mr. Hayes, what organization made the largest contribution to your last reelection campaign?"

Hayes paused. "It might have been Profacci and Bellino."

"To the tune of two hundred thirty thousand dollars. No other contribution came close. How do you explain that?"

Slate watched Hayes shift in his seat. "I don't know. My campaign manager handles all of that."

"How convenient. DeMeo is the front man at court, then your campaign manager is your front man for reelections, but you remain pure."

"Objection. Pure harassment," DeCenzo said.

Lyon sat down.

"Strike Ms. Lyon's last comment.

"That is your last witness, Mr. DeCenzo?"

"Yes, your honor."

"We'll break for lunch and resume at 1:00 p.m. since we're leaving early," Judge Secrest declared.

"We're close, Ed," Lyon said as the courtroom cleared out.

"What do you think?"

"I think we have an excellent case. Your investigation brought it all together."

"You got DeCenzo a little aggravated. I wouldn't think the jury would take long, given what we have, Paula."

After lunch, Judge Secrest announced, "We're ready for the closing arguments." He looked at ASA Lyon.

"I'm ready, your honor."

"Proceed."

Lyon stood with her notes and walked in front of the jury to her right. Slate wondered again why a woman with her looks and abilities had never married.

"Ladies and gentlemen of the jury, I'm not going to belabor the issue and recite all the facts you have just heard. We know you are a very responsible group of citizens who want our society to be one based upon just laws that protect the weak and the strong alike. Therefore, I'll be brief.

"We have a Circuit Court judge hearing felony cases and accepting bribes to enrich himself, rather than obeying the law himself. W. C. Hayes owns property in Illinois, Michigan, and Florida, all debt free. Still he's on his third marriage, pays child support, and does not come from a family with money. He drives a seventy-thousand-dollar car. All of this with an annual salary of one hundred sixty-three thousand dollars.

"Alderman Steven Bryan, a former Naval officer, husband, and father of two young sons, was murdered in order for someone to get a casino built on Sheridan Road rather than a condo development. A casino will allow the Outfit to buy into the deal or skim a part of that income each month. The man charged with that murder was found not guilty by a directed verdict rendered by W. C. Hayes rather than allowing the jury to decide the case when probable cause was clearly present."

She checked her notes. "A waste hauler was robbed and two trucks stolen and run into Lake Michigan over a bidding war. One hauler had Outfit connections. The defendant was found not guilty by Hayes even though a witness identified him as being near a stolen truck on the day of the crime and his fingerprint was found on the door."

Lyon moved to another position in front of the jury as she checked her notes. "Then a furrier's shop was burned and the owner's son killed, actually cremated by the explosion of cleaning fluids while he slept, because Mr. Yost, a retired naval captain, refused to pay street tax to protect that business.

"Evidence was also collected from a tracking device placed on the car of Mario DeMeo, office administrator to W.C. Hayes, and Mr. DeMeo was found meeting with a made guy, Carmine Vaccaro. Before his throat was cut, Mr. DeMeo admitted to me and to Lieutenant Slate that he and Hayes had been paid hundreds of thousands of dollars over the previous five or six years for fixing cases and that some payments came from Vaccaro.

"A tape recording shows the judge and his office administrator extorting an additional fifty grand, on top of the original seventy-five grand paid. You have heard the saying there is no honor among thieves, and this conduct certainly proves that. You have heard the recording of Mr. DeMeo's offer to me for a plea bargain and his willingness to testify against Hayes, Profacci, and Vaccaro."

Lyon paused and moved again to a new position. "And you have nearly a quarter million from Profacci's law firm going to Hayes's reelection campaign fund. You have the motive: to protect the Outfit and their income. You have the opportunity: trials to render justice being used to set criminals free and to enrich a judge and his office administrator. You have the means: the Outfit's money to have a casino built and provide the Mob's take, the waste business contract and the Outfit's take, and finally, the verdict that protected the Outfit's guy, Danny Fischetti, who collects street tax from Chicago business owners.

"You have the investigation reports, telephone recordings, the record of calls between DeMeo and Profacci, and the bank records of Hayes and DeMeo. You have the recording of the meeting DeMeo had with Lieutenant Slate and me, and his homicide shortly thereafter to silence him, and the arson of Mrs. Delaney's home in an attempt to keep her quiet. This, ladies and gentlemen, proves our case for a criminal conspiracy beyond a reasonable doubt. And again, we have only filed on the third trial. The evidence is overwhelming, and that case has been proven. I am confident that you see the need for justice in these matters and will find both defendants guilty as charged."

Lyon returned to her seat.

"Mr. DeCenzo," the judge said.

DeCenzo stood and adjusted his trousers again. He strode toward the jury. "The Assistant State's Attorney is a good speaker, but don't let her verbal skills confuse the facts. My clients are honest professional people trying to earn a living, like all of you. Yes, the Chicago Police lost some cases, but that doesn't mean something illegal was going on. It means they didn't do their job and establish a solid case before going to trial.

"Lieutenant Slate," DeCenzo turned and pointed to Slate, "took it upon himself to start a crusade. Religious zealots have started many crusades and wars throughout world history. He convinced a retired school teacher that a crime was being committed. Moving trial dates is a normal and frequent event in every court.

"Bank records mean nothing. We all have money to deposit as we sell or trade investments. Houses burn every day, but it's not due to arson. Circumstantial evidence is the weakest evidence.

"Mario DeMeo was likely confused and thought the police could somehow convict him and was trying to save his own neck by telling them what they wanted to hear. Even if it could be proven that he had been selling favors, Judge Hayes wasn't aware of any wrongdoing. And Mr. DeMeo was no doubt the victim of a robbery gone bad."

"Ladies and gentlemen of the jury, W. C. Hayes comes from a working-class family. He attended night school for many years. He served as a public defender and worked in the family grocery store. He worked in traffic court. From there he was selected to fill a term of office after the death of a judge. Finally he was appointed and then elected to his Circuit Court office, where he has served the people of Chicago and Cook County for fifteen years. Please do not allow a crusade by one police lieutenant trying to make a name for himself to ruin this fine man's reputation and career."

DeCenzo moved to a different spot in front of the jury.

"Then we have Mr. Anthony Profacci, who has been practicing law in Chicago and the suburbs for twenty-six years. The Profacci and Bellino law firm handles many trials each month and it is frequently necessary to move trial dates. That may be due to a conflict with another trial, or a client or witness may have an emergency. Neither Judge Hayes or Attorney Profacci has ever been involved in criminal activity, and their clean records prove that. Mr. Profacci's firm also handles cases without a charge for those who cannot afford to hire an attorney.

"Put yourself in these men's places. Would you want to be convicted of such charges when there is no proof of a crime and no proof that money was every exchanged? The cases that were lost were weak cases and a just verdict was rendered in each. It is your duty to find both of my clients not guilty. Thank you."

DeCenzo took his seat.

At a little after 2:00 p.m. Judge Secrest gave the jury their charge. He explained probable cause, direct and circumstantial evidence, and beyond a reasonable doubt. He read from Chapter 38 of the Criminal Code paragraph 33.3, Official Misconduct, and Chapter 33.2, Failure to Report a Bribe. The jury was then escorted to a room down the hall to consider the facts of the case.

CHAPTER
34

SLATE TOOK A walk to get a cup of coffee and relieve some of the tension. When he returned to the courtroom he sat down with Lyon for a while, discussing the penalty of the two laws. He bought a Sun Times and sat on a bench in the hall to read. Late in the afternoon he went back into the courtroom. Lyon was doing some paperwork at her table, and Hayes, DeCenzo, and Profacci were now at the defense table, on the left.

"Nothing yet?"

Paula leaned close and whispered. "I don't like this, Ed. They've been out three hours."

"I could go back to Area 3 and move my own paperwork, but I'd like to be here when Hayes and Profacci get the verdict." He offered her his newspaper.

They talked and read until 5:40 p.m., when .Judge Secrest and the jury entered the courtroom. "The jury is still deliberating," the judge said. "We are adjourned until 9:00 a.m. Tuesday." He cautioned the jury not to discuss the case with anyone but another juror.

Looking over at the other table, Slate was annoyed to notice that Profacci, Hayes, and DeCenzo were all wearing grins.

Slate checked out his Dodge and headed south to Area 3. Given the evidence and the way Lyon had built the case, why would a verdict take this long? The jury had seemed solid.

In his office he reviewed several investigation reports that had to be moved and checked his phone messages. He was about ready to head home when Commander Arnold stopped by.

"How's the trial going, Lieutenant?"

"Jury has it, but they were out from 2:00 p.m. until nearly 6:00 p.m. and no verdict."

Arnold studied Slate. "What do you think?"

"Not sure. I figured it was a slam dunk in Lake County."

"If it's lost, we'll really have trouble."

Slate nodded. "I know. Anything more from Deputy Chief Urbanski?"

"No. I figure he, and maybe some others, are waiting to see how the trial goes."

From the way Arnold had come in and questioned and exited, Slate knew the commander was worried about his own career.

On Tuesday morning the court was called to order at 9 a.m. sharp. The jury foreman stood and asked the judge to repeat the charge about guilty beyond a reasonable doubt. Judge Secrest reviewed the material and released the jury to deliberate.

ASA Lyon worked on her paperwork. Slate walked the hall and drank coffee. At 11:00 a.m. the bailiff came to the hall and said court was ready to reconvene. Slate sat at the prosecutor's table with Lyon.

"Have you reached a verdict?" Judge Secrest asked the jury.

The foreman stood. "We have not, your honor, and we are deadlocked."

Judge Secrest studied Lyon, then DeCenzo. He looked at the foreman. "We are going to break for lunch, then the jury will resume at 12:30 p.m."

Lyon and Slate walked to the restaurant near the courthouse for lunch.

"This isn't good, Ed."

"You're right. What do you think the roadblock is?"

"It's solid. I can't see why they're having a problem."

"I agree. You screened the jurors."

"I felt good about all twelve. Did you detect any antipolice types?"

"No. They looked good to me. Actually, more professionals than I expected."

"That's Lake County. There's more money in the suburbs and most of these homes are out of my range," Lyon said.

"And mine."

———

The court resumed after lunch and Lyon and Slate sat and talked. At 3:00 p.m. the jury returned. "Have you reached a verdict?" the judge asked.

"We are deadlocked," the foreman reported.

Judge Secrest scrutinized the jury, then Lyon and DeCenzo. "We have a hung jury, ladies and gentlemen," he finally announced. Then the judge addressed ASA Lyon. "The State will have to decide if they want to retry the case. This court is adjourned." Judge Secrest struck his gavel. Slate looked over to see Hayes pumping DeCenzo's hand and smiling broadly.

Slate and ASA Lyon had just stood when Candice Bryan approached. She looked defeated.

Slate made introductions. "Paula Lyon, Mrs. Bryan, the alderman's wife."

They shook hands. "I can't believe what I just heard any more than I can believe justice was served in the verdict concerning the murder of my husband," Mrs. Bryan said. "What's happened to our justice system?"

"We're not sure," Lyon said. "The case was solid, but all it takes is one juror to disagree."

"Now what?"

"We'll try to determine the problem, then decide whether to retry the case."

"I'll keep you informed, Mrs. Bryan," Slate added.

Candice Bryan turned slowly and exited the courtroom.

———————

As Slate drove home he tried to come to terms with the reality that they had lost the trial. And that threat from Hayes to sue was not empty words, Slate knew. He was at the breakfast bar drinking coffee when Rebecca got home and found him.

"Good news?"

"We ended with a hung jury."

"Meaning they could not decide?"

"It only takes one of the twelve. But they all looked good. ASA Lyon did a good job of screening the jurors and she presented a solid case. It should have been two quick guilty verdicts."

Ed felt his wife looking deep into him as she commented, "Think of all Mrs. Delaney has gone through. Her life threatened, then moved out of her home, then it's destroyed by an arsonist and now she is trying to decide how to move on."

He nodded. "All that because I got her involved."

Rebecca moved to the counter beside Ed. She put her arm around his shoulder and kissed him gently on the cheek to offer comfort. "You did your best. What about us? Are we safe now?" she said.

Ed couldn't express what was going on inside. All that came out was, "I can't believe we lost. It was solid! I still want Hayes and Profacci. Maybe the FBI can get them on the conspiracy charge, but this loss hurts their case." He paused. "And if we have brass involved, they may come after me. And Hayes may sue us."

"And you'll have to testify in an FBI trial?"

Ed nodded.

CHAPTER
35

SLATE STOPPED FOR his Starbucks and Danish on his way in Wednesday morning. The Chicago Tribune he carried had been opened, folded, reopened, and refolded. He sat at his desk and read the headline again: JURY HUNG: JUDGE RETURNS TO THE BENCH. The article below gave an overview of the trial and then quoted DeCenzo as saying that an overzealous police lieutenant had created the entire myth. The defense attorney was also quoted as saying the case harmed not only the reputation of Judge Hayes, but the City of Chicago, and the Chicago Police Department.

Sergeant Rick Waddell knocked and entered, carrying his coffee. "What happened, Ed? I see they're already on you."

"Yeah. We didn't get our verdict. And I had been expecting we could get back to normal."

"Do you want me to keep the coverage on Delaney?"

"For now. Let me talk to Lyon. The State's Attorney's office needs to give our witness some help if she wants to relocate."

Slate moved part of the backlog of investigation reports, then called Lyon. The ASA agreed to fund Delaney's move to any place she wanted to go in the U.S. and place her in witness protection if the witness wanted that.

Slate pointed out that the Bureau could subpoena Delaney for their RICO charge. Lyon would have to explain that to her. He would pull the detectives who were protecting her once Lyon and Delaney finalized their plan. He gave Lyon Waddell's direct line.

"Ed, I'll be calling jurors this week to see if we can find out what was going on to end up with a hung vote. For starters I'll find out how many holdouts there were and who they are."

Slate called Waddell to keep the detectives on Bernice Delaney until he heard from Lyon. He had just hung up when Commander Arnold entered and shut the office door behind him.

"Doesn't look good, Lieutenant."

"I know, but the case was solid."

"What happened?"

"Not sure. Lyon is going to call some jurors. The group looked good. All suburbanites."

"Maybe one had an Outfit connection."

"I've been wondering about that."

"You know Urbanski will be on our asses."

Slate held his boss's eyes. "I expect so. Cops, lawyers, a judge, a court administrator, the Outfit, and who else? Alderman Bryan is killed and his wife and kids are left alone, DeMeo's killed, Ruggerio killed, a house is torched, I'm threatened, my wife is threatened, a bomb is placed on my car, an ASA is threatened, but no one is guilty." Slate shook his head. "Justice has gone to hell in Chicago!"

"If you want to take some vacation, I'll approve it. I'll let you know when I hear from the deputy chief."

Slate just nodded.

After the Commander left he managed to move some more investigation paper before he got up and went to the squad room for another coffee. Several detectives commented about the case and the screwed up justice system.

Before lunch he went down to Technical Services with the tape from Michigan that he had enhanced to have Ernie Shimp make copies of the enhanced part, where Deputy Chief of Detectives Urbanski was mentioned. When Shimp had finished making copies, Slate had the original on an evidence form from Sergeant Morrison in Benton Harbor, plus a copy of his own, and three copies of the part where Urbanski was mentioned. Shimp agreed to keep it confidential.

Back at his desk Slate replayed in his mind what he knew about the FBI and their potential RICO case. Could they make a case on all the suspects? When he had finally moved all the old paperwork, his mind started replaying the idea of getting out four years early and moving to Wisconsin. Police work itself was stressful enough, but when it included a corrupt system and threats to the family and witnesses, it was beyond what anyone should have to endure.

Just before Slate was ready to close up and leave, Arnold called with word that Urbanski wanted to see Slate at 10:00 a.m. the next morning.

Ed felt relieved that he had followed his hunch earlier in the day as he responded. "Commander, you remember I have Urbanski's name mentioned on a tape from the Hayes house in Benton Harbor, Michigan. Hayes, DeMeo, Profacci, and Vaccaro are discussing the grand jury indictment and the need to hit Delaney. I want Internal Affairs to hear a portion of the tape dealing with Urbanski as an information source. Do you want to deliver that, go with me, or shall I go on my own without your knowledge?"

There was a long silence.

"Come on down and we'll discuss it."

Slate headed down to Arnold's first floor office, closed the door, and sat in front of the desk. "I don't intend to see Urbanski until Internal Affairs hears this tape." He played it for Arnold.

Arnold shook his head. "He's dirty. How much you can prove is something else, but he's dirty. I'll go with you to Internal Affairs or meet you there."

"How about we meet there tomorrow at 8:00 a.m."

CHAPTER 36

THE NEXT MORNING Slate checked the lime in his driveway for footprints again but found none. He went directly to the Michigan Avenue Police Headquarters Building, where he met Arnold.

His boss told the receptionist they needed to see Deputy Superintendent Palmer regarding an emergency. In a few minutes a Lieutenant Harwood came out to the waiting area and introduced himself. "What's the problem, men? The receptionist said it was an emergency."

"It is, or I would have made an appointment," Arnold replied.

"Can you give me something for the Deputy Superintendent?"

"No. We'll talk to him."

Harwood hesitated for a moment. "Okay, this way." He led them to Palmer's office and made introductions. "Commander Arnold, Area 3, and Lieutenant Slate, Robbery/Homicide."

"Have a seat," Palmer said tersely, motioning to the chairs in front of his desk as he dismissed his staff man.

"Just what brings you here without an appointment?" the deputy superintendent started. He looked at Slate. "Are you the one on the Hayes trial?"

"Yes, sir."

Arnold said, "Lieutenant Slate has conducted a very good investigation and the case should have been won. During the investigation he had authorities in Michigan bug a house owned by Hayes. On the tape, Hayes, the trial lawyer Profacci, Hayes's office administrator DeMeo, who was killed, and Vaccaro, an Outfit guy, are discussing the grand jury indictment. They discuss hitting Slate's witness Delaney. And my boss, Deputy Chief of Detectives Urbanski, is mentioned as a person who can find out what we have. Now Urbanski has called Slate in for a 10:00 a.m. meeting."

Slate jumped in. "I don't intend to meet with him again, sir, unless you order it. He had me in once and was pissed because I wouldn't tell him what I knew. Then he had both of us in after the indictment. This thing is too big to cover with you this morning, but we have possibly two department retirees with Outfit connections, in addition to those on trial, and this guy Vaccaro."

"The FBI refused to help us prosecute our case with a RICO charge so I could use the Michigan tapes. They wanted to take over the case. I said we would give them what we had after we finished our trial. And a hit man out of Florida may also be involved. We think he's the one that hit DeMeo who had met with ASA Lyon and me, trying for a plea-bargain arrangement. ASA Paula Lyon prosecuted, and her boss, State's Attorney Erwin, oversaw the grand jury work. The case was solid and presented well. The jury looked good."

"You have a tape?" Palmer asked.

"Yes sir." Slate dug into his briefcase. "Here's a copy. And here's a copy with just the part involving Urbanski." He handed the two tapes to Palmer.

Slate felt the deputy superintendent trying to measure him as he asked, "How did you get into this case as head of Robbery/Homicide?"

"I knew we had lost some trials in Hayes's court, but after I was promoted last fall, I saw that we were losing even more. Then detectives came to me complaining about Judge Hayes and their two trials lost."

"You had the serial killer last year?"

Slate nodded.

Palmer continued. "Forget about your appointment with Urbanski and get me a copy of your investigation."

"I brought a copy." Slate handed it to Palmer.

"Anything else?"

Arnold looked at Slate. "That's it, sir."

Palmer stood and shook hands.

———

After the meeting in the deputy superintendent's office Slate stopped for his coffee and Danish before reaching Area 3. He had just keyed in and sat down when Arnold walked in. "What's your next move?"

"To find out what Lyon learns about the jury. We could retry the case, but with all this flak in the paper, Erwin may not be interested."

Arnold nodded. "I wish we knew how much the feds know and whether they could make all of them on a RICO."

"You know the Bureau, Commander."

"How about Delaney?"

"Lyon's on that. We're keeping the four detectives on her until Lyon finds out what Delaney wants to do. She'll probably move near one of her kids."

"Your ASA also needs to see that your Unit's cases aren't heard by Hayes."

"Good point. I'll tell her."

"So, in addition to losing the Hayes and Profacci trial, we have the hit on DeMeo, and Delaney's arson unsolved," Arnold said.

"Right. But DeMeo's hit was in River Forest, and Delaney's home was in Oak Park. RICO can bring them all in, including the Michigan tape, and maybe the Florida hit man who got DeMeo," Slate paused, "and maybe Fischetti for extortion and conspiracy. And if one of them wants to deal, maybe Carbonaro for whacking Alderman Bryan."

"What a mess. Keep me up to date, Ed."

Slate spent the remainder of the day moving the case investigations and cold case supplements from twenty-seven pairs of detectives. He sensed that maybe he wasn't being quite as critical about the details missing in the reports as usual, and he knew why. He had lost the trial of his career, and that didn't set well. If he survived the backlash from the department, he would bring every damn one of them to justice if it were the last thing he did. But right now, he wasn't quite sure how.

About mid morning ASA Lyon called.

"What do you have, Paula?"

"I was able to reach three jurors, Ed. The count was eleven to one."

"Do you know who that was?"

"The jeweler from Highland Park. A Jacob Walberg."

"He's the one with a place on Michigan Avenue?"

"That's him. He seemed fine when I screened them. I guess he thought there was not enough proof. He didn't like the code talk idea and not seeing any money exchanged."

"Think we should have looked closer at the Chicago connection with his business?"

"That may be it."

"Paula, Commander Arnold mentioned that we need to keep the Robbery/Homicide trials out of Hayes's court."

"We've talked about that."

Slate briefed her on his contact with Internal Affairs.

"How about a pen register on Walberg?" Slate asked.

"I've been thinking about it. See who's calling him, but after the jury was impaneled."

"Right. What about me giving him a visit?"

"Let's check the records first. If he were to go to the media about a visit from you, you'll really get beat up."

"Yeah, you're probably right. I'll run some checks on him, but he's probably clean. Would Erwin let us retry Hayes and Profacci?"

"Hard to say. He doesn't like the flak we're getting. But if we find a juror was bought, I'm sure he would. On Delaney, she's going to move to Phoenix, near her daughter."

"When can we pull the coverage?"

"She's moving in with a neighbor tomorrow and will try to salvage some things from her home, but I guess there's little left. So after today."

"I'll tell Waddell."

Slate called Waddell regarding withdrawing the coverage when Delaney moved. He then used his notes from the jury selection and ran a record check with the State Police Law Enforcement Automated Data System and the National Crime Information Center. Neither LEADS nor NCIC had a record on Jacob Walberg. The jeweler was fifty-two and lived in Highland Park along Lake Michigan north of Chicago. Highland Park PD had nothing on Walberg either. Slate then called Hal in the Intell Unit but they had nothing that would connect Walberg to the Outfit.

Later in the week Arnold stopped in again at Slate's office. "Have you heard?"

Slate gestured with his hands open.

"Urbanski announced his retirement."

"Effective when?"

"Immediately."

"Internal Affairs moved on our info then. That's one problem out of our hair. Maybe the Bureau can make him."

"We'll need to run that by Internal Affairs before we give what you have to the feds."

"Okay. Think Palmer will come up with any more of ours that's dirty?"

Arnold shrugged. "Hard to say."

"Any idea who's replacing Urbanski as Deputy Chief of Detectives?" Slate asked.

"I hear it may be Newcomb, Commander in Area 1."

Slate nodded. "After the Southwest Side, he should know how to deal with crime. Do you know him?"

"Just from some meetings we've attended. Seems sharp enough. Any more on the trial?"

"Lyon says the jury was eleven to one. He's a jewelry store owner from Highland Park."

"Where's his store?"

"Michigan Avenue."

Arnold seemed to gauge what steps Slate might have taken with the information. "You check him out?"

"No record, but I wonder about his store." Arnold nodded in agreement as he left.

Slate was moving his pile of paper the following Monday morning when he took a call from Special Agent Dodd.

"Good morning, Dodd. What's on your mind?"

"Assistant Director Millburn asked me to give you a call. We arrested the Professor in St. Louis over the weekend."

"Really."

"We got him attempting to hit a witness in a conspiracy case there."

"You had somebody on him?"

"We were covering two guys from Miami, and this one panned out."

"Good. Anything on my case?"

"That's what we wanted to know. Are you ready to give us what you have?"

"Maybe, but I still want Hayes. Can the Professor give him to me?"

"Not sure, but he wants to deal. He's offered to give us something on DeMeo if he can walk on this last attempt. We think you
should come to St. Louis and talk to this Delbert Brunk, AKA, the
Professor. Then see if we can work a deal that suits both of us."

"Where can I get back with you?"

"In St. Louis." Dodd gave his number.

"I'll be in touch."

Slate called Arnold about meeting with regard to the arrest of
Brunk. Arnold agreed to come to Slate's office.

Slate shut his door and unlocked his whiteboard on the wall
beside his desk. He erased the notes regarding Arnold, now convinced that his boss was clean. He added the trial lost by a hung jury,
the arrest of the Professor in St. Louis, and the check on juror Walberg. He sat on the end of his desk evaluating the issues.

In about ten minutes Arnold knocked and entered the office.

"Commander." Slate moved a chair from the table to in front of
his desk so Arnold could view the board.

"The Bureau has the hit man in custody?" Arnold asked.

Slate nodded. "In St. Louis."

"Where does that leave your case?"

"They want what I have and want me to come to St. Louis to give
it to them."

"Fine. Go ahead."

Slate motioned to his board. "See if I'm missing anything. On my
case we had Hayes, DeMeo, and Profacci. I think the feds can make
Profacci and Vaccaro on an interstate conspiracy charge with the
tape where they discuss the grand jury indictment, my trial, and the
plan to hit my witness, Delaney. And they talk about getting information from Urbanski.

"DeMeo, of course, is gone, and Ruggerio, the one that was
involved in the robbery and truck theft of the waste hauler and then
was hit by the Outfit for talking too much. Hayes isn't heard on the
tape though. That leaves Seryak's threat to me, which isn't enough to
file on, and the threat to my wife about me, which may have been
Seryak. Whether Seryak's boss, Vaughn, is involved, I don't know.
Then, my car bomb. But the FBI may be able to learn more after a
couple arrests."

"Seryak had Urbanski's spot before retiring, and Vaughn was a
Commander in Area 4," Arnold commented.

Slate nodded. "That means they may be able to charge everyone
if someone, namely Profacci, gives up Hayes."

"That could get him killed, Ed."

"Yeah. But with my information, the tape from Michigan, and what the FBI has, they might get most of them on a RICO charge. And find out who placed the car bomb and torched Delaney's place. Easier than having us, River Forest, and Oak Park prosecuting."

Arnold studied the board, then Slate. "See what they have in St. Louis. You shouldn't be gone more than a day, then we'll talk again. I'll call Palmer in Internal Affairs before we release what you have to the Bureau."

"Good. Maybe we're still in the game."

CHAPTER
37

SLATE MET SPECIAL Agent Dodd at the St. Louis PD a little before 10:00 the next morning. Dodd escorted the lieutenant to a small conference room. "They'll bring Brunk up in a few minutes," Dodd said as they took seats at a small table. "Chicago ready to move on this?"

"We want to hear what you have and talk to Brunk first. You're sure this is your Professor?"

"Yeah, it's him."

"Who is he?"

"A retired Navy Seal. Owns a health club in Miami."

"He's how old?"

Dodd checked his notes. "Forty-one."

"Any idea how and when he started this new profession?"

"He's been out three years. We have several hits with a knife over the past two years."

"What's he admitted?"

"Nothing really. But I think he did DeMeo."

A St. Louis detective knocked and opened the door. "Brunk's in room 3."

"Thanks," Dodd said. Looking to Slate, "Let's see what you can get out of him."

The officers walked two doors down to the interrogation room. Brunk was sitting at a table, facing the door and the two-way mirror. He was cuffed on his left wrist, then locked to a chain that extended from a ring secured into the floor. Dodd took the seat to the right end of the table and Slate took the one facing Brunk. Slate figured him at maybe five-ten, medium build, with longer thick blond hair, and a full beard trimmed to about one inch. Not handsome, but neat, clean, and confident. He seemed small for a Seal.

"This is Lieutenant Slate, Robbery/Homicide Chicago. Delbert Brunk."

The Professor had cold eyes, Slate noticed, and he looked at Slate without blinking.

Slate pulled his notes from his briefcase and set them on his lap where Brunk couldn't read them.

Dodd started. "You have been advised of your rights in the early interviews, and we're taping this one. Sign here to acknowledge all of that."

Brunk signed and dated the form and Dodd signed as a witness. Dodd nodded to Slate.

"Special Agent Dodd tells me you may be able to help clear up some of our Chicago cases."

"That depends on what Agent Dodd will do for me."

"You did twenty as a Seal?"

Brunk nodded.

"A little young for Vietnam, I guess."

"Did some work in the Persian Gulf. You a Seal?"

"No. Marine Corps. But we worked with them in Vietnam a few times. Bunch of bad asses."

Brunk lifted a corner of his mouth in agreement.

Slate moved on to his cases. "I think we can tie some of our court officials in with Carmine Vaccaro, a made guy. And we think we can prove that Vaccaro paid you for the hit on Mario DeMeo in River Forest. Actually you were paid to hit a Bernice Delaney in Oak Park, but when they learned that DeMeo wanted to deal and you saw we had Delaney covered, they moved you to DeMeo."

Bruner kept his unblinking eyes focused on Slate without acknowledging anything.

Slate turned to Dodd. "What will the Bureau do for him if he pleads to DeMeo and gives you Vaccaro?"

"What will it take?" Dodd asked.

"I walk on everything."

Dodd shook his head. "Damn. Sure you don't want some reward money too? There's no way any assistant U.S. attorney will buy a walk for the Chicago hit and the attempt here. Can you prove the hit on DeMeo, and Vaccaro's payment to the attorney? We got you cold here, Brunk. You're looking to be in a federal pen for a long time on interstate conspiracy and attempted homicide of a witness in an organized crime case. Federal judges won't play with you like state courts. Your nice retirement checks will be of no value, and your health club business in Miami will be gone. You're going to miss a lot of life."

Brunk leaned forward and pinned his eyes on Dodd. "I would have to see the deal in writing, and signed by a U.S. attorney or an assistant U.S. attorney. Then I might tell you that I know DeMeo drove a black Lincoln, lived in River Forest, Illinois, and died in his garage."

"How about the payment? And from who?" Dodd asked.

"I might find a bank transfer record to an off shore account, and have a name and telephone number."

"How about Judge W. C. Hayes?" Slate asked. "Have you worked for him, or can you tie him into any crime?"

Brunk turned his eyes to a wall and his shook his head.

"Need an answer for the tape."

"No."

Slate continued. "How about the attorney, Profacci? Can you give us anything on him?"

"No."

"Anyone in my department that has used your services."

"No."

"How about a retired cop, Seryak?"

"No."

"A retired cop, Vaughn?"

"No."

"Or a cop named Urbanski?"

"No."

Dodd said, "You want a pass on this St. Louis attempt charge and the DeMeo hit, then you'll produce proof to convict Carmine Vaccaro in court for paying for the hit on DeMeo?"

"And I want into a witness protection program."

"I'll check, but you may have to give us more than just Vaccaro to avoid some time. And a deal may be conditional to convicting Vaccaro."

"You haven't worked for Seryak or Vaughn?" Slate asked. "Retired cops that run Vaughn Security in Chicago?"

"No."

Dodd and Slate left the interrogation room and returned to the conference room. "What do you think?" Dodd asked.

"Sounds okay on DeMeo and Vaccaro. I think he knows something about Hayes."

"Your question surprised him. What do I tell my boss?"

"I'll check the CPD brass. If they agree, we'll give you a copy of my investigation and a tape from my Michigan bugs in Hayes's summer home, and I'll testify in your RICO trial. But I want the freedom to go after Hayes, Urbanski, Seryak, and Vaughn if I can get them on a state charge."

"Some of your own, huh?"

"A dirty cop is worse than these guys."

"What's on the Michigan tape, Slate?"

"Urbanski, our former Deputy Chief of Detectives, retired the day after I turned my tape over to Internal Affairs. He was named as an information source on that tape. Profacci is also on the tape, talking about hitting Delaney, my inside witness. He's the lawyer that was code talking with DeMeo on my phone tap."

Slate continued. "And Vaccaro talks about calling Miami for the Delaney hit. DeMeo's hit was in River Forest after he met with the ASA and me. Delaney's arson was in Oak Park, but I had her in a safe house. Not sure who torched it."

"Will we have any trouble getting cooperation in either of those cities?" Dodd asked.

"I don't think so. Call me if you do." Slate paused. "So you can't make Hayes either unless Vaccaro or Profacci give him up?"

"No. Your jury was hung?"

"Eleven to one.

"I'm going to talk to Brunk again before I go, but I'll let you know within a couple days if it's a go for CPD."

Dodd followed Slate back to the interrogation room.

Slate pulled out a photo and handed it to Brunk.

"What's this?" the Professor asked.

"We figure that's you in a Chicago condo hitting Judge Hayes's second wife."

Brunk glanced at both of them. "What's this shit? You two trying to frame me for another one to work your deal?"

"Look at the side profile. It looks like you even with the hooded coat."

Brunk studied the photo from the surveillance camera. "It could be anybody. All you can see is his nose and cheek."

"Yeah, but see the beard."

"When was this taken?"

"The date's on the back."

Brunk turned the photo over. "Oh, 1992. I was in the Navy, scouting the shorelines of Kuwait, Iraq, and Iran until near my retirement."

"What was your retirement date?"

"June 16, 1992. I went in right out of high school in '72."

Slate exhaled a deep breath that expressed his satisfaction with the answer. "Juantia Hayes, age thirty, was hit on October 7, 1992. Killed in her own home early in the morning with one stab wound to the heart. A victim who married the wrong man. Now, if you can tell me her husband, W. C. Hayes, paid for the hit and can prove it, we can deal, Brunk."

Brunk laid the photo down on the table. "I was working to get my health club going then."

Slate studied Brunk for several seconds. "When the FBI profiler names you in this shot," Slate reached over and picked up the photo, "the deal is off. And when Agent Dodd gets done with you, I'll take you to Chicago to face this charge. But if you can give me the guy who hired you, you might walk on most of them."

Brunk stared at Dodd. "You heard my deal."

CHAPTER 38

THE NEXT MORNING Slate called ASA Lyon regarding his visit to St. Louis and the FBI request. "Paula, the question is, do we give them what we have, or do we retry Hayes and Profacci? If we give it to them, I told Dodd I want to able to go after Hayes, Urbanski, Seryak, and maybe Vaughn on a state charge, if I can."

"What did they say?"

"He's going to check."

"Erwin's not keen on trying a Circuit Court judge a second time. What's your department say about that?"

"I haven't asked. I'll tell Arnold when we hang up. I say give the Bureau what we have so we can put some of them away. We may get more from the RICO trial that we can use here for a second trial against Hayes."

"You got Deputy Chief Urbanski out of CPD."

"I'm afraid there may be more, Paula."

"Not Arnold?"

"No, he's clean."

"I would give what you have to the feds, Ed. It won't hurt our case if we file later. And like you said, we may flush out more material to use against Hayes."

Slate briefed Arnold regarding his visit, the Bureau's request, and Lyon's position. He was relieved to hear Arnold offer to talk to Palmer in Internal Affairs.

Slate moved the two days of paper from his IN box, but he stopped twice during the day to open his whiteboard and sit on the end of his desk viewing his notes, trying to find a way to bring all the corrupt to justice.

The next morning Lyon called.

"What's on your mind, Paula?"

"I had an intern going over Jacob Walberg's phone records. He came in this morning and reported that he sees nothing suspicious from the calls from or to his home or business."

"Well, maybe he can't see anything in the phone records. But I'm sure they got to him."

About 11: 30 a.m. Slate headed to Smokey's for lunch. It was sunny and warm as spring had finally turned to summer in Chicago. The sun lightened his spirit a little, but losing the jury trial haunted him. Suddenly a car pulled up right beside him near the curb. Slate jerked sideways to face the threat and grabbed his pistol on his left front.

Barona lifted both hands from his steering wheel and called, "Eating alone, Lieutenant?" through his open window.

"Trying to get your ass shot off, Joe?"

"Sorry I startled you."

Barona pulled out and parked near Smokey's. As Slate entered the restaurant Barona caught up with him and apologized. "Sorry. I should have known better."

"You've been around long enough to know not to pull a stunt like that on *any* cop, Joe."

"I wasn't thinking."

They found a table in the rear corner and ordered.

"I am so glad that Delaney detail is over. What a boring assignment," Barona offered.

"I'm sure. But you kept her alive. She's moving to Phoenix near her daughter."

"How do you feel about heading Robbery/Homicide now?"

Slate paused, mentally flipping through the cases they had worked in the two years before his promotion. "I miss being out there digging, Joe."

"I see in the *Tribune* that Hayes's attorney, DeCenzo, is after you. How did you end up with a hung jury?"

Slate shook his head. "Not sure. I would have bet anything we had two convictions. We moved the trial to Lake County so we could get justice. Then this."

"Hayes is back on the bench. How about our cases he hears now?"

"Lyon's going to see that he doesn't get any of them."

"What's the story on Urbanski retiring so quickly?"

Slate considered the question. "Outfit connections."

"And you found that."

"Joe, would I be so cunning?"

"What's next?"

"I was just in St. Louis. The FBI got the Professor on an attempted hit there."

"Really. Is he talking?"

"Maybe. He's trying to work a deal."

"Does he admit the hit on DeMeo?"

"Maybe."

"Can he make Hayes?"

"He denies hitting Hayes's second wife, but I think he did it. I think he figures they may let him walk on DeMeo or the attempt in St. Louis, but not two or three, so he's hedging on that one."

"You figure the street tax guy is their man?"

"Fischetti? Yeah, he's a collector for the Outfit. So what's new with you, Joe?"

"I did well on the sergeant's exam," Barona said.

"Good."

"So what do you know about Detective McFall?" Barona asked. "She's not a great looking gal, but she's single and really built."

Slate eyed Barona with a disapproving expression, more emotion than he usually let himself display. "You and Maria still having trouble?"

"Yeah. I think she'll leave me after her MBA."

"Joe, you know the rules. If you get involved with Debra McFall or another detective, you'll end up back in uniform. And I won't try to protect you."

Barona waved a hand in resignation to the rules. "I know. And losing this trial is driving you crazy, right?"

Slate nodded. "And all the city and department crap we have to deal with."

"Let me work it with you and we'll keep digging until we get all of them."

"Can't. Arnold doesn't like me working cases." Slate stood. "Well, let's get back to work."

"Right. With the high salaries, we shouldn't be loafing. Want a ride?"

"No, thanks. I'll walk. It's a good way to get chance encounters with friends."

———

After checking with Rizzo and switching his Dodge for a silver Ford pickup at the police garage, Slate pulled into an alley three doors from Custom Jewelry on Michigan Avenue. A young woman working in a showcase near the door greeted him as he entered the store.

"I'm here to see Mr. Walberg."

"Your name?"

"Lieutenant Slate, Chicago Police." She walked to the rear and Slate moved toward the rear. In a minute she returned. "Go on back."

Slate strode to the rear of the store where Walberg was working. The owner briefly glanced up from his bench without acknowledging Slate.

"How's the jewelry business, Mr. Walberg?"

"A little slow."

"We're talking to a few jurors, wondering what happened at the trial."

Walberg laid down his tools and carefully made eye contact with Slate. "We couldn't all agree," he said slowly.

"What was the problem?"

"Most evidence was circumstantial."

"The taped telephone conversations between Profacci and DeMeo weren't."

"But what did it mean, moving a trial several days?"

"It meant a thousand dollars for each day referred to."

"But there was no proof. No money was seen."

"You heard the tape from DeMeo during his meeting with ASA Lyon and me. You saw the bank deposits immediately after the calls. How many of the twelve had trouble with our evidence?"

"I think that should remain confidential, Lieutenant."

"You mean confidential like the Holocaust? The six million Jews killed was a private, internal German problem?"

Walberg's face flushed and his jaw tightened. He glared at Slate. "What are you implying?"

"That only one juror of twelve had a problem with the evidence. And if I found out that this guy here," Slate moved closer and held the mug shot of Danny Fischetti a few inches from Walberg's face, "warned you that your store could be torched, or he paid you off, you'll be the next guy we prosecute."

"This guy torched Yost Furrier on Huron because Mr. Yost wouldn't pay the street tax. Yost's only son died in that fire. Before that, an alderman was killed because he intended to vote for the condo development his constituency wanted rather than a casino that the Outfit could manage. Now that alderman's wife is raising their two little boys alone. A waste hauler was robbed and his trucks ruined to protect the Outfit's waste contract. Then Mario DeMeo was killed and Mrs. Delaney's home, with all her possessions in it, was burned. My wife was threatened and I find a car bomb under my floorboard."

Slate stepped back. "I don't see how a juror could sleep at night if, in fact, he sold his vote to protect this," Slate waved the photo in his hand, "and people who corrupt the system, murder, and plant car bombs."

Slate moved toward the door, then turned to face Walberg. "Can you imagine how a Jewish juror will feel as he stands in God's courtroom beside Hitler? Hitler will plead that he was trying to establish a superior race, and a Jewish juror will plead that he sold his soul to protect his precious business."

Slate turned and exited. He knew there would be trouble if Walberg went to the media. But the jeweler wouldn't do that if he were guilty. Now, if he could prove the payoff.

———

Back at Area 3 Slate opened his whiteboard and noted his contact with Walberg. He sat on the end of his desk studying the board, wondering what kind of deal could he make with ASA Lyon if Walberg came forward and confessed. They could retry Hayes and Profacci if that happened.

He was in deep thought when Arnold knocked and came in. "Talked to Internal Affairs. Deputy Palmer's okay with giving your investigation to the Bureau. Anything new?"

"No, but I just talked to the holdout juror. I still want Hayes."

"Damn, Slate! You're on thin ice messing with a juror!"

"I know."

"So?"

"I think his business was threatened by the same guy that torched Yost Furrier."

Arnold glanced at Slate's board to find the name. "Fischetti?"

Slate nodded.

"You don't think the feds can get Hayes on their RICO?"

"Doubt it. He used DeMeo for the contacts, and he's not on the Michigan tape. And Brunk, the Professor, is in too deep already to admit hitting Hayes's second wife. But he did it. Even if he admitted it. Hayes is smart enough not to have ordered the hit himself. I'm sure he used DeMeo or Vaccaro, so it's not likely I could get Hayes even if the Professor admitted the hit. But damn, I want Hayes!"

"I wouldn't push the juror anymore." Arnold turned to leave then stopped. "You checked the juror's phone records?"

"ASA Lyon found nothing."

Slate called Lyon to clear the move with assisting the FBI on their RICO, then had his entire case investigation record copied. He included the original tape from the Benton Harbor bugs along with the chain-of-evidence form for the tape. When he called Special Agent Dodd to let him know, Dodd reported the Bureau was okay with Slate going after Hayes and any in CPD and that he would pick up the investigation ASAP.

Before he called it a day Slate phoned Sergeant Morrison at Benton Harbor PD to give him a heads up on the feds' RICO case and provide Dodd's number.

———

The failure to convict Hayes and Profacci continued to dog Ed Slate every day. The FBI's RICO trial date hadn't been set, but it appeared that Delbert Brunk, AKA the Professor, would testify against Vaccaro for the hit on DeMeo, and the Michigan tapes should get Profacci on conspiracy. Unless Chicago could retry their case, it looked like Hayes would survive. Slate felt pretty sure that Erwin, the new State's Attorney would be unlikely to retry Hayes with an election coming up.

Slate went to Technical Services to check out two Tele-Track systems and a camera with a long lens. Ernie Shimp agreed to log them out to Barona and Ingram.

Back at the office he ran a registration check by name on Larry Seryak, the retired Deputy Chief of Detectives whom Urbanski had replaced and who had given Slate the warning at Smokey's restaurant. Registration showed that Seryak lived in Oak Park at 917 Forest, near the Frank Lloyd Wright Studio building. He owned a 1995 Buick Regal and a 1994 Cadillac Deville. Slate figured the small Buick was the wife's.

The phone directory indicated that Vaughan Security was located on Kedzie, just off Logan. That placed the business just south of Area 3. A registration check on Danny Fischetti showed him in Cicero at 2310 Cermak Road. He owned a black 1987 Cadillac Eldorado, a classic.

Slate leaned back in his chair and thought about Arnold. He knew the Commander would not want him going back after Fischetti, and investigating a retired Deputy Chief of Detectives like Seryak. But after the threats to Rebecca and Lyon, the car bomb, and fixed jury trial, he wasn't backing off. He would get every damn one of them one way or the other!

After a quick lunch at Smokey's, Slate decided to patrol the Loop in his Ford pickup, figuring the truck would be taken as a delivery vehicle, thus allowing him to find Fishcetti unnoticed. He put on his sunglasses and headed out. He had just turned north from Ohio onto St. Clair when he spotted Fischetti's black Caddie parked in an alley.

Slate turned around at the next alley. He then came back past the Caddie and double-parked across the street and two doors down as if making a delivery. Within a few minutes Fishcetti appeared on the other side of the street, walking toward his car. Slate got his camera ready.

Slate figured the man at about five-nine and around one-ninety. He was balding with longer hair just on the sides and rear. Fischetti was wearing black slacks, a navy blazer, a bright red shirt open at the neck. He felt sure Fischetti was armed while collecting the street tax, and with his connections he probably had a concealed weapon permit from the Cook County sheriff. Slate snapped two photos as the man approached his car.

Fischetti pulled out and moved north on St. Clair. Slate quickly backed his pickup into the alley and turned around to follow him north. When the Caddie pulled into the next alley and parked, Slate wondered if the local beat sergeant had been paid to allow Fischetti to park in the area as he collected the payoffs each month.

Slate double-parked on the street and waited. Fischetti made the rounds in and out of most businesses on each side of the street, circling the block. Slate moved with him in his pickup and snapped photos as the collector entered and left the businesses. Then he snapped one more as the Outfit's collector got into his car.

At the next alley Slate waited until Fischetti had parked and entered the second business place moving north. Then he pulled into the alley beside the Cadillac and quickly placed the four-by-six-inch monitoring unit on the bottom of the black Cadillac's gas tank. The four magnets snapped into place. He drove on through the alley. Before entering Fairbanks he stopped to check his monitor. The signal was strong.

The following day FBI Special Agent Dodd called to update Slate that they were shooting for a RICO trial date within the next month. Slate agreed to meet with an assistant U.S. attorney when they were ready to go over his evidence and testimony.

On his way home Slate decided to locate Seryak's house. If he could arrest Seryak or Fischetti on any charge, it would at least be a start on his long list. And maybe that arrest would lead to some of the others.

At North Avenue he headed west. At Austin he made a left and proceeded south, then picked up Chicago Avenue heading west into Oak Park. He made a right to Forest Street and found 917. At the next street he made a U-turn and parked along the curb facing south a few doors north of Seryak's home.

Just before 6:00 p.m. a black Cadillac approached from the south and pulled into the driveway on the south side of 917. Slate had hoped the car would be parked on the street so that he could attach the monitor after dark. After a few minutes wait he pulled out and slowly drove past the house. The Cadillac was not in the driveway and the garage doors were closed.

––––––––

He drove home and parked the borrowed pickup near his own garage. As Rebecca met him at the back door, he noticed that the pistol from the bedroom still lay partly concealed on the counter near the door.

"How are things in your department now?"

"Pretty quiet. FBI says we'll go to trial pretty soon on their conspiracy charges."

"That's against the Outfit guy and the attorney?"

Ed nodded. "Vaccaro and Profacci. The hit man will testify that Vaccaro paid him to hit DeMeo, the one who was killed after meeting with Lyon and me. He was actually hired to hit Delaney, but we had her covered."

"What about Mrs. Delaney's house?"

"Not sure who did that. Maybe that will come out in the trial. I guess she's moving to Phoenix, to be near her daughter."

"But the FBI can't get Hayes?"

"No. The sucker isn't heard on the Michigan tape."

"Think they'll retry the case?"

"No."

"Are you okay in the department?"

"I figured they might move me out of Robbery/Homicide after we lost the trial, but it seems okay with Urbanski gone." Ed paused and looked into Rebecca's eyes as he offered his next comment. "I'm trying to get a couple right now that may cause me some trouble. One's a former deputy chief of detectives. Had Urbanski's spot. So I'm thinking I may have to get out early."

"Is that smart, Ed?"

"Maybe not, but I just can't let all this corruption pass if I can stop it."

Rebecca studied her husband without saying anything.

"I've thought about taking a four-year leave, until I can draw retirement."

"What would you do for four years?"

"Move all of you to Wisconsin, then hunt, fish, and maybe rearrange the furniture each week, I guess."

"Ha!" Rebecca studied Ed for several seconds. "I *would* like a safe place, Ed, but you would be miserable then. And that would drive *me* crazy."

He nodded and hugged his wife close. "You're probably right."

The next morning he stopped for a Starbucks and a Danish, then headed for Vaughn Security on Kedzie. He hoped to find Seryak's Cadillac parked on the street, and he wanted to get a look at the layout. The business was in a narrow storefront adjacent to a parking lot for a small condo building. Seryak's car was in the corner of the lot, near Vaughn Security. Slate turned the pickup truck around about a half block away and drove back past the area. There was both pedestrian and vehicle traffic. It was just too exposed to place the monitor without being seen.

He made his way to Area 3. Traffic was heavy and slow, giving him time to drink his coffee and think. He did like the challenge of policing. Bringing robbers and killers to justice made him feel needed. But the politics that had taken over the system was making the struggle for justice more difficult. Or were his twenty years taking their toll? The Hayes trial still haunted him. He didn't like losing at anything, least of all a trial involving a corrupt judge.

———

At Area 3 he reviewed homicide and robbery investigations, conscious that his own investigation of Hayes, Seryak, and Fischetti was playing in the back of his mind. An arrest of any of them would bring more pressure on him. At late morning Arnold called.

"Yes, sir?'

"Our new Deputy Chief of Detectives is Newcomb, and he wants to see both of us at 1:00 p.m."

"Now what?"

"I expect he wants to know about the Hayes trial and if the case was solid."

"And if I'm causing trouble for the department."

"I expect."

"I'll meet you out back about 12:30 p.m."

Slate wondered what he should expect from Newcomb. He didn't know the man. He decided not to take any paperwork since he hadn't been told what the meeting was about. The day was sunny and warm when he headed to Smokey's for an early lunch.

He was at the rear entrance to Area 3 when Commander Arnold came to meet him. "I'll go with you," Arnold said.

"I'm driving a pickup."

Arnold looked at him. "Drive mine, then." He handed Slate the keys. They got into the unmarked Ford and headed south to see Newcomb. "Do we assume he's clean, Commander, or tell only what we have to?"

"I've done some checking. I think he's okay. You know he's black?"

"Yeah."

SLATE PARKED ARNOLD'S car at the rear of the Michigan Avenue building. Arnold keyed them in through the rear door. Deputy Chief of Detectives Newcomb was on the third floor. At 1:05 p.m. a lieutenant approached. "Lieutenant Zolinski," he said, extending his hand.

"Commander Arnold and Lieutenant Slate," Arnold said.

"This way."

Newcomb stood and Zolinski made introductions. At six-two, Newcomb appeared to be all business. He was in uniform, unlike most deputy chiefs, who wore civvies. Slate figured it was because he was new in the position. He thought of how little he himself spent on clothes.

Arnold and Slate took the two chairs in front of the desk. Zolinski pulled a chair from the conference table to the side and moved it to the end of the desk.

"I wanted to talk to both of you to get a clear picture of what we have with the trials lost, the Hayes trial, and this Outfit talk." He nodded to Arnold to start. Arnold and Slate brought the new deputy chief of detectives up to date and he seemed satisfied.

———

Before noon the next day Slate was in the pickup, waiting down the street from Vaughn Security. Seryak's Cadillac was in the lot. About 12:10 p.m. Seryak came out and got into the car and headed south on Kedzie. Slate followed at a distance. At Armitage, Seryak's car pulled into the lot beside Franky's Bar and Grille. Slate pulled to the side and waited.

After Seryak entered Franky's Slate pulled in and circled the lot, just to be sure Seryak was not coming right back out. He then pulled in behind the Caddie and placed a monitor on the bottom of the trunk. The magnets snapped in place. He was back on Kedzie heading north in a few seconds. The signal on the monitor was strong.

He hoped his suspects wouldn't think to check for a bug. The Hayes trial would have made them more alert, he knew. But Fischetti was still collecting the street tax. Slate thought about Seryak's job offer and the threat he made in Smokey's before the Hayes trial.

Back at Area 3 he was moving paper when Special Agent Dodd called.

"What to you have, Dodd?"

"The assistant U.S. attorney wants to meet to discuss our RICO. You available in the morning at 9:00 a.m.?"

"I can be. The Federal Building?"

"Room 412."

"You have the copy of my case?"

"Right, and he's reviewed it."

"Is this an experienced attorney?"

"Joseph Kiefer. He's out of New York. A tough prosecutor."

"How about Sergeant Morrison in Michigan?"

"He's been notified."

CHAPTER 40

THE NEXT MORNING Slate met with Assistant U.S. Attorney
Joseph Kiefer, along with special agents, Milburn, Dodd, and
another agent named Kilmer. Sergeant Morrison from Benton Harbor, Michigan PD was also present. Slate's first impression of Kiefer
was good. The attorney was tall and lean, maybe in his mid forties,
with longer brown hair. After introductions they all took seats
around a large conference table.

"I've reviewed your investigation, Lieutenant Slate. Quite an
impressive and in-depth investigation, especially for a Unit manager."

"Thanks."

"The tape in Michigan looks good for Profacci and Vaccaro on a
conspiracy to hit your witness here, providing Brunk can prove the
payment from Vaccaro."

"What about the charges River Forest could bring on the DeMeo
hit?" Slate asked.

Kiefer shook his head. "We've talked to River Forest. They're
okay with us charging him. The only way Brunk will give us Vaccaro
paying for DeMeo's hit is to walk on that charge. But we still have
him on the attempt in St. Louis."

Slate nodded.

Kiefter continued. "I'm not sure we can make Hayes. The code talk is vague."

"Hayes is there in Michigan when the hit on Mrs. Delaney was planned. And you have the bank records and the tape from DeMeo telling Lyon and me they had been on the take for years. So it's all tied together," Slate said, expressing some frustration.

"Still not real strong."

"Then you have them renegotiating the fee *after* Hayes had heard the arson and homicide case involving Yost Furrier, and DeMeo referring to Hayes as the schedule setter."

"Yes, but it's still the code talk with DeMeo and Profacci, and Hayes's name isn't mentioned." Kiefer paused. "With the hung jury, charging Hayes again without more evidence looks bad. If Vaccaro or Profacci gives us Hayes, we'll charge him. But given the risk from the Outfit, I doubt they'll talk."

Slate blew out a long breath to relieve his aggravation. He knew the federal boys wanted only a sure thing. "I think Hayes's second wife was a hit too. Burglars don't work a sixth floor condo at night, knowing people are likely to be home. And I think Brunk did it but he won't admit it with facing the two other charges. Maybe you noticed that Hayes married number three shortly after number two was killed."

Kiefer nodded but said nothing.

Millburn asked, "So Dodd got all you have, Slate? Your investigation and the Michigan tape is the extent of your records?"

"That's it." He looked at Morrison. "Sergeant Morrison here can cover the Michigan bugs. Oh, you also have the trial transcript from Lake County?"

"Yes. We've ordered that."

"You might talk to our Intelligence Unit and to Internal Affairs Assistant Superintendent Palmer. Commander Arnold and I met with him."

"You're convinced that Hayes is dirty?" Millburn asked.

"Absolutely. They should have both been found guilty. The case was solid, well presented by ASA Paula Lyon. And like I said, his second wife looks like a hit."

"We'll talk to Lyon," Kiefer said.

"Is DeCenzo still defending them?" Slate asked.

"Yes. He had the Hayes and Profacci trial, didn't he?"

Slate nodded. "How long before this RICO goes to trial?"

"Shouldn't be too long, but I can't give you a date yet."

"I'd like to get our former Deputy Chief of Detectives, Urbanski, too, from your trial."

"He's the one named on the Michigan tape?"

"Yes. And he suddenly retired after I met with Internal Affairs."

"Okay, Slate. We'll see if Profacci or Vaccaro will implicate him, as well as Hayes."

"I still think you got enough on the Michigan tape to try Hayes as a part of the conspiracy."

"We'll see," Kiefer acknowledged.

They went over the Michigan tape and what Sergeant Morrison could add about the vehicles at Hayes's summer home. Then what Bernice Delaney could testify to concerning the discussion between Hayes and DeMeo regarding twenty-five days for an arson and death, which allowed Slate to tap Hayes's office phones.

CHAPTER

41

SLATE DECIDED TO call ASA Paula Lyon regarding his photographs of Fischetti collecting his street tax on St. Clair. The ASA agreed to meet at 11:00 a.m. Slate managed a good bit of his departmental paper and still was at Lyon's office in the Cook County Courthouse on California by 10:50. At 11:05 a.m. another associate left her office and she waved him in.

"Good morning, Paula."

"Ed. How's it going? I see you have a new deputy chief of detectives. What's his name?"

"Newcomb."

"What do you think?"

"The Commander and I met with him the other day. I think he's okay."

"What's on your mind now? More trouble?"

"Isn't that why the big salaries?"

"You're speaking of the police, I guess."

"I wish. But even with the salary change when you left the business world, you're having more fun here than handling malpractice suits. Right?"

Paula nodded as she opened up the file for Slate's investigation. "I'm fine. Your investigations help keep me on my toes."

He briefed her on Fischetti's street tax collection and the Tele-Tracks on Fiscetti's and Seryak's cars. "I want to charge them and anyone else involved."

Paula flipped to the paperwork already completed about the two suspects. "Extortion I guess, but I'll have to research the best charge. We'll need written statements from several business owners about these payments. You know, no written contract offered and no visible services, but warnings of risks like a fire or a break-in if they don't pay, and they are willing to testimony in court."

"Okay, I'll start with Kim, the one you used in the Yost arson."

"The Korean dry cleaner. If you get three or four statements and the people willing to testify, then some photographs of him working the stores, then get him with the cash, I think we're okay. I'll have to talk to Erwin. He's still getting heat over the Hayes trial and he's facing an election. I'll also research the best charge to file."

"Good. Keep in mind that Fischetti collects the first week of each month."

So you need an answer soon."

"Right. I'll get some help with the surveillance and arrest."

"You think this Seryak is involved?"

"Not sure, but he offered me a job, along with a warning of risk when I was investigating Hayes. Vaughn, *his* boss, heads Vaughn Security and is a retired CPD commander. He may be connected to the Outfit."

For the next two days Slate continued to plan his next move as he reviewed investigation reports and ran Area 3 Robbery/Homicide. Lyon called to say the State's Attorney would charge Fischetti with extortion if Slate had several witness statements, the people were willing to testify, and the cash was confiscated.

After lunch the next day Slate drove to the Loop Cleaners at 112 Huron Street. He parked his pickup at a meter and paid the charge. He didn't want the local officers to know he was in the area as he didn't know if the beat sergeant or any of the traffic officers might be involved with Fischetti.

A Korean woman was working the front counter as he entered Loop Cleaners. Slate displayed his star and ID. "I'd like to speak with Mr. Kim."

"I'll tell him."

James Kim approached with a worried look on his face.

"Mr. Kim, I need to talk with you in private."

"Come back," he said and motioned. Slate followed him to a small office in the rear corner behind the racks of cleaned clothes hanging on the conveyor. Kim took a seat behind a small desk. Slate sat down on the only chair in front of the desk.

"You know about the arson trial we lost?"

"That was a bad trial."

"Are you still paying the monthly fee?"

Kim didn't respond.

"You're not in trouble, Mr. Kim. I'm still after Danny Fischetti."

"I pay every month."

"Still no contract, or reports, or photos of security risks from Fischetti?"

Kim shook his head no.

"I think you're an honest businessman, Mr. Kim, like most business owners in the area. What I need from you is a written statement of Fischetti first coming to you, what he said, and the monthly payments you make. Then explain there is no contract, no reports, no photos ever provided to you concerning any security problems, and you have never seen him in the area in the evenings or on weekends when you're here."

"Then what happens to my store? He's in the Mob."

"When I get several statements like yours, we'll arrest Fischetti with the money he has collected. He won't try anything if he's out on bond, and he'll do some time for extortion. You'll appear as one of several witnesses."

"He'll go to jail?"

Slate nodded.

"But when he gets out?"

"He'll know it isn't safe to work this area."

"He'll go away?"

"I think so. While you're writing your statement I want to get a couple more here business owners on Huron. Do you know of another owner who might cooperate?"

"Mr. Wang in the restaurant next door pays too. We have talked, but he's afraid of the Mob."

"That helps. I'll talk to him. Anyone else?"

"On Michigan Avenue, at Alice's gift shop. Mr. and Mrs. Weber pay. We have talked at our Loop merchants' meetings, but they're afraid not to pay."

"Okay. Make your report and I'll talk to some of your neighbors then stop back."

Kim nodded. "I will do it if you get more."

"I understand."

Slate went into Wang's Chinese Restaurant next door and found Mr. Wang at the cash register. Slate displayed his ID and asked to speak with him. They took a table in the rear corner. Slate explained that Mr. Kim was giving a statement and that his detectives were the ones who had arrested Fishetti for the arson at the Yost fire.

Wang eyed Slate cautiously. "But he beat the charge. This could be very dangerous."

"How long have you been paying?"

Wang didn't answer.

"I know you're paying. I've talked to others in the area."

"Several years."

"At a hundred per month, twelve hundred per year, five years is six thousand dollars, Mr. Wang. Do like wasting that kind of money? Business must be good."

"Maybe he protects the place while I'm closed."

"Do you have a contract?"

Wang shook his head.

"Ever receive a record of security risks or photos concerning a problem?"

"No."

"I'm getting some other business people along this street to make statements. When I get several statements, we'll arrest Fischetti and put him away. The State's Attorney's office has agreed to prosecute him."

"But there may be others who will take his place."

"Then we'll arrest them."

"I don't want to have trouble, Lieutenant."

"What if I show you statements from other merchants?"

"You and the officers can't always be around. Yost's business was burned."

"So you're okay with the Outfit stealing from you?"

Wang didn't respond.

"Here's my card. Call if you change your mind."

Slate moved on west to Alice's Gift Shop. He made the same pitch with Mr. and Mrs. Weber. They agreed to provide a statement and appear in court if James Kim would do the same thing.

Slate headed back toward the Loop Cleaners and stopped at Gibbs's Leather Apparel. He had seen Fischetti go into the shop the previous month. Mr. Gibbs played it dumb, however, and refused to cooperate.

Mr. Kim had his statement ready. Slate thanked him, then drove to Alice's Gift Shop and obtained their statement. A quick flip through the pages assured Slate that Mr. Kim's and the Webers' statements were well written with good detail.

Slate then moved to St. Clair Street and parked. He contacted five merchants and obtained two statements about the terms Danny Fischetti demanded in exchange for "security" to their businesses. That gave him a total of four.

The next morning Slate took a call from FBI agent Dodd with notification that the RICO trial had been scheduled for the second week in June, about three weeks away.

Slate called ASA Lyon regarding the four statements he had obtained from merchants who were paying Fischetti the street tax. With those things in place, he left a message for Barona and Ingram to see him whenever they could stop by later in the morning.

He was just finishing his Danish and coffee when Barona and Ingram knocked at his office doorway and came in.

"Shut the door and have a seat." Slate gestured toward the table to the side of his office.

They all sat down. "Joe, Pam, how's business?"

"Good," Barona said looking very focused. "Our clearance continues to be above average, Lieutenant."

"Keep it up. But that's not what I want to talk about. Remember Danny Fischetti on the Yost arson?"

They nodded.

"I have Tele-Tracks on his Eldorado Caddie, and on Larry Seryak's black DeVille. Seryak is a retired deputy chief of detectives. A couple weeks ago I got several photos of Fischetti collecting his street tax on St. Clair. Then I obtained statements from four merchants about paying the fee and they agreed to testify. ASA Lyon has agreed to an extortion charge if we can get Fischetti with the cash as he leaves the stores."

"He's still working the same area even after the arson?" Barona asked.

Slate nodded. "Feels safe after his court experience, I guess. What I want to do is monitor his collecting again on St. Clair and then photograph him collecting on Huron. Then with your help, tail him as he finishes on Huron to see where he goes and arrest him and whoever he delivers to."

"So we need to change cars," Barona noted.

"See what Rizzo has that will blend in. And tell Sergeant Waddell you're working a special detail for me."

"I see you have a pickup," Ingram said.

"Yeah. I had the BMW at the Hayes trial, and when I found the bomb."

"You think there's still some danger, even after the hung jury?" Ingram asked.

"The FBI's RICO trial is scheduled for mid June."

"And you'll testify in it?" Barona asked.

"Right. Along with several others. You two can get a monitor and a camera from Tech Services after you switch cars. My equipment was checked out in your names. Tell them you need another set. Then be ready to monitor Fischetti the first of June. He starts on St. Clair and works north."

"Is he covering the entire Loop, or is he working with someone else?" Ingram asked.

"I'm not sure. Maybe you two can check that out. When you see him start, let me know. Take photos of him going in and coming out of several stores and to his car. I'll join you there on Huron. We can both take photos, then follow him to his delivery point, make the arrest, and confiscate the cash. And remember to let me know what you're driving."

When the detective team left, Slate updated his whiteboard with the plan to arrest Fischetti. There were enough other ongoing investigations in Area 3 to keep him busy, but he still stopped other work occasionally to make notes for the RICO trial and to review the best way to handle the arrest of Fischetti. Was Vaccaro Fischetti's contact? Or was Vaughn Security the front for the Outfit's business?

He added a note to have Barona and Ingram check out the beat sergeant in District 18 to see if he was involved in the collections. Much of the Outfit's crime was like the corrupt city politics. It had become a way of life and was just accepted. The street tax didn't fit exactly under Robbery/Homicide, but it was being ignored, and Fischetti was part of the bigger package of corruption that he was committed to clearing out.

Before heading home Slate checked with Barona. The detective team had a monitor and camera and planned to be in the Loop the first of June. Barona also reported they would be driving a gray Lexus 300. Slate reminded him to use the surveillance frequency to avoid being monitored.

ON TUESDAY, JUNE 2, Slate was moving paper when about 9:20 a.m. Barona radioed that he had movement on St. Clair.

Slate locked his office and headed for the pickup. Using the surveillance frequency, he radioed as he neared St. Clair. "768 to 954. Status report."

"Running the first block and about ready to move to the next."

Slate drove southbound slowly on St. Clair and found Fischetti's Cadillac in an alley just off the street. Barona and Ingram were parked at a fire hydrant about a quarter of a block south of the Caddie. Slate stopped opposite them. "I'll pick him up as he works back south in each block. That way he won't make us."

Slate circled the area and came back through the alley, ready to pick up Fischetti as he collected on the other side of the street. They continued this pattern while taking photos until Fischetti finished St. Clair and moved north to Huron Street. Slate radioed Barona that he would cover him westbound and Barona and Ingram should get him coming back east on the other side of the street. On Huron, Slate parked at the curb near where he had first picked up Fischetti the previous month. He checked his camera and waited.

About five minutes later the black Eldorado appeared and parked in the first alley to the north. Slate waited until Fischetti entered the second business, then moved up and stopped near the parked cars as if making a delivery. He photographed the Caddie, then Fischetti as he exited the business and entered the third one. He moved and photographed six times.

Barona and Ingram picked up the suspect as he made his way back east on the other side of Huron. Slate moved to the next block west on Huron and waited. They continued changing off photographing Fischetti in each block until he reached Michigan Avenue.

As Fischetti came back to his car and headed north, Slate followed him for several blocks then radioed Barona to take him. They continued switching tails as Fischetti drove northwest. Slate was behind him on North Avenue when he saw Fischetti use his phone.

He radioed Barona. "He's arranging a meet. Get ready."

Slate checked his Tele-Track monitor and radioed Barona. "Seryak's Cadillac is in the lot at Vaughn Security." Barona and Ingram moved in close behind Slate's pickup.

At Kedzie, Fischetti headed north. Slate radioed again. "The meet may be at Vaughn's, just before Logan."

Fischetti slowed at Vaughn Security and pulled into the lot. A black Cadillac was stopped in the lot, facing the entrance. Seryak was in it and Fischetti pulled up alongside Seryak's car.

Slate touched his mike button without removing it from the dash and yelled, "Pin them!" He then pulled in and quickly passed the two stopped cars on the left, then turned sharply right behind Seryak's car and in front of Fischetti's. Barona and Ingram turned into the lot to block the two cars on the opposite side.

Slate came out of his pickup with his pistol drawn, and Barona and Ingram followed. Startled, Fischetti and Seryak looked to the front and then to the rear. Leaning over the edge of the pickup Slate yelled, "Shut off the motor and throw the keys out!"

Nothing happened for several seconds. Slate repeated the order. Both suspects shut off the motors and dropped the keys beside their doors.

"Now, get out with your hands up!" Slate yelled.

Both drivers got out and Slate, Barona, and Ingram moved up.

Seryak yelled, "What the hell is this all about, Slate? You're forgetting that I'm a retired deputy chief!"

Slate placed Seryak against his own car, then handcuffed and frisked him. He took a pistol from Seryak's waistband.

"That weapon is legal."

Barona and Ingram cuffed Fiscetti. Ingram took a snub nose revolver from Fischetti's sport coat pocket.

"You're both under arrest for extortion."

Seryak turned and glared at Slate. "You're a dead man, Slate!"

"You have the right to remain silent. Anything you say can and will be used against your in a court of law. You have the right to have an attorney present. If you can't afford an attorney, one will be appointed. Do you understand?"

"You're in over your head, Slate!"

Fischetti was silent as Barona read him his rights.

Slate moved Seryak near Barona, then recovered a briefcase containing cash in a variety of denominations from Fischetti's passenger seat. "Have the cars towed, Joe."

"My car is in the lot. You don't have to tow it," Seryak said.

Slate radioed for a paddy wagon to pick up the two prisoners.

"You won't survive this one, Slate!" Seryak threatened again.

Slate moved close to Seryak's face. "You're just a common criminal, Seryak. Do you think the Outfit gives a damn about you? You need to ask yourself, 'Will they hit me here, or in the pen?'"

"Slate, listen to me. This is bigger than both of us. The Outfit controls more than you realize. It's smarter to go with the flow."

Slate directed Ingram to remove both monitors before the cars were towed. The paddy wagon transported the prisoners to Area 3 and Slate followed them in. Barona and Ingram waited for the tows to be completed.

At Area 3, Seryak asked to talk to Commander Arnold. Slate ignored him. Barona and Ingram arrived and processed both prisoners. Neither would give a statement. Fischetti was also charged for a concealed weapon since his permit had been issued by the former Cook County Sheriff. Then both were transported to the Cook County jail. Slate let Barona and Ingram carry the arrests.

Slate headed to Arnold's office and briefed him on the arrests.

Arnold repeated the names from Slate's investigation. "Seryak and Fischetti?"

"Right. Extortion."

"The street tax?"

Slate nodded.

"What did they say?"

"Seryak said I was dead, then asked for you when he was booked."

Slate felt his boss taking his measure again, weighing what his lieutenant must have been doing to bring his investigation to this point. He knew Arnold was considering the ramifications of charging a retired CPD deputy chief. He added some details.

"Both were armed. Fischetti's weapon permit was expired, so we hit him with CCW as well."

"I hope this case is solid, Slate."

"ASA Lyon approved it and she ran it by State's Attorney Erwin. I have statements from four merchants who pay the street tax, and they'll testify."

"This will stir the media and the brass—a retired deputy chief of detectives collecting street tax. I wonder where he was taking it. How much did they have?"

"Haven't counted it. I thought about waiting to see where Seryak would take it, but I figured we have two for sure, and I didn't want him to get inside someplace and lose the bag of money."

"Now what do they do with Seryak?" Arnold asked.

"Ignore him or hit him, I guess."

"And they can get to him even in jail or the pen."

Slate nodded. "He'll bond out quickly."

Arnold continued. "A deputy chief of detectives with a good retirement, working with Vaughn, and working for the Outfit. How do you figure that?"

Slate thought about Seryak's neighborhood and big house. "Makes me wonder if he was ever one of us. You'll give Newcomb a heads up, I guess?"

Arnold nodded. "Wait until it hits the morning paper. The Hayes trial, then this. You're getting to be popular with the media, Slate."

Slate nodded. "I wonder if either will want to cut a deal. The Bureau could use them on their RICO trial."

Arnold considered that. "That might be interesting. I wonder who else Seryak could finger in CPD."

Slate took his lunch break late at Smokey's, then spent the remainder of the day completing the extortion investigation report. He stopped several times to replay the insult of Seryak's job offer at Smokey's before the Hayes trial. He ended the day by updating his whiteboard.

That evening he briefed Rebecca on the two new arrests and warned her to be alert. Just to be safe he asked her to ride to work with someone else again for a while until things settled down.

The next morning Slate grabbed the newspaper in the driveway. The front page of the *Chicago Tribune* proclaimed, RETIRED DEPUTY CHIEF OF DETECTIVES ARRESTED FOR EXTORTION. As he considered the implications, he wondered about his pickup. He had stopped using the lime.

He studied the door carefully for any sort of jimmying before unlocking and opening it. Then he released the hood latch and checked under the hood. Everything under the hood looked okay. He stood there thinking for a moment, then went into the garage and grabbed a canvas tarp he used to drag yard waste to the street for pickup. He spread the tarp under the driver's door, laid on it, and checked under the floorboard, then made his way to Area 3. Robbery/Homicide was buzzing like it had been after Hayes was charged.

Sergeant Waddell followed Slate into his office and shut the door. "You're in the paper again, Lieutenant."

"Afraid so, Rick."

"Seryak's working for the Outfit?"

Slate nodded as he sat down at his desk.

Waddell pulled at chair from the table and sat at the end of the desk.

"What did he do when you arrested him?"

"Said that I was dead. I told him he was the one at risk."

"I read your report before I went home last night, and Barona and Ingram's report this morning. I see the count in Fischetti's bag was over three-thousand. They're still collecting street tax after the Yost arson trial?"

"Yeah. He must have had some of Monday's tax with him on Tuesday. And he must have collected some from other businesses before we got on him yesterday. Think what they collect in the entire city."

Rick shook his head. "They'll claim they're providing a service, I guess."

"My witnesses will counter that. I got four of them to come forward. Now we got to keep them safe, Rick." Slate handed him the list of the four witnesses.

"What's the status on the FBI's RICO case?"

"Coming up in a couple weeks."

"Think Seryak and Fischetti will cut a deal?"

"Hard to say. If they don't cut a deal, they'll do some time. And if they do time, Seryak may not survive the pen."

"I guess that depends on how much damage they can do to the Outfit. I wonder if Seryak will name anyone in the department. Getting any heat from Arnold?"

"No."

Later in the day Slate called the Cook County jail, but Seryak and Fischetti had both bonded out.

43

SLATE HAD JUST sat down the next morning when Special Agent Dodd called.

"Morning, Dodd," he greeted the agent. "You've called to report that Seryak wants to deal."

"You're right."

"How about Fischetti?"

"He's not talking, Lieutenant. What I need to know is, will you drop Seryak's state extortion charge if he cooperates with us on our RICO case?"

"Just before the Hayes trial that asshole tried to offer me a job, then warned me about how dangerous things could be for me. On my charges, any deal would depend on how much he could give you, or rather who. Then Commander Arnold and the State's Attorney's office would have to agree."

"Yeah, but you have the influence there, Slate."

"Do you know what he's offering?"

There was a long silence. Slate knew it was the Bureau again. Wanting, but not giving.

"We can't be sure right now."

"Which means he's told you what he has, but you haven't checked it out yet. So here's the deal, Dodd. You tell me and the ASA exactly what and who Seryak will give you, then we'll talk. If he can give you Hayes, I'm interested."

"I'll get back to you."

After that call Slate sat back in his chair and fumed a little about the problems in dealing with other agencies. Every damn piece of information had to be forced out of the Bureau. And they wondered why the locals didn't like or trust them. When Slate gave ASA Lyon a heads up concerning the FBI's call, Lyon agreed with his position.

The next morning Dodd called and asked Slate to a 3:00 p.m. meeting with Assistant U.S. Attorney Kiefer and himself, Larry Seryak, and Seryak's attorney, Stanley O'Neil.

Slate moved some paper, then opened his whiteboard. He studied the list of names, thinking about the RICO trial and how many that trial might get. He added some details to his notebook in preparation for the meeting and the RICO trial before turning back to the routine paperwork.

Shortly after 2:00 p.m. Slate headed south toward the Dirksen U.S. Courthouse. On the seventh floor he was escorted to a large conference room. Kiefer was seated at the head of the table at the far end of the room and Dodd sat to his right. To Kiefer's left was a man Slate figured would be O'Neil. Seryak sat to O'Neil's left.

"Lieutenant Slate, glad you could make it." Kiefer gestured to his right. Neither O'Neil nor Seryak spoke. Slate moved up beside Dodd. As Seryak eyed Slate, the lieutenant immediately found himself thinking of Seryak's threat to him, the threatening call to his wife, and the car bomb.

"Mr. O'Neil has said that Mr. Seryak will provide some information on the Outfit if he gets probation and if we put him in witness protection with a new identity," Kiefer led off. "Lieutenant Slate heads Robbery/Homicide in Area 3 and has agreed to listen before proceeding with his state extortion charge against Mr. Seryak. Mr. Fischetti, who is represented by Mr. DeCenzo, has not offered to talk."

Slate nodded.

"So, what can you tell us that we don't already know, Mr. Seryak?" Kiefer asked.

"I can give you some people and I will testify against them."

"Who? And what kind of a crime?"

"Carmine Vaccaro for extortion and paying for a hit."

"We already have him," Kiefer said.

"And Charlie Dorman for hiring the hit on Alderman Bryan on the city council casino vote."

"That could be of interest, if we could prove his payment and get the hitter too." Kiefer looked at Slate. "Does that interest you, Lieutenant?"

"If he can prove it."

Kiefer glanced over at Seryak.

"Dorman had orders to get a casino built on Sheridan Road rather than a condo. He hired Frankie Carbonaro to stage an accident and kill Alderman Bryan, who was going to vote against it and he held the swing vote on the council."

"Who gave Dorman the order?" Slate asked.

"I don't know that."

"How can you prove this?" Kiefer asked.

"It's a lead to follow up on."

Kiefer looked at Slate. "Anything you can pursue, Lieutenant?"

"It's nothing. We can get stuff like that on every corner."

Seryak slapped the table. "A good detective could work it!"

"How about Judge W. C. Hayes?" Slate asked, "What can you give us on him?"

"You had a weak case. That's why you lost," Seryak shot back. "I was deputy chief of detectives!"

Slate thought of the threat at Smokey's. "You were a mobster, Seryak, and you won't survive long enough in the pen to need a change of clothes." Slate stood. "I'll go with my charges."

CHAPTER 44

ABOUT TEN DAYS later, on a Wednesday morning, Slate arrived at the Dirksen U.S. Courthouse before 9:00 a.m. for the FBI's Racketeer Influenced and Corrupt Organizations trial. He figured this RICO trial should put away attorney Profacci and the Outfit's guy, Vaccaro, but it galled him that "His Honor" sat untouched on the Circuit Court bench hearing felony cases despite all the evidence of his corruption.

On the right side behind Kiefer's table Slate saw Mr. Yost, the furrier owner, and the witnesses that had testified at the trial of Danny Fischetti for the arson death of Keith Yost. Mrs. Bryan, the alderman's widow was sitting about one third of the way back on the right side also. Slate took a seat with the other witnesses.

At exactly 9:00 the U.S. District Court was called to order and Judge Rubin Wesley took his seat. Due to the small number of black judges in both the State and Federal systems, Slate was surprised to see he was an African American. Wesley was a big man, maybe in his late fifties with thick gray hair. His glasses hung on a cord around his neck and his black robe had a gold-colored trim. Slate had been impressed with Assistant U.S. Attorney Joseph Kiefer at the pretrial meeting. He hoped Judge Wesley was of the same caliber.

Slate glanced over toward the defense table to the left. He recognized DeCenzo, who had defended Hayes and Profacci in Lake County. Sitting to Profacci's right was a shorter baldheaded man maybe in his sixties. Slate didn't remember ever seeing Vaccaro in person, the Outfit's made guy. His appearance wasn't impressive but he had ordered the hit on Delaney, Slate's witness, and then moved the hitter to DeMeo, who was looking to be a State's witness.

Slate wondered about the car bomb and how many hits Vaccaro had ordered over all.

Delbert Brunk, AKA the Professor, was sitting with a U.S. Marshall just behind the defense table. Slate felt thankful again that he had gotten Bernice Delaney covered before Brunk arrived from Miami, and out of her house before it was torched.

After the judge's comments to the jury and counsel, Assistant U. S. Attorney Kiefer led off screening and excusing potential jurors. Then Defense Attorney DeCenzo challenged several jurors. Jury screening went faster than in Circuit Court and concluded Wednesday afternoon.

On Thursday and Friday, Slate, and several others testified regarding the arson death at Yost's Furrier and the trial of Fischetti, the phone tap that recorded the payoff negotiated before the trial between defense attorney Profacci and DeMeo, then the additional fifty thousand demanded before the verdict. Sergeant Morrison of Benton Harbor, Michigan PD and Slate covered the Outfit's Carmine Vaccaro ordering the hit on Bernice Delaney when at Hayes's summer home in Michigan. Slate also testified concerning DeMeo's contacts with Vaccaro and DeMeo's meeting with ASA Lyon and himself. The tape recording of that meeting was played.

———

On Friday afternoon Slate checked some of the paperwork at Area 3, then headed home. He slept in on Saturday and had a late brunch. He mowed the yard and tried to relax, but he had too many investigation points rolling around in his head to really let go of the pressures.

On Sunday after church he and Rebecca met Roger Daniels and his friend, Grace, for brunch. Daniels, his radioman in Vietnam, had been partially disabled by a head wound from a sniper.

That night he had trouble getting to sleep. Then about 3:00 a.m. he heard Rebecca yelling and felt her shaking him.

"What wrong?"

"You were having another nightmare."

Ed wiped his sweaty forehead with the sheet. "What did I say?"

"'Hang in there, Sarge. Hang in there. The chopper's on the way.' Roger Daniels?"

"Yeah. Why the sniper shot my radioman instead of me, I'll never know. At least Rog is alive and able to function even with the disabilities to his arm and leg."

———————

On Monday morning, Assistant US Attorney Kiefer then called Delbert Brunk, AKA the Professor.

Brunk took the stand and was sworn. The man glanced at Slate as he took his seat. Slate was still surprised by the small stature of the former SEAL that he had interviewed in St. Louis.

Kiefer stood and approached Brunk. "Please tell the court your name, your background, and your business."

Brunk sat up higher in the seat. "Delbert Glen Brunk. I retired after twenty years of service as a U. S. Navy SEAL, then started a health club and martial arts training facility in Miami."

"Did you serve in clandestine operations in the Middle East, in which you killed people?"

"Yes."

"How many people did you kill while serving your country, Mr. Brunk?"

"That's classified information."

"Why did you become a hit man after retiring from the Armed Forces?"

Brunk shifted in his seat and glanced in the direction of Vacarro. "It cost more to get my club started than I planned on, and it didn't take off like I expected, so I needed more cash."

"Tell the court how you became involved with killing Mario DeMeo."

Brunk glanced again at Vaccaro. "I was paid to hit a Mrs. Delaney, in Oak Park."

"By 'hit' you mean what?"

"Kill her."

"Who contacted you?"

"I didn't know at the time."

"Why is that, Mr. Brunk?"

"I normally get an anonymous call. When I take the job a down payment is arranged to be transferred to my account in the Cayman Islands. And the final payment is wired, but with a later release date. The job is done, and the final payment is released. I normally don't know who hires me."

"What was the payment in this hit?"

"Twenty-five thousand dollars."

"But in this case you did find out who ordered the person killed, didn't you? Tell the court how that happened."

"I came to the Chicago area and found the target. I saw she was covered each time I checked her place in Oak Park. I then called home for messages and had a message to call someone here due to a change of plans."

"Then what happened?"

"I called the number in River Forest and was told to hit DeMeo ASAP rather than the woman."

"Then what happened?"

"I demanded another five thousand for wasting my time finding the woman."

"What happened then?"

"The caller agreed, so I hit the guy in his garage."

"You cut Mr. DeMeo's throat as he got out of his car?"

Brunk nodded.

"Is that true?"

"Yeah, I did him."

"Then you were arrested while on another assignment in St Louis. Is that correct?"

"Yeah."

"And that second call you received in Chicago—to move from the woman to DeMeo—the message you recorded in your notebook— was then traced to who, Mr. Brunk?"

Brunk pointed to Vaccaro.

"Let the record show that Mr. Brunk has identified Mr. Carmine Vaccaro, a made man in the Chicago Outfit."

Kiefer entered Brunk's notebook with Vaccaro's phone number, and Brunk's bank records and the transfers as Exhibits.

DeCenzo countered that Brunk had received a reduced sentence on his case in St. Louis for this testimony and that the word of a hit man should not carry any weight in a court of law.

Neither Vacarro or Profacci took the stand in their own defense. At 3:20 p.m. the judge released the jury to deliberate.

Slate moved to a bench in the hall and dove into the stack of robbery and homicide investigations he had in his briefcase. He hoped the verdict would be quick, sending Profacci and Vaccaro on their way to the Federal pen. He could then move on to the others still on his list.

At 6:00 p.m. the jury was still out so he headed to Area 3, where he went through part of his IN box, placed the remaining paperwork in his briefcase, and headed for home.

––––––––

When he returned to court before 9:00 a.m. on Tuesday morning, the jury was still out. He processed paperwork until 10:00 a.m. then went to a coffee shop in the building and continued checking investigation reports.

At 10:30 a.m. he was back in the courtroom. At 11:40 a.m. the jury entered the room and the court was called to order. Slate tried to read jurors' faces. What he saw made him feel pretty confident.

"Have you reached a verdict?" Judge Wesley asked.

The foreman stood and answered, "Yes, we have, your honor."

"Please read the verdict."

"We find Anthony Profacci and Carmine Vaccaro guilty as charged."

Profacci lowered his head into his hands. His law career was over. Vaccaro showed no emotion but due to his age, he would certainly die in a Federal prison.

Judge Wesley scheduled sentencing for a week from today.

To Slate, the convictions made the trial lost in Lake County a little less painful.

––––––––

After lunch Slate ignored the piles of paper in his IN box and unlocked the doors to his whiteboard. He studied his notes of the last few months, then began a new listing that showed the suspect and the agency that had made the case.

Convicted: Carmine Vaccaro, Anthony Profacci by Robbery/Homicide CPD / Benton Harbor PD / FBI RICO. Danny Fischetti, Larry Seryak by Robbery/Homicide CPD

Pending sentencing: Delbert Brunk by Robbery/Homicide CPD / FBI St. Louis
Dead: DeMeo, Ruggerio by the Outfit
Retired: Urbanski by Robbery/Homicide CPD / Benton Harbor PD
Pending: Hitter on Alderman Bryan, Frankie Carbonaro, Judge W. C. Hayes, juror Jacob Walberg

He stepped back and sat down on the end of his desk to study the big picture on the board. What had started with losing some solid cases in a Cook County Circuit Court in Chicago had developed into a major investigation with both State and Federal charges.

He headed to the squad room for coffee and had just returned to his office when Commander Arnold stopped by.

"Commander."

Arnold looked at the list. "Now what are you up to? Causing me more trouble?"

"Probably. What do you think?"

"Looks like you got eight of the eleven, with a little help from Michigan and the feds. Three to go. Think you can make the case?"

"Hayes is the one I really want."

"Carbonaro was the hitter on Alderman Bryan?"

"Right."

"Walberg is the one who hung the jury on the Hayes trial?"

"If Lyon will allow him to walk with a fine, I'm going to see if he'll cooperate now that Fischetti will be in prison."

"Find out who paid—or threatened—him to hang the jury, then retry Hayes?"

"If State's Attorney Erwin will agree."

"Judge Hayes," Arnold said, looking at Slate.

Slate nodded. "The key player is still on the bench hearing cases."

"And Hayes's first wife left him, and your think his second wife was a hit?"

Slate nodded.

Arnold turned toward the door and stopped. "Get this cleaned up ASAP so you can get back to concentrating on the clearance rates for the rest of the department."

"I want Hayes!"

His commander didn't respond.

Slate moved the paper, then called ASA Paula Lyon.

"Who are you after now, Ed?"

"I want to offer the juror Jacob Walberg a deal if he will confess to being paid off or threatened, and gives us the name."

"What kind of deal?"

"A fine only if he testifies and we convict the guy."

"Erwin may not want to retry Hayes, Ed. An election will be coming up."

"Can you feel him out?"

"I'll try."

Slate then briefed her on the RICO trial of Profacci and Vaccaro.

"On Fischetti and Seryak," Lyon said, "they have two weeks to get their personal affairs in order before beginning their sentences."

"Three years for Fischetti and one for Seryak?"

"Right."

"I just listed the group on my board. So far we have eight of eleven, Paula."

"But Hayes is still on the bench."

"Do you have any problem of me talking to Walberg again while you're checking with Erwin?"

"Go ahead, but I doubt he's going to cooperate."

CHAPTER

45

AS SLATE DROVE toward the northwest side and home a few days later, he mentally replayed key events of the past months. So much ground had been gained, but how could he make the case on Hayes? Could he get the State's attorney to take on a sitting judge a second time?

As he drove west he noticed a car about half a block behind him. It had been following him for most of the drive, he realized. The risk with Carmine Vaccaro's conviction occurred to him, but this car looked like an unmarked squad car, probably another officer heading home to the northwest side. He wondered why this was the first time he'd ever seen it.

He parked the pickup on the right side of his driveway so Rebecca could get their car into the garage. He had just opened the truck's door and stepped down when a shot rang out. He dropped to the ground and two more shots were fired. The glass from the opened driver's door glass shattered and fell on him. He looked toward the street and saw a black Ford speeding away to the east. Then he saw the car that had been behind him make a skidding bootlegger turn to pursue the black Ford.

Slate jumped back into the truck, backed into the street, and headed east at top speed. About three blocks from his house he heard three shots. Then he came upon the black car in a yard on the left side of the street, up against a tree. Barona and Ingram were running toward the car with their weapons drawn.

Slate skidded to a stop on the left side of the street and ran toward the car, pulling his weapon as he ran. He saw that the driver was slumped down in the front seat against the left front door. Barona moved to a position behind the driver's door and yelled for the driver to get out. Ingram approached from the passenger side and Slate ran toward her.

"He's hit," Ingram said.

Barona pulled the driver's door open and Danny Fischetti fell out onto the ground. He was bleeding from a hole in the back of his head. Slate moved around near Barona as he placed his pistol against Fischetti's head and pulled both of his arms out away from his body.

"Gun on the front seat," Ingram notified.

Barona felt the man's neck for a pulse. "He's dead."

Ingram opened the passenger door and grabbed the pistol by the trigger guard. Slate reached in and shut off the motor.

"Was that you two behind me?" he asked.

"We thought you might need some help," Barona answered.

"Where did he come from?"

"From the west toward us. He was waiting for you."

Slate moved back and looked at the shattered rear window of the Ford Fischetti had been driving.

"I got off three rounds," Ingram explained.

Slate moved back up close to Fischetti. "One got him in the head."

By now the neighbors were standing in their yards and on their porches. Slate radioed the shooting in. Barona and Ingram spread out and kept the neighbors away.

In about twenty minutes Commander Arnold and the Forensic team reached the scene. "What do you have, Lieutenant?" Arnold started out.

"It's Fischetti, the street tax punk. He fired three rounds at me in my driveway." Slate motioned down the street. "As I got out of my pickup. Barona and Ingram had followed me home and they turned and pursued him to this point."

"Wasn't he sentenced?"

"They gave him two weeks to get personal things in order."

"Who got him?"

"Ingram got off three rounds through his rear window. One got him in the back of the head."

Arnold moved over to talk to Barona and Ingram.

Doctor Kimball from the ME's office arrived and performed a quick on-site exam on Fischetti, talked to Barona and Ingram, and left.

The scene was processed by Forensics. While Arnold talked to Barona and Ingram, Slate called in the registration on the Ford Fischetti was driving and it came back to a car rental in Cicero. The ME's van arrived and removed the body. Slate ordered a tow truck for the Ford.

Arnold, Barona, Ingram, and the Forensics team followed Slate home to examine the first shooting scene. The assailant's first shot had missed Slate. The second or third shot—that broke out the driver's door window—could not be found. The garage door had two holes. One of those also went through the rear garage wall, but they found no entry hole in the neighbor's house or garage to the rear. One shot stopped in a studding in the rear garage wall. Forensics recovered the slug in the studding, took photographs, then left.

"You're lucky he missed with the first shot, Lieutenant," Barona said.

"He must have been shooting through his open passenger side window."

Arnold looked at the shattered door glass. "That was close, Ed." The Commander shook Slate's hand. "Glad you're okay. Take tomorrow off if you want to."

Slate turned to Barona and Ingram. "Thanks for watching out for me, guys. Good shooting, Pam. It's you two's case." He shook their hands.

"The Commander asked us to keep an eye on you," Barona answered with an odd expression on his face.

Slate nodded. "Fischetti will collect no more street tax, and the merchants will be relieved."

When Rebecca pulled into the driveway Ed was sweeping up the glass from his broken window. She pulled up just enough to get off the street, got out, and walked up to her husband. "Ed, what happened?"

Slate stopped sweeping and looked at his wife. "A guy took a shot at me. But we got him."

"Are you serious?"

"Afraid so."

Rebecca gestured wildly as she cried and yelled, "Edward, this kind of living is absolutely impossible! These people know where to find us now! I can't stand it anymore!"

"I'll put your car away once I have this cleaned up," Ed responded in a very controlled voice.

Rebecca managed to get a grip on herself before she asked, "Who was it?"

"Fischetti. The guy who torched the furrier business where the owner's son was killed. He's the one we just arrested with Seryak."

"I thought they were sentenced."

"They were both given time to get their personal matters in order before they reported."

"Did you shoot Fischetti, Ed?"

"No. Barona and Ingram had followed me. Ingram got him."

Neither Ed nor Rebecca had any appetite for dinner, but they pieced nervously all evening long. Ed kept flipping through TV channels to keep from talking. Every time Rebecca tried to bring up her worries and fears, Ed headed her off. Whenever he started saying something, they ended up in an argument. Neither one could sleep when they went to bed. It was a long night. But he didn't want to take a day off. He wanted to get on with the next step toward putting away Hayes and whoever else was involved.

The next day Slate answered questions from several detectives who expressed satisfaction about Ingram—one of their own—getting Fischetti. As he reviewed the homicide and robbery investigations, he kept being distracted by thoughts of how close he had come to dying in his own driveway. It did seem like the time had come to start looking for that place on a Wisconsin lake.

Sergeant Moore, from the shooting team, called for an appointment with Slate, Barona, and Ingram at 9:00 a.m. the next morning.

Before lunch Slate took the damaged pickup to the police garage and picked up his unmarked Ford. Slate told Rizzo not to repair it until the shooting team saw it. Since the pickup hadn't kept Fischetti from finding him, he felt he no longer had a need for a surveillance vehicle.

After lunch at Smokey's Slate headed for Custom Jewelry on Michigan Avenue. He parked in an alley and entered Walberg's business. The same sales associate as before greeted him, and he asked to see Mr. Walberg. Within a few minutes Jacob Walberg came out to the front. Slate figured he didn't want to talk so he came out front rather than asking Slate to the back of the store where they had talked before.

"Mr. Walberg, I need a minute of your time." He motioned and added, "Let's move to the front of the store."

Walberg remained behind the counter but did move to the front of the store. The associate returned to her work near the rear. Slate stepped closer to the counter. Walberg eyed him warily.

"Are you aware, Mr. Walberg, that Danny Fischetti and a Larry Seryak have been arrested for collecting street tax, protection money from merchants, and that Fischetti is now dead?"

"I saw it in the paper," Walberg said, still looking very cautious.

"Fischetti tried to kill me yesterday afternoon, but he's the one who died instead. That means that merchants like you are safe. You don't have to pay an extortion fee anymore."

Walberg said nothing.

"If you were willing to cooperate with my department and the State's Attorney's office and tell us who threatened or paid you for hanging the Hayes jury trial, I'll try to get you off with just a fine. You would then be a law-abiding citizen again and your conscience would be clear. And we could retry Hayes."

"I have nothing to tell you, Lieutenant." Walberg turned to leave.

"Sir."

The jeweler stopped but avoided making eye contact with Slate.

"When I get the guy who paid you or threatened you, and he wants to deal for a lighter sentence, we'll prosecute you to the fullest extent of the law." Slate moved to the front door and exited the store.

The next morning Slate sat studying his whiteboard as he drank his coffee and ate his Danish. He moved Fischetti's name from the **Convicted** column to the **Dead** column. But W. C. Hayes was still hearing cases.

Just before 9:00 a.m. Slate, Barona, and Ingram headed downstairs together to Commander Arnold's conference room to meet with shooting team members Lieutenant Wolfgang and Sergeant

Moore. Sergeant Blazack, the Commander's assistant, was also present. Slate had known both Wolfgang and Moore from previous shooting investigations. Wolfgang concluded that the Office of Professional Standards would rule the killing of Fischetti by Detective Ingram a righteous shot.

Slate returned to his office and found a message from Special Agent Dodd stating that Profacci and Vaccaro had both been sentenced from the RICO trial to twenty-five years.

He opened the doors over his whiteboard and added the two sentences. He then sat on the end of his desk, studying his many case notes. Under his **Pending** heading: Walberg, Carbonaro, W.C. Hayes. He wondered about the former deputy chief of detectives, Urbanski, how deeply he was connected to the Outfit. No doubt Larry Seryak was already dirty when he held that position. He wondered momentarily if Seryak would survive the State pen, not that he really cared.

While Slate rested over the weekend he repaired the bullet hole in the garage door and the one that exited the rear. He knew that Rebecca didn't need that reminder. After brunch and church Sunday they took an afternoon nap, then walked in the neighborhood after a light dinner.

"When will everything finally be over, Ed?"

"We've gotten most of them, but Hayes is still on the bench."

"Has Chicago always been corrupt?"

Ed paused. "With the size of the city and of our department, there's always been corruption. But it's become worse in recent years. Probably the worst part is that after a while the corruption just kind of becomes the norm. With six hundred homicides each year, I guess many Chicagoans feel the corruption is the 'less serious' stuff."

"We ought to encourage the kids to choose another place to live," Rebecca said.

"What if we stay here after retirement ourselves?"

"Do you really want to do that? We've talked about Wisconsin, near my folks. It would be safe, and the cost of living is much lower."

"Someplace warmer would be nice, but that would have to be south, not farther north."

Ed moved close and placed his arms around his wife's shoulders. "I guess this life has been hard on you, babe. I have started thinking seriously about getting out early, but I want Hayes before I hang it up."

On Monday morning he started reviewing the pile of homicide and robbery investigations and the many cold case supplements. With over thirty percent of homicides still open, the supplements never stopped.

ASA Lyon called. "Good morning, Ed. I see that people are still shooting at you."

"Ingram nailed him with one of three rounds through his rear window."

"How did she get in on it?"

"The news reporter didn't know the entire story. They followed me home"

"Did you know it?"

"I saw a squad behind me about half a block back."

"I guess you're used to watching your back by now."

"Yeah, but Fischetti came from the other direction. He was waiting for me to get home."

"You got most of them Ed and you're still alive. How's your wife holding up?"

"The car bomb and Fischetti trying to whack me shook her."

"But your four years short for retirement right?"

"Yeah, but if I could get Hayes I might go early."

"Glad you're okay.

CHAPTER 46

SLATE HAD JUST sat down at his desk on Monday morning when the phone rang.

"Slate."

"Lieutenant, this is Sherri Herman, sister of Karen Hayes."

"Right. In Wisconsin."

"Yes, Stevens Point. Our mother passed away a few weeks ago, and while going through her things I found something that you should know about. My mother had a letter from Karen dated January 1984." Eleven years ago, Slate calculated immediately. He wished he could remember the date of Hayes's first marriage.

"I'll read you part of the letter. 'You know, Mom, what I've been putting up with for six years. He's been violent, and now I think he's corrupt, because he spends more money than we make. I can't take any more. I was packing to leave him when he came home unexpectedly and found me with things spread out in the bedroom. I told him I'm moving back to Wisconsin for a while and that I might ask for a divorce. He grabbed and slapped me, then said, 'You're not going anywhere! I have an election coming up in the fall. Unpack now!' While I unpacked he said, 'If you're *ever* disloyal to me, Karen, I can make one phone call and your life will be over.' Mom, I'm afraid to stay and afraid to leave."

Slate was already considering his next moves as he asked, "And your mother never said anything about this letter to you?"

"No. Her mind was failing by then."

"I need that letter, Ms. Herman. Make yourself a copy and ship me the original by UPS or Priority Mail. Attach a handwritten note to me with the date you send it. This may be the break I've been looking for."

"I've read about some of your work since we last talked, Lieutenant. The Chicago Outfit is involved, I see. And W. C. was not convicted in the trial?"

"No. The jury was hung. One person voted not guilty. Have you had any contact with W. C. since Karen came up missing?"

"No. He was only up here once that I can remember."

"And you said before that due to your age difference, you rarely saw Karen?"

"I was already in college when she was born. A surprise baby."

"Have you gone through all of your mother's things?"

"Yes. There were some other letters, but not like this one."

"Letters from Karen?"

"Yes. Five or six."

"Send them too. That will help identify her handwriting. Oh, and in your note to me list how many letters and the date of each."

"All right, I will. You'll let me know what you find?"

"Absolutely."

"I'll send them today."

"Thanks for your help, Ms. Herman."

Slate got up with his empty cup and headed to the squad room for coffee. He got a refill, pulled the investigation report on W. C. Hayes, and returned to his office. The marriage information Detective Brandi La Rue had researched for him was right on top.

Karen Olson of Stevens Point, Wisconsin, age twenty-four, had married W. C. Hayes in 1978. Wife number two, Juanita Jameson, age twenty-five, had married Hayes in 1985. And wife number three, Carmel Destazio, age twenty-eight, had married Hayes two years ago, in 1993. Karen Hayes's letter of January 1984 was written just before she disappeared, and the year before the judge's second marriage.

Slate moved departmental paper, but paused several times to think about his own investigation. He was playing the attempted hit from Fischetti in his mind again when his phone rang. It was Barona, asking to meet him for lunch at Smokey's.

As Slate took his lunch break from Area 3 he realized that spring had turned into summer. It was sunny and about eighty degrees.

Detective Joe Barona was waiting in the lobby when he got to Smokey's. As they shook hands Barona greeted him with, "Anyone shooting at you today, Lieutenant?"

"No. I considered leaving my coat and gun belt in my squad when I saw how warm it was, but decided against it."

"You're wearing your ankle piece?"

Slate nodded.

As they took seats at a rear table Slate followed up on Barona's concern. "I really appreciate you and Pam looking out for me, Joe. I heard Ingram is at the doc's today. The shooting's not the reason, is it?"

"No. It was her first one, but seeing you shot at probably helped set her off. She seems okay. I think it was just a routine appointment she had made. What else have you added on your investigation since you last updated me?"

Slate decided to keep Sherri Herman's call to himself for now. "Stop in and look at my wall board."

"How many have you got so far?"

"Eight of the eleven, counting Urbanski's retirement, and the Bureau's and Benton Harbor's help getting Brunk, Vaccaro, and Profacci. The Outfit got Ruggerio on your waste hauler robbery, and they got DeMeo with Brunk's hit."

"Yeah, but all of them came off our cases. I wonder how deep Urbanski was connected to the Outfit."

"We'll probably never know. I'm sure Internal Affairs checked him out as best they could, when they told him to retire."

"I keep waiting to hear that you've given up your lieutenant rank in order to return to sergeant and regular detective duty with me again." Barono baited. "Of course, I don't know why you would want to. You're still working cases while running Robbery/Homicide."

"I do see a need for a better way to work major crimes like this one."

"Like a white-collar function?"

Slate nodded. "Something like that."

As Slate started back to his office from lunch he formed a quick plan to pay a visit to his old high school friend Michael Vansant at his sporting goods shop on Broadway. He noticed that his unmarked Ford squad felt awkward compared to the several vehicles he had been using as he made his way north.

He parked at the curb near Mike's Sporting Goods. Mike was checking an invoice when he entered the shop.

"Well, what brings my buddy up this way? I see you're still living dangerously, Ed. That sounded like a close one in your driveway." Mike paused. "How's Rebecca taking it?"

"Same as always. Threatening to leave me and move to Wisconsin."

"How about you?"

"I've started thinking about leaving early."

"Another detective got the guy?"

"Yeah. They followed me home."

"He was the one arrested for the protection money thing?"

Slate nodded, then got to his purpose for the visit. "Mike, have you ever been approached about paying street tax?"

"No. I think the alderman in this ward is okay. He would be on it."

"I'm still interested in the Hayes family, Mike."

"Right. Especially W. C."

"You read about that trial too, I guess."

"A hung jury, huh? How did that go over in CPD?"

"No big problem. You told me a while back that Hayes's first wife, Karen, left him and went back to Wisconsin."

"That was the story."

"How do you know that?"

Mike shrugged. "That was the word when she came up missing. She was working in the store one day and gone the next."

"You saw her?"

"No. A disabled vet who loafs in the neighborhood and helps me sometimes said he bought groceries from her one day but the next day someone else was there and they said she had left W. C. and gone back to Wisconsin." Mike paused. "Do you think there's something wrong?"

"Not sure, so keep it between us, okay?"

Mike nodded.

Slate returned to his Ford trying to sort out the facts. If Karen Hayes *had* gone back to Wisconsin, why had no one in Wisconsin seen her or heard from her in eleven years?

He knew the house Hayes had lived in near Wrigley Field was gone and the space was now part of a parking lot. He wondered what year the houses had been removed and the lot built.

He pulled out and made a U-turn. The fire station for the Broadway area was a couple blocks south. At the firehouse he parked on the approach to the doors but to the side and placed his blue light on the dash. Inside, he asked for the captain in charge and was directed to an office in the rear corner.

The doorway was marked with a sign: Captain Paul Buronski. The door was open so he knocked and entered. "Captain Burnoski? Lieutenant Slate, Area 3, Robbery/Homicide." He displayed his star and ID.

The captain stood and shook hands. "Have a seat, Lieutenant." Buronski motioned to the lone chair in front of his desk. "I don't have a firefighter as a victim of a robbery or homicide, do I?"

"No. Just need some information. How often does your house inspect commercial buildings in this area?"

"We aim for yearly, but don't always make it."

"Who here would inspect C & D Grocery and Liquor back north on Broadway?"

Burnoski got up and collected several folders from a filing cabinet in the corner of his office. He came back to the desk and examined two of them. "Looks like Incandella did the last one. What's the problem?"

"I need to know the layout of the building. Do you have floor plans of the buildings in your district?"

"Only the ones built since 1978."

"What's Incandella's full name?"

"Jovan Incandella. He goes by Dell."

"Is he working?"

"He's off right now, but he moonlights detailing cars for a dealer here on Broadway."

The captain checked a list under the glass on top of his desk and gave Slate two telephone numbers.

"Got his and Weston's address?"

Buronski got up and checked another file.

"Incandella's at 5217 Ashland. An apartment I think. Weston Chevy is only four or five blocks farther south on Broadway."

Slate stood "Thanks, Captain."

Slate pulled into Weston Chevrolet and parked near the showroom door. He was directed to the rear of the service area and the wash rack, where he observed a man drying an older Corvette. Slate approached him with his ID out. "Mr. Incandella?"

The man nodded.

"I need to talk to you."

"Trouble at home?"

"No trouble. Let's go outside where we can talk." Incandella put down his cloth and stepped outside through the open overhead door with Slate.

"I talked to Captain Buronski and he said I could find you here. Dell, right?"

"Yeah."

"The captain said you inspected the C & D Grocery and Liquor store on Broadway, a couple blocks from the firehouse."

Dell nodded.

"I need to know the layout of the building—rooms and number of floors."

"What's this about?"

"It's a confidential police investigation, so don't discuss this with anyone, or you could get charged with obstructing justice."

Dell frowned. "Do you have a paper and pen?"

Slate pulled his notebook from his sport coat pocket and opened it to a blank page then handed it and his pen to Dell.

Dell squatted, laid the notebook on his knee, and began drawing. "The place isn't very big. There's the grocery area, with two rooms and a restroom in the rear. The liquor side is smaller to the north with one medium size room to the front and one small room to the rear. Toward the rear of the grocery side there's an archway between the grocery area and liquor store. It's an old building.

"Oh, and below the liquor store is a small basement. They say it was used during Prohibition to store booze, when both sides on the first floor were the grocery store. You know, during Capone's time."

"When did you last inspect it?"

"During the winter. Before Christmas, I think."

"The basement is small?"

"Real small. They still store liquor and some cartons of canned goods in it, but nothing flammable."

"What are the measurements of the room?"

Dell thought for a moment. "Maybe ten by fifteen."

"Concrete floor and walls?"

"The walls are mortar over stones, I think. The walls are real rough."

"The floor?"

"There's wood platforms to walk on. I don't know what's under them, but it smelled musty."

"Okay, Dell. I appreciate your help. And let's keep it between us for now."

Dell stood and returned Slate's notebook and pen. Slate shook his hand.

As they walked back inside, Slate commented, "Nice Vette."

"I wish I could afford one, but not on firefighter pay."

———

Slate grabbed a stack of reports that had to be processed from his IN box, but the unanswered questions about Karen Olson Hayes kept nagging at his attention. She would have been thirty years old when she wrote her last letter.

He closed his door and opened the doors to his whiteboard. Under his **Pending** heading he noted what he had learned from Sherri Herman, Mike Vansant, and firefighter Incandella. He sat on the end of his desk and studied all of the notes. When someone knocked he closed the doors over his board and opened his office door.

"Lieutenant, got a few minutes?" Sergeant Waddell asked.

"Sure. Come on in and shut the door." Slate grabbed his tablet and moved to the table to the side of his office. Waddell followed.

"What's on your mind, Rick?"

"Any problems with Ingrams's shooting? She and Barona said the shooting team was okay with it. I knew you would go, so I didn't attend."

"It was a good shoot. Fortunately none of the rounds struck a house in the area. She took the rear window out, and the other two rounds stayed in the car."

"How's your wife taking it?"

"Not good. I'd like to wrap this whole case up so we could get back to normal."

On Tuesday morning Slate found the letters delivered by UPS from Karen Hayes's sister, Sherri Herman. He carefully read the seven letters and made notes. The marriage had been in trouble for a long time. When he called Paula Lyon to ask for a meeting, the ASA scheduled him for 1:30 p.m. That left time for a quick lunch stop at a Wendy's on his way.

———

Slate was on California at 29th by 1:30 p.m. and briefed Lyon on the call from Sherri Herman, the letters, and his plan of action. Lyon picked up the latest folder she had on the Hayes case. "You think Karen Hayes was killed rather than just leaving him?"

"She never showed up in Wisconsin. Nobody in her family followed up with a missing person's report even though no one has seen or heard from her in eleven years. And the letters sent to the mother say she felt she was in danger."

"The mother had dementia?"

"Right. Hayes's wife number one, Karen, was a late birth and this older sister, Sherri, was already in college then. So they weren't close."

When Paula tapped on the opened folder without speaking, Slate knew she was mentally investigating the case. "And you think this Brunk, the Professor, hit wife number two?"

Slate nodded. "He didn't admit it, but I think he's the one. And another thing, Paula. I talked to Walberg, the juror, again, but couldn't move him. If I can ever prove he was bought, I want to prosecute him to the max."

Lyon nodded. "I'll need to talk to Mark Erwin before we act on Hayes again, due to the hung jury and media coverage. How about the PD? Will they back you?"

"No problems since Urbanski retired."

"I'll need the letters."

"I figured that. Here's the chain of evidence form. I made copies for my investigation." Lyon signed for the seven letters Karen Hayes had written and sent to her mother.

———

Slate stopped at Forensic Services when he returned to Area 3 and let them know he would be asking for their help soon with another part of his investigation.

Two afternoons later Lyon called, then faxed a search warrant for C & D Grocery and Liquor. Slate called Forensics for a team to meet him at the store the next morning at 9:00 a.m. with all their equipment. He also notified Waddell to have Barona and Ingram join him there.

He was restless all evening long, wondering what he would find the next morning. If he found nothing and word got out, the department and the media would be all over him. And maybe Hayes would sue, as he had warned.

AT 9:00 A.M. the next morning Slate pulled in front of the C & D Grocery and Liquor. Barona and Ingram were waiting and approached him as he got out.

"Good morning, Lieutenant," Barona said. "Is this your answer?"

"I hope and pray."

Slate made eye contact with Barona's partner and greeted Ingram with, "Morning, Deadeye."

The look of satisfaction on Ingram's face spoke for her.

While they were talking, a man arrived and unlocked the front doors to both stores. Slate figured it was Dewayne Hayes, brother of W. C.

As they approached, the man offered a "Good morning."

"Mr. Hayes?"

"Yes."

"Lieutenant Slate, Robbery/Homicide, Area 3," Slate announced, displaying his star and ID. "I have a search warrant for the basement of your liquor store."

"A search warrant?"

As they started to enter the grocery the Forensics van pulled up in front. Technicians Bauer and Young quickly followed them in, carrying a gas monitor and two probing rods.

The store's proprietor stared in astonishment at the police team and their equipment.

"Is it Dewayne Hayes?" Slate asked.

The store owner nodded.

"Here's your copy."

Dewayne scanned the warrant. "There must be some mistake!"

"No mistake. Show us the way down."

"I may call my lawyer. You're the one who charged W. C. with corruption?"

"That's right. And you can call anyone you want. Where's the stairs to the basement?"

Dewayne obviously struggled to grasp who was there and what was unfolding at his store before he answered, "On the other side, just inside the second room to your left."

While Dewayne Hayes studied the warrant, Slate walked back in the grocery area, then crossed over to the liquor side through an archway toward the rear. Then he turned right into the second room on that side. There was a small door to the left as he entered the second room.

He opened it and found a narrow and rather steep wooden stairway leading down to a dark room. He found a switch just inside the door to his right and flipped it. A light above the stairs and several lights in the basement below came on.

"Watch your step," he cautioned as he started down the stairs. Barona, Ingram, and the forensics team followed down the stairs into a room that ran east and west.

The basement was larger than the firefighter had remembered, about fifteen feet wide and maybe twenty feet long. Shelving ran along both side walls with another wide section of shelving in the middle of the room with storage on both sides. Slate and the others moved around, scanning the room. The ceiling was less than seven feet, making the ceiling a bit threatening to those six feet or over.

The flooring was made of wooden pallets that ran east and west parallel to the shelving. The boards that made up the pallets were about one inch apart. Slate lifted one section and found a dirt floor.

"Okay, guys. See what your gas monitor tells us," Slate directed.

Bauer turned on the monitor. The device had long shaft with a wide disk-shaped bottom and a meter and handle at the top. He started at the northwest corner of the room, under the stairway where they entered, placed the probe just above the floor, and moved slowly away from the stairs, walking east between the north wall shelves and the center shelf. He swung the probe to the right, then to the left. The probe was silent.

He then moved back to the northwest end and moved the probe toward the southwest corner of the room. Again the probe was silent. Bauer then moved east between the center shelves and the shelves along the south wall. There was no sound on the south side until he reached the southeast corner. Then, the probe gave a loud buzzing sound. "We have gases here," Bauer said.

"Circle the room again," Slate directed.

Bauer retraced his earlier steps. The probe was silent until he reached the southeast corner again. Then it buzzed loudly.

"Okay, everybody, let's get the wooden pallets up and use the rods to probe."

Barona and Ingram joined Bauer and Young with removing parts of the wooden floor in the southeast corner. They set the pallets on an edge along the north wall shelves. That created an open dirt area of about eight by six feet in the southeast corner. Bauer moved the gas probe around the corner until the signal was strongest and placed a rod in the ground.

The probing rods were about three eighths of an inch in diameter and five feet long with a sharp point on one end and a wooden handle on the top.

Dewayne Hayes came down the stairs just then. "What's going on? What was that buzzing I just heard?"

"Our monitor shows the presence of methane gas in an area of this basement," Slate said.

"Which means?"

"A decomposing body gives off methane gas."

Dewayne paused. "A body? Could it be an animal?"

"Try the rods," Slate said.

Young began to probe with a rod. "It's loose here." After about five minutes of probing Bauer and Young halted and reported, "We have a softer area about six by three feet, Lieutenant."

"Okay. Did you bring shovels with you?"

Bauer looked at Young, who leaned his rod against the shelving and started up the steps. "Bring a plastic tarp too," Bauer said.

Dewayne Hayes had been standing near the stairs watching. "What are you looking for? Some sort of grave?"

Slate nodded.

The owner turned and headed back up the stairs, likely to call an attorney, Slate guessed. He hoped Dewayne wasn't yet connecting the dots to W. C.'s missing wife and the possibility of finding her body.

Young returned with two shovels and a tarp. They spread the tarp along the north edge of the area where the dirt was softer, and he and Bauer began to dig, throwing the dirt past their tarp and against the pallets stacked against the north wall.

As the Forensics team dug, Slate felt mixed emotions. Maybe he now had a case that showed Hayes's real character, a case W. C. could not beat even with the Outfit's help. Then there was Sherri Herman, Karen Hayes's sister in Wisconsin. At least their mother would never hear her baby girl had been murdered.

The Forensics team dug steadily for several minutes, then stopped to rest. Bauer looked at Slate. "Who are we looking for?"

"For a woman, about thirty."

"Know how old this grave is?"

"About ten or eleven years. What will be left?"

Bauer shrugged. "Hard to tell. It depends on how they're buried . . . bare . . . in their clothes . . . a blanket . . . plastic sheet . . . a box. We've found them about every way you can imagine. And in all kinds of condition."

The men went back to digging. They dug and rested several more times. The pile of dirt along the north wall was getting deeper.

"You should be getting close," Slate said.

The two men continued to dig. Finally Bauer announced, "Okay. I've hit something different."

Slate moved closer. "How deep are you?"

"Maybe four feet."

"Okay. Go easy now and scrape the loose dirt away."

As they carefully removed six to eight inches of dirt, something black appeared. The smell of death was present.

"A plastic bag or tarp," Slate said. "Pull on it to see if it's a bag or a tarp."

"It's a tarp," Bauer said. "See the cloth and plastic where our shovels tore it."

Slate pulled a pair of latex gloves from his jacket pocket and put them on. He then eased his way into the side of the hole and helped pull up about three feet of tarp and fold it to the side to expose the area below.

Slate examined it. "A vinyl tarp, like I use to drag leaves to the road. Let's pull up on one side to see if we can expose the body." They pulled on the north side but it would not move. "Okay, try the other side." The south side of the tarp pulled up out of the soil and back from covering the grave site, but they could not pull it completely out. Slate bent over and picked up a piece of rotting material that had been under the tarp, then another one, and another. He laid the items on the north edge of the hole where Young had spread their work tarp.

Ingram stepped closer and examined the pieces. "Women's clothing."

Slate said, "My guess is he buried her in the tarp, then placed her clothes on top of her, then folded the tarp over the clothes."

Bauer, Young and Slate began pulling pieces of clothing from the pile and placing them on the tarp beside the hole. The stench became much stronger. Barona and Ingram spread the clothing on the tarp.

Slate stood to straighten his back and look at Ingram. "It's dry enough that the clothes didn't rot completely."

"Look here," Bauer said. He placed several rotting shoes up on the edge of the hole, then two purses.

Slate studied the items. "Looks like he buried her with all her clothes to make it appear she'd taken her stuff and left. I think we'll find her under all of this."

"Here's a box," Bauer said. He laid it at the edge of the hole.

"A jewelry box," Ingram said.

After they had removed clothing, shoes, and purses, Barona joined them in the hole. The four of them lifted the entire black tarp up and onto the side of the hole between the clothes and shoes and the pile of dirt to the north.

"Not very heavy," Barona noticed.

They carefully unrolled the tarp and found a body dressed in women's clothes. She appeared a little over five feet tall.

Slate moved closer and studied the body. "I'm sure this is Karen Hayes, his first wife. Radio for the ME, Pam."

"The judge's wife?" Bauer asked.

Slate nodded.

Bauer and Young grabbed their shovels, rods, and gas probe and returned the equipment to their van. They came back with photography equipment and evidence bags. They photographed the basement, grave, articles of clothing, shoes, purses, jewelry box, and the body. They then tagged and bagged all the items and placed them in large evidence bags. But a check of the grave with luminal for blood yielded nothing. After spending most of the morning digging and preserving evidence, the Forensics team was ready to leave.

Barona said, "What a case, Lieutenant. Looks like you've finally got His Honor!"

"We still need DNA. Mark the basement entrance as a crime scene, Joe."

Slate found Dewayne Hayes in the store. Clearly the man was uneasy. But when Slate informed him the basement was a crime scene and not to be disturbed until he was notified, Hayes was shocked. "There's a body?" he asked.

"Yes. In a black vinyl tarp. With women's clothing and shoes piled on top of it."

Slate paused. He wondered what Dewayne Hayes might know. "Your former sister-in-law, is my guess. If you warn your brother, I'll charge you with obstruction of justice."

Dewayne didn't respond.

"Do you understand?"

Dewayne nodded. "I understand. I knew he was different, but I never imagined this."

"The restroom is back there?"

Dewayne pointed to the rear of the grocery.

Slate and Barona used the facility and washed their hands and cleaned their shoes.

About forty minutes later Dr. Kimball arrived. Slate explained the situation, who he thought the body was, and that he needed DNA, ASAP. He and Kimball went down to the gravesite. When the ME finished, he called for transportation to the morgue.

"We're done with the scene, Doc. Will you need to see it again?"

"No."

"How soon can I get DNA?"

"I'll ask the State Police to rush it."

"I'll be getting a sample from a sister in Wisconsin for comparison."

Slate and Doctor Kimball went back upstairs. Slate told Barona and Ingram the scene would be clear when the body was removed. Slate went to his car and made several bulleted notes in his notebook. When Forensics and the ME were finished and the body was taken away, Slate notified Dewayne Hayes. He would let the grocer deal with the hole.

Standing in front of the store, Barona asked, "Now what?"

"Get some DNA from her sister in Wisconsin. Then I go after Hayes. You two know where I can get an assist?"

"You're damn right," Barona said.

Checking his watch, Slate announced, "It's lunch time. I'm buying."

———————

At Area 3 Slate went directly to Commander Arnold's office, knocked, and entered.

Arnold stopped writing and looked up. "What did you find?"

"One small woman's body, with a bunch of clothing, shoes, and purses piled on top of her."

Arnold stood. "In the basement?"

Slate nodded. "I thought you'd want to know, and to tell Deputy Chief Newcomb."

"Can you keep it quiet?"

"I doubt it. I'll request a court order to pull Hayes's passport."

"The Outfit could get him out of the country without it," he observed.

"I thought of that, but State's Attorney Erwin won't let me charge a judge with homicide without the DNA."

"You're probably right. And the word will get out. How about the brother?"

"I've warned him with an obstruction charge if he tells W. C."

"You could put a tail on the judge, but that takes a lot of manpower. And Delaney has already cost you." Arnold sat down. "So who are you missing on your list?"

"Carbonaro, who hit Alderman Bryan. And Walberg, who hung the jury on Hayes's trial."

"Not bad, Lieutenant. Not bad."

"I'll call ASA Lyon about the passport, unless you have something better."

At his office Slate called ASA Lyon, who agreed to go for a court order to require Hayes to surrender his passport pending the DNA check. Then Slate placed a call to Sherri Herman to tell her of the body.

"Is it my sister?"

"Can't tell after maybe ten years, but I think so."

"That dirty bastard!" There was a long silence. "It's better that Mom never knew. I wish my mother had shared her letters with me. Maybe I could have done something. When will you arrest him?"

"Not until your DNA is compared with the body. Give me time to call the Stevens Point PD for arrangements, then you call them. We'll need your sample as soon as possible."

Slate contacted the Stevens Point Police concerning Sherri Herman and the needed DNA sample. They would ship the sample ASAP to the Illinois State Police Lab in Elk Grove Village.

With the follow-up to the morning's work completed, he leaned back in his chair and noticed his IN box was full. That could wait, he told himself. What else could he do to assure Hayes's arrest? A tail on him would keep the man from leaving the country, but would the Outfit help him on a crime that could not be tied to them? He thought not. In fact, now Hayes had become a liability to them.

He lunched alone at Smokey's and spent the remainder of the day with his door shut, moving the backlog of paper, then updating his own investigation report and the notes on his whiteboard and adding the discovery of the body. Later in the day Lyon called to report that Erwin approved pulling Hayes's passport and she would process that through court. The next morning ASA Lyon called to report the order to pull Hayes's passport was approved and that she had made the contact with his attorney, DeCenzo.

It was midafternoon when he took a call from Special Agent Dodd in the local FBI office. "I understand you found a body, Lieutenant."

Slate wondered how he could know already. "And what body would that be?"

"Karen Hayes. The judge's first wife."

Slate waited.

"Attorney DeCenzo contacted us and asked for a meeting with W. C. Hayes and himself with Assistant Director Wisner. Wisner gave it to Special Agent Millburn. You met him when we came over there."

"And you're calling me for what?"

"Milburn wants you there for the meeting."

"Hayes wants to deal?"

"DeCenzo didn't say, but I expect that's the agenda."

"He'll give you some Outfit guys to save his neck."

"I wouldn't be surprised."

"He knows we won't deal after losing the jury trial, but he isn't waiting on the DNA."

"Probably figures he's at risk from his friends in the Outfit. Not because of your body, but from his business with them if he starts talking."

"When's the meeting?"

"They wanted to meet tomorrow, Friday, but Millburn has a major case going and can't meet until a week from Monday 1:00 p.m. Can you make it?"

"It's a state homicide. And I want Hayes. He'll give you his Out-fit contacts and you guys will try to get him a pass on his wife's homi-cide."

"He asked to talk to us, Slate."

"Because he knows he won't get off again with me."

"You're probably right."

"He murdered and buried his first wife, had the second one hit, and he's still on the bench, Dodd."

"How about the meeting?"

"I'll let you know."

Slate hung up his phone and slammed the desk with his fist. "I want Hayes!" He said it out loud. The Bureau couldn't give the man a pass on the state homicide charge for Karen Hayes, but they would try to persuade the Cook County State's Attorney to reduce the charge if they got a good RICO case on Outfit members.

He called Commander Arnold and briefed him. They reviewed what Slate had set up on the DNA and blocking the judge from flee-ing, then decided it would be best to see what developed during the next week. Slate then briefed ASA Lyon.

On Friday, Slate was still angered about the Hayes ploy to talk to the FBI to avoid a murder charge. He called the State Police lab and talked to the director, explaining his lost trial, the two wives killed, and the FBI getting involved again. The director agreed to process the DNA immediately.

Dr. Kimball called to report the body was a female, about thirty to thirty-five years old. She was five feet four inches, small frame, and she died from a blunt-force trauma to the skull. He would have the detailed final report soon.

Over breakfast on Saturday morning, Ed tried to talk through things with Rebecca and to reassure her, but had little success. He worked in the yard, but his mind was on Hayes. They ate out Sunday after church, and talked about their future and the things they needed to get in order to start looking for that house on a lake in Wisconsin. But his mind was on getting back to work and arresting W. C. Hayes. And he didn't like the damn FBI trying again to get involved in his case.

The backlog of homicide and robbery investigations, and writing his own investigation report from the notes on his whiteboard kept

Slate occupied Monday, Tuesday, and Wednesday. On Thursday he had just sat down with his Danish and Starbucks when the State Police lab called. The DNA of the body was a match with Sherri Herman. They would fax a copy of their report and then send the original.

Slate called ASA Paula Lyon.

"Morning, Ed."

"We got him, Paula."

"You have the DNA report?"

"Right. And the ME IDed the body as a female, age thirty to thirty-five, and five feet four inches, with a fractured skull. I want to grab him before he meets with the feds."

"That's Monday, right?"

"Right. Can we get the warrant ready for tomorrow morning?"

"Fax the DNA report and I'll brief Erwin. I'll go with you to arrest him."

"Fine. I'll take Barona and Ingram."

Slate thought back to the trial Lyon had lost with one juror making a hung jury and felt some satisfaction at being able to get the truth about W. C. Hayes out there with hard evidence that nobody could call circumstantial.

CHAPTER 48

SLATE HAD JUST sat down at his desk on Friday morning when
ASA Lyon knocked on his open door and entered. "Good morning, Ed."

"Paula. Are we ready?" The ASA handed him the arrest warrant.

Slate read it. "'W. C. Hayes, for homicide.' We've finally got him."
Slate called Arnold with a heads-up. "We'll stop by Sergeant Waddell
on the way and have Barona and Ingram meet us at the courthouse."

———

When Slate and Lyon pulled in front of the Cook County Courthouse on California at 29th, Barona and Ingram were waiting.

"Joe, Pam. ASA Lyon will accompany us."

Lyon checked her watch. "I'd like to get him in his chambers,
before he's on the bench."

"Okay, let's go," Slate said.

They quickly made their way past the screeners and to the courtroom on the third floor. The courtroom was about two-thirds full
when they entered. Slate and Lyon approached the bailiff, a Cook
County Sheriff's deputy. Barona and Ingram followed. Slate showed
him the arrest warrant. The deputy stared, speechless.

The door to the left rear corner of the courtroom opened just then and Judge W. C. Hayes entered the courtroom, carrying a folder. He had taken just a few steps when he recognized Slate and stopped.

Slate quickly pulled his pistol from his cross draw holster under his sport coat and held it down along his right leg as he walked to Hayes. Two camera flashes went off. The talk in the courtroom stopped. Barona and Ingram followed Slate with weapons drawn. Lyon hung back a few steps.

Slate carried the arrest warrant in his left hand and held it up so Hayes could see it. "Wilbur Clarence Hayes, you are under arrest. Turn around and go back to your chambers."

"Bailiff, remove these people!" the judge ordered in a raised voice.

The bailiff didn't move.

"Move back into your chambers," Slate repeated as more cameras flashed from the area behind him.

Instead of moving, Hayes leaned toward Slate and said in a low voice, "I have an appointment with the FBI."

"Frisk him," Slate directed.

Barona and Ingram moved in. As Barona removed a snub nose revolver with a hammer shroud from the right pocket of Hayes's robe there were more camera flashes.

"Now go back into your chambers, or I'll cuff you right here," Slate said.

Hayes finally turned and went back through the doorway. Lyon followed them in and shut the door.

Inside, Hayes threw his folder on the desk, then turned and yelled, "You're done, Slate! I'll have your job for all this harassment and sue your ass for every cent you have!"

"Remove the robe."

"You're a punk cop on a crusade. I beat your ass once and I'll beat you again. You're screwing with a Circuit Court judge!"

Slate holstered his pistol, handed the arrest warrant to Lyon, then quickly moved close. With his left hand he grabbed the chest area of the robe. "Remove this robe or I'll tear it off!"

Hayes unzipped the robe and laid it across his desk.

"You're under arrest for homicide."

Hayes looked stunned. "Homicide? The charge was bribery!"

"The homicide of Karen Olson Hayes."

"Let's see the warrant."

Lyon moved closer and handed it to Hayes. He turned pale and broke out in a sweat.

Slate took the arrest warrant from him. "Cuff him," he directed. Barona handcuffed the judge.

Hayes looked at Slate. "She left years ago. I've never seen her or heard from her since," Hayes countered.

"But she's been close."

Hayes gave Slate a blank look but said nothing more.

Slate said, "You have the right to remain silent. Anything you say can and will be used against you in a court of law. You have the right to consult with an attorney. If you can't afford an attorney, one will be appointed. Do you understand these rights?"

Hayes stood silent.

"Do you understand?"

The judge nodded.

Slate stepped back to Lyon. "Unless you have something more, we're ready to book him."

"I'll tell the bailiff to see a supervisor about the scheduled court session." She turned and left to take care of that matter.

Slate handed the arrest warrant to Barona. "Book this man for the crime of homicide."

Barona and Ingram led Hayes out of his chambers and into the rear hall. Two reporters were waiting and flashed several shots.

Lyon returned to the judge's chambers. "We're going to be in the paper Ed."

He looked at Lyon with satisfaction, "That felt good!"

She nodded.

As they went back through the courtroom two reporters approached. The *Tribune* reporter, Stanley Zack asked, "Lieutenant Slate, what's the charge against Judge Hayes?"

"Assistant State's Attorney Paula Lyon and I, with the assistance of Detectives Barona and Ingram, have just arrested W. C. Hayes for the homicide of his first wife, Karen Olson Hayes. After the booking you can contact our department for more details."

The noise in the courtroom increased and there were more questions and photos, but Lyon and Slate proceeded through the crowd and out of the courthouse.

———

While Barona and Ingram booked Hayes back at Area 3, Slate and Lyon grabbed coffee before entering Slate's office. Lyon sat at his side table.

"Care for half of a Danish, Paula?"

"No. The coffee is fine."

Slate brought his roll to the table but didn't sit down. "Now that's the way to start a morning." He took a bite and a drink, then set his coffee down and opened the doors of his whiteboard. He added the arrest of Hayes.

"They won't let Hayes bond again, will they?" he asked.

"I doubt it, on a homicide."

"If he does get bond, we'll need to freeze his passport again."

Paula nodded.

Slate moved back to the table and picked up his Danish and coffee then turned to view the board with Lyon.

Convicted: Outfit's Carmine Vaccaro; Attorney Anthony Profacci; Hit man Delbert Brunk by CPD Robbery/Homicide, Benton Harbor PD, and FBI RICO.

Dead: Court administrator Mario DeMeo by Brunk, AKA the Professor; robbery/truck theft, Frank Ruggerio by unknown hit; street tax extortion, Danny Fischetti by CPD Robbery/Homicide

Retired: Deputy Chief of Detectives Urbanski, by CPD Robbery/Homicide

Prison: Street tax extortion, retired Deputy Chief of Detectives Larry Seryak by CPD Robbery/Homicide

Pending Court Action: Judge W.C. Hayes by CPD Robbery/Homicide

Pending: Hit man on Alderman Steven Bryan homicide, Frankie Carbonaro; juror Jacob Walberg; Hayes trial for homicide

"You got most of them, Ed. I didn't think you would ever get Hayes."

"He'll try to bargain with the feds, then they will try to bargain with you and Erwin. Even if the Bureau can charge him with an Outfit connection, I want us to try him first."

"We'll see what they come up with. Well, it's Friday and I still have more than a day's worth of work to get done." Lyon stood and they shook hands to congratulate each other. "Another outstanding investigation, Ed, and you're still alive."

After Lyon left he called Media Relations and briefed them on the arrest of Hayes, then called Arnold with an update. "Given this case, Commander, and some other tough ones we've had in recent years, I think we need a Major Crimes Section within Robbery/ Homicide." He also thought about the threat to himself and his family, knowing the Outfit liked to settle scores.

"You may be right. And, you know who could head up a Major Crimes Section. Right?"

"I do."

"I'll give it some thought, Ed."

He then called Sherri Herman in Wisconsin and informed her that Karen's body had been positively identified and Wilbur Clarence Hayes had been arrested for homicide.

———

On Saturday morning Slate checked around and under his car, then grabbed the *Chicago Tribune* from his driveway. JUDGE HAYES ARRESTED ON HOMICIDE CHARGE was the headline. Below were several photos of the confrontation in the courtroom. One photo showed Slate confronting Hayes with his pistol drawn, and another with Barona and Ingram frisking and removing the pistol from Hayes's robe.

He was surprised to see that Hayes had been released on a ten-million dollar bond from Cook County Jail, wearing an ankle-monitoring bracelet. How could he have posted bond money like that, Slate wondered. All of Hayes's properties might match the ten percent, the one million required. Had the presiding judge thought it was a weak charge since Hayes had beaten the jury trial for bribery? Or was that judge also on the Outfit's payroll?

A long article followed, covering the earlier jury trial lost in Lake County, Slate's previous shootings and Fischetti shooting at him in his own driveway. It also mentioned Deputy Chief of Detectives Urbanski's sudden retirement, and Seryak, who previously held Urbanski's position, being charged with extortion and now serving time. Slate read the entire article twice as he ate breakfast. He felt a great deal of satisfaction and relief to have so much behind him from his original investigation into cases that had been lost in one judge's courtroom. Now, to see Hayes convicted of homicide. He was sure he could have also charged Hayes with arranging for the homicide of his second wife if the FBI had given Brunk a break, but that was not to be.

———

Monday morning the office was noisy with discussion on the arrest. When Ed stopped into the squad room for coffee, several more detectives complimented him on getting Hayes.

He read the Monday morning edition of both the *Chicago Tribune* and *Sun Times* over his coffee. Both were still covering the earlier jury trial, the homicide arrest, and Hayes's marriages. The *Sun Times* carried a photo of the gravesite in the basement of the liquor store. A photo of Slate, his background, and some of his recent cases were included in the *Tribune*. He had just finished when Detectives Joe Barona and Pamela Ingram knocked and came in.

"Well, here's my arrest team. How did 'His Honor' like the booking?"

"He was a jerk all the way," Barona said.

Ingram said, "I'm surprised he was allowed to bond."

"His buddy DeCenzo was waiting when we finished," Barona added. "What do you think of the coverage, Lieutenant?"

"Both pretty good articles."

Barona nodded. "The shot of Pam and me frisking him is good."

"Yes it is. But now *you* may be on a hit list. I forgot to mention that Friday."

"We can handle it," Pam said.

"I think you can. Know how his bond was posted?"

Barona shook his head.

On Tuesday the media was still on the arrest and the squad room was still noisy. Slate had hoped that things would return to normal after Hayes was convicted, but there was nothing normal in Robbery/Homicide. As the week progressed things began to quiet down.

As Slate headed for the northwest side and home on Friday evening, he promised himself that he would sleep in Saturday and relax the entire day. It had been a tough and dangerous investigation, but the judicial system and the city would be in better shape as a result. And Sherri Herman now knew what had happened to her young sister, Karen.

He was still in bed Saturday morning when he heard the phone. Rebecca was up and answered it.

She then came to the bedroom. "It's the department," she reported.

Slate rolled over and grabbed the phone. "Slate."

"It's me, Lieutenant," Barona answered.

"You working?"

"No, but I picked something up on my monitor. Schneider and Dolsi are at the Townsend Building on North Avenue, unit 349."

Slate sat up in bed. "Hayes's townhouse?"

"Right. They've called for the ME."

Slate thought of wife number three. "I'm on my way."

"I'll meet you there."

Slate skipped the shower and shave and headed for the Townsend Building. As he hurried through traffic he wished he had a strong coffee, but that would have to wait.

CHAPTER

49

LIEUTENANT ED SLATE parked in front of the building and placed his blue light on the dash. Barona met him at the front door and gave him shoe covers to put on.

As they entered townhouse 349, they saw a man in dark blue pajamas hanging by the neck from the upper area of the open stairway. A rope was wrapped around three vertical spools that secured the handrail to the steps, then around the man's neck. The body slowly twisted to the right, then to the left, as if Hayes was still struggling to stay alive. Slate figured it was due to a twist in the rope, but it was a chilling sight

As they viewed the body, Detective Schneider approached. "I was just ready to call you, Lieutenant."

"How about the wife?"

"She's the one who found him." Schneider glanced over his shoulder and up in the direction of the body. "He won't fix any more trials or buy any more jurors, Lieutenant. The ME isn't here yet, so we didn't want to cut him down."

"Forensics have photos and everything they need?"

"They're going over the place now, mostly his bedroom."

"His wife found him?"

"Yeah. She moved out the same day you arrested him. I guess she came back real early today with a friend for the rest of her personal things." Carmel Destazio Hayes approached just then, concerned about what personal items she could remove and when. Schneider told her to wait off to the side.

Slate hadn't seen the third wife until this crime scene investigation. She was very attractive. And obviously much younger than Hayes, he noted. The thought crossed his mind about how the first Mrs. Hayes and her possessions had ended up. This time it was Hayes himself who was dead.

"Any note?"

"No. And nothing has been taken as near as she can tell. The door was locked when she arrived. The technicians say it looks like he was dragged from his bed on the second floor and across the bedroom and hall carpets to the stairway."

Slate nodded as he looked back up and studied the body on the rope and the monitor on the man's right ankle just below his pajamas. Schneider approached Mrs. Hayes.

"Who do you think whacked him?" Barona asked.

Slate surveyed the scene again, then looked back to Barona. "This may answer the bond question, Joe. He knew too much for the Outfit to let him go to trial or plea bargain."

Barona nodded.

"They could have provided the one million and bought another judge to allow him to bond out on a homicide," Slate speculated. "If the Outfit did post his bond, now they'll get it back, and Hayes won't be making any deals." He paused. "Maybe Mrs. Bryan will have some closure this way, even if we don't get Carbonaro."

"No forced entry though."

"Locks don't stop them if they want you, Joe. I'd have liked to hear what he had to offer about the Outfit, maybe other judges, and some in CPD."

"You figure they heard he wanted to deal? Like with DeMeo? Or they just eliminated the risk?"

"Hard to say. I doubt the FBI had a leak. The Outfit knew he would try to save his own ass." Slate looked up again at Hayes twisting on the rope. "He's saved us another trial Joe, but his information could have been a gold mine."

Slate looked toward the crime scene detective and raised his voice. "Schneider, you have everything you need?"

"I think so."

"Good. I'll call the Commander."

"Okay, Lieutenant."

Slate and Barona went outside in front of the townhouse and Slate called Commander Arnold. As he waited, he wondered how much Hayes's current wife knew about his other life. She might be a good source.

When Slate finished the call, Barona asked, "How do you figure it, Lieutenant? The guy's an attorney, a Circuit Court judge, has a good income, three homes, a beautiful woman, a big Mercedes. And he's an Outfit guy?" Barona paused. "It's scary to know we can be appearing before judges that may be on the Outfit's payroll."

Slate studied Barona for several seconds before responding. "He resented his upbringing and lacked a value system. He went with the Outfit to get the things that were important to him." Slate paused and put his hand on Barona's shoulder. "But when he stands in God's courtroom, all of those achievements will be ruled inadmissible."

As they walked toward their cars, Barona said, "You got most of them, Lieutenant. But what about you and your family? The Outfit tends to settle a score, even if it takes years."

"Yeah, I know. And it *is* hard on the family," Slate agreed. "I've considered bailing out early, and Rebecca is certainly ready, especially since Fischetti tried to whack me. But the city needs guys like you and me, Joe. Guys who live for the challenge of bringing assholes like Hayes, Profacci, and Vaccaro to justice. And to tell the truth, loafing along a lake in Wisconsin would drive me crazy."

"Maybe after you do your thirty."

Slate nodded. "With Fischetti dead, I'll never get Walberg for hanging the jury in Lake County. But maybe I can get Carbonaro for his next hit."

THE END

COMING IN EARLY 2013
another Detective Ed Slate novel

SPOT OF BLOOD

Inspired by an actual homicide
Dale F. Shaffer

"This is one of the best police novels I have ever read. Dale Shaffer takes you on a ride through a homicide investigation that has all the twists and turns of a real investigation. If you want to understand how moral decisions, the chain of evidence and legal constraints impact on an honest detective then this is the book for you. I felt like I was back investigating homicides as I read and enjoyed every page."

Dale P. Bowlin
Chief of Detectives, Retired
Miami-Dade Police Department

Lieutenant Ed Slate and Sergeant Joe Barona walked to the room and stopped at the door to put on their foot covers. Barona removed the police tape from across the doorframe and unlocked the door. A flip of the light switch revealed the young woman's jacket hanging over the back of the chair at the computer desk. Also a purse and a ring of keys laying at the end of the desk. A strong spring breeze howled through Chicago's Loop and against the wall of the medical student's eighth floor room at Northwestern University. Slate glanced out the window to choppy Lake Michigan and wondered if that was where they would find the missing medical student.

"The blood spot is there." Barona pointed. "Out about four feet from the desk, where I laid the pencil."

Slate moved up to the pencil and bent down to examine the dried blood. He looked back at Barona and stood. "You talked to her mother?"

"Yeah. She said Susan didn't call this last weekend, so they called the University PD. Now, see the big smear closer to the desk where the blood's been wiped up?"

Slate moved closer to the desk. "Yeah....a pretty big area. Gordon have anything on this . . ." Slate checked his notes, "Susan Thanajaro?"

"No. He's looking for a janitor that works here. Her folks are on their way up from Champaign."

Slate stepped back toward the door, avoiding the spot of blood, then turned back and bent over again to study the one small streak of blood out from the smeared area.

Barona stepped up beside him.

Slate pointed. "If she was shot in the heart, this spot out here could be from the heart pumping after the shot and the large area that was wiped up is where she fell. He missed this spot."

"Or maybe the blood's from her period?"

Slate grabbed the pencil and moved it along the narrow pattern of blood about three inches long. "No, it looks like it was sprayed out here. See the pattern. It's not a spot but a long and narrow splash."

Barona nodded. "We found no brass, but the shooter may have used a revolver. Why whack a medical student?"

"And why no body?"

Barona hesitated. "He could be a collector and buried her near his place, you know, so he could visit her."

Slate nodded, "Maybe. Okay, let's see what this janitor has to say. The witness saw a black guy in the elevator early in the morning?"

"Yeah, and we IDed her boyfriend, and her former boyfriend. Gordon will get her current boyfriend in. Right now he's checking on her car. I talked to her parents. The notes are on your desk. I'll meet with them while you and Gordon interrogate the janitor."

"You notified Forensics?"

"Told them about both blood spots."

Slate placed the pencil back alongside the narrow streak of blood.

———————

At the Area 3, on Belmont Avenue, Detective Gordon strode through the CPD detectives' large squad room and to the rear corner, then knocked at Slate's open door and entered Slate's office at Major Crimes. Gordon moved to the front of Slate's desk.

"Barona and I ran the janitorial and physical plant maintenance lists through the National Crime Information Center and the state Law Enforcement Agencies Data System. NCIC and LEADS had two hits. One of the maintenance people had a domestic violence charge about seven years old.

"However, this janitor, Jessie Adams, an employee of A-1 Cleaning, has a rape charge that's about five years old. He also has a battery charge about six years old. I talked to the detectives in Gary, Indiana. Apparently the battery charge was also sexually related, but reduced to battery. He did three years on the rape charge. He's been out two years and with A-1 cleaning for one year. Black male, twenty-eight, lives in an apartment in a tough area of Gary. Here's his rap sheet. I have him in the interrogation room."

"He give you any trouble?"

"Yeah. He's pissed about being brought in. Oh, Student Affairs has nothing on Williamson, her current boyfriend."

Slate sorted through the papers on his desk, looking for Barona's note. "Our third suspect is an old boyfriend. The Thanajaros said he went from the University of Illinois at Champaign to law school at the University of Michigan at Ann Arbor. I need data on him so I can run LEADS and NCIC checks. Here's the name. Phillip Caldwell, c-a-l-d-w-e-l-l. White, twenty-six, and probably has his JD."

"Okay. I'll check the universities at Champaign and Ann Arbor when we finish Adams."

"You and Barona are checking on registered sex offenders in the Loop area?"

"Right. And spot checks of students in Abbott Hall. If I miss you with the Caldwell information, I'll put it on your machine."

"Okay. Let's see what Adams has to say."

CPSIA information can be obtained at www.ICGtesting.com
Printed in the USA
LVOW13s0740170114

369783LV00001B/52/P